DR. Sherrill —

If you have any trouble with the medical terminology used herein, please call!

All the best,

Leelapp '09

About *Into the Storm…*

"Experience firsthand the struggle of characters who must overcome fear with faith as they turn trials into triumphs. I highly recommend this novel to readers of all ages." Bill Ewing, producer, *End of the Spear*

"An inspiring, courageous, action-packed story around a common-man hero." Anne Marie Gillen, executive producer, *Fried Green Tomatoes*

About *With Hearts Courageous…*

Nappa's prose is at its lyrical best in this book. His rhythm and the British voice he captures are hypnotizing. I immensely enjoyed reading these pages. As always, his action scenes are tremendously done. In addition to the feeling of authenticity in this courageous novel, I'm simply gripped by the writing. But I think Nappa may have outdone even himself in the final 30 pages of the novel. When Fletcher comes calling and that amazing series of incidents occur, I was absolutely mesmerized. JG, editor

These Storm Warrior stories are fantastic. The planning and preparation that went into them are obvious. The narrative is just great and the plots are fluid and engaging. They will be well received by a wide audience. LC, editor

A great, great story written in a great, great style. JS, editor

The detailed description puts you right in the middle of stormy seas while your muscles strain at the oars. Nappa never misses a beat, tacking and jibing at just the right times. An incredible adventure made all the more so when you realize how factually inspired it is. JN, reader

This book is definitely a must-read for anyone who feels like a failure despite maximum efforts. There's a sobering message in this book that will grant hope and the courage to never give up. BC, reader

WITH HEARTS COURAGEOUS

WHEN EVERY EFFORT FAILS...
WHERE DOES HOPE COME FROM?

A Novel

JON STEVEN NAPPA

Storm Warriors International

With Hearts Courageous
When every effort fails...where does hope come from?
All Rights Reserved.
Copyright © 2010 Jon Steven Nappa
v3.0

Cover design by studiogearbox.com

Storm Warriors International, Inc.
Charlotte, NC
www.stormwarriors.org

ISBN PB: 978-0-615-32395-4
ISBN HB: 978-0-615-32391-6

Library of Congress Control Number: 2009910570

Storm Warriors International, Storm Warriors Press and their respective logos are trademarks of Storm Warriors International, Inc.. Absence of ® in connection with marks of Storm Warriors International or other parties does not indicate an absence of registration of those marks.

PRINTED IN THE UNITED STATES OF AMERICA

For Christi Fisher
1957–2008
Though you rest in your winter repose,
Like a perennial flower you will bloom again.

Acknowledgments

Thank you to Jeff Gerke for his quintessential editing, David Radcliffe for his excellent research, Manx National Heritage and the RNLI for their encouragement, Robert L. Hofmann for his suggestion of the title, Betty Mayes for use of the cabin in the woods, and my wife and children for being my number-one fans.

Part 1

Virtute nihil invium.
With courage, nothing is impossible.
Sir William Hillary

Chapter 1

I am unjust and will judge you harshly.

I will roar upon you until you shout my name in fear. I will not cease lest you think your cry does satisfy my aim. I will press you and harangue you and break your soul to pieces.

I clash with my three brothers as we battle for first in line, but we take it out on you and the puny works of your feeble hands. We neglect not your lands, but it is from the seas we take our strength. We feed you to the waters. May you rot beneath the watery shroud.

Which of you does turn my tap and choose my rate of flow? From where do I come and to where do I go and in what place do I hide? You barely know. Yet you try.

I will snap your spine of oak into splinters and shred your garments of white into paste. I will claw and rake the seas with blasts of rage. I will shove and beat and freeze and pummel until content. I am never content.

You've angered me, you have, with your meager arks of wood. With their flimsy accents of cork and pockets full of air, you face me with paltry paddles and heaving breaths. I will strain you until I curl your nerves of steel like thread.

Alas, there lies one of your arks, derelict and forgotten. My chilling fingertips reach to rock what my growling stomach aches for. I cramp with delight. Is this what has become of your warrior? Is this what I am to fear? Is this now the fruit of your first reply?

I rush atop the Irish Sea and race to break the heart of man. The isle that bears his name is like sand that flows through my fingers.

I rush with saline saliva foaming from my mouth. Seaweed streams between my teeth and I arrive.

Your craft is aged and soaked to rotting. It is brittle and frail. I tempt it with a foaming roller, and it foolishly points its nose. I blast it with spray and gusting blows while its bluff bow rises and pierces the crests of sea. Foam spits from its wedge. It offers a pathetic attempt to return to former glory.

Curse it to deposit on the ocean floor with mollusks and sponges and other blind creatures, a testimony to man. He who launches but seldom maintains, who knows joyful beginnings but disappointing ends and does not comprehend the middle, he has not the fight within him.

I lift the craft to point high and snap its backbone keel in two. The timbers crumble and shatter as the seas rush from all sides. I withdraw my breath and the waves crash down, smashing the wooden carcass to disjointed smithereens. Its body is broken, and I have won. I swallow it and pass it to sea.

Compassion but not courage means my way in the end, blown in every direction with no sight of promised land. I am the South Wind this day upon the Irish Sea, and I care not whither I go.

I know what I come for, what I always come for, and what I will come for again.

Chapter 2

Sir William Hillary peered out his large window in the great room of his home on Prospect Hill, the *Isle of Man Weekly Gazette* clutched in his hand. He gazed across the crescent-shaped Douglas Bay barely a half mile away, quickly glancing past the stony outcrop in the center known as Conister Rock. He focused on the headland shore beyond Douglas Harbor to his right. Situated on that hill, called Douglas Head, was the magnificent Fort Anne residence. He admired it. It reminded him of Danbury Place, the estate he had enjoyed with his first wife and two children.

So many things had changed.

His eyes wandered about the picturesque scene along the coast of the Isle of Man, pausing to note some fishermen gathered along the shore of the bay. Several of them huddled together. A few pointed out toward the falling morning tide. Already it had ebbed a hundred yards away from the shore, baring a maze of jagged rocks laced with veins of dark green weeds. He wondered if the men were investigating something left behind by the sea. He hoped all the fuss wasn't over some flopping creature.

Fishing didn't interest Sir William. Nothing did. Not anymore.

"Good morning, dear," Emma said as she entered the room.

Sir William heard the rustling of his wife's dress. He turned from the broad window and beheld her lovely form: her morning attire elegantly sweeping the floor, her sleeves worked with extravagant lace and tucked neatly beneath her bracelets, her green eyes as deep as the Irish Sea, her rich red curls mostly hidden beneath her cap.

"I need some air," he said as he passed her en route to the hall, dropping the newspaper onto a chair.

"Dear?" she asked.

He hesitated. His dark mood fought his every effort to employ his kinder ways. He took a half step toward the exit, stopped again, strained his neck to gaze upon his wife. A shiny red curl dangled atop her gently sloping forehead, her soft skin as white as a cloud. Part of him longed to smile. She didn't deserve this treatment.

But his self-absorption won out. He brushed by her with a wave and threw an overcoat over his fine suit. He grabbed his hat, his scarf, his gloves, and his cane.

"Dear?" Emma called after him.

Sir William's boots tapped against the hallway floor, clapped the wooden deck of the porch, and scraped along the native rock of the front path. His strides were long and fast, and his walking cane never touched the ground.

He reached the gate and stopped only a moment to gaze upon the garden covered in winter white. Not a sign of life. Only sticks.

He missed the blossoms.

He slammed the gate and moved on.

He reached the center of the muddy lane and glared. The pockmarked road twisted down toward town. He stood checked by indecision: walk upward toward the frozen countryside where he could meander and regret or walk down the steep and crooked descent into a town with few attractions. He lifted his top hat and ran his hand through his thick locks. Despite the cold air, he perspired.

He stared toward the wide-open fields and bordering woods and watched the south wind rattle the limbs. He replaced his hat, briskly rubbed his long arms, adjusted his overcoat, widened his scarf, and turned around.

Going to town seemed the lesser of two evils. The town of Douglas on the Isle of Man was meant to have been a new beginning, but it was boring the life out of him. All forty-three years of it.

He headed quayside, rushing past the street leading to St. George's church. He had no interest in detouring for a chat with the vicar—too much lamenting in that. Of course he missed his son and daughter. Terribly so. He didn't need the vicar or anyone else to remind him of his failures. How could he forget? At least Frances, his first wife, forgave him and Emma loved him now. The children were too young to understand.

Did they ever think of him? He wondered how they looked these days. Seven years was a long time.

As the road bent, he came face to face with the bitter cold of the south wind blasting from the sea. It funneled between buildings and through broken tree lines. He leaned forward and suddenly changed direction, away from the quay, and made a steady tack toward the barracks of the old Manx Fencibles, the former local militia that used to station at the edge of town, near the bay. He had no idea where to go or what to do. Impulse was his guide.

He saw Lieutenant Colonel Ambrose St. John emerging from his flat alongside the old barracks building, the green-gray waters of the bay moving restlessly in the background. As usual, his old friend wore his former military uniform, now faded and too tight in some places.

The former officer looked up. "Good day, Sir William," he said, his voice feeble but friendly. He made short strides to come nearer.

"Colonel, it's good to see you," Sir William said, intentionally straightening his posture.

"It's the duel for you for lying," Colonel St. John said with a slight rising at the corners of his mouth.

"Whatever do you mean, old friend?" Sir William asked, extending his hand.

The colonel shook it, his grip as firm as ever. "You're wearing a face that could sink a fleet," he said. "I'm supposed to be the grumpy one, not you. *Good* to see me! Ha! Who are you trying to bluff?"

Sir William sighed and raised a hand. "I am in a sour mood, I confess."

"I see," Colonel St. John said. "Trouble with Emma? How can that be? She's a radiant angel."

"No," Sir William said. "We're content. There are other things that consume me. Or not enough, maybe."

"You'd be hopeless if you weren't happy with her. There was more than one who sought her hand before you arrived." Colonel St. John lowered his chin as his eyebrows lifted high. "You're a lucky man, Sir William."

"As you've reminded me many times," Sir William said. He patted the colonel's shoulder. "Emma is my only joy these days. But I think I need something beyond domestic felicity."

"Perhaps my daughter should visit you two. Sarah's always a charm; you know that. She brightens every house."

"How could I forget, old friend?" Sir William asked with a mild chuckle. "She's always welcome, and should she visit today she'll find my Emma at home. But not me."

"I'm heading to the pier to sit and talk with the seagulls," Colonel St. John said. "Care to join this old half-pay man? We can reminisce about our former glories, when we both knew the thrill of land-based militias!"

"I'm afraid not," Sir William said. "We've done that too much of late. I think it depresses me more than lifts my spirit."

"Well, then," Colonel St. John began, rubbing his short white whiskers with one hand. "Have you read the paper today? We can talk about that if we really want to get depressed." He thought a moment. "Although I'm not sure the birds will like it."

"The new laxity for creditors? It's partly to blame for my mood," Sir William said. "Yes, I saw it. The isle is no longer the safe haven it was."

Colonel St. John moaned. "The dogs!" A flash of spirited fight, such as worn by a fresh recruit making his first charge, flashed across the colonel's face and then disappeared. The old man's countenance became wistful, and he fell into a blank stare as though he were an ocean away.

"With Napoleon all but dead," Sir William said, trying to step into his friend's gaze, "I feared such changes would come. They wasted no time."

"Eighteen-fourteen may yet mark the year of my departure." Colonel St. John sounded trancelike. His lips trembled. "I may well be ruined."

"Nonsense!" Sir William hooked his walking cane on his arm and gently held his friend by the shoulders, squeezing them. "You are the former MP for Callington. You served in the Second Worcester Militia, where you performed honorably. There is no forgetting that, and with such remembrance will come all due arrangements. You'll see. It will not be the end."

The colonel focused on Sir William. His eyes widened with sudden recognition. "Sir William!" he said. "Ah, yes." He shook his head. "I wish I had your financial security. I really do."

Sir William felt his stomach knot. He unhooked his cane and lowered his arms. "Actually, I need a plan myself in light of this latest development." A flood of self-criticizing thoughts overran him. His tenuous finances. The ache for his absent children. His need for renewed purpose. He stopped as his gaze wandered toward the shore of Douglas Bay. A sight in the distance interrupted his self-pity.

"What?" Colonel St. John asked, turning around.

Sir William pointed. "I saw them from my front window this morning—those fishermen. Has something of interest washed ashore?"

"As long as it's nothing that disrupts our peaceful settlement," Colonel St. John replied. "I've not much concern whatever it is." He turned back to Sir William. "What say now? To the birds?"

"Come now, Ambrose," Sir William chided. "Clearly there's more to our purpose than keeping the peace and feeding the birds."

"We've been over this before, Sir William. I've purpose enough in that. That and staying one step ahead of creditors." His face darkened. "The dogs!"

"Hear, hear," Sir William said, his tone brightening. "We'll get to the birds soon enough. Let's first discover what this activity is about." He cupped his hands around his mouth. "Ahoy! Kellerman? Is that you?"

"How on earth do you even know their names?" Colonel St. John asked.

The small gathering of fishermen broke asunder and turned. Michael Kellerman stood in the center and raised his hand. His gray gansey hung loosely over his baggy black pants. He clutched his rain hat in his other hand. One of his fishing partners, Joseph, stood beside him, portly and grinning as usual. "Ahoy! Sir William," Michael said. "It's me, well enough!"

"And they address you so directly!" Colonel St. John said. "You came over to this island so much later than most of us, yet you know so many of the commoners."

Sir William waved Michael over. "It's not hard to do."

"I swear, I think those Quaker roots of yours predispose you to an unhealthy affection for the dregs."

"I'm not ashamed to take an interest in those less fortunate. What difference is there between them and us but for our wallets?"

"I should hope it's more than that," Colonel St. John said, nearly spitting as he emphasized. "Curiosity is excusable, maybe, but interest? I have other interests needing my attention. Good day, my friend."

"Hold on, Ambrose."

"I'm afraid I've work to do," Colonel St. John said, his tone very different from what it had been at the outset. He turned his head toward the pier. "I'm going quayside. The birds are expecting me."

Sir William tapped his cane on the cobblestone street. "Very well. I'll catch up with you this afternoon. We can reminisce then, perhaps over lunch at the York Hotel?"

"Hanby's place? Whatever you say." Colonel St. John turned his back and slowly walked away. "Of course, I may be bankrupt by then."

"I'll buy," Sir William said as he watched his old friend moving away like a tug not yet up to steam.

Michael Kellerman arrived, breathing hard and bending over at the waist, his hands on his knees, his fishing hat still crumpled in one hand. "Good day, sir."

"Good morning, Michael," Sir William said. "I spotted you and the others from Prospect Hill this morning, all gathered up and pointing to sea. What's the lure?"

Michael stood up, his bushy black eyebrows arching high. "You haven't noticed?"

Sir William looked again at the shore many yards away. His eyes scoured the mucky surface of the bay floor, lying exposed by the absent tide. He saw the rocks and the seaweed, perhaps an ancient chunk of wood or two, but nothing else of any meaning. Farther out, he saw the ebbed green-gray waters splashing about Conister Rock. "Apparently not. What is it?"

"The lifeboat, sir. She's gone. Washed to sea. Nothing but some driftwood remains. I fear the south wind took her."

"Oh," Sir William said. "What of it?"

Michael nodded. "She was a bit of a derelict, it's true, sir. But for those of us who work the sea, she was plenty comforting to have around." His leathery face wrinkled.

"I'd half forgotten we had one," Sir William said. "I don't recall it being used the few years I've been here."

"Aye," Michael said. "But you know the storms, sir. Or maybe you don't. They're cyclical-like. There were days we needed lifesaving regular."

"Not since I've been here," Sir William said.

"There's a saying among the fisher folk," Michael said. "It's been handed down in the old Gaelic tongue. *Yn chiuney smoo erbee geay jiass smessey jee.*"

Sir William laughed. "That's impressive, Michael! What does it mean?"

Michael didn't laugh. "The greater the calm, the closer the south wind."

"I see."

"It's been a while maybe," Michael said, "but it felt a mite safer knowing the boat was nearby. It was modeled after the Lukin style, you know. Then again, no one took good care of her."

"Well, maybe you should have if it meant so much."

"There's the rub, Sir William. Who can afford to maintain it when keeping your own vessel afloat is tricky enough?"

"It's that tight?" Sir William asked.

"Tighter, sir,"

"I'm sorry."

Michael shrugged and squinted into the morning sun. "The lighthouse is gone too."

"The lighthouse? The one at the end of Red Pier?"

"She's the only one we had, sir," Michael said. "Busted over by the evening storm. The south wind dined upon Douglas last night."

"That sounds dangerous, man." Sir William turned to look toward the pier but couldn't see it from where they stood.

"We've rigged a lantern on a pole," Michael said. "It'll have to do."

"Are there no funds set aside for such eventualities?" Sir William asked.

Michael laughed. "By who, sir? It's the fisherman's lot."

"Thanks for the insights, Michael."

"You're quite welcome, sir." Michael stared toward the bay. "I suppose when it's needed again, there'll be a cry. Always seems that way. Good day, sir." He jogged away.

Sir William watched Michael as he rejoined his mates. They took such a peculiar interest in the loss of the boat. Sir William looked past the ebbed water line, farther out toward Conister Rock, also known as St. Mary's Isle, and watched the foam-riddled rollers crash against its jagged terrain.

Chapter 3

"Rot! These infernal potholes!" Sir William's face contorted. Emma and Sarah rocked and swayed, rustling and crinkling their grand dresses.

"The dogs!" Colonel St. John grumbled. "They'll collect a tax but God only knows what they spend it on."

The rented carriage bumped wildly despite the agonizingly slow pace.

"I've heard, Father," Sarah said, holding her feathered hat pressed to her towering coiffure, "there may soon be an end to the income tax in England. Perhaps there shall also be to some of the fees on the isle."

"Really?" Colonel St. John replied with a trace of sarcasm. "And there's been talk of roads made of crushed stone, but talk it remains, you'll notice." His head bobbed, forcing him to make a hiccupping sound.

"Speaking of laws," Sir William interjected, "I've been meaning to have a talk with you on that subject, Ambrose. You'll recall—"

The carriage suddenly jolted and tilted down.

"Whoa!" the coachman cried. The coach was instantly motionless.

Major Caesar Tobin rode his horse up to the coach. "Whoa," he said, stopping to peer inside. "Are you in a comfortable state?"

"Hardly, brother!" Emma said, helping to upright Sarah's hair.

Colonel St. John leaned over. "Caesar, if the governor insists on throwing a Christmas extravaganza in Castletown, he might leastways make a road to get there!"

"You know the score, Colonel," Major Tobin said, steadying his uneasy mount. "If it's to be a governor's holiday, then the capital city it is. No matter, it's needless to fret, old chap. I'll push you out."

The major dismounted and handed the reins through the window to Sir William.

"Shall we disembark?" Sir William asked. "Lighten the load?"

The major removed his uniform dress helmet, tucked it under his arm, and placed his hands along the bottom side of the window to lean in. Though the Fencibles had disbanded years ago, Sir William's brother-in-law still wore the uniform dress, especially on occasions like this. His slender frame flexed admirably for a man in his upper-middle years. His matted black curls still bore the ringed impression of his headdress.

"To request such an exodus would be to suggest an abundance of weight I daresay is not consistent with the cargo inside." He smiled at the ladies, his perfect teeth as white as his military collar.

"Haw!" Sir William laughed. "I protest! It was the weight on this side I was referring to." He rapped his knuckles on the side of the coach, prompting the major to reverse the direction of his head.

"I say," Emma said, tapping her umbrella on the carriage floor, turning the major's head once again. "Am I to be so insulted as to be referred to as mere cargo?"

"Oh, dearest sister," Major Tobin said, "it appears I cannot win under such flanked position." He withdrew from the carriage. "Stay where you are, I'll have all of you free in an instant."

"Coachman!" Colonel St. John bellowed. "Work with him."

The grunts of the major, the hollers of the coachman, and the whinnying of the horses were easily heard within the carriage. It suddenly lifted and lurched to roll forward a foot. Major Tobin's face again appeared. "And not a spot of mud on my breeches!"

"Dashing!" Sarah said.

"Quite!" Major Tobin replied, regaining his reins and mounting his steed. "We are resumed." He galloped ahead, and the carriage rolled forward.

"It could be worse," Sir William said, again jostling. "We've normally snow this time of year."

"If it were snowing," Colonel St. John said, "we'd have no reason to make this wretched trip."

Sarah tapped his knee. "Father! And miss all the fun! I hear there will be waltzing this night. Sir William, you must do me the honor."

"Waltzing?" Colonel St. John asked. "What in King George's name is that?"

"Really, Father, you are behind the times," Sarah said. "It is the latest dance."

"The fashionable dance," Emma added. "Although with quite a few turns."

The colonel looked at Sir William and rolled his eyes.

"Cheer up, old man," Sir William said. "When tonight comes the morning after will be all the nearer. Such torture won't be eternal."

"It should take us all night to get there," the colonel said. He looked out the window. "This is no happy expense to me."

Sarah pouted. "Father, don't be such a black cloud."

"Don't take him too seriously," Sir William said. "It's just this miserable journey. He'll straighten up once the destination is attained. Isn't that right, old friend?"

"Humph." The colonel leaned back in the cramped quarters, folded his arms, and closed his eyes.

"A rough road is a small price," Emma said. "Soon we will forget the bumping and the gaiety will be well worth it."

"I think not," Colonel St. John said with eyes closed. His face rocked back and forth.

"Courage!" Sir William said. "You know the old Hillary saying: With courage nothing is impossible."

Emma laughed. Sarah burst forth a piercing giggle and then covered her mouth.

"And what, pray, is so funny?" Sir William asked.

"Oh, nothing, dear," Emma said. "It's just that you invoke your motto so often yet still surprise me where you find it applicable. This time you mean to inspire courage in the carriage, I suppose."

Sarah filled the coach with joyous laughter.

"Really?" Sir William said somberly. "I do not think it was quite that funny."

"I think it was, dear," Emma said.

"As do I, sir," Sarah added, failing to restrain herself.

Colonel St. John opened his eyes and smiled broadly. "It was somewhat amusing."

"Ha!" Sir William exclaimed. "I see the plot. Quick to reply at my expense, aren't we?"

The others laughed as the coach bounced along.

"I do believe you are now praying your food to take flight, Sir William," Sarah said from behind her gloved hand.

Sir William limply turned his entrée over with his silver fork. "No, dear Sarah," he whispered, amused. "Though you are correct in pointing out my distaste for water fowl, this isn't seabird. The soup was pheasant. This also is, only larded."

"And what of the partridge, hey, Sir William?" Lieutenant-Governor Cornelius Smelt asked from the opposite end of the long table, which was surrounded by guests. His stately figure was impeccably arrayed in full regalia, including a gold epaulette on each shoulder. "Is it to your liking?"

"It seems you're both mistaken," Emma whispered with a smirk.

"Just now moving in on the—er, partridge, Governor," Sir William replied, holding high his forkful of food and then sliding it into his mouth. "Mmm, as tasty as the first course was stimulating, sir."

"Excellent! A toast, then," Governor Smelt said, lifting his glass of Madeira. "To each of you who managed the journey from anyplace other than Castletown. Remarkable spirit."

"Hear! Hear!" Sir William responded with a tip of his glass. Around the table, ladies and gentlemen joined the chorus of salutations.

Sir William chewed the wild game. It was tougher than he preferred. He glanced around. With Emma on his right, Sarah on his left, the large dining table filled with foods that flowed in courses á la russe style, and uniformed men and their ladies in attendance, Sir William knew he should feel as light as a feather.

He used to love the jocular atmosphere of formal dinners. He had once moved easily within such environments, especially during the first few years after his arrival, and had always been delighted to see his many recent friends in attendance.

He looked at his wife. She ate daintily and conversed easily. It had been only sixteen months since their wedding vows, but it felt as though they had been married at length. Sometimes, while in the tenderness of her embrace, he nearly forgot the life he had before. No, the emptiness in his soul wasn't due to her. Even her brother, Caesar, had embraced him as though he had been a childhood friend. All was well in that department.

Sir William swallowed the partridge, aided by the wash from his glass of cider, and tapped his lips dry with linen. Too much lard.

The dinner proceeded through several courses, featuring removes, entrees, and desserts. Tarts and compotes, fish and puddings, duck and creams and figs all found their way around the table until at last the women retreated to a fire-warmed drawing room and the gentlemen remained to stand and dialogue, many with small glasses of port in their hands.

Sir William approached the two gentlemen warming themselves at the fireplace across the room. At a little over six feet, they stood nearly as tall as he. Sir William bowed his head. "Graves! Burbridge!" he said, extending his hand. They each shook it vigorously. "With the table conversation going as it did, I didn't have opportunity to comment. I half-expected to see at least one of you on the road to Castletown today. You must've left much earlier than I."

Lieutenant Burbridge snorted. "Earlier than that, I'd say."

"We arrived together yesterday," Lieutenant Graves said, "having made arrangements with Smelt to come a day earlier."

"That explains it," Sir William said.

Lieutenant Burbridge set his glass on the mantle. "A happy morning of pheasant hunting urged us to do so," he said, mocking up a rifle-toting position.

"A plentiful bag, I hope?" Sir William asked.

"The hills are full of them," Lieutenant Graves replied.

"And the wives?" Sir William asked. "They are enjoying the trip?"

Lieutenant Burbridge retrieved his drink. "Most giddy, I must say. There's plenty of gossip to catch up on."

"Apparently our good old town of Douglas doesn't provide them with near enough," Lieutenant Graves said.

"I don't know." Sir William chuckled. "There aren't many secrets that survive Douglas."

"There's a bet you won't lose," Lieutenant Burbridge said, gulping his port and belching. "If you want it known, share it there!"

"Did you see the papers?" Lieutenant Graves asked. "About the removal of our beloved isle's protections from English creditors. I saw it coming, of course."

"A most unfortunate development," Sir William said.

"Only for those concerned," Lieutenant Burbridge said, raising his glass. "To us who remain unaffected! Hear! Hear!"

"Hear! Hear!" Lieutenant Graves answered the toast.

"Unfortunate for some but surely anticipated by most," Burbridge said, exchanging his empty glass for a full one from the attending servant.

"It was predictable," Lieutenant Graves said. "There was ample time to make preparations." He raised his glass. "Assuming someone needed to do so."

Burbridge acknowledged the toast. "Defensive formations were always your suit, lieutenant. There was never a shudder in the men while you were in charge. Always prepared with countermeasures, your men were."

Lieutenant Graves smiled, bowing his head.

"Hear! Hear!" Sir William said with less excitement than before, beginning to feel some indigestion. He recalled the larded partridge.

"You're looking somewhat pale, Sir William," Lieutenant Graves said. "Are you all right?"

Sir William forced a smile. "Yes, quite all right. I was only thinking, that is all. I was considering the toast and the reference to your former naval exploits. Clearly, nothing beats a good defense."

Graves nodded.

"Nothing except perhaps a small fortune!" Lieutenant Burbridge snorted a thick laugh. "Jolly for us who can manage a few advances! Eh?" He raised his glass and then gulped much of it down without waiting for replies. "My troops were always the brave and ready when time to rally a charge, eh?" He took another swig, a small amount spilling over the rim. "As were you, Sir William. No! No! I must switch to your other most honorable title. Lieutenant-Colonel Hillary, commander of the once great and impressive Essex Legion—than which there was no land-based militia as large or as well financed in all of England."

Sir William felt the bittersweet pain of the memory.

"Something we shall not overlook." Lieutenant Graves smiled and sipped his port.

Sir William lifted his glass but stopped short of drinking. "Gentlemen, I do believe I'm ready for some night air. Excuse me." He looked at both of them square on, endeavoring to sport a smile.

Lieutenant Burbridge motioned to the passing servant, acknowledging Sir William while eyeing the tray of brimming wine glasses. "Until our next rendezvous, Sir William."

"Good evening, sir," Lieutenant Graves said.

Sir William took full advantage of his long strides to retreat toward the large second-floor veranda. It would be cold but entirely better. Few would be gathering there, though he had noticed Ambrose venturing that way only moments before. There was something more than larded partridge coming back to threaten his comfort. It needed to be addressed.

As Sir William neared the doors, Colonel St. John returned from the veranda. "Brr! Not a night for standing among the sculptures, I'm afraid."

Sir William grasped his friend's arm and turned him back to the veranda.

"Good heavens, Sir William, did you not hear my weather report?"

Sir William forced their retreat to the drafty location. "Ambrose, old friend," Sir William said softly, "we must confer. It is most important we do so."

His friend's face wrinkled. "What is it? Can we not do it indoors?"

"No," Sir William said. "I'm afraid not."

Colonel St. John stuttered.

"It's personal," Sir William said.

Slowly, the colonel's face relaxed. His eyes softened. "What is it, Baronet?"

Sir William smiled. "You always do that, good friend."

"Do what?" Colonel St. John asked, appearing dumbfounded.

"Don't play dull with me. Whenever you detect me to be in pain, you invoke my title," Sir William said. "It is appreciated."

"It is a well-deserved title," Colonel St. John said. "You honored all of England with the legion you mustered in defense of her shores."

"Ambrose," Sir William said. "You are correct in sensing my pain. I am a mix of frustrations, I admit. And fears."

"You? Hogwash! Moody as of late, yes, but fearful? Never! Do you so quickly forget your own motto? You invoked it for the thousandth time in the carriage only this morning. Courage!"

"Courage for what?" Sir William blurted, throwing his hands up. "That's part of the problem, I think. I am as restless as a fish on a rock!" He crossed his wrists together. "Only my hands are tied!"

"How so?"

"For one, everything is lacking meaning. I have no sense of mission." Sir William walked to the edge of the veranda and peered over the waist-high wall into the moonlit gardens below. The statues looked like dark hulks.

"You have a good life here," Colonel St. John said. "What more do you want?"

Sir William faced his friend. "I had purpose with the Essex Legion," he said. "I don't know where I'm going from here."

The colonel's nostrils flared. "I see. I think." He paced along the wall. "You are having a personal crisis. Am I right? There are no wars to fight. There is no gold strike to run after. There is no heart to be won. Is that right?" He looked up.

Sir William spread his arms wide. "I don't know. Emma is lovely, and I do love her. I have no desire in those respects. It's the lifestyle that bores me. What are we doing? I become depressed when I realize, especially since the creditor protection has been lifted, that I likely can't afford to do anything meaningful even if I could think of something meaningful to do."

The colonel clasped his hands behind his back and paced several long, slow strides and then turned around. He walked close and looked up into Sir William's face. "Have you had too much brandy?"

Sir William shook his head. "No, old friend. And then there's the financial matter."

"You know I'm one of the last people you should ask for help in that area."

"Perhaps," Sir William said. "But I've been trying to figure out a way to protect my assets should this recent change of law seek to adversely affect me and my station. I think I have an idea, but it involves your daughter and therefore your permission."

"Do not disappoint me," Colonel St. John said, raising a hand between them and moving back a half step. "I would not be able to bear it."

"Without question." Sir William stood straighter. "My integrity remains intact, as does hers. That most certainly was not my meaning."

The colonel nodded, briefly closing his eyes and lowering his hand. "Very well." He glanced up at his friend, one eyebrow cocked. "But we must not forget her initial fascination with you when you first arrived."

"Of course. But you know that to have been a mere child's fancy on her part, and never an ounce of intention on mine," Sir William said. "That has long since passed, and you know she has been as a daughter to me and a trusted friend to my betrothed."

"Your *second* betrothed," Colonel St. John said, firming his countenance.

Sir William lowered his gaze then immediately righted his attention to meet the colonel's eyes. He set his jaw. "Such an unfortunate fact is partly the issue at hand."

"Has the former Lady Hillary changed her mind about the present arrangements?"

"No, nothing like that. All matters pertaining to my marriage to Emma are as agreeable to all parties as before." Sir William hesitated. "It is with regard to that estate and the assorted financial matters therein that I mean this plan to address."

"Recall to whom you are speaking, Sir William! I am nothing but a half-pay man. Packs of creditors nip at my heels."

"All the more reason you should understand," Sir William said. He could taste the partridge again and felt seriously ill. "I also have concerns over creditors."

The colonel's eyes widened. "You? Former commander of the Essex Legion? With private income from the Danbury estate?" The colonel shook his head. "I don't believe it." He said nothing more for several moments.

Sir William wanted to explain but waited for his stomach to settle.

The colonel resumed. "The baronet ruined? Impossible."

Sir William exhaled a long, slow breath and looked up. "Not ruined," he said. "Vulnerable."

"What do you mean?"

"When all was said and done," Sir William said, "the Essex Legion cost over £20,000, seriously drained the estate, and largely ruined the marriage."

The colonel's eyes widened again, his mouth dropped open. "The very cause of your being given the honor of a baronetcy was also the undoing of your first marriage?"

"In a way, yes," Sir William said. "There were other issues, of course, but in my zeal to raise a proper militia to protect our shores, I, well, should I say, 'lost sight' of at least a proper measure of prudence."

"Overzealousness is something I've noticed in you before, more when you first arrived than now," Colonel St. John said.

"I've had difficulty in finding my passion these days, it's true."

Colonel St. John placed a hand on Sir William's shoulder. "But those were threatening times. It was widely held that Napoleon would cross over at any minute."

"But he didn't."

"But if he had—"

"But he didn't!" Sir William snapped.

The men stared at each other. Sir William's eyes burned as he saw the colonel's filling.

The colonel removed his hand. "You said this concerns my daughter."

"I have other sources of income," Sir William explained, "mostly due to the sale of my family home and the death of my brother Richard, whose Jamaican plantation afforded me some benefit."

"Sugar?"

"Yes," Sir William replied.

"So the worldwide glut of sugar has made that benefit somewhat smaller, I suppose."

"Precisely," Sir William said. "That, when added to the currently precarious position of the Danbury estate, meaning it is not clear whether or not it shall fail—when these circumstances are considered—"

"You are telling me much more than I have a right to know," Colonel St. John said.

Sir William ignored him. "When these circumstances are considered in light of the recent tax laws and changes in creditors' rights—"

"I see it!" Colonel St. John said. "The new creditors' rights! The isle is no longer a safe haven from debts incurred in dear old England. Therefore, given the present state of your affairs, you are vulnerable should the estate fail and the dogs come after you here! Is that right?"

"Right again," Sir William said, feeling somewhat relieved over getting it across, but not too well since the threat remained.

"Is the estate at risk of foreclosure?" Colonel St. John asked.

"Not so far as I know. But it has the potential to be should market forces make it so."

"So, though you hid it well—better than most, I'd say—like so many others here, you really did come to the isle as a haven from such an eventuality should your financial situation never right itself."

"Yes, old friend," Sir William said, feeling as though he were admitting some sinful behavior to a clergyman. "That, and the isle's own currency being worth fourteen pence to an English shilling."

"Beats the usual twelve, doesn't it?" Colonel St. John asked, rubbing his chin and nodding.

"You know that some of the others who've migrated here have been absconders. I wasn't and still am not," Sir William continued. "I am current with all debts. But in the event things turned for the worse, and in light of the marriage having buckled under all that pressure, this was a wise place to settle."

"You are quite the mix of emotions, Sir William," Colonel St. John said. "And circumstances." He walked back and forth a few paces, briskly rubbing his hands over his arms. "Rotten cold, it is." He turned around. "If I'm to understand the purpose of these confessions, it is to say that you are, as of yet, not in any real trouble of insolvency. However, should the Danbury estate eventually collapse and the creditors be yet unsatisfied, they might elect to seek you out since there now remains not even a vestige of the old law providing shelter."

"You have deduced it brilliantly," Sir William said, moving closer, also feeling chilled.

The colonel cocked his head. A frown appeared, and his eyes seemed to scan Sir William from toe to head. His head trembled slightly from side to side and his eyes again grew moist. "I am pleased that you feel so trusting of me to share such exposing things. I reserve no disappointment due to these details, believing your predicament has come about from noble efforts to defend your country rather than mischievous scheming or reckless imprudence." He stepped closer and whispered, "You have risked no danger of these details being repeated in any circle." His face brightened with a soft smile. "But I need ask you, what does this have to do with me and my youngest daughter?" He shrugged. "You know my situation." He began to drift into that faraway look.

Sir William placed his hands on the colonel's shoulders. "Ambrose—"

The colonel surprised him with an interruption. "Unlike you, I have debts accrued upon this lonely isle," he said. "I am unprotected regardless of what the old law was or new law is. I have no station to offer you. I am no safe harbor. Why do you come to me?"

Sir William was relieved his friend hadn't fallen into one of his remorse-filled trances. He looked deep into the moist eyes of his closest friend on the isle. "Your permission and blessing is essential to my plan."

"A plan for purpose?" Colonel St. John asked. "I don't see how."

"No," Sir William said. "I've not figured out a plan for that yet, but as far as my finances are concerned, I do have a plan."

"Well, whatever it is, I advise you to not leave your Emma behind," Colonel St. John said.

"I wouldn't dream of it," Sir William said.

"I don't exclusively refer to the literal sense," Colonel St. John said, holding up clenched fist and pointing his thumb at Sir William. "I mean let not your obsessions remove her from first place in your thoughts."

"Sage advice, old friend," Sir William said. "She is the center of my heart, I assure you."

The colonel walked away and lifted both hands into the air. "Then what, pray tell," he asked with bemused smile, "is your plan?"

"There you are!" Major Tobin shouted from the entrance to the veranda. "Are you already so drunk that you dread not this cold?" The major strode into their midst. "Come, you must discover the pleasantry of Felton's new pocket billiards. The governor has recently received it from England and has for several minutes been calling for you to compete with him."

"Very well," Sir William said. "Of course." He motioned indoors with his hand. "Colonel?"

"Mysteries upon mysteries," Colonel St. John said grumpily. He shuffled toward the interior of the home.

Sir William stared hard at his friend, attempting to warn him not to let on about their conversation, but it was too late. The colonel's back was toward him, and he had already stepped inside.

"Mysteries?" Major Tobin asked, following the colonel alongside Sir William. "Whatever do you mean?"

The colonel turned around to answer. Sir William felt ill.

"I'll tell you," Colonel St. John said, his face wrinkling. "First I hear of something called a 'waltz' and now I hear report of 'billiards' on the isle! Will this world never stop spinning?"

"I should hope not," Major Tobin said with a laugh. "What say you, Sir William?"

"Sir William has spoke enough," Colonel St. John said. "Lead the way, Major. Show us what is to be made of this game."

Major Tobin smiled and whispered to Sir William, but loudly enough to be heard by all three. "Crusty old chap, I daresay."

"Quite!" Sir William said. "Do lead the way, though."

Major Tobin strode forth, Sir William right behind, and Colonel St. John lagging in third. "The world marches on," Major Tobin said gleefully.

"And the dogs chase it!" Colonel St. John said.

"Dearest Amelia," Phillip Garret said, his sparkling blue eyes bright and clear and never removing their fix upon her as he stepped first to one side and then the other while holding her hand. "It has been too long since this pleasure has been mine to cherish."

"My honorable friend, Phillip," Emma said, slightly bending her knees and tipping her head. She walked past him and then turned to face him again as they danced the quadrille. "You know it has been many years since I preferred that choice of address." She smiled.

"Ah, yes," he replied in kind tone. "Forgive me for not mentioning it. It is only that having to say 'Lady Hillary' is a stabbing pain in the heart of every man who knows she is not to be of his household." He raised her hand high enough for her to walk under.

"'Emma' will do," Emma said, moving on to the next in line.

As she stepped and dipped and twirled her way through the line of Manx society, composed mostly of former military men on half-pay, erudite types who sought the isle as creative and restorative refuge, and younger men of considerable social standing from the mainland sent here for unknown reasons, Emma could not keep from reflecting on Phillip and his words. She looked forward to the opportunity of circling back to him, which the dance was faithful to provide.

Phillip Garret was known as one who excelled not only at performing the quadrille in perfectly timed steps and rhythm, but also in effecting the most entertaining and flattering conversation. Yet her interest was not a romantic one. Despite his being a fashionable businessman with success and renown in privateering, speculation, and whatever else his imaginative mind could think to conquer, Emma did not regret rejecting his proposal so many years ago.

He was dashing, no doubt, a perfect gentleman, her childhood friend, and a close friend of her family, especially her brother, Caesar. Despite all these perfectly aligned attributes, he simply wasn't one who had successfully stolen her heart. That honor was reserved for Sir William alone, and it was a choice she did not regret. However, she did enjoy conversation with Phillip, and it was to such conversation she was happy to return.

"Ah, Lady Emma," Phillip said, "I can breathe again."

"Indeed, breathe!" Emma said. "I thought it strange that your face was closely matching your eye color."

"Not only that," he said, again flashing his bright and handsome smile, "it is my heart that is bluest of all that again we must soon part." He lifted her hand, and she stepped under and moved on.

"Will you be prone to learning a new dance tonight?" Lieutenant-Governor Smelt asked Emma. "I've just returned from playing your kind husband in billiards that I had shipped from London." His stalwart frame perfectly filled out his many-buttoned uniform. "But the women shall not be trapped in yesterday's delights, either. There's a new dance being introduced tonight. It's called waltzing." He stepped first to one side and then the other while squeezing her hand.

"So I have heard," Emma said, again bending her knees and tipping her head, walking past and turning around. "I think I may."

"Then you will add to the perfection of the evening," Lieutenant-Governor Smelt said. He lifted her hand and nodded his head as she walked under and stepped away. She cast her eyes downward with respect.

"My lady!" she heard a very familiar voice say. She looked up and smiled. "Kind sir," Emma said, curtsying in exaggerated style and tipping her head sideways. "I am delighted to witness your arrival."

"It could not be too soon," her husband said. "A moment longer and the wolves might have carried away the desire of my heart." Sir William, resplendent in his highly fashionable dress, gently held her hand as she traced the floor with her foot, sliding first to one side and then the other.

"That is impossible," Emma said, deeply curtsying and tipping her head, then walking forward to brush against him. She turned sooner than usual in order to face him in close quarters. She wanted him to feel her breath. "As impossible as it would be for my husband to be found without honor and courage above all others."

"You must have married well," Sir William said, lifting her hand to his mouth. His kiss was warm.

She stepped under his arm and whispered as she moved past, "*Very well.*" And she moved on without looking back.

"Ah, Lady Hillary," Lieutenant Burbridge said, holding her hand a mite too hard. "You are all the more striking each time I see you. I believe I see a most angelic glow about you."

"I believe you are correct," Emma said.

"I have been known to produce such effect," Lieutenant Burbridge said, snorting a chuckle.

Emma smiled politely and stepped back.

Chapter 4

Several days later, in the early hours of a Douglas dawn, Michael Kellerman craned his neck to search the December sky. The horizon-hugging sun shone bright, and the azure dome was naked of cloud. Golden light crept over the harbor community like a garment of sheer chiffon.

Michael helped his six-year-old son, little Mike, get into the simple boat to sit near his portly partner, Joseph. Four other men—Red Kelly, Hunter Barnes, and the Miller brothers—were already aboard the large rowboat with a single bare mast. They each gripped an oar.

The narrow harbor lane, lined on one side by the rocky cliffs of Douglas Head and protected on the other by the stone pier, was peppered with small boats voyaging out to sea. Hundreds of seven-man fishing vessels had already rounded the end of the pier and were heading northward in search of speckling phosphorescence, the telltale signs of the coveted shoals of herring.

Into this exodus of nearly three thousand fishermen composed of grandfathers, sons, and grandsons, rowing and steering among nearly four hundred boats, Michael launched his.

"I'm betting Clay Head," Michael grunted as he put his back into it.

"I—don't—doubt it," Joseph said, matching the rhythm of the row.

"That's where the fish will be! You wait and see!" Red Kelly said.

"Is that far, Poppa?" little Mike asked, beginning to untangle a net.

"Not as far as it would be if we had a headwind to battle," Michael said. He grunted. "A few miles north."

"Miles? Is that why we left so early?" little Mike asked.

"We always—leave—early—little Mike," Joseph said.

Little Mike giggled. "You talk funny when you row, Mister Joseph."

"Ha!" Joseph blurted out. "I'm trying—to keep up—with your—father's—pace!"

"We launched early, you're right, son," Michael said. "We all need to leave harbor before the tide retreats. She'll ebb later." He rowed hard.

"Then how will we get back?" little Mike asked, reaching for another net.

"Those nets—look—fine—little Mike," Joseph said. "You're doing—a good job—for your first—fish."

"Thanks," little Mike said. "It's not my first, Mister Joseph."

"I meant—first—all day—fish," Joseph said, his forehead already a spate of sweat.

"You remember ebb and flow, don't you, son?" Michael asked.

"Yup," little Mike said.

"Be careful with those nets," Michael said. "Don't tear them. You're doing well, but don't rush none."

"Yes, Poppa."

"The tide will begin ebbing not long from now, but it will flow this evening," Michael said. "We'll time it to come back rightly."

"It's—an all day—fish," Joseph said.

"Oh," little Mike said, holding up a net and looking through it at his father. "Is this good?"

"Quite the fisherman, you are," Michael said. "Starboard oars!" He ceased rowing on one side and continued with the starboard oar. Joseph and the others did the same, and the boat turned left to head northward around the end of the pier. The makeshift lighthouse—little more than a pole with a lantern—hung loosely at the end of Red Pier.

"There—be not a—trace—of wind," Joseph said.

"All oars!" Michael commanded as the tiny boat straightened. "Calm as I like it!"

"Me too, Poppa."

Michael glowed on the inside as brightly as the rising sun shone on the side of his face. He loved to fish for herring. If all went well, they would haul in enough of the tasty fish during this one day alone to sell to the merchants and wholesalers for enough money to give his wife and children a decent Christmas.

Morning was almost done by the time they reached the place where the herring were running in record numbers. By midday, Michael and the rest of the Manx fishermen were repeatedly casting and hauling nets fattened with bustling fish. Little Mike's mouth and eyes were opened as wide as they could stretch as he watched the catch pour in.

Michael noticed his boy's dark hair being stirred. The wind was blowing from the south. He searched the horizon. The radiant blue sky met the line of distant sea with a hazy swath of gray.

Hours later, in the sanctuary of his hilltop home, Sir William tossed in his sleep. He kicked off his covers, causing Emma to stir.

"I'm sorry, dear," he mumbled. "I was dreaming."

Emma offered no reply but her slow, deep breathing.

"Did I wake you?" he asked. "I was dreaming I was in quicksand."

The howling wind answered.

Sir William sat up. The fire was still crackling, though a downdraft in the chimney coughed smoke into the room. He peered at the large windows facing the bay. The sheers were drawn but there was no mistaking the sound of the wind. He saw flickers of light filtering through his curtains and wondered if it were lightning. It looked like a swarm of fireflies. He crossed to the window and tugged open the curtains.

Douglas Bay was filled with hovering pinpricks of light. Bobbing lantern lights.

He unlatched the window and pushed it open. Cold air rushed in. The wind blew like great guns from the south, sweeping away the smoke. Leaning his head outside, he noticed another line of light— torchlight—along the shore of the bay. It appeared as if the entire community had gathered there, mere feet from the foaming chops of water breaking near the shore, where rocks protruded like deadly spears.

As his eyes adjusted, he better understood what he was seeing. A powerful gale had moved in from the south. The herring fleet was anchored in the bay, waiting for the flowing tide to reach a safe level before daring entrance to the harbor. The waves were tall and the troughs deep. Vessels bobbed and plunged, some of them with a lone light in their forward section. Some of the lights disappeared under clouds of salty spray.

Sir William crossed to the table at the side of his bed and quickly located matches to light his lamp. "Emma," he said, nudging her.

She stirred but did not open her eyes.

"My love," he said louder, shaking her more. "Wake up."

Emma opened her eyes. "William?"

"My dear," Sir William said. "We must dress and hurry to town. I'm afraid there may be a crisis developing."

"What time is it, dear?" Emma asked, rubbing the sleep from her eyes.

He helped her sit up. "I don't know. It's late. The seas are rough, and the herring fleet is anchored in the bay."

"Are they in danger, dear?" she asked.

"They may be," Sir William said. "It seems the whole town is out with torches. That is not a good sign."

"Very well," she said. "I will join you. Maybe we can help in some way."

"Let us hurry," he said.

Michael Kellerman had little Mike huddled between his legs and covered with a tarp.

Another wave splashed over the side.

"How much longer do you think?" Joseph asked.

"A bit," Michael said. He noticed the white-knuckle grip his friend had upon the oar although the oars were shipped for now. "Save strength, Joseph."

"The anchors are barely holding, Kellerman," said Hunter Barnes, a lanky mate with hollow cheeks and a pointed nose, seated in front and holding the lantern.

"I've noticed," Michael said. "We're creeping closer to the shore. We must stop that."

Red Kelly, brawny and square-jawed, looked up from under the brim of his soaked hat. "We ought to run for harbor, Mike. We don't want to strike rocks between here and shore."

"Yup," Michael said. "Only it's not certain there's enough deep in the harbor. We could run afoul rocks if we move early."

"Then we ought to row out along the anchor lines," Kelly said. "Buy time."

"We should've run north to Ramsey like some others did," Hunter Barnes said.

Booker and Brodie Miller, the remaining two of the crew, voiced their agreement.

"That's twelve miles," Michael said. "Could have been the right choice. Maybe." He looked southward into the face of the wind. Hundreds of boats were dragging their anchors, trying to hold out long enough for the harbor waters to return to sufficient depth. No one seemed willing to make the first run to port.

The wind grew fiercer and the waves raged tall. He looked to the shore of the bay. There were many boats close to grounding. Suddenly, he saw the first vessel founder. "Yonder boat!"

The crew saw the embattled fishermen. The unfortunate boat had swept in ahead of the flowing tide and struck rock. It turned sideways and flooded with gushing seas. Seven fishermen were sucked out of the boat. The crowd along the beach watched and shouted.

"That's Fergie's boat," Hunter yelled.

"No," Joseph said. "It's Mallard's."

"I can't tell," Red said. "Pray they make shore."

"The currents are frightful strong," Hunter Barnes said.

"There be many rocks between them and safety," Michael said. "Red, we'll row out."

"Aye, along the anchor line," Red Kelly said. His unshipped oar splashed into the sea. The rest did likewise.

"Poppa?" Little Mike peeked out from under the tarp.

"Not now, son," Michael snapped, quickly covering his son. "Be still."

"Oars!" Michael yelled, and the men pulled in unison into the oncoming rollers.

Another boat glided stern-first alongside them toward shore despite the frantic attempts of the men rowing within it. Its southerly facing bow dragged a snapped anchor line. There was nothing to keep it from shoving toward shore. The powerless boat suddenly struck rock. It spun sideways to the waves and flipped over, its hull glistening atop the sea.

"With all your strength, men!" Michael yelled. He examined his anchor lines. He knew they could make headway so long as their two bow anchors held. The lines were still taut. Michael whispered a prayer. "Don't fail us now."

Suddenly, a man from the overturned boat bobbed out from under the water. With one arm reaching upward he cried out, "Help!"

Booker, the younger of the Miller brothers, let go of his oar and reached over for the man.

"Avast!" Red yelled. "Man your oar, Miller!"

Brodie also let go and assisted his brother.

"Belay those actions!" Michael shouted. "Man your oars!"

It was too late. The sudden lessening of oar power was all that was needed to offset their movement against the violent seas. The boat lurched and pulled hard on the taut anchor lines. They snapped, and the boat turned sideways and rapidly rode a white crested wave toward shore.

"Poppa?" Little Mike yanked back the tarp and tilted his face up.

Michael saw his son's eyes wide with fear. He released his oar and leaned forward to take hold of him.

The boat tipped over, and the cold seas rushed in.

It seemed to Sir William that almost all of Douglas, most of them common fishing folk, had left their homes to congregate on the shore.

He and Emma worked their way among them along the beach. People were shouting, praying, and crying. It was chaos. Some ran into the rising waters to pull out floating bodies. Some of the fishermen emerged alive, though barely so. Others were battered and dead.

Men yelled. Women screamed. Many cursed the wind.

Sir William scoured the white-flecked waters curling around their feet. A man's body slid right past him, face down in the surf.

Another man splashed through the waves and flipped the body over. "It's Booker Miller!" he cried. "He's gone." He struggled in the surf to carry the man to dry ground.

"I'll help you," Sir William shouted, leaning to assist.

"Leave him alone," the rescuer said. "Nobody touch him." The man shoved Sir William aside and resumed his task alone.

"William, what do we do?" Emma asked. Already her dress and her winter cloak and cap were soaked with salt spray.

"I don't know." Sir William licked his lips, tasting the salt there. He looked around and saw boats swamping just yards away but the violence of the wind and waves turned the scene into a death trap with sharp rocks and entangling seaweed.

He looked toward the distant pier at the entrance to the harbor. There were more lights over there. Perhaps some were making it safely home. He looked back at the bay.

The number of foundering boats and washing bodies was incomprehensible. A woman's scream riveted his attention. He recognized her. It was Michael Kellerman's wife, Anne. "Emma, come." Sir William ran to the woman.

Anne Kellerman dropped to her knees in the brine-soaked sand, one fist clutched at her heart. In her other arm was her infant, Peter, wrapped in a swaddling tarp. Three-year-old Sylvia stood clinging to her neck. The small girl had a patched winter coat but no head covering. Her gnarled blonde locks were matted across her thin face. It was only then that Sir William saw Michael, his forehead bloodied by some sort of blow, walking in dazed circles, scouring the waves.

Sir William removed his overcoat and gave it to his wife. He pointed to Anne. "Wrap her in this. Stay with her." He ran to Michael. "Michael, it's me. Let me see your head."

Michael's gaze was eerie. Blood trickled between his eyes and over the bridge of his nose. "My son," he said. "I must find my son."

"Little Mike? Little Mike is out here?"

Michael's face contorted with grief. "My boy."

Sir William pulled two hankies from his vest pockets and wrapped his friend's head while looking in every direction for Michael's son. He cinched the makeshift bandage with a wet knot then moved his friend onto dry land. "Emma! Bring Anne and the children over here. It's dry. Don't leave them."

Emma struggled to get Anne to move. Sir William assisted and was able to help the despairing family trudge over to Michael, where Anne finally crumpled into a sobbing heap.

Sir William ran along the beach, his boots plopping in and out of the deepening muck. He tripped over rocks, got snagged by seaweed, but never stopped racing through the surf. He hauled bodies to shore, called others to attend them, and then moved on, searching for a body that could pass for a boy.

He saw Joseph, gasping and coughing in the rollers. He hauled him out and set others to take care of him.

"Thank you, Sir William," Joseph said, his round face dotted with wet sand.

"Sir William!" a voice cried out.

Sir William turned around. It was his brother-in-law, dressed in a nightshirt tucked into uniform pants. He wore a heavy coat, unbuttoned, and his feet were bare. "It is a catastrophe, man!" he said, his coat flapping like a torn sail. "I just came from the pier. Some boats got in safely, but one struck the pole holding the lantern marking the entrance. It was knocked into the sea and a pileup followed. It was horrible to see! Many smashed into each other and the pier."

"We aren't faring much better here, I'm afraid," Sir William said. "Have you, by chance, seen a boy among the rescued?"

"I have," Major Tobin said. He pointed.

Sir William felt energized. "Show me. Hurry!"

Sir William followed his brother-in-law back to dry ground, where several bodies lay surrounded by grieving friends and family. Off to one side was the body of a lad.

"No," Sir William cried. He ran to the boy, knelt beside him, and turned him over. The boy was limp, his face blue and puffy, and no breath lifted his chest. Sir William stared at the face.

It was not Michael's son. But it was someone's. "God bless your soul, lad," Sir William said shakily. He gently laid the boy down. He was reminded of his own son, Augustus, and was grateful his boy was not in danger this night. Wherever he was. He stood up. "Caesar, we must search for another boy."

Major Tobin nodded, and the men split up.

Sir William hunted through the swarm of anguishing souls. His heart ached for their loss. Scores of lifeless bodies washed up at the feet of torch-bearing loved ones. It was madness.

He saw another man in deep surf only yards away. Though he appeared strongly built, he offered no fight. Sir William lifted his knees and stepped high as he ran to him. The man clung to something, a barrel or a clump of net.

"I'm coming, man," Sir William yelled. "Hold on, friend."

He reached the man and grabbed his hair to yank his mouth out of the water. He didn't recognize the face. It was square-jawed and the matted hair was blazing red. Sir William partially broke the man's grasp of his cargo to make it easier to tow him. Sir William gasped and fell backward. "Heaven be praised!"

It was not a clump of net.

It was little Mike.

Sir William clambered to his feet and pried the young boy from the strong man's protective arms. He bent the boy over his shoulder, then gripped the man by the collar and dragged him far enough to be free of the rollers. Pulling little Mike into his arms, he studied the pale face.

Little Mike's eyes were closed, his lips slightly parted. Sir William pressed his cheek close to the boy's mouth. There was a faint breath. "Michael!" he shouted. "Little Mike!" He shook the boy.

Sir William jerked the boy's body and shook him again. He turned him on his side and squeezed his stomach. He rolled the boy onto his belly and pressed his back. Water flowed from the lad's mouth. Little Mike coughed.

Sir William waited until the water had drained from Mike's lungs into the sand, then he straightened the boy and beheld his eyes. They were half open. He looked sleepy. "Little Mike."

The boy coughed and sputtered. "Where's my poppa?"

Sir William hugged the boy. He looked down at the strong, redheaded man who lay battered and pale. His eyes were closed, his chest still. Sir William knelt beside him and whispered, "You did well."

"Where's my poppa?" little Mike asked. "I want to see my poppa."

"Ahoy!" Major Tobin ran up. "You found him."

"Thank God you are here," Sir William said. "Yes, this is the boy. Now I need you to attend this good man. I must take the boy to his parents."

"Red Kelly," Major Tobin said, dropping to his knees and examining the man. "It is a shame. He's dead."

Sir William stared at the red-haired rescuer. Then, saying nothing more, walked away with little Mike in his arms.

While he walked he saw some people ecstatic with relief having found family members alive. Many others wailed in torment as they cradled the limp body of a lost father or son.

When Sir William at last found Emma, only Anne and her two children were with her. Emma held the infant in one arm, and Sylvia sat curled up in a ball beside her. The wailing mother, still draped with his overcoat, was as limp in Emma's other arm as some of the bodies washing ashore.

Sir William saw Emma lock her eyes on him as he approached. He saw her whisper into Anne's ear. Little Mike's mother raised her head. Her forehead wrinkled, and a flood of tears washed over her face. She leapt up, Sir William's overcoat falling from her tiny frame, and ran toward them.

He lowered the boy.

"Momma!"

Anne Kellerman dropped to her knees and seized her son.

Sir William picked up his overcoat and draped it over the two of them. Emma walked up, little Sylvia gripping her free hand.

Sir William placed his arm around his wife. "Where is Michael?"

"Searching," Emma said, checking the cradled infant in her arm. She wiped her tears with a corner of the baby's swaddling. "Where did you find him?"

"In the arms of a fisherman," Sir William said.

"Mikey?" Michael Kellerman's voice rang out in a pitch that barely sounded like his usual voice.

Sir William and Emma turned to see the boy's father staggering toward his wife and son in disbelief. "Mikey?"

Anne released her grip and let little Mike run to his father.

"Poppa!"

Michael caught his son and lifted him high with both arms. He pressed him close while the rollers washed in the dead and the living and the south wind blew.

Chapter 5

"Blustery though it is," the vicar said, standing alongside Sir William in front of St. George's gates, "at least it's not snowing hard today."

"The day isn't over," Sir William said from behind the scarf wrapped tightly around his neck and the lower half of his face, just below his prominent nose. His gloved hands were shoved deep into his overcoat pockets, and his top hat tucked tightly onto his head with the help of the second scarf he wore wrapped around his head and ears. He could feel the swirling flurries landing cold and wet on his nose and cheeks.

"It's no wonder to expect more," the vicar agreed. He shivered. "I haven't seen this much December snow in a long time. It makes a bitterly cold shroud for the dead. I never imagined it."

It was December twenty-third, one week since the holiday dinner at the governor's in Castletown, several days since the great tragedy of the shattered herring fleet, and the day after the well-attended community church service in honor of those who had perished.

Sir William spoke through his muffler. "You needn't confess to me, Vicar. I fall far short of prophetic insights myself. No one was guessing weather like this, and certainly no one could foretell such large losses of life. It is horribly sad."

"You sure you won't stop in the rectory to warm up?" the vicar asked.

"No, I must walk on," Sir William said, waving. "Too late to delay any further. Despite the somber circumstances, the Christmas season is upon us. There are preparations to complete."

"Merry Christmas, Sir William," the vicar said, absent any joy.

"I pray it can be," Sir William said.

He trudged on through the heavy snow. The road was dangerous enough during dry times but presently too deep and icy for his horse, too steep for a sleigh, and impossible for a carriage. His boots felt tight, and his feet were cold.

His mind was awhirl with disjointed thoughts as the spinning flurries gusted around him. The mass of dead bodies. The wrenching sight of heartbroken widows and orphans. The red-haired man who had saved little Mike, only to lose his own life. The Kellerman family united, others broken forever.

He also felt anxious about his finances. No opportunity had since prevailed in which he could impress the details of his plan upon the colonel. On the carriage ride home from the governor's party, they had been joined by Lieutenants Graves and Burbridge, along with their wives, making it a very bumpy and crowded journey, with no opportunity for candid conversation.

Of course, the colonel and Sarah, along with Major Tobin and a few others, would be attending his house on Prospect Hill for a Christmas Eve celebration, but that would likely not produce opportunity either.

He reached the base of the hill at the edge of town and sighed. Even through his muffler, he could see his foggy breath. He felt guilty for thinking of his financial situation in the wake of so much death and despair.

He headed for a section of town he rarely visited. It was the extreme south side. He crossed over the footbridge that spanned what was left of the narrowing harbor waters to reach the tenement houses snugly tucked in the bowels of Douglas.

The streets were narrower and crazily crooked, slippery with snow and grime. The tall brick buildings helped block the wind but also trapped the smell. There was the obvious odor from the open sewers on both sides of the street, but there was also an acrid smell in the air. Black smoke wafted from the countless chimneys, but it didn't smell like wood. Sir William lifted his scarf to cover his nose.

A handful of open barrel fires burned between stairwells, their flames jumping and licking the edges of their rusty hearths. They spewed black smoke reeking with the odors of the crates and soiled rags burning within. Families huddled and shivered around them.

Sir William turned onto Enders Street and walked as swiftly as his cold and aching body permitted. The brick row houses were heavily shuttered and deathly quiet. Suddenly, a baby's cry rose up, a cat shrieked, and some kind of iron clanked. But all grew quiet again by the time Sir William reached the home of his friend.

He saw Michael sitting on his stoop, his head lowered, his arms resting atop his legs. Sir William tugged his scarf down from his mouth. "Michael?"

The fisherman, dressed in heavily patched garments, a knit cap, and gloves without fingertips, looked up. "Sir William?" Michael appeared surprised, though his countenance remained dark.

"Merry Christmas," Sir William said, crossing over and sitting down beside his friend.

"I'm afraid not, sir," Michael said.

"Don't let the grief of these recent days get you down, Michael," Sir William said. "We've got our health, man, and our families, now don't we? Little Mike is alive."

"The entire crew, except for Joseph, was lost, sir."

"I see," Sir William said. He wanted to say something more but found no words.

"The man who saved my son was named Red Kelly," Michael said, looking straight ahead. "I fished with him for seven years."

"He died a hero," Sir William said. He clasped his hands, locking and unlocking his fingers. The odors were strong, but Sir William resisted pulling up his scarf.

"A hero?" Michael asked. He turned his head and looked at Sir William and then resumed looking down. "A hero who doomed his family."

"I don't follow," Sir William said.

"Who will take care of his brood? I owe him everything, but I cannot take his family in."

"He saved yours," Sir William said. He stared at the side of Michael's head, hoping he'd make eye contact. "That was a noble and courageous act." Sir William offered a smile. "Right?"

Michael looked up and half-smiled. "Why are you here, sir? What brings you to our streets?"

"I'm here for you, Michael."

"Me? Why?"

"You lost your boat, didn't you?"

Michael's expression turned sour. His cheek rippled as he clenched his jaw. "Yes. I can't provide for my family any more than Red can for his. The boat is gone. The crew is gone. We might as well have all perished."

"We must repair such situation," Sir William said. He stood up and brushed off the back of his coat and the bottom of his pants. He stood before Michael, who sat there watching him.

"Without boat or crew, I've no means to catch. And without catch, no means to provide a right meal for the wife and brats, sir."

"What have I told you about calling them 'brats'?" Sir William patted his friend on the shoulder.

"Just an expression. There's no lack of affection, I assure you, sir."

"I know that, Michael," Sir William said, withdrawing his hand. "There's no better father than you, not that I know of. Every one of your children would agree. Little Mike, Peter, and Sylvia never doubt it. Neither does your lovely Anne."

"I appreciate you remembering their names, sir, and the missus," Michael said. "But a good father feeds his family." Michael stood up and loudly exhaled. "I'm sorry but I need to be going in."

"Now wait a minute, Michael." Sir William replaced his hands on Michael's shoulders and made him look square. "Now, now," he said softly, "there may be the loss of a boat, and there's the loss of good men, but there's no loss of hope, man. Courage is needed."

Michael squinted. "Courage won't feed the family, sir."

Sir William straightened, dropping his hands to rest on his hips. "I think it might."

Michael cocked his head sideways.

Sir William glanced at the door behind his friend. "Suppose we consider that while we visit your family inside."

Michael's face loosened. Sir William wasn't sure if his friend was relieved or disappointed. Michael turned and led the way into his flat.

The dwelling was smaller than Sir William could have imagined. "Oh!" Anne exclaimed. She looked startled or embarrassed, Sir William wasn't sure. She wore a long thick skirt of gray. It was well worn but not patched. Her dark blue blouse was tucked into her waist and buttoned to her collar. Her face was neither attractive nor unappealing, being so tightly cropped by her tied-on bonnet. A few strands of either light brown or possibly gray hair stuck out at the top of her forehead. Her eyes looked soft though a little baggy. She stood with her baby, Peter, cradled in one arm, her other hand held up to her mouth. "Oh," Anne said again, looking to her husband.

"Anne," Michael said, motioning to Sir William, "you remember the baronet, Sir William Hillary of Prospect Hill?"

"Yes," Anne said. She pecked her husband's cheek and then turned to Sir William. "You brought our son to us." Her voice sounded softer than it had that night along the beach. She lowered her eyes. "Thank you."

"Well," Michael began. He crossed the square room to sit in a wooden chair with spindle legs aside the fireplace. In the hearth, a gaggle of ropes and broken crates burned. He slumped into his chair, which creaked so loudly, Sir William was certain it would break.

Anne stared at her husband. She glanced at Sir William. "W-would you like to sit?" Her voice quivered.

It was only then Sir William realized he was bending over slightly to keep from hitting his head on the ceiling. He surveyed the room. There were no other doors. The floor was stone though a few throw rugs covered a spot here and there. A loom was in front of the fireplace and many implements such as kettles and bowls and spoons and fireplace tools hung from hooks all around it. At one end of the room was a large wooden bench with high ends and a flat hard surface for a seat. A sheet and blanket were folded at one end and a crumply feather pillow was at the other. It wasn't a bench. It was likely a bed.

A circular table leaned in the center of the room, and there was a bowl of dried flowers, mostly brown, atop it. Sir William wasn't sure if they were for decoration or something to eat. Scattered around the table were potatoes and leeks and a single knife blade with no handle. On the lower tier of the table was a triangular shelf filled with bowls and what appeared to be dried oatmeal. For the first time he saw the two other children crouched behind it, oatmeal on the corners of their mouths, their eyes wide with either curiosity or fear. They peered at Sir William as though he were a perfect stranger.

"Michael?" the woman asked, her voice trembling more.

The couple seemed so uncomfortable with his presence that Sir William decided to get to the point at once.

"Hanby's!" Sir William pointed toward the harbor.

The woman turned and stared at him. "I'm sorry?"

"The York Hotel," Sir William stuttered.

"I don't understand," she said.

"It's—it's a surprise, sort of," Sir William said. He noticed Michael staring at him as if he were a strange fish. "Michael wanted to let you know he'd be late tonight, but you'll see," Sir William said. "It will turn out well." He crossed to Michael, being careful not to hit his head. "Let us proceed there straight away." He placed an arm around his friend's shoulders and pointed him toward the door. "We'll see what courage might do for us today."

Sir William forced a quick pace toward the door. He turned his head for one last glance at the children, who had moved slightly to keep their eyes upon him. He smiled and glanced at his downcast fisherman friend. "Cheer up," he said to all. "Your father and I have a plan!"

Anne watched them as they backed out the door. "Good day, sir," she said. "Do come again." It was more a question than an invitation.

Matthew Hanby's establishment was a brown box of a building with symmetrical rows of vertical windows on all but the first floor, where two large, hand-lettered windows displayed, York Hotel. It sat quayside near the back of the harbor.

Most of Douglas had one oil lamp on each street corner with long stretches between, but Hanby's hotel had a row of them along the front porch. As Sir William and Michael approached the front door, Matthew Hanby, short and round and wrapped in coat and scarf, walked out with stepladder in hand.

"You're lighting already?" Sir William asked as he and Michael stepped up.

Matthew loosened his scarf. "It seems that a great many clouds are headed in," he said with a tiny voice. "No doubt it will darken early." He opened his ladder and situated it under a lantern. "What brings you to the harbor, Sir William? The Whitehaven packet isn't expected until tomorrow. Weather delayed."

"So I've heard," Sir William said. "You know Michael Kellerman?"

The two men nodded. Matthew reached into his pocket and pulled out a tinderbox. "You'll excuse me, gentlemen. I've some tasks."

Sir William climbed a step and placed his hands upon one knee. "Actually, I'm wondering if you might be of assistance to us."

Matthew tightened his small mouth, and his eyebrows lifted. "Yes?"

"It seems," Sir William said, "Michael had a most unfortunate incident, as many have recently, and lost his boat and very nearly his life."

"That is unfortunate," Matthew said, shifting his feet. "Sorry to hear it, Kellerman. Many sorrows these days. It's a sad holiday."

Michael shifted. He appeared uncertain where to cast his eyes.

Matthew stared at Sir William. "Well?"

"It being near Christmas," Sir William said, "and knowing how much our fishermen rely upon their vessels for food and trade, I thought you might be willing—"

"Sir William!" Matthew said, his tiny voice suddenly pitched with indignation. "The kitchen in this place only survives through paying customers. Otherwise it's my own family that goes hungry. I might have some bread or something, but—"

"No, no," Sir William said, raising his gloved palms from his knee. "You misunderstand my meaning."

Matthew's eyes jumped to survey Michael. "Well, then? What is it?"

"Sir William," Michael interjected, "I thank you, but charity wasn't my aim, sir."

Sir William smiled and extended his arms. "Gentlemen, I have a different idea than either of you are thinking. I'm referring to those!" He pointed across the quay.

"The harbor?" Matthew asked.

"Your rowboats."

"My rowboats? What about them? They are for the pleasure of my guests, as you know. And only in better weather than this."

"Of course." Sir William stepped back to the street and moved one step closer to the boats. "But they're never all used at once, and I was thinking, it being Christmas and all, you might lend one today. Lend it long enough for Michael to make a catch."

Matthew's chin pressed inward and his eyebrows rose. "Oh."

"As in you agree?" Sir William asked.

Matthew reddened. "Very well."

Sir William turned to Michael. "What say you get your gear and load up one of those boats?"

Michael looked back and forth.

"Take the closest to the base of the pier," Matthew said, pointing it out. "It's rarely used, but she's dry and she floats."

"And I'll be joining you, Michael," Sir William said.

"You, sir?" Michael asked, his voice cracking.

"Get your gear and load her up. We'll want to do what we can before the weather does darken." Sir William turned back to Matthew. "I do hope you're wrong about it getting dark early."

"Right away, sir," Michael said, running down the pier toward the fishermen's shacks.

"I didn't know you to be a fisherman," Matthew said, his tone indifferent. He put the tinder box into his pocket and folded the ladder.

"Are you not going to light them?" Sir William asked.

"I'll not curse the weather while you two are out and about. Let's hope the darkness holds off until darkness is due."

"I appreciate the thought," Sir William said, ascending the steps and extending his hand.

Matthew looked at it and smiled. He placed his pudgy hand firmly in the grip of Sir William. "I'll rent it regular to him for cheap, since his own is gone."

"I knew you had a soft spot, Matthew," Sir William said.

"I can't be promoting handouts and giveaways," Matthew said. "You know what sort of parade that starts."

"I understand. We both know a rowboat doesn't replace a fishing vessel, but it's something for him to work with until he can recover." Sir William peered down at the tiny boat. "How much will you sell that boat for?"

"I'm certain he can't afford what it's worth," Matthew said, his forehead squeezing tighter. "I'll have to think about it."

"I can afford it, Matthew," Sir William said. "Make it a fair price and put it on my account."

"*That* I can do, sir." Matthew smiled, his forehead relaxed, and a tiny peep of laughter escaped.

Sir William nodded and headed for the harbor.

"Merry Christmas, Sir William," Matthew said. "You're a good man, sir."

"Merry Christmas, Matthew," Sir William said from halfway across the street. "It's you who are kind. I knew I could count on that."

"I'll price it as low as I can, sir."

"Really, sir, I should like to be the one rowing," Michael said. "It's not right that a gentleman should be doing so."

"Nonsense," Sir William said, his voice slightly strained as he pulled, lifted, and pulled again. They cleared the harbor and rounded the end of the pier into rougher waters.

"I never knew you to be the type to enter such frail craft, sir."

"As long as we do not repeat your earlier performance at the beach," Sir William said, grunting. "And I insist we stay far from Conister Rock. No need to greet her unfriendly borders. I'm not a swimmer, you should know."

"You can't swim?"

"Not a stroke."

"Yet you insist on accompanying me to fish from a rowboat in December? Right game of you, sir."

"I'm not foreign to navigation and a little trimming of sail," Sir William said. Water splashed over the side.

"Then you've some experience, sir?"

"Not fishing," Sir William admitted. "However, as an equerry to Prince Augustus I had a time of beating about in more than one stormy sea around the coasts of Italy and thereabouts."

"You've been around royalty?" Michael asked.

"There was a time I knew one or two personally."

"You have known many privileges, sir," Michael said, pointing off the bow.

Sir William adjusted course to follow Michael's direction. "I named my son after the prince."

"You have a son?"

"And a daughter. Elizabeth."

"You are full of surprises, sir."

"And regrets," Sir William said, pulling hard on the oars.

"That's enough, sir. We shall first cast here."

Sir William ceased, and Michael threw out the first part of the net and marked it with a buoy.

"What did you mean when you said Red Kelly's family was doomed?" Sir William asked as he watched his friend work the netting.

Michael banged his thumb on the oarlock as he threw the remainder of the net. "Ouch!" He sucked the welt. "With Red gone, there's no one to provide for his wife and brats—er, children. He's got no brother or other surviving family to care for her. She'll likely move in with her sister, Dora. They're already hard-pressed."

"Oh."

Michael lowered his head. "He rescued my son and doomed his." He rubbed his thumb along his pant leg. "Most men don't dare to try to rescue others when they know they're desperately needed themselves. It's not our own lives we cling to. It's worry for those needin' us that keeps a fisherman sharp and scared. Red proved the fears. Who's to help his family now?" Michael pointed. "We need to go that way, sir."

Sir William rowed. His muscles felt strong, but his stomach hurt. He couldn't make all the problems go away. He wished he could. He had sometimes thought about sailors trapped at sea and figured he was brave enough to assist a wreck if a need arose. But what comes when a sailor or would-be rescuer drowns? He'd never thought about that.

Per Michael's instructions, he ceased pulling with his right and pulled hard with his left arm, then pulled a few more strokes with both before stopping so Michael could cast the next net.

"We'll not haul herring here, but this will do for other kinds, still edible," Michael said. "We'll go there next, sir." Michael pointed. "Shall we switch positions?"

"Not at all," Sir William said. "You're the net caster, I'm the lackey."

"You are no lackey, sir," Michael said, facing him. "You are very generous *and* very different from most of the 'Come-overs.' Many fishermen agree on that, sir."

"Thank you, Michael," Sir William said. "But let us not heap praises before we know if we're to go home with a catch or not."

"True enough," Michael said, pointing to the next spot. "We'll cast there."

Sir William rowed hard. His muscles were beginning to ache, but the exercise felt good, and he felt strong enough to handle a little more. He was certain he could row all the way across the bay and back if the situation needed it, but he hoped it didn't. He reached the spot and stopped. "Michael?"

"Sir?"

"It's no replacement for what you've lost," he said. "I can't replace your crew, but this boat is yours to help you get through."

Michael stopped his preparations to throw, and his eyebrows drew close. "Sir?"

"Merry Christmas, Michael. This boat is a gift from Lady Emma and myself."

Michael stared at him for several long moments. His eyes glistened. "Best of the catch to the Hillary household, sir," he said, tossing the net off the bow. "Merry Christmas."

"Hear! Hear!" Lieutenant-General Stapleton said in reply to the toast by Lieutenant Burbridge. Everyone raised a glass.

Hattie lifted the cover and steam rose like fog lifting from the sea to reveal a hot plate of broiled cod. The salty fish scent filled Sir William's nostrils as he leaned his head into the rising cloud and deeply inhaled.

"Careful you don't singe your insides," Hattie said. "That steam is mighty hot."

"The baronet loves the bounty of the sea if it's without wings," Sarah said, opting for the curried rabbit passed by her father, Colonel St. John. "No limit to what he'll risk to partake of it."

"Indeed I do enjoy a good fish," Sir William agreed from his seat at the head of the table. He helped himself to a large portion from the steaming plate. Hattie filled the glasses with more wine and disappeared into the kitchen.

"Particularly when he's had a hand in the catch," Emma added, seated to her husband's right.

"I wonder what his appetite is for flying fish?" Major Tobin asked.

"There's an untested query!" Lieutenant-General Stapleton said with a laugh from the opposite end of the table. His wife, Lady Margaret, sat around the corner from him on his left side.

"I am fascinated," Colonel St. John said. "How is it you can find a comfortable station to join a lowly fisherman in his rowboat? Don't you think it to be a mite unbecoming a baronet?"

"I think it honorable to aid the poor, Father," Sarah said.

The colonel lifted a basket of biscuits. "Then help yourself, my dear."

"Father, really!" Sarah said, reddening as she reached for her glass.

"You must note, dear Sarah, Sir William did get the best of the catch," Major Tobin said, spearing a large roasted potato. "Perhaps he's more enterprising than noble!"

"Brother, how dare you," Emma teased. "And at Christmas. Good will toward all, I say."

"Touché, Major, touché," Lieutenant-General Stapleton said, sipping his wine. "Sir William is no dolt in the presence of the working classes."

"I might be more duplicitous than most suspect," Sir William said.

"I think not," Emma said, caressing Sir William's hand resting atop the table.

"You can never be called duplicitous, my friend," Colonel St. John said. "Wearily undiscerning of dangerous precedent, perhaps, but never insincere."

Sir William raised his glass and nodded. "Thank you. I think."

"Dangerous precedent?" Lieutenant Graves asked. He and his wife were seated at the middle of the table, opposite Lieutenant Burbridge and his wife. "What sort?"

"Mixing with the dregs," Colonel St. John explained. "What good can come out of it?"

"Really, Colonel," Emma said. "How can one as sentimental as you feel so harshly toward those less fortunate?"

"I am hardly sentimental," the colonel grumpily replied.

"That's rightly said," Lieutenant Burbridge joked. He passed the rabbit to his wife, Jane, who sat beside him and playfully tapped his wrist.

"Forgive my husband's humor," Jane said, accepting the dish and extracting a small piece. "He's sometimes the rogue at dinner."

"Ha! Yes, well, rightly spoken again," Lieutenant Burbridge said with a wide grin.

Sir William laughed. "You don't fool me, Colonel, old friend. You call them 'dregs' and you claim to shun them, but there must be some other concern you haven't made clear."

"It is quite clear to me," Colonel St. John said.

"When one takes the time to understand their plight," Sir William said, feeling a rush of sentiment. He cleared his throat and continued, "One may be surprised at what becomes clear."

Hattie returned with another covered plate.

Major Tobin cut in. "I say. What are we talking about? Nothing is clear to me! Hattie, why is there none of your famous duck? I tell you, that is what most compelled me to journey up Prospect today. I held out hope for your marvelous fare."

"You'll not be disappointed in this house," Hattie said, lifting the cover and displaying the very object of the major's appetite.

"Ah." The major pretended to faint. "The Hillary house made into heaven. It ought to be the toast of the isle."

"You mean it is not?" Sarah asked. She lifted her glass. "To the preservation of my illusions, for I have often perceived this home as heaven itself!"

"Hear! Hear!" the lieutenant-general said, and he was echoed around the table.

"When does the Madeira arrive?" Major Tobin asked with a wink.

"He just asked for duck and now presumes the wine!" Hattie said as she approached with a decanter upon a tray. "He knows my every move, he does."

The celebrations and libations continued until evening. After dinner, everyone gathered around the Christmas tree in the parlor to sing Christmas carols and tell stories. Sir William told his favorites about the Essex Legion at its height, Colonel St. John recounted highlights from within the Worcester militia, and Major Tobin shared some concerning him and his brother John when they had sailed the Irish Sea as privateers and secured for themselves a considerable sum.

The ladies laughed along and later retired to the drawing room while the men moved to the great room where the large windows overlooked the bay. The light of the half moon made the bay appear as black ink mapped with white veins of chopping seas.

"I have news of a most interesting development, I think you should hear," Lieutenant-General Stapleton said. He stood in the center of the room and commanded the attention of the men. "It concerns an opportunity that may arise in Laxey."

"Laxey?" Colonel St. John grumbled. "Is there anything good in Laxey?"

"He's got you there, General," Lieutenant Burbridge said. "It's said that if you want to find anything worth finding in Laxey, you'll have to dig deep for it."

"Precisely the sort of opportunity I am alluding to," the lieutenant-general said, smiling and circling to make eye contact with each of the men.

"You refer to mining?" Sir William asked.

"I'm getting it," Major Tobin said. "It seems to me there is a dormant mine there, is there not?"

"There is." The lieutenant-general nodded to the major. "It's only seven or eight miles away, easy enough to investigate. I'm thinking of visiting there after the first of the year. Anyone care to join me?"

"She's a derelict mine," Colonel St. John said. "She's been stripped long ago."

Everyone waited for more to be said, but Stapleton casually walked over to a large painting on the wall. "What is this piece, Sir William? I've often admired your collections throughout your home, but I do not recognize the style of this one."

Sir William crossed to stand beside the painting. "It is not an artist you would know, though I'm happy to acquire the masters when I can. This one was a local artist from near where I grew up in England. The painting is of a place very near to Birkrigg, where I was born."

The others moved closer to inspect.

"It looks like it could be any scene of our own hills on the isle," Lieutenant Burbridge said. "I'd always assumed it was."

"No," Sir William said. "It is from England. I quite agree, however, it does appear similar to here, which may be one reason why I am so fond of being a Manxman."

"No one, save you," Colonel St. John said with a scoff, "would consider any of us Manxmen. We're 'come-overs' and no more."

"The colonel is quite right on that point," Lieutenant Burbridge said.

"I imagine those hills in the painting hold precious memories for you, Sir William," Lieutenant-General Stapleton said.

"You imagine correctly," Sir William said. "Shall we move to the gallery? There are some other exciting pieces you might enjoy, and I'm certain you'll recognize by whose hand they were fashioned. I am especially fond of my biblical collection, particularly the one of Joseph in prison. It's quite moving, I think."

"No," the lieutenant-general said, moving to a chair and sitting. "I have a mind to tell you more about Laxey, whose hills, like those in that painting, are filled with precious items that could prove profitable to us all."

"Tell me more," Lieutenant Burbridge said, sitting nearby. "Indeed, I like the sound of clinking gold."

"More like copper, lead, and silver," the lieutenant-general said, his eyes narrowing as his smile lengthened. "At least, that's the rumor."

"I believe I'll peruse the paintings you spoke of, Sir William," Colonel St. John said. "I've no wish for fanciful thinking about a long-derelict mine." He shuffled out of the room.

Sir William smiled but moved to where the others were seating themselves and stood among them. "Do tell, General," Sir William said. "You're not a man who speaks without something to say."

"Thank you," Lieutenant-General Stapleton said, tipping his head to Sir William. "If an adventurous search for piles of riches seems a worthwhile thought to any of you, then listen to my plan for a new endeavor, proposed to be called the Kirk Lonan Mining Association."

"Who proposes?" Major Tobin asked.

"Those who have already purchased shares and seek your purchases as well," the lieutenant-general said. "Have you any smokes in the house, Sir William?"

"Forgive me for not having produced them earlier," Sir William said, crossing to the fireplace mantle. He retrieved several from a box and returned to distribute them, taking none for himself.

"No offense, Sir William," the lieutenant-general said, puffing his cigar to a deep orange glow. "I know you're not a smoking man just as I know you've been reluctant to invest in anything here on the isle since you came here, beyond lines of credit with a few merchants. But this opportunity is, well, let us say, extraordinary, and we can all be the richer for it."

"No offense taken, of course," Sir William said. "But isn't the mine as the colonel described? That is, derelict?"

"Not derelict," Lieutenant-General Stapleton said. "Just abandoned." He filled the room with the smoke of his cigar and the words of his scheme.

The other men spoke little but for a few clarifying questions, which Lieutenant-General Stapleton addressed at length. "Technology today permits more effective means to strike the mother lode," he said. "The miners of old lacked what progress has bestowed upon us. We may be the fortunate few."

Sir William felt his personal interest piqued and admitted to himself, given the stated history of the mine, that it could remain stocked with precious metals, especially in light of the newer technologies. This venture would dig deeper than before, and there was no telling how much might remain buried.

"Well?" the lieutenant-general asked after nearly an hour of enlightening the men.

"Count me in," Lieutenant Burbridge said. "It's worth the £50 investment."

"That's per share?" Lieutenant Graves asked, his hand resting on his chin.

"And only twenty shares to be issued," the lieutenant-general reminded them.

"I'll take the ride to Laxey with you after the first of January," Major Tobin said. "I want to reserve my decision until I see for myself."

"And what about you, Sir William?" Lieutenant-General Stapleton asked, rising to his feet. "Surely you'll not have me leave tonight without at least knowing what you think of my proposed adventure." He patted Sir William's shoulder.

Sir William headed out of the room, the lieutenant-general at his side and the others following. "I admit to a heightened interest."

"Capital!" the lieutenant-general exclaimed.

"Though," Sir William continued, "I'm not one to make rash decisions."

"Ha!" Major Tobin said.

Sir William looked at his brother-in-law.

"You most certainly are not rash." Lieutenant-General Stapleton slapped Sir William's back. "I am all the gladder for that. You take your time to consider my proposition and reply to me in whatever way you determine."

They came upon Colonel St. John asleep in a chair in the gallery. After some playful prodding by Lieutenant Burbridge, the colonel fumbled a bit but rose and accompanied the men to attend the ladies.

By one in the morning, all the guests had departed but for Colonel St. John and his daughter, Sarah, both of whom were to stay the night. They joined Sir William and Emma to sit comfortably in the drawing room.

"It is time to retire to bed," Colonel St. John said.

"Hold on, dear man," Sir William said. "If you might indulge me a moment or two longer, I wish to speak of something I've desired to speak of for many days but haven't had occasion to do so."

"Let us not detain you from doing that very thing," Emma said, starting to rise. "Sarah and I shall make straight away to our bedchambers."

Sarah rose.

"No," Sir William said. "Honestly, I must speak with all of you. It is urgent. I beg your indulgence."

"Very well, love," Emma said, sitting straight and turning to Sarah. "Sarah?"

"I am awake enough to hear whatever you say, Sir William," Sarah said. "So long as you first permit me to say it has been a wonderfully enjoyable affair this evening. I welcome the opportunity to stay the night at this most holiday time of the year. It is very much a merry Christmas for my father and me." She curtsied and bowed her head. She resumed her seat and settled comfortably.

"I do so love you," Emma said, patting Sarah's arm.

"Am I to understand this," Colonel St. John began, then after interrupting himself with a great yawn, continued, "to be pertaining to that matter you first began at Smelt's? The financial plan you spoke of?"

Sarah yawned. "Oh, Father. I really wished you hadn't done that."

Emma yawned. "Forgive me, William. Go on, dear."

Sir William felt irritated. "It is for the future of Miss Sarah and for her importance to my wife, along with consideration for the best interests her father could have for his daughter, that I seek to propose a most mutually beneficial arrangement." He straightened his vest, tugging it from the bottom. "Yes, I do have a financial plan to propose. Much has been happening within me."

Sir William surveyed his small assembly. They were blank faced. His irritation grew. He cleared his throat. "It is with the highest regard for our closeness as friends who are indeed as close as any family could be that I make such a generous," Sir William said, walking three steps away and whirling around, "and daring, proposal."

"And on the eve of Christmas!" Sarah said, her face full of youthful admiration. "Very inspired timing, Sir William!" She bounced in her seat.

Sir William was taken aback. "Uh—yes, of course."

"Mind you," Colonel St. John added with a smirk, "he's been trying to open this present for over a week now!"

Emma laughed and leaned forward, waving her hand at the colonel. "You are such a heckler, Colonel!" She looked up at Sir William, her face kind and her attention fixed. "Go on, dearest."

"Oh, rot!" Sir William threw up his hands and waved them off. He stormed several paces away then returned, his face feeling hot. "I have need of special measures, and I hope our friendship is such that I might secure your assistance."

"Spit it out, man," Colonel St. John said, gruffer than usual. "Make your request."

Sir William surveyed each of them. The colonel was leaning forward, his countenance perkier than it had been all night. Sarah was angelic, totally unaffected and patiently awaiting his continuance. Emma, her deep green eyes soft and inviting, jerked her head as if to say "Speak now!" He did.

"I wish to pass all of my assets outside of the isle to Miss Sarah."

Emma gasped.

"Our families have been close these many years since having ventured to the isle," Sir William said. "Such an arrangement of mutual trust will inure to the benefit of all parties concerned." He stood still.

"What?" Sarah asked. "Pass what?"

The colonel hadn't moved or blinked or breathed.

Emma placed her hand to her neck and inhaled deeply. "William, what are you saying?"

Sir William exhaled slowly. "I am proposing Miss Sarah be the very person in whom we place our most sacred faith as a reliable trustee of my entire income that flows from England."

The colonel blasted forth with a venting breath and then sucked in what seemed like volumes of air. He stood and then sat and then leaned forward, his hands resting on his knees. "For heaven's sake, why?"

"What does this mean?" Sarah asked, looking back and forth among them. "Sir William? Can you explain?"

The colonel rose again and this time took several steps away before turning around. "Indeed, explain this foolhardy idea to all of us, Sir William. It is most puzzling."

"It is not foolhardy," Sir William said. "It has been done before by others, and I am proposing to do the same. It is a wise strategy to employ. Of course, it must be done in ultimate secrecy."

"But the risk," Emma said, rising to approach her husband. "I mean no disrespect to Miss Sarah or the colonel, but the risk. Have you not considered the risk?" She lightly touched him. Her hand trembled.

Sir William embraced her. "Emma, Emma, my queen. Of course I have. To not locate a trustee may be the greater risk. That is the point. Whom do we trust more? The creditors from Danbury or dear Miss Sarah? As my wife, you are no haven from creditors who could come calling."

"I don't understand," Sarah said, also rising. "Someone please explain what we are talking about."

"Lieutenant-Colonel Hillary," Colonel St. John began, stepping forward so that all four were facing each other in a small circle. "Sir William Hillary, the baronet, is proposing that you become the rightful owner of his entire range of assets outside of this island."

"In law the owner," Sir William pointed out. "In truth, a trusted but mere holder of them to pass cash forward to Emma and myself as we have need. It is an essential layer of protection from creditors who may come in search of my wealth, now that the once comforting shield has been legislated away."

"But why?" Sarah asked.

"The creditors would have no legal right to his wealth if it were stashed in the name of someone other than Sir William or his wife," Colonel St. John said somberly.

Sir William turned to Emma. "If I put them in your name, they remain unprotected," he explained. "But if we pass them into Sarah's name, they are safe forever."

"But," Colonel St. John said, stomping his boot on the floor, "Sarah will have the legal right to do with the money as she sees fit."

"She will see fit to do with it only what I instruct. That shall be our agreement," Sir William said. "Such is the value I place upon her moral character."

Sarah beamed like a full moon upon the sea. "It is safely placed, Sir William. I would never take for myself what is rightly yours. I should dare to suppose that I would barely seek what is rightly mine if it meant harm to dear Emma or to you, sir."

"It is a dangerous thing you propose," Colonel St. John said. "Such temptation is far too great for even as gentle a soul as my daughter's."

"Father! Do you question my honor?"

"I merely point out what is in all men," Colonel St. John said. He suddenly appeared sluggish and returned to his seat.

"Emma," Sarah said, taking hold of her hands. "If such a thing is necessary to do, surely you know I am your humble servant to do as you need."

Emma tossed her head from side to side, her usually peaceful countenance flushed and wrinkled. "Oh, Sarah, it is not your character that pains me. You are unimpeachable, dearest." Emma sat down, pulling Sarah to sit down beside her.

Sir William noticed his wife's tears. He stood in their midst and opened his arms wide. "Emma, Ambrose, Sarah," he said. "Fear not. I have meditated upon this course for many days. It is a sound plan.

And with it comes security for both of our families."

"How so?" Colonel St. John asked. "Other than my lovely daughter being placed into a most impossible position that will certainly set her up to disappoint you and justify what might otherwise never occur to her moral mind."

"Nonsense!" Sir William said with force. "You have made no secret to us of your precarious position, Colonel. This arrangement, should Sarah never marry or should she not have the right opportunity of marriage come forth, will permit Sarah to always know the joy and security of being a member of this household. Forever, Colonel."

The colonel looked up.

"Yes," Sir William continued. "She will be sustained by and be a central part of this household for as long as she wishes. You needn't worry how she will carry on once you are gone."

Colonel St. John became wistful and began assuming that faraway look. He rested his chin on his clasped hands.

"Ambrose?" Sir William spoke loudly. He didn't want the colonel retreating to his confounded trance. "Ambrose!"

Colonel St. John looked at Sarah. "It is true I have so little to leave you, daughter," he said, sadness filling his voice. "I am certain we will soon be poor."

"I have your love and your name," Sarah said.

The colonel stared into empty space. "I have feigned superiority over the dregs because I know I am one myself, I'm afraid," Colonel St. John said.

"Emma, Colonel," Sir William said, his voice gentler. "This is no occasion for mourning. This is reason for celebration. With such a plan in place there will never again be the threat of the Danbury estate creditors coming to rob us of all we have. We can, at last, be free."

Emma shrugged and smiled weakly. "Perhaps, my dear. It may be."

"Of course," Sir William said, kneeling down in front of his wife. "Any business we do locally we do not pass to Sarah. We do not want anyone save this tiny circle of knitted hearts to know of our arrangement. Local affairs we can keep in our name—in yours alone, if you like."

"That is not necessary, William," Emma said, resting her face against his chest and sobbing.

"Emma," Sir William said softly. "Trust me. This plan will prove to be the joy of all of us here. We will prosper without fear of raiders, without fear of ruin, and without fear of betrayal."

"That is certain," Sarah said, moving to hug Emma. "I will be as I have been, your most trusted and only daughter."

Emma lifted her head and smiled. She caressed Sarah's face. "You are precious to us, dear Sarah. I do love you."

"And I, you," Sarah said. "Forever." She touched her father's cheek. "Father, I know how you have feared leaving me with nothing. This will provide hindrance enough to that!"

Sir William rose up. "I, too, fear poverty. What man does not? That is the reason for my proposal." He looked at the colonel. "Well, dear friend, what do you say? Will you bless this financial plan for freedom?"

The colonel pursed his lips, and his eyebrows connected into a large wrinkle. "Freedom to do what?" he asked. "Have you thought of that?"

"Ah!" Sir William beamed. "The tragedy of the herring fleet has opened my eyes to an extraordinary need. There are exploits to be done greater than those any land-based militia ever dreamed about. There is a mission before us, I say, that far exceeds any glories of the once great Essex Legion!"

"A mission for what?" Colonel St. John asked, his eyebrows now twitching.

"I haven't worked out the details," Sir William said. "Something to help those who are wrecked domestically because of wreck at sea."

"What?" Emma asked. "What idea is this?"

"It's been growing in me as of late," Sir William said. "I've been bored and restless upon this island. Ever since the day the Essex Legion dissolved, I've been a man in search of his place. I may have found an object that makes my blood flow. I'm not sure."

"What makes it flow?" Emma asked, appearing earnest, her head tilted and her eyes fixed upon him. "What exactly are you seeing, dear?"

"I'm not seeing it clearly yet. It's more like—I'm still discovering— yes," Sir William said. "I'm feeling my way to a strategy, if you will, to help families who lose their loved ones at sea." Sir William searched the faces of his inner circle. They were all motionless. "I never understood their burden, though it is great. Sometimes, it may be the ones who survive the storms that are in greatest need. Has anyone been thinking of that?"

The colonel slowly rose. His face relaxed. "I know I haven't," he said. "Whatever your aspirations, it is your financial plan that leaves my Sarah in a position that could well test her character." He stared at Sir William. "But it is no greater a test than you shall face, having placed so great a trust in another." He turned and looked down at Emma seated in her chair. "Lady Emma?"

Emma returned his gaze.

"Have you thought less of me, knowing my finances to be unsophisticated?" he asked.

"You know better than to ask that," Emma said.

"I have thought more of you, knowing you are well off," Colonel St. John admitted. "It follows you should think less of me for my state."

"It does not follow," Emma said firmly. "Circumstances alone do not adequately testify to the merits or nobility of a man."

"That is why I love her," Sir William said, grinning. "She speaks the truth, Colonel. A man's financial condition does not necessarily tell his story."

"Let us hope you are both right," Colonel St. John said. He reached for Emma's hand. "May fears and cautions be found out to be misplaced, and may the future bring with it the kind of security and felicity so proposed by this man we all admire. If it meets with your acceptance, Lady Emma, I shall grant mine."

Sir William looked at his wife.

Emma dipped her head to one side. Her face softened, and her deep green eyes glistened. A red curl dropped down atop her forehead, her skin as white as cloud.

Chapter 6

S everal weeks later, Sir William walked tall in his fine suit, hat, and tails. The warming weather and drier skies made for a less hazardous trek, and there was the fragrance of spring in the air.

He strode up Athol Street, the widest and straightest in town, into the midst of the Douglas business district. He passed the law offices of Bluett & Dumbell, the lone architect's office, both of the Douglas physicians, the offices of the fledgling shipyard company, and several lodging houses before reaching the section just before the harbor bridge. This was where the finer restaurants were. Lieutenant-General Stapleton stood in front of one.

"Good day, Baronet!" Lieutenant-General Stapleton said, extending his hand. "A good day for a shareholders meeting, eh?" He laughed.

"A good day indeed," Sir William said, shaking hands vigorously. "Am I early or late?"

"All but St. John are here. I'm told he's not feeling well," Lieutenant-General Stapleton replied as the two men entered the establishment. "He's not so poor as to risk missing such an opportunity with an excuse of ill health, is he?"

Sir William stopped and stood very straight. He felt his lips press tight together as he carefully weighed his words. He spoke evenly. "No, that is not it at all. If he's reported himself ill, I'm sure he is." He removed his hat and looked around.

"Of course," Lieutenant-General Stapleton said.

"Where are the others?"

"They're all here," Lieutenant-General Stapleton said, leading the way. "Garret, Burbridge, Graves, and, well, you know, all the fellows! The fortunate few, I say."

Sir William followed Stapleton to the back room where several friends sat. In addition to the ones named, Sir William noticed his lawyer, Willard Dumbell, and two others he didn't know.

"Gentlemen," Lieutenant-General Stapleton said. "Sir William is now present and this meeting may convene."

"Hear! Hear!" Burbridge shouted, standing with drink in hand and spilling some. "May we all strike it rich in copper and silver!"

"Don't forget lead," Phillip Garret said, rising to shake hands with Sir William. "There's supposedly lead in there too!"

"We can all hope," Sir William said.

"Sir William," Phillip Garret said, motioning to the two men Sir William didn't recognize. "This is John Wulff and Edward Forbes. They've recently opened a bank here in Douglas." The men nodded.

"Yes, I've heard," Sir William said. He shook hands. Forbes seemed friendly enough, smiling and returning a big handshake, but Wulff seemed fidgety and nervous, his eyes darting back and forth. "Pleased to meet you, gentlemen."

Sir William thought of his good friend the colonel and wondered how he might describe this assembly.

"Well, whatever the mix," Burbridge said, "may we dig until we strike something!"

"Hear! Hear!" the men said in chorus.

Except Sir William. He was thinking about the colonel and how much he had hoped to see him here. Sir William was confident this was a reasonable investment to take a poke at and had privately offered to lend the colonel the purchase price of one share, if need be.

Of course Ambrose had refused, stubborn man that he was, but he had promised to be here on his own accord and with money in hand. What had intervened?

"Now," Lieutenant-General Stapleton began, "for the matters at hand, let us discuss our intentions as the newly forming Kirk Lonan Mining Association."

Colonel Ambrose St. John was agitated. The walk across town was not an easy endeavor, yet his conscience prodded him on.

The streets were crooked and uneven, and, to make it worse, the break in the weather had brought out youngsters chasing hoops. At first he determined to take a longer route to avoid being spotted, but eventually he chose to walk the length of Athol Street to alleviate some of the challenges of the lower roads.

He figured it was late enough in the day that Sir William and the others would already be underway with their meeting—a meeting he had no desire to be a part of. He had no business being a part of it either. In truth, he had no business at all. He scowled at the thought and was painfully aware what his expression must look like. He was certain the corner of his mouth could travel farther down than most.

He didn't want to be a part of this other thing either, but his own heart insisted he must. A man knows when his days are short, and some things can't wait a day. He would do this last important thing or die trying to do it. Right now he was sure he would die trying.

He turned toward the south side. He trudged down the narrow, grimy streets past the vacant area where a shipyard was supposedly planned, and finally reached Enders Street and the fisherman's door. He was about to knock when Michael Kellerman opened the door. "Good, good," Colonel St. John said. "My regards." He shuffled through the door and scraped his head on the ceiling. "Blast!"

He saw a woman seated on a wide bench at one end of the room, an infant cradled in her arms. Two other children, a boy and a girl, clung to her from each side. He nodded. "Pardon me, I, uh, hit my head." He looked for a chair and spotted one near the fireplace. He crossed to it, being careful to protect his head.

Upon reaching the chair, he studied it and then tested its strength by pressing down on it with one hand. It squeaked but seemed solid. A hot pain cut through his gut and momentarily bent him over. He clenched his jaw tight until the pain passed. Slowly, and with much difficulty, he sat in the chair. He stared at the family. The fisherman had joined his wife and children to sit with them on the bench.

He wondered if that furniture was bed or bench, noting the blankets and pillow on the floor in front, and then drew in a slow, shallow breath. He coughed on his own saliva. He turned his head and addressed his mouth with his hankie. He tucked it away and cleared his throat. "Thank you for making yourself available."

"How may we help you this day, sir?" Michael asked.

"I want to return a favor to you," Colonel St. John said.

"I am not aware of having done anything for you, although I would've been glad to if I could."

"No, no," Colonel St. John said, waving his hand. "You wouldn't be aware of it. I was barely aware of it myself, but it is true. You've done me a great service."

"How can we be of further service, kind sir?" the woman asked.

The colonel smiled. He liked her voice. It sounded far younger than she appeared. He wondered what one of Sarah's dresses might look like on her. "No, you misunderstand," he said. "I have determined to be of service to you."

"But why, sir?" Michael asked. "As we've said, we—"

"Confound it, people." Colonel St. John raised his hands. "Please slow down. Just wait. Give this old, dying man some time to think and speak, will you?" His voice was far more agitated than he intended, but he wasn't sure he could remain strong enough to finish what he'd come here for. He wanted to do it quickly and be certain it got done.

"My apologies, sir," the woman said, lowering her head. The children cowered.

"Now, now, see what you made me go and do?" Colonel St. John said. "You made me be like I really am, and I'm wanting to be more like you."

"Sir?" Michael's face twisted. "I ought to be out fishing. Might you explain why you asked to come here?"

The colonel nodded his head in an exaggerated motion. "Yes, yes, exactly what I've a mind to do. You know my friend, Sir William Hillary?"

The fisherman smiled, and his wife looked up. "Yes. He is our friend."

"He is a saint," the woman said.

The colonel chuckled. "Yes, indeed he is. A saint. Yes, I think you've got that right. He told me something once, and it sort of stuck with me."

"I know what you mean," Michael said. "He often speaks with wisdom."

"He told me circumstances do not rightly measure a man," Colonel St. John said. He slowed down his words and thought of that day in the drawing room when Sir William and his wife had shared these sentiments with him. It felt good to remember.

"Sounds like something the baronet would say," Michael said.

"Yes, well, said it he did, and I haven't forgotten it," Colonel St. John said. "It got me thinking, and I realized I have been unjust. I have often judged men by their wealth. If they had it, I knew them to be a better man than I. If they didn't have it, then I knew they must be of the vilest stock because I knew what kind of flawed man I was. And if they were poorer than me, well, it just stood to reason, you see?" He waited for a response but found them staring at him. He cleared his throat. "Yes, well, I was wrong."

The fisherman and his wife offered slight smiles. The woman nodded as if permitting him to speak on. He did. "There's fortune and there's misfortune. There's integrity and there's corruption. Well, I guess what I want to say is that maybe there's no correlation between the two, or the four, or whatever. I mean maybe there is but not necessarily. It's not open and shut, you see? Do you see?" He waited for some indication they were listening.

Michael nodded, but his wide-eyed stare made him appear uncertain.

"I am a poor man, though I'm mostly thought of as a gentleman," Colonel St. John said. "And I've been unkind to your kind because, privately, I knew I wasn't any different, and I was very angry about that." His eyes filled. "I haven't a long time left, and I can't afford to pay my creditors. The dogs! So I'm not going to give them anything, how about that?" He reached inside his vest and pulled out a clinking bag. "They stopped making these over ten years ago." He tossed the bag on the floor at the feet of the man and woman. "They're gold English guineas."

Michael Kellerman's eyes widened as far as the colonel could imagine them capable. It struck him as funny. He laughed and then coughed. He coughed so hard it took him several minutes to recover. The searing pain in his gut returned, and it was several more minutes before he could straighten up in his chair. The bag still sat on the floor.

"Go on," Colonel St. John said. "They won't solve anything, but they'll help with some things—clothes and food and such. Won't buy a house though. Just stay here and budget some, and they might last awhile." He stood. "At least that's the best plan I can figure. 'Course, I may not be the best one to ask." He shuffled to the door.

"Sir," Michael said. "Please take your coins with you. We are grateful, but we don't need the charity."

"Blasted man!" Colonel St. John yelled. "Don't lie to me. We all need charity! And I'm not giving it to the dogs. You're no less and no greater than any other man. You sweat and you toil and you live. You're as good a man as any, and better than most, from what Hillary says. My own offspring is taken care of, and I have no need of it. Now allow a dying man his last wish and make some sense with what I've done for you. And what I've done for me, I tell you. I did it for me, too." The colonel left the tiny dwelling and slammed the door hard, hoping they'd understand not to open it while he was still around.

The walk home took longer than the walk there, but it felt sweeter.

The colonel arrived at his flat in terrible pain and mightily fatigued. He kept his boots on and lay on his bed. He chuckled. He started laughing hard enough that tears rolled down his cheeks. He felt giddy. He tasted the salt of his tears and thought of Sarah. Outside, a dog barked in the alley. Ambrose smiled.

"You're too late."

Chapter 7

Spring arrived and departed quickly. By early summer the colonel had failed considerably and by mid July he was dead.

Sarah sat opposite Sir William and Emma, staring out the carriage window in the direction of the retreating gravesite. Her cheeks and forehead were moist with sweat.

"I will deeply miss him," Sir William said, his eyes welling.

"We will all miss him," Emma said, her hankie muffling her voice. She was dressed in black. "We had no other friend like him." She dried her eyes and nose and leaned close to Sarah. "One consolation though: You will live with us now."

Sir William looked at Sarah's perspiring face and reasoned it a mix of the hot day and her black paramatta mourning dress, but also her stubbornness. She had yet to cry over her father's passing. He glanced out the carriage toward the cemetery. The small assembly of mourners had already dispersed.

They traveled back to Prospect Hill from the open countryside. Sir William didn't get up this way often but it was pleasant. He and the colonel were planning to hike here but never did.

"Sixty-three," Emma said.

"What?" Sir William broke from his reflections.

"Ambrose was sixty-three years old," Emma said. Her head was tilted. She smiled while she gazed, as if remembering something pleasant.

"July twelfth is a day I shall always mourn for my friend," Sir William said. "I miss his wonderful grumbling already."

Sarah looked up with a trace of smile. "He was adept at complaining, it's true."

"The dogs!" Sir William said, imitating his friend.

Sarah sobbed.

Emma held her gently, as best as their mourning dresses allowed. "Cry, dear. We all miss him."

Sarah lifted her face, now streaked with tears, and spoke between sobs. "He really was so softhearted, you know. Underneath it all."

"We know," Sir William said. "Never a doubt about that. And he was true to the end."

"I am glad about residing with both of you, truly I am," Sarah said, managing a pretty smile. "I just never expected him to be gone so soon."

"You have been our utmost confidant and truest friend along with your father," Sir William said, his voice quivering with his own distress. He cleared his throat. "You will now enter into my household with full provision, just as we have always agreed."

"I think I prefer being a spinster if I can have such a warm place to be one," Sarah said.

"Enough," Emma said. "You are still very young, and who knows what the future holds? For whatever length of time, you are family in the Hillary home."

"Forever, I think," Sarah said, resting her head on Emma's shoulder.

"If it is forever then it shall be forever," Emma said. "We shall see, but we will not worry, will we?"

"No, I think not," Sarah said.

Sir William observed his wife and the young lady who was now his daughter. It would be easy to provide for her. His love for Ambrose made it easy. His love for Sarah made it easy. Emma's love for Sarah made it easy. Sarah's submissive role regarding their financial arrangement made it easy.

Sir William stared out the window as the coach neared his home. His eyes lowered from the bouncing horizon to the surface of the road. He smiled as he remembered how aggravated the colonel used to get about bumpy rides.

Summer passed without remarkable incident. There were summer balls and fancy dances. Sir William and Emma remained selective, attending only those events whose hosts would view their absence an insult. Sarah joined them to reside at Prospect Hill but did not attend any of the socials due to her official status of mourning.

The mining operation was getting underway, though no real progress was expected anytime soon. To his relief, most of Sir William's England-based sources of income were producing nicely, and the financial concerns of the recent past melted away under the hot summer sun.

Not knowing what to do with his time, Sir William wandered aimlessly about his grounds atop Prospect Hill. The morning grass was wet green, the trees were full, the weather was warm, and his wallet was fat. He approached the garden, staring at the blossoms, and noticed a bucket with a spade. *If I'm content, why am I so uneasy?*

A loud screech drew his attention upward. A lone seagull coasted high upon a sea breeze.

Sir William chuckled as he remembered the way he and the colonel used to sit at the pier and tell each other tales of the days when land-based militias gave them a place to belong. His mouth tightened. He desperately missed the companionship of his old friend and wondered if he should go to the pier and talk to the birds like Ambrose would do. *I am restless. What to do?*

He knelt down, but he didn't pray.

He dug.

He poked the spade into the rich soil and turned it over.

"I planted the periwinkle in tribute to you," Emma said from over his shoulder, startling him.

He dropped the spade and stood up fast, brushing his knees free of dirt.

"I planted the chrysanthemum for Sarah, and the rose is my own personal favorite," Emma said, pointing to the flowers. She looked peaceful. She was dressed in a light, flowing dress, and a large white hat with a wide brim shaded her porcelain face. She carried a basket of clipped flowers.

"The garden is quite colorful," Sir William said.

"What were you digging?" Emma asked.

"I—I wasn't digging," Sir William muttered. "Not really. I was . . . Well, I was—"

"Digging," Emma said, squeezing his arm. "You want to help?"

"Restless," Sir William said. "No. Not really."

"In that quadrant"—Emma pointed as she spoke—"are wallflowers and polyanthus. Over there are marigolds and hydrangeas." She stepped to the far end of the garden. "This is where I get the carnations I'm always putting in your button holes!" She knelt down, clipped off a carnation, and stood up. She looked straight at him, the bright sun making her green eyes sparkle as she fastened the flower to his lapel.

Sir William reached for his wife and drew her close. He kissed her full on the lips for several long seconds and then drew his head back to see her soft face. "I couldn't resist."

"I'm so glad," Emma said, tilting her head and not moving away. A red curl dangled upon her forehead.

"You say you planted the periwinkle for me?"

"It's a royal color. I think it noble."

Sir William returned his gaze to the garden. "Tell me more."

She hooked her arm in his and led him beside the length of the plantings. "As far as I know, I am the only one cultivating pheasant's eye on the entire isle."

"Remarkable," Sir William said. "It really does resemble the bird's eye."

"I just love the colors and scents," Emma said. "They're all so different but all so lovely, don't you think?"

"For the most part," Sir William said. "There's a dead one, I think. I'll pull it."

"That stick?" Emma tugged him backward. "I think not! It blossoms later."

"It's a stick."

"In the dead of winter, when this garden is bottled up like a clam and barren as a desert, you'd see little but sticks. If you pulled them out, there wouldn't be any of the colors you see now."

"You mean that's a flower?" Sir William asked.

"That one happens to be an herb," Emma said. "Follow me, and I'll teach you a little about gardening, Sir Green Thumb, who's eager to dig today!"

"Ha! I'm found out!" Sir William said with a laugh. "It's true. I'm so bored today I was thinking to uproot your entire garden just to make sport. Of course, the periwinkle would remain." He kissed her again.

Emma playfully pushed him back. "Hold on there," she said with a laugh. "That's unfair! I can't think straight when you do that."

"My plan is uncovered," Sir William said, leaning in close.

She offered a peck and then fended him off. "Some flowers are what I call 'respecters of the seasons.' They have their appointed times."

"What does that mean?" He lowered his eyes and watched Emma's mouth form each word. "They are subject to times of repose," she said slowly. "But you mustn't uproot them. Their colors arrive in their own due time."

He could feel her warm breath and saw her face flushing deep red. "Is this the appointed time?" Sir William asked.

"For which one?" she asked.

"For this," he said. He kissed her briefly and then embraced her and kissed her passionately.

After a long while, Emma said, "Dear?"

"Yes?" He relaxed his embrace.

"Let's meet in the garden more often." She sauntered away, calling back to him, "I expect to see you for tea."

Sir William laughed and watched her until she disappeared around the corner of the house.

He looked down at the colorful garden, with its multiple flowers and assorted plantings and occasional barren sticks. He sighed. He placed his hands on his hips and looked around. He stepped toward the house and then stopped. Turning, he walked to the far edge of the yard and looked out over the bay. It was as smooth as glass.

He surveyed the beach, barren of all but two boys running in circles on the sand.

He thought of little Mike and the Kellerman family in their modest flat. He hadn't seen Michael or Joseph or any of the fishermen in a long time. The summer schedule had moved him far from their experiences.

He remembered little Mike coughing up the seawater and recalled the surge of emotion it had filled him with. He could feel his heart pound. He thought of his own son, Augustus, and wondered if Augustus ever thought of him. *I wonder what Frances has told him about me.* He thought of his little girl, Elizabeth, and imagined her with pigtails and summer dresses.

He squinted at the late-morning sun high above the horizon.

The yellow rays warmed him. *The light over the Isle of Man.* He smiled. *The light of man.* He liked that thought. He closed his eyes and tilted his face until the heat felt warmest, absorbing the rays for as long as he could bear.

The days lengthened until the summer heat was followed by a drenching fall and a heavily blanketed winter. Sir William's skin remained bronzed from the August sun, but it was the log-burning hearth of his home from which he found winter warmth as he hibernated in the comfort of holiday gatherings and domestic tranquility. He slept deeply and at length and often snored loudly.

Eight years later, on a windy January night, destiny barged into his cave.

Part 2

Write the vision and make it plain.

Chapter 8

"We'll shelter here!" Captain Reid bellowed to his crew.
The *Vigilant* was only a cutter, but it was a vessel of His Majesty's Service, and Reid was proud to be a lifelong naval man and happy to command her. He stood as lean and straight as his ship's lone mast, arms folded behind his back. He inhaled deeply, feeling his brass buttons tightening down the center of his uniform, and carefully watched his men take in all three sails.

With the gale force winds blowing hard from the northwest, he had ordered his double-ended cruiser into Douglas Bay, using the rocky isle as a protective barrier. He had chosen well—the bay was relatively calm. Once the mainsail, staysail, and jib had been furled and anchors set, he allowed himself a sweeping view of the area. He could feel the evening chill.

Several other vessels had chosen the same precaution. Reid noticed a couple of schooners, three sloops, and a brig—all local variety, no doubt, nothing too impressive. One of the sloops caught his attention.

Similar in size to his own vessel, but with one fewer headsail and a single mast placed more toward the front than center of the ship, it was rudely jibing past another sloop on a starboard tack—clearly an imbecile was in command. The starboard tack always had the right of way, but the impertinent pilot was brazenly and dangerously crossing in front of the one who was in the right, forcing the responsible seaman to pull a hard rudder while frantically commanding the release of sail, narrowly but successfully avoiding a catastrophic collision.

"Jolly good for him," Captain Reid said to his mate. "Let us be certain not to run afoul of that other beast of a boat lest we have to evade as well."

"Aye," the mate said. "Pleasure boater, for sure."

Reid smiled. Both he and his mate had spoken the classic insult of calling a ship a boat. He turned and surveyed the large island of rock in the center of the bay. "It's officially called St. Mary's Isle, but to most it's been known as Conister Rock for ages."

"What's that, sir?" the mate asked, stepping closer.

Reid pointed. "That outcropping there. Do you know what *Conister* means?"

"No, sir."

"It's a corruption of the original Gaelic. It means *head of reef*." Turning away, Reid crossed the length of his vessel. Sailors moved out of his path. He walked slowly and inspected every feature of the *Vigilant*.

As he neared the bow, he scanned the fine homes on the steep hills high above the shore of the bay, just as the sun was beginning to disappear behind them. He was surprised by the relative barrenness of the coastal shoreline, and was amused by the complicated network of narrow and crooked streets coursing through the town of Douglas at the south part of the bay, all packed at one end.

The rows of tall brick and stone buildings were crammed tightly beside each other to hug the long, narrow harbor formed by the Red Pier and the rugged face of Douglas Head. "You don't want to be walking those streets at night," he said. He waited for a response. He raised his head and turned around, intentionally wrinkling his forehead. A mate was bent over coiling a line at amidships. "You don't want to be walking those streets at night!" Reid spoke loud.

"No, sir," the mate replied, rapidly finishing the coil and rushing to stand near his captain.

Reid smiled and walked away. "I'll be below."

His berth was the largest in the vessel but was nevertheless extremely small, as most of the men had only space enough to lay their bodies down. Reid had the privilege of a doorway leading to his. His bunk was neatly made, his shelves neatly arranged with a shelf guard in place to maintain order on blustery days. His trunk was secured and perfectly stacked—trousers on the right, shirts and vest on the left, underclothes atop, and two of his three coats hanging from brass hooks. He was nearly always wearing the third except when he slept. He hung his cap on the last hook.

Reid stretched out on his bunk, propped his two pillows behind his lower back, and assumed a semi-seated posture. He placed his hands behind his head and exhaled. He reached to the small table anchored to the floor beside his bed and picked up his navigational guide. He flipped through the worn pages, scanning sections he'd read thousands of times. He lowered his book to his flat belly and closed the hatches of his eyes.

He recalled heaving and hoisting protocols, trimming and sheeting commands, and imagined longitudinal lines traversing the unruly surface of the seas. A familiar feeling rose up within him, one he welcomed and thoroughly enjoyed. It was that family tradition of secure contentment. The Reid peace he liked to call it. A certain gladness and rest rooted in the satisfaction of being a learned man with royal connections.

His usual naptime mantra, *It's smart to be smart*, washed back and forth over his mind like a tiny wave lapping at the bow.

"Captain! Wind's backing!"

The mate's voice startled Captain Reid.

"Sir?" the mate repeated.

Reid surfaced from his nap somewhat disoriented. It was cold. "Hello!" he said. "What?" It was far darker than he was prepared for.

His navigational guide slid from his belly to the floor. He saw a lantern dangling in the air. He sat up to see his mate's face only one foot away, holding a light over their heads. His skinny nose and large eyes contorted to form an unpleasant sight.

"What is it, man? Is it worth disturbing a short nap?" Reid didn't like the quality of his own voice, still weak from having been asleep. He pulled down on his vest and cleared his throat and then boomed. "Confound it, man, what is it?"

"The wind, sir," the mate said. "She's backing."

Reid leapt to his feet, grabbed his hat off the hook, and blew past his mate, nearly knocking him down. His boots clapped as he raced up the ladder to the main deck. He twirled around in a complete circle, his eyes squeezing narrow in the face of the strong wind. He looked to the top of his lone mast and saw the telltale streamer. It was fluttering wildly in the direction of the coast. Above it, the night sky was only speckled with stars as ashen clouds coursed by.

"Confound it!" he said. "The wind has backed completely around." He noticed the bottom crescent of the moon and wondered how much light might survive to pierce the thickening clouds. He had slept too long. He cupped his hands. "All hands, prepare to raise anchor and head up!"

Reid's crew of half a dozen men raced to his commands. Two of them raised anchor with a small capstan, rapidly wheeling around. Others raced to unfurl sails. Reid rushed to the tiller.

Scanning the bay, Reid noticed other ships rocking wildly at anchor. This helped him understand the backing wind must've happened too fast for anyone to be prepared for. His mind was awhirl with angles and equations.

"Jib!" one of his crew yelled, indicating the foremost headsail was full and operating.

Reid pulled the tiller hard to port, knowing the combination of that action plus the strong headwind striking the narrow jib would begin to swing the bow to starboard side.

"Anchor aweigh!" his anchor crew yelled as the anchor became clear.

"Stay sail!" another crewman shouted as the second headsail forward of the mast rose high. The ship answered even more aggressively, swinging to the right and beginning to creep forward.

Reid knew he had to find the perfect position for the rudder. Not enough and they would be dead in the wind. Too much and they would blow around to face shore—a deadly option.

He could feel the resistance as he pulled back slightly. He couldn't make the command for hauling the mainsail too soon or the wind would back it into his face. He had to swing to starboard just enough so that the high force wind would strike the mainsail at the perfect angle. *Now*.

"Haul mainsail!" he shouted. He heard the men hoisting and the sail rising up the mast. *Hoist and rise. Hoist and rise.* "With backbone, men!"

As the main sail rose, it flapped for a moment, cueing Reid to tiller slightly more to port. And then he heard what he longed to hear—a great filling of sheet. It sounded like one great snap of a rug just like he used to hear when his mother shook out carpet on the front stoop. It now meant a sail with a belly full of wind.

"Mainsail!" his mate shouted. "Sheeted home!"

The weather darkened. Reid made out silhouettes of the other ships, and he knew the large blot of black straight ahead was Conister.

"St. Mary's Isle dead ahead," the mate shouted from the bow.

Reid wasn't worried. He knew they would be cutting it close but they could clear the inconvenient reef along its south side.

The challenge was that cutters were known for being less effective when sailing into the wind. This was a cruising ship that displayed greatest agility when running with the wind or when the wind was perpendicular and abeam to their direction of movement.

If he pushed the tiller too far to port they would fall off the wind too much and swing wide to starboard, possibly shedding enough speed to lose forward movement. If he rode too high on the edge of the wind, they'd risk running straight into the rocks. It would take precise operation with the rudder and some ongoing trimming of the sails to keep them close-hauled to the wind. He needed faultless execution.

As soon as they were past the rocky outcrop and to the right of it, he planned to call for a reversal of tack, pushing the tiller far over to allow the sails to fill on their reverse sides. His vessel would cut back left and rush past the ship-threatening obstacle on a tightly executed starboard tack.

The wind picked up to gale force strength, and darkness swallowed the bay. Reid felt beads of water above his upper lip, either sea spray or sweat. A roving blur approached. He knew what it was and straightened the bill of his cap. The rogue rainsquall pelted them from bow to stern as it passed and moved on.

There was yet no fog to blot out the numerous dots of lantern lights now appearing throughout the bay like ghostly apparitions. The black and ominous hulk he knew was Conister Rock grew larger. The *Vigilant* drew disturbingly near. Reid held his breath, but he steered safely and cleared the deathtrap, moving on with relative ease.

The crew cheered. Reid smiled and barked out commands to change tack. The men loosened sails, and Reid pushed the tiller to the right. The bow turned, and for a moment the sails sagged but then quickly filled from the opposite side.

"Sheet 'em home!" he yelled. He felt perfect tension in his grip of the tiller arm. His men had rightly secured the sails.

The sails filled well, the ship answered the helm, and the *Vigilant* set off on a new tack, cutting diagonally to the left to move past the eastern side of the dangerous Conister reef once and for all.

"Sloop to starboard!" one of the crewmen cried.

Reid snapped his attention to his right. His face grew hot. "Imbecile!"

The reckless sloop he had spotted earlier was now hurling straight across the *Vigilant's* bow, a violent collision imminent. Unless.

Reid pushed the tiller all the way to his right, causing the bow to swiftly veer left. The offending sloop rushed by, moving swiftly on its portside tack, the two ships barely missing each other.

Reid watched the cursed ship slide past, only inches away, his eyes locking hard into the bleary eyes of the sloop's captain, who stood with white face and mouth agape. Reid let rip a string of obscenities like a condemning judge pronouncing a deserved death sentence.

The other sloop disappeared into the dark, and Reid knew he was doomed.

"Breakers on the lee!" his mate shouted.

They struck Conister Rock. The Reid peace was shattered.

"What was that?" Sir William sat upright in bed. Emma stirred.

A second loud bang pierced the night. It was still dark, much too early for the horn announcing the passenger steamer to Liverpool. But what else could it be? A third sound boomed, this time sounding more like a rocket.

Sir William threw back the covers and hurried to peer out his bedroom window, which overlooked Douglas Bay from one floor above his great room.

It was a maroon—a signal rocket launched from a vessel in the bay, often used by naval ships. Someone was in trouble. Sir William scrambled to get dressed, pecked his sleeping wife on the forehead, and rushed out of the house into the cold, blustery dark of pre-dawn.

The steep road from Prospect Hill had recently been surfaced with crushed slate from the quarry behind the South Quay, and most of the potholes were filled with gravel from the beach. Most of them.

Sir William stepped into one that had since been reopened by galloping hooves and heavily weighted carriage wheels, and tumbled head first into the dark.

He slammed hard into the cold damp surface of the road but managed to break the impact somewhat with his arms and shoulders. He rolled two complete revolutions, using his momentum and the aid of gusting wind to spring back to his feet and continue on. He felt a surging pride about his strength and stamina for his fifty-one years of age.

Another maroon-fired rocket shot high over the bay, splaying across the darkness with a burst of momentary brightness. Whoever they were, he knew their situation must be desperate. Sir William slipped again, this time his boot heel sliding on the slick surface. He barely kept his balance but rushed on to the bottom of Prospect Hill.

He charged through the crooked, narrow streets of town. Most of the Douglas roads remained packed dirt, and the tall stone buildings, jammed side by side, blocked the brunt of the cold and forceful wind.

The streets were dark. None of the few street lanterns were burning—either blown or burnt out, Sir William wasn't sure. He noticed some windows glowed amber and supposed the exploding rockets in the bay had awakened others as well.

He rounded a tight corner at full sprinting speed, his knees lifting high and his clenched fists pumping at his sides.

His face met a sudden blast of cold wind as he turned to run alongside the more exposed quayside area. He was hoping to see what boats might be readily available in the harbor and whether anyone else was there to help mount a rescue attempt.

"Impressive, man!" Lieutenant Burbridge said. "Did you run the entire way?"

Burbridge looked so much better without a drink in his hand. Sir William was surprised at his first thoughts when his friend suddenly appeared in front of him. He stood there in resilient pose, his legs braced to stand firmly in the wind, his arms cocked and ready to grapple, and his clothes flapping in the wind. His hair was tousled, and his face appeared resolute.

"I did indeed," Sir William said. "There's no time to lose."

"There's no lifeboat, sir," Michael said, stepping forward from a group of fishermen. "But I'll gladly lend the use of my boat, if she's wanted."

Michael was dressed in his working clothes, oilskin breeches and thick grey gansey. He wore tall, loose-fitting black boots and a large brimmed rain hat. His hands were covered in worn-out wool gloves with the fingertips cut off.

Sir William squeezed Michael's shoulders. "Good man!"

Men were running to harbor from all directions. Hotel windows and tenement houses glowed with lantern light as onlookers gawked from overhead to spy out the streets below. Someone shouted from an open window, cursing the crowd and demanding peace and quiet. No one acknowledged him.

"I've been to the beach," Lieutenant Graves said, jogging up to Sir William and the growing crowd around him. "It's a navy cutter afoul St. Mary's."

"Aye," Michael said to Sir William. "And no fewer than four other ships in perilous ways."

"And no lifeboat?" Sir William asked quietly, stroking his chin.

"We do have a fleet," Matthew Hanby said, his small voice barely perceptible above the din, "of sorts."

"A fleet of what?" Lieutenant Burbridge asked.

Hanby extended both of his short arms toward the harbor. "The York pleasure boats. What else might do it?"

"Rowboats?" Lieutenant Burbridge asked, the pitch of his own voice ranging unusually high. "A fleet of rowboats?"

Hanby shrugged and then looked at Sir William. "What do you think?"

Sir William cupped his hands about his mouth. "Yo! Mates! Gather around!"

Many looked but did not budge.

"We've got a naval cutter hung up on Conister," Sir William said. "It's likely to break up at any minute. There may be as many as a dozen men aboard, maybe more. Atop that, there are several other vessels anchored in the bay. They may not be able to beat out and could end up fighting for their lives."

One fisherman approached. "I hope they're up to snuff with their Maker." He was of average height and build, and his face was taut and scarred.

"Who are you?" Sir William asked.

"The name is Jones. Monty Jones."

"The sea gods are angry tonight," said another as he stepped up. He was a puny man with a thin mustache. "There's no appeasing them until the tale is done. Morning light will show the score." He stepped closer. "And the name is Jimmy O'Leary, if you're wantin' to know."

"The question is," Sir William said loudly, squeezing his eyebrows tight, "are *we* up to snuff with our Maker?"

"What's that supposed to mean?" Monty Jones asked with a snarl.

Sir William placed a hand on Matthew's shoulder. "The good proprietor of the York Hotel has made a generous offer to lend us his boats in order that we may cast off."

"Cast off?" Jones asked, his face twisting up.

"Cast off," Sir William repeated, his eyes fixed on Jones. "In effort to assist those now fighting to survive."

"I'll not be launching into such a scourge," Jones said. "There'll be no result other than death."

"Aye," O'Leary said, bobbing his mousy face. "It's suicide."

Several nodded and raised voices to agree.

Sir William bit his bottom lip. "Who is with me?"

"I'll go," Matthew Hanby said. Some scoffed, others laughed.

"And I," Lieutenant Graves said, standing alongside Sir William.

"Jolly right, chap," Lieutenant Burbridge said, clapping the heels of his boots and straightening up at attention. "Just like old times, eh?" His eyebrows arched high, and a boyish grin spread over his face. "To the oars, I say!"

"You won't get out of the harbor," Monty Jones said, throwing his hands down in disgust and walking away. He rallied others to retreat with him, then turned back. "The only sensible thing is to move to the beach and behold the spectacle. Pray if you like, but don't be fool enough to step aboard anything tonight. A seaman knows tonight is an anchoring night."

Michael stepped up. "Remember the tales from Ramsgate, mates. They proved what a brave bunch of fishermen could do."

Monty Jones spun around, his face ablaze with reddened fury. "Ramsgate? Look around, Kellerman. There be no lifeboats or cork jackets here. You'll all be dead come the first wave."

Many of the fishermen moved away from Sir William to gather near Jones. But Michael and his fishing partner, the portly Joseph, remained. "Like I said, sir. I'm ready to help, and my boat is available," Michael said.

"Aye," Joseph said.

"That makes six," Sir William said. "We need at least three boats with five men in each. In seas like these, we will need all the strength we can cram onto each oar."

"Each boat a grave," Monty Jones said from the center of his huddle.

Sir William suddenly stepped forward five paces to peer down at the man. "Listen up!" he shouted, making Jones flinch. "Every second we banter about there are men and maybe women and children in desperate need. There's no time for cowardice and self-interest. It's courage that's needed. Nothing is impossible if we have courage!"

The wind gusted and blew a fisherman's crate along the street

Jones stepped back, and though he was visibly shaken, he shouted, "Courage? I spit on your definition of courage. And what becomes of our wives and brats should we perish out there, as likely we would? Tell us that."

"It's a risk we take," Sir William said. The wind gusted again, setting him back on his heels.

"Ah, yes," Jones said. "A tidy formula you have. What do you know of risk? You have incomes that continue after you're gone. Your household's preserved. What do we have? The poorhouse!"

"Debtor's prison! The millhouse wheel!" Jimmy O'Leary said. "That's what we get. Monty is right! It's an uneven sea!"

The cluster of reluctant fishermen grew firmer in their resolve to offer no aid as they raised their fists and voices. Some cursed Sir William to his face.

Sir William remembered what Michael had told him long ago about the man named Red who had saved little Mike but doomed his own house. It was all coming back.

"I—I don't—" Sir William stuttered. He felt guilty for having forgotten. Had he really forgotten or had he neglected? It was painful to consider.

"Yeah, that's right!" Monty Jones said, a thin smile on his face. "Nothing to say!"

Sir William straightened up. It was not time for self-pity. He remembered his creed. "No excuse, men!" Sir William snapped. With his boot, he flipped over the crate that had blown up the street and then stepped atop it. "I'll personally guarantee a financial reward to anyone who gets in a boat and takes an oar."

He glanced over each one and liked what he saw. He added fuel. "By late morning you'll be safe in your homes, your pockets full and your hearts satisfied for having done a bit of good. You'll even have a tale to tell the children, and you'll note a warm smile on the face of your beloved, if not a bit of admiration."

"Aye, that would play well," a stout fisherman said, looking nearly as muscular as Red Kelly had been, only with dark complexion and boyish face. "Guaranteed?"

"What's your name, brave soul?" Sir William asked.

"Tom," the big man said.

"Guaranteed, Tom. Now, what of it, men? Can we find some courage among our number?"

The small cluster of fishermen stirred with mumbles and sideways steps. Beards were stroked and heads scratched. The expressions remained dark and moody but with discomfort. "Are you a man of your word, Sir William?" Tom asked.

"Don't insult him," Michael said, stepping forward. "If he said it, he meant it."

"Well," O'Leary said. "He did say it."

"And I meant it," Sir William said. "Now, we mustn't delay further."

Tom smiled, his boyish appearance somewhat lessening as his smile revealed unsightly teeth. "I'm in."

"And I," Jimmy O'Leary said.

"I'm no money grubber," Jones said. "I'll be no part of it."

"To the oars men," Michael said. "It's a fair offer."

Sir William nodded to Graves and Burbridge and waved all to the pier.

In all, there were fifteen of them who had found the courage to launch three rowboats. Burbridge was in the first boat along with O'Leary and Tom. Sir William, Joseph, and Graves in the second, Hanby and Michael in the third. Monty Jones and the others disappeared into the dark.

In each boat, there were four men on two oars and one in the stern helping to steer with an improvised third oar. Sir William manned an oar along with Joseph. It was cumbersome but each pulled hard. Sir William's back ached as they cleared the end of Red Pier.

They aimed the bows of their little boats straight into the teeth of the storming sea. This was the hardest kind of rowing as both the wind and flowing tide pushed against them. With rollicking bow to the unceasing, white-crested waves, the men put their backs and legs into it. They nearly stood in order to get enough leverage to pull the oars through the churning seas. At the end of each stroke, when they lifted the oar out of the water to swing it back toward the bow, the sudden absence of resistance tempted them to rest.

Sir William knew hesitation risked having them be pushed by wind and tide, absent any gain. His lifted the oars from the surf by pressing down the oar handles from his chest to his torso. He pushed them across his thighs and past his knees. He pulled the handles up, feeling the paddles break into the violent surface. They were instantly seized with enormous resistance.

Sir William gritted his teeth so hard he could hear them scraping. He dug his heels into the bottom of the boat and pulled with all his strength. It felt like a thousand tentacles gripped the oars beneath the surface of the angry sea, threatening to snap the wooden sticks on every stroke.

Slowly the oars powered through the thick water until the handles once again attained his chest and he pushed down, sending the paddles into the air and momentarily ending the torturous cycle. The temptation to quit returned. "Courage won't quit!" Sir William grunted.

"Aye," Joseph replied, along with several gasps.

Sir William flexed his legs and ground his boots into the bottom of the boat. His thigh muscles flexed, rippling like the sea itself. His breeches were soaked and freezing.

He pulled the oar handles tight to his chest. His bottom lifted off the seat until the entire length of his body was rigid and extended. His back muscles flexed in a succession of movements as each made way for the next. His triceps burned and knotted, reluctant to relax until the hot pain was overtaken by sudden burning in his bulging biceps at the midpoint of each stroke.

Over and over he pushed and pulled, straightened and sat, pushed and pulled, straightened and sat. His muscles felt like singular organs flexing and folding, mirroring the beating of his pounding heart. They seemed out of sync and more massive as larger sections of his body felt seized up and knotted, tearing and burning.

Out of the corner of his eye he saw Joseph. The man's face was strained and twisted. It didn't seem like he was adding any assistance to the pull of the oar, but his arms were indeed flexed and his fingers as white as snow as they clutched the oar handle near his own.

Sir William's whirling mind thought of lying in bed and kissing Emma, of tipping a bowl of hot mutton stew to his mouth and slurping it dry. He saw himself rolling head over heels down Prospect Hill while running toward town and then being smashed into pieces by an enormous wave, his body separating into various muscles and washing away to sea like a school of dead fish. He forced his mind into a narrower channel.

Like a fast-flowing river, knowing full well its way, he focused his energy into the exclusionary concept of being a machine that lived only to row, only to push and pull, to straighten and sit. And thus, back and forth, like ebb and flow, Sir William alternated between focus and confusion, between strength and exhaustion.

"Lift oars!" Graves commanded.

Sir William hadn't realized his eyes were closed until he opened them.

Lieutenant Graves was kneeling, soaked, at the stern and pushing the modified tiller oar far to starboard. His coat wrapping oddly from the wind, his hair blown wildly back, and his eyes only slits. "Starboard oar, ready!"

Sir William pushed his oar handle down and forward, his forearms resting on his thighs, his fists side by side, the oar clinched between his knees.

"With a will!" Lieutenant Graves shouted.

Sir William and Joseph pulled the starboard side oar handle, sending the paddle to splash into the Irish drink. They dug in their heels, straightened their forms, lifted their bottoms, and strained with their might.

"Row!" Lieutenant Graves commanded a second and then a third time as he held the tiller oar pushed far to his right. The bow answered and slowly veered to port.

Sir William and Joseph pulled several more times, the tiny craft turning left until the bow pointed toward the bay.

"Ready port oar!" Lieutenant Graves said.

The two fishermen on the other oar assumed their position.

"All oars, men! Snap to it!" Lieutenant Graves bellowed.

The two oars plunged into the sea, and the men pulled hard. The boat lurched forward, seemingly flying over the crests. They had turned to flow with wind and tide and the difference was amazing. The tiny craft bounded over the waves, nearly leaping from crest to crest, icy spray behind them and the dawn just appearing as a dull grayish glow from the east.

Sir William knew the current and the wind would sweep them along northwesterly toward the deadly Conister Rocks. There was also the cluster of rocks just north of the end of the pier to be aware of, known as the Pollocks. He hoped they had rowed out far enough so that upon turning to ride the wind and tide they would clear the intermediary reef and shoot straight for the place where the cutter was foundering. That was the plan.

As a rower, Sir William's back continually faced the destination. He trusted Graves to steer by the dullest of twilight. The gale force winds had churned the entire bay into one mass of molten sea.

The Pollocks would not advertise their location. The treacherous rocks would be masked by leaping waves of frothy white, similar to any other expanse of foaming sea. Sir William hoped Graves had a sharp eye to make a reasonable judgment. To guess wrong could spell disaster.

He studied Graves as his eyes roved back and forth. He appeared keenly alert. Beyond him, Sir William saw his first glimpse of the other two boats. Neither had turned to ride the tide as they had. He hoped they would not turn too soon.

"Pollocks!" Lieutenant Graves shouted.

Sir William felt a shiver through his veins for an instant. Then he realized there was no alarm in his friend's voice, only relief, and a smile to boot.

"We're clear and clean!" Lieutenant Graves grinned from ear to ear. "Clear and clean!"

"It's a pleasure working with you," Sir William said out of the side of his mouth to Joseph, who panted heavily beside him.

"Aye, sir," Joseph blurted. "Pleased."

The other boats reached the required distance and turned. Sir William looked toward the bow. His twisted back rapidly tightened, but the sight before him erased his concern over such matters as back-wrenching spasms.

It was a naval cutter. He recalled seeing her anchored in the bay the day before. She was sideways to the incoming rollers and clearly hung up on the massive reef. The unceasing waves battered her.

Her rudder and sternpost had been ripped out. She rose and fell, rocked and moaned. It was clear the tempestuous sea had forced her up the rocks to become stranded on the largest ones that rose like barriers. She was being pummeled. The men aboard her could be doomed.

"Sir William?" Lieutenant Graves called.

Sir William turned and saw Graves leaning far forward. "Lieutenant," Sir William replied.

"We've need of a plan," Lieutenant Graves said.

"There is only one that I can think of," Sir William said. "We ask the cutter for hawsers to be tossed to each of our boats that we may venture to tow them off the rocks and back to harbor."

"That will be quite the feat," Lieutenant Graves said. "I fear she's too far wedged for any hope of a tow, especially one powered by so few oars."

"What do you suggest?" Sir William asked. "Be snappy, we're drifting in very close."

"Drifting close is my suggestion," Lieutenant Graves said. "We get in close enough that those men may leap aboard us."

"Look again at the churn," Sir William said, pointing to the cutter. "The chaos about her is impenetrable for rowboats. These aren't like the Lukin or Greathead boats. We'll be capsized. We've no life jackets, don't forget."

Lieutenant Graves studied the wreck and nodded.

"Let us row to her north," Sir William said. "The hawsers will keep us in place until the others are in position. We try to pull her off. If we can't, perhaps the men can ride the hawsers to safety in a bosun's sling or something."

"Well thought," Lieutenant Graves said. "Let us hurry, we are getting too close."

Sir William and the others rowed hard while Lieutenant Graves steered them to pass the length of the cutter.

"Hawsers!" Lieutenant Graves shouted through cupped hands to the captain of the cutter, now peering over the side. "For towing!"

"Aye!" the cutter captain replied.

"Ahoy!" Lieutenant Burbridge shouted, his boat coming up fast on wind and tide. The last boat followed close behind. The commanders of each vessel shouted through wind and wave until the plan was clear. Within twenty minutes the boats were connected to the cutter with hawsers. The heavy ropes were tightened and loosened as the crafts pitched and rolled.

"What are they doing?" Joseph asked, pointing to the mast of the cutter.

Sir William saw some of the cutter crew laboring around the mast. It began to teeter. Others were pushing a large black object through an opening in the rail. "I'd say the captain has made a difficult decision," Sir William said.

A cannon suddenly rolled over the side of the cutter and splashed into the sea. Stores and tackle streamed over the side like so much waste. Next, a great snapping preceded the mast falling over. The crew guided it to fall onto the isle of rocks.

"He's making it easier to tow," Sir William said. "Lightening the load."

"I think he thought right," Lieutenant Graves added. "We may succeed at it now."

Sir William seized his oar handle. "Let us pray we can."

"Ready oars!" Lieutenant Graves shouted so that all three boats could hear.

"Ready oars!" Lieutenant Burbridge echoed.

"Ready oars!" came the command from Michael's boat.

"Heave!"

The three rowboats strained the lines connecting them to the cutter, being careful not to crash into one another. Sir William felt immense pressure against his oar as the weight of the cutter seemed immovable. He straightened his body rigid and pulled with all his might. His teeth seemed to loosen as he clamped them hard.

A great scraping sound scratched through the howling wind followed by snapping timber and then cheering voices rose from the cutter. The ship was slowly scraping off the rocks.

"Don't stop now," Lieutenant Graves shouted, leaning forward, reaching between Sir William and Joseph, and trying to help pull the oar back. It helped.

The cutter whined as it dragged over the reef. Sir William wondered if she was being holed below her waterline. If so, they would only be towing her out a very short distance before she would fill and sink.

All three boats rowed until the cutter suddenly lurched. It plunged into deeper water.

"We must see if she sinks," Sir William said.

All waited.

The cutter rose higher.

And rocked.

"She floats!" the cutter captain yelled, one hand gripping the ship's rail. He waved his cap. "You have saved us!"

"There's a grateful soul," Sir William said. "Let's tow her home, mates." He looked to the far side of the bay where other boats still rocked at anchor.

"We—did it, by—goodness," Joseph said, breathless. "We really did it."

"Feels good, doesn't it, my friend?" Sir William asked.

"It does, indeed, sir."

The three rescue boats rowed across the bay, struggling with the wind and tide angling against them, making good progress with the tow. Lieutenant Graves used a lantern to signal the other boats to learn if they desired a tow but all waved him off.

"I hope they know what they're doing," Sir William said.

"They're well anchored vessels, sir," Joseph said. "They may hold."

"They may not," Sir William said.

"Aye," Joseph said. "It would be tough for us to row across the bay again and again. We need more men. And a lifeboat wouldn't hurt us, sir. "

"Aye."

The tow was slow, but they reached the harbor slightly after the fullness of dawn. Rockets from the pier fired hawsers to the stricken vessel, and with help from men ashore, including Monty Jones, the lines were pulled hard to bring the *Vigilant* to safe moorings.

As he and the others stepped out of the rowboats, Sir William looked across the bay to watch a schooner and two other vessels still rocking. They bucked like stuck pigs but their anchor lines were holding.

"Those lines look strained," he said.

"What's that?" Lieutenant Graves asked, stepping beside him.

Sir William shook his head. He said nothing but prayed hard the vessels wouldn't snap their lines or there would be more trouble. He feared no strength was left in the rowers to help them.

Lieutenant Graves grabbed Sir William's hand and shook it. "That was quite the thrill," he said. "It was enlivening to do a maneuver again. Good night, Lieutenant-Colonel!" He winked. "I'll see you after I've had a day or two of rest." Sir William nodded and watched his friend walk away.

Exhausted and cold, Sir William and some of the other rescuers landed themselves in the York Hotel to be wrapped in warm blankets and succored with hot drinks. He sat at his favorite table in the back with Matthew, Michael, and Joseph. The tea warmed his insides, but his feet were beginning to itch from within the wet cocoons of his socks.

The captain of the cutter entered and stepped up to their table. "Captain Reid of His Royal Majesty's Service and commander of the *Vigilant* at your service," he said with a salute.

"The honor is mine," Sir William said, moving to stand.

"Please," Captain Reid quickly interjected. "Please, don't get up. Your rest is well deserved."

Sir William remained sitting. "Then I insist, do sit with us."

Joseph drew out an empty chair.

"It is a privilege," Captain Reid said as he sat across from Sir William. "You have done me a great honor and, frankly, saved me a considerable embarrassment."

"There is no shame in battling the south wind," Sir William said.

"Aye, none," Michael said.

"You did well considering the predicament," Sir William said. "You are clearly an officer and a gentleman."

"I won't be understood a gentleman should I get my hands on a certain sloop captain." Captain Reid raised his gloved hand and shook his head. "As it is, I shall be embarrassed enough, but it will not cost me my ship or my rank. For that a great debt is owed."

"You owe us nothing," Sir William said. "We didn't do it for reward."

"Then the king shall hear of this," Captain Reid said.

"Begging your pardon, sir," Jimmy O'Leary said as he approached the table to stand close to Sir William. "Some of us did, sir."

Sir William looked at the little man, whose eyes sparkled above his grin. Sir William recalled his guarantee. "Of course," he said and then turned to Matthew. "My good friend, might you fetch ink, pen, and some sheets of paper? I've some IOUs to write."

Matthew Hanby stood up, a look of disgust on his face. "Aye, but you needn't write any to me." He headed for the front desk mumbling the entire way.

"Nor me," Joseph said.

"Me neither," Michael said.

"Well, you need to write one to me and a few other blokes," Jimmy O'Leary said, his grin widening. He held out his hand.

"Soon enough, O'Leary," Sir William said. "I'll call you back shortly."

Jimmy O'Leary remained standing with his palm out.

Sir William stared hard until the man wavered and slowly retreated to his own table. "Your word is your word," Jimmy O'Leary said before turning around to sit.

"And a good word it is," Michael said, his tone rising. He stood.

Sir William waved his friend down and returned his attention to the captain after Michael resumed his seat. "What were you saying about the king?"

"Yes." Captain Reid flashed a perfectly proportioned smile. "I move in some circles of royalty, and I shall seek to submit a commendation to the king for the service you have done this night. It is the least I can do."

"The king, you say?" Sir William asked. "I once rubbed shoulders with Prince Augustus, many years ago."

"The son of King George III," Captain Reid said with a nod. "I do not personally know him, but I've heard about him. Quite the idealist, I understand. And sickly, if I recall."

"Yes, right on both accounts," Sir William said. "I was his personal equerry while he journeyed about Italy and Malta. It was quite the adventure." He grew quiet for a moment to collect his thoughts. "If you indeed have audience with the king, there is something you might do."

"Please," Captain Reid said, opening his hands. "You need only say it."

"I need no pecuniary award, but some of the men involved would benefit from such." Sir William motioned toward Jimmy O'Leary with his head. "I agreed to provide it in order to—uh—encourage their participation. Do you see?"

"I think so," Captain Reid said. He scanned the entire room as if taking a closer look at the gathering. "What do you need?"

"Some sort of recompense to the fishermen who risked their lives would be no disservice," Sir William said. "But actually, I've been imagining something far more substantial that would serve not only the isle but the entire nation."

"Indeed?" Captain Reid leaned forward. "I'm intrigued."

Matthew returned with the pen, an inkwell, and scraps of paper. "Will these do?" he asked, his frown still fixed to his face.

"Thank you, Matthew," Sir William said. He arranged the papers neatly and dipped the pen. He looked up at the captain. "I envision an organized effort for lifesaving, and afterwards."

"Afterwards?" Captain Reid asked.

"Precisely," Sir William said. "Rescue at sea and on shore."

"On shore?"

Sir William wrote on the paper and looked across the room. "O'Leary!"

The little man scurried over and snatched the paper out of Sir William's hand. He studied it and smiled. "This will do fine, sir," he said. "You are a man of your word." He turned around and held it up for others to see. "Two pounds!"

Some men cheered. Others began to stand in line.

Sir William began writing another and resumed his conversation. "It seems that some men are reluctant to venture a rescue due to fears of leaving a family behind if they should perish in the attempt." He finished several more notes and held them up for the fishermen. They were grabbed away. "It's a reasonable concern, don't you think?" Sir William looked straight at the captain.

"Well, er, yes, I think so," Captain Reid said, his eyes roving back and forth between the lineup of fishermen and Sir William.

"And in the case of a drowned fisherman, whether a rescuer or a sailor aboard a sinking ship," Sir William said as he wrote yet another note, "the problem of a fatherless home remains."

"Indeed it does," Captain Reid said. "But what do you propose?"

Sir William stopped writing and returned his gaze to the captain and then stared out the window behind him into the half-light of dawn. "I don't know. I'm still considering it."

"Well, when you do, you need only write to me. I will leave my address with this hotel. In fact, I suggest you write down your idea, even a proposal, if you will, and I will do what I can to place it before royal eyes. It is the least I can do for the man who saved my ship." He stood up. "I will be here for several days for repairs. If you compose your plan before my departure, I'll take it with me. If not, you may send it by packet, and I will make certain to follow through as I have said." He extended his hand.

Sir William rose and shook it. Pain burned in his legs and back. "You are a gentleman," he said, trying not to grimace from the discomfort.

"As are you," Captain Reid said. He looked at Matthew. "And now, Mr. Hanby, I will need rooms for me and my crew."

"Of course," Matthew said, his face now happy and content. He crossed to the front desk.

The captain tipped his head and followed.

Sir William sat down and reached behind his back to rub the pain. It was no use since his arms equally ached. He fidgeted in his chair to find a comfortable position. He felt chilled.

Several minutes later, Matthew Hanby returned. "I've done a good bit of business just now, no little thanks to you. I want you to receive a favor from me in return."

"Yes?" Sir William looked up at his friend. He wrapped the blanket more tightly around himself.

"It's cold for sure, but there's no snow, and the roads are traversable enough. I'm providing a coachman and carriage to take you home."

"You needn't bother," Sir William said. "I can do that myself."

"I insist. The discussion is over. It's out front. Go home and sleep."

Sir William smiled. "Thank you, Matthew." He stood, pain in every limb. "What's the state of the ships in the bay?"

"Never you mind," Matthew said. "Go home and sleep."

"If they get into trouble, send word to me," Sir William said.

"Good night, Sir William," Matthew said. "And take the blanket with you."

"One more thing," Sir William said. He scratched out two more IOUs and held them out to Joseph and Michael.

The two fishermen didn't reach for them. Michael shook his head.

Sir William smiled and left the papers on the table. "Allow me the joy of knowing you'll take these home." He nodded to his friends and walked slowly to the carriage in front.

As he bounced up Prospect Hill, he once again surveyed the ships still rocking at anchor in the bay. They looked like toys in the hands of bully waters. He prayed for their preservation.

Preservation. He liked that word.

Upon entering his home, he was surprised to find Emma awake. She looked stupefied by his blanketed appearance.

"Good morning, love," was all he could think to say.

"When I awoke to find you missing," Emma said, speaking rapidly,

"Sarah and I convened in the parlor to worry and wait. What on earth have you been doing?"

"Not on earth," he replied. "On sea."

Sarah stood beside her, equally dumbfounded. "You look dreadful!"

After being assisted by Emma into dry bedclothes and then into bed, he explained the early morning ventures, though with little animation. Emma and Sarah stood with mouths open and heads shaking.

Emma tucked him in. "I'll fetch your bed cap," she said. "We can't have you catching cold."

Sir William offered the best smile he could and then lowered his eyelids.

He didn't know how much time elapsed before her return or if she returned more than once, but at length he felt her tipping him onto his side and slipping fire-warmed water bottles under his neck and lower back. He knew her touch, though he didn't open his eyes to confirm it. His eyelids were snagged shut like an anchor clinging to weeds.

He could hear the surf, the deafening surf, buttressed by the howling wind filling his ears, and though it felt all consuming it was comforting to him as all turned black and still.

Chapter 9

Sir William woke up after a deep sleep. Emma sat beside his bed reading the *Isle of Man Weekly Gazette* under the light of an oil lamp. A full fire blazed in the hearth, and dim light filtered through the curtains of the bedroom window. Something pelted the glass.

"What time is it?" he asked.

Emma looked up. "Good afternoon, dear." She smiled warmly. "It's nearly four o'clock, I think. Listen to this." She thumbed back a few pages.

There was a knock.

"Yes, come in," Emma said.

Sarah cracked open the door. "Is he awake yet?"

"Yes," Emma said. "Come in, darling."

Sarah pushed open the door. "Hattie has a brunch prepared if Sir William is hungry."

"No brunch," Sir William said. "Breakfast, please."

"Good day, Sir William," Sarah said. "It's good to see you rested. I'll tell her." Sarah shut the door.

"Listen to this, dear," Emma said again. "Storm Reports. One week ago. Twenty miles south of Douglas a captain and several of his crew were swept clean from their deck and thrown into the sea. A succeeding wave flung the captain and some of his crew back aboard but left the remainder somewhere at the bottom, not to be found."

The pelting continued. "Is it still storming?" Sir William asked.

"Yes, dear, but don't you think it amazing that men were tossed so easily by the elements?" Emma asked. "I'm glad that wasn't your experience last night."

Sir William sat up and set his feet on the floor. His back felt weak, and his legs pulsed with pain. He forced himself to the window.

"Be careful, dear," Emma said. "You overexerted yourself, I'm sure."

Sir William pulled the curtains apart. It was hailing. He gasped. Several ships remained in the bay, obviously dragging their anchors as he had earlier feared. "They're in trouble."

Emma stepped beside him. "You'd think it was dusk, the sky is so dark."

"Emma," Sir William pointed to the bay. "Those ships are in trouble."

"They are having a rough time," Emma said. "But they're big ships. They should be able to ride it out, don't you think?"

"I don't know," Sir William said. "They seem closer to shore. They may be dragging anchors."

"It's these winds," Emma said. "It's hail, not rain!" She tapped the newspaper in her hands. "The paper says there have been numerous storms beating different parts of the coasts. I think we got ours last night."

"And right now," Sir William said. He crossed to his wardrobe. He could feel his legs burning with soreness. "I must get dressed."

There was another knock on the bedroom door.

"Who is it?" Sir William asked as he opened the cabinet doors to his wardrobe.

"It's me," Hattie said from outside the bedroom. "I've prepared some tea and toast and cheese for you."

"Come in," Emma said.

The door opened and Hattie walked in with a tray. Sarah was behind her.

Sir William pulled out a pair of black trousers and a tan shirt. "Where are my sweaters?" he asked. "I need a warm sweater." He looked at Emma.

"Put the tray over there, Hattie, thank you," she said. "If you two would excuse us."

"Wait!" Sir William barked. "Sarah. I've written a few papers of credit to some fishermen. I'll need you to withdraw twenty-four pounds this week and pass it to me. Don't forget, please."

"Of course," Sarah said. "Whatever you desire. As always." She tipped her head and immediately turned around. She and Hattie exited the room.

"Twenty-four pounds?" Emma asked. "For what?"

"I'll explain later," Sir William said, beginning to change.

"Dear," Emma said, "why get dressed? You need rest. Here, have some tea."

"Where are my sweaters?" he asked, pulling on his trousers. He turned back to his wardrobe and examined the many shelves. "I can't find them."

"William!" Emma said, somewhat louder.

He turned.

"What are you doing?"

"I'm getting dressed. Those ships are in trouble. They need help."

Emma approached and touched his arm. "Dear," she said, more softly than before, "you've been out there once. You needn't go again. Please. You must preserve your strength."

Preserve. He remembered thinking about that on the ride home from Hanby's.

He faced her squarely and placed his hands on her arms. "Emma," he said as kindly as he could, "I think I've come up with something. I must do this."

Her countenance fell. "William, you'll catch your death if you go out there again. Please." She laced her arms around his waist and hugged him. "It's too dangerous."

He hugged her for several seconds and then forced the two of them apart. "I must."

"Why?" Emma asked as he hurried to dress.

"Because I'm the man who always says it's impossible to fail with courage. Now where are my sweaters?"

"I'm not telling," she said, folding her arms and turning her back.

"Emma," Sir William said with no trace of humor.

Emma crouched and reached deep into the bottom shelf and pulled out a navy blue sweater. She held it out without looking at him.

"That's my lady," he said. He grabbed the sweater and swiftly left the room.

Less than twenty minutes later, he stood in front of the York, peppered by stinging hale, a familiar circle of fishermen gathered around him. "I'll personally reward any man who agrees to help." Burbridge and Graves weren't around. Neither was Monty Jones. But Captain Reid was present, standing among his own men.

"Were at the ready," Captain Reid said.

"The weather's far too miserable now," Jimmy O'Leary said. "It was the luck of the Irish with us last night, but this is now a fiercer storm."

"I'm not Irish," Sir William said. "Not that I'd be unhappy if I was. It's just that it's better to count on courage than to hope for chance—that, and maybe some Providence if you believe in that sort of thing. I know I do."

"I'm not a betting man," Jimmy O'Leary said with a smirk.

"That's a fish tale, O'Leary, and you know it," Joseph said. "Next you'll tell us you don't like potatoes."

The fishermen chuckled.

"The ships in the bay need assistance for sure," Captain Reid said. "But what of that ship farther out, she's in a sorry state."

Sir William looked out to sea, directly north of the harbor entrance, and saw a large ship rollicking in a tempestuous sea.

"That's the *Two Sisters*," Michael said. "I know her lines well. I'm not sure we could help her. She's a brig, you understand."

Matthew Hanby stepped up beside Sir William. "Hawsers maybe."

"We might tow lines from the harbor," Captain Reid said. He turned to his men.

"Hmm," Sir William looked about. "We'll need nearly a mile of line." He glanced at Michael and Joseph, who shook their heads, and then at Matthew.

The hotel proprietor rested his lips on his knuckles. His face suddenly brightened, and he perked his head high. "We've got quarter-mile coils intended for rope walks," Matthew said. "I do believe we've even four of them. It could work."

"That's the plan, then," Sir William said. "We'll need four boats heading north to the brig, a coil in each. You'll have to fasten them well so others can haul on them from shore. The rest of us need to row into the bay and offer assistance, or they'll beach disastrously."

Captain Reid turned around. "My crew and I will carry the lines. It's a long row, and we're likely more rested than the rest of you," he said. "Where do we set up?"

Sir William tapped Matthew's shoulder. "Hanby, you help the captain. Get him the lines and four of your boats and a few more men if you can."

"Aye," Matthew said. He waved Reid and his men to follow.

"Good luck, mate," Captain Reid said to Sir William as he passed.

"All success to you, Captain," Sir William said.

"Your offer of a personal guarantee still stands?" Jimmy O'Leary asked. "We still run the same risk."

"Of course," Sir William said. "The offer remains unchanged."

O'Leary and the others agreed. Within minutes a fleet of pleasure boats from the York Hotel were outfitted and manned. One end of a great coil of line was fastened to a sturdy post at the end of the pier and then placed in a Hanby boat. Three other boats were also filled with identical coils and launched under the command of Captain Reid. The lines were to be plied out and spliced as the men rowed north of the bay until they reached the distant *Two Sisters*.

Sir William was in the second fleet of four boats headed for the bay. This time he manned the tiller. Michael, Tom, Joseph, and Jimmy O'Leary comprised his crew.

Sir William sat at the stern while the fishermen rowed hard. The hail stung their faces and bruised their hands. The icy waters swept over them, soaking them to the skin when they were barely beyond the pier.

The closest sloop, named *Eliza,* was reached first. She bobbed erratically, pitching and rolling in the throes of fitful seas.

Sir William surveyed the scene. "She's clearly dragging her anchors," he said. "See how she moves with every roll?"

"Aye," Michael said. "She'll shoal if we fail to pull her out."

"Not a moment to spare," Sir William said. He half-stood in the boat, hoping to get the attention of his small fleet of Hanby pleasure boats. The hail felt like frozen pine needles in his face. The other three rowboats were downwind and flanked him on the left.

The steersmen watched him. He motioned the closest one to swing closer to his boat and then mimicked a throwing motion to the others, hoping they'd understand.

"Cast lines!" he shouted, knowing the wind and hail likely dwarfed his voice.

The boat farthest from him understood his motion and immediately cast a line to the embattled sloop. The crew aboard the *Eliza* caught it and made it fast.

"Excellent," Sir William said. Suddenly, his own boat pitched high, and he was slammed hard to the bottom of the boat.

Michael helped him up. He peered over the side and saw another line cast and secured. The other rowboat rocked close by.

"Swing around with us," Sir William shouted. "We'll cast our lines from this side."

The two boats clawed with oars and cast lines one after the other. The toss from the other boat missed, but Sir William's throw made good. "We'll hold her steady," he yelled. "Cast again!"

The second throw made it, and all towlines were set. Sir William motioned his rescue fleet to row homeward. Against wind, hail, and rollers they slogged, being careful to stay clear of Conister.

It took more than an hour to tow the *Eliza* close enough to the pier that rockets could fire additional hawsers. A group of fishermen pulled from atop the pier and helped drag the sloop home. When the sloop cleared the end of the pier, Sir William stood up. He ran the edge of his hand across his throat, signaling the sloop to release the lines from the rowboats. As soon as they did, he sat back down. The rowboats hauled in their lines.

"What say, men?" he asked. "There's yet more out there. Do we go again?"

Jimmy O'Leary winked. "At two pounds a trip, I'm with you until the bay freezes solid."

The others nodded. Sir William motioned to the three other rowboats. "If you're up to it, men. We've others to tow." He turned to his crew. "We'll see who follows."

After a few strokes, the other rowboats hadn't moved from their positions. They bobbed and splashed, but their oars were shipped.

"I don't think they're coming, sir," Michael said.

Jimmy O'Leary let go of his oar and stood up so fast he nearly fell overboard. Joseph and Tom steadied him. "Hey, all you bloody mates! Two pounds a trip! Sir William has guaranteed!" He sat down. "Don't worry, blokes, they'll be coming. I'll guarantee that." He resumed his hold on the oar. "C'mon, mates. Bloody well row!"

Michael, Joseph, and Tom resumed their rowing. Sir William watched the other boats and, sure enough, one by one they followed all the way across the bay until they reached the schooner named *Content*.

Being there first, Sir William cast a line upwind and then ordered an anchor thrown overboard. "We can help her keep from dragging until the others get here."

The captain and crew of the schooner hailed them and cheered. "We never expected you to return," the captain shouted through a funnel.

"What's a little wind and hail?" Sir William offered in return. "Hold fast, we'll tow you soon." He saw the other three rowboats approaching and repeated the same instructions he'd given earlier. Two of them cast lines downwind of the vessel and the third rowed in close and tossed an upwind towline. Sir William looked to the far side of the bay and saw the last remaining sloop.

"She's the *Merchant*," Michael said.

The medium-sized vessel was moving quickly toward shallows. "She can't wait," Sir William said. "We need to attend her now." He called to the nearby rowboat. "We're hauling our anchor and retrieving our line. You lead the tow back. We'll attend the sloop. Return when you can."

The steersman in the other boat waved his reply and shouted to the other boats, miming Sir William's commands and motions.

"What will we be able to do?" Tom asked, his voice slightly wavering. "We're just one boat."

"Anchor and cast a line to her," Sir William said. "We should be able to slow her some."

"She seems heavy," Joseph said. "Look how low she sits in the water."

"We can try," Michael said.

"Men"—Sir William looked at each of them—"it's up to you. What say?"

"Like I said," Jimmy O'Leary said, "I'm in until the bay freezes solid."

The men exchanged glances. They were soaked and breathing hard, but they all nodded.

"Aye," Sir William said. "There's no lack of courage here." He turned to see the other three rowboats successfully towing the *Content* toward harbor and clear of Conister. He looked at his men, already rowing toward the last boat in distress.

"Don't worry," Jimmy O'Leary said. "For two pounds a trip, at least two of 'em will be back, maybe all three." He rowed hard and swift.

Sir William noted the wiry muscles in the arms and neck of the little man. He hadn't really cared for this fisherman named Jimmy O'Leary at first, but the little mouse of a man had real spirit.

A powerful surge in the wind roared from the south and their speed increased.

"Whoa!" Jimmy O'Leary squealed.

Sir William tightened his jaw. It was a welcome push, but it would be a difficult resistance on the return. He looked up to see the *Merchant* turning dangerously.

"What?" he yelled. The sloop had either snapped a line or the captain had done something foolish. Suddenly, the sloop's bow turned toward Sir William and his crew.

"Is she thinking to beat out?" Sir William asked. "Doesn't she see us?" He tilted his head high to see a row of heads peering over the sloop's rail. The one with the captain's cap was either shaking his fist or waving.

The wind surged again.

The *Merchant* lifted high and turned sideways to the rollers. It sounded like a cannonade as the surf lifted and slammed the vessel against serrated rows of rocks.

"She has struck!" Sir William shouted. "Hard to starboard!"

The foundering sloop ripped open, and thousands of bushels of oats flowed into the sea. Her deck buckled, and the crew was scattered into the deadly surf.

"All hands to oars!" Sir William shouted, unable to hear his own voice above the howling wind. From his seat in the stern, he reached forward and grabbed the oars, hoping to help his four crewmen row. The small boat tilted. "Ride the rollers!"

Suddenly, his back twisted with a ripping spasm. He jerked backward, losing his grip and collapsing into the bottom of the boat in massive pain.

A towering wave loomed high. It drooled with foamy crests and teetered. Sir William folded his arms over his face and squeezed his eyes shut. An immense weight collapsed over him, forcing the air from his lungs with a single blast.

Sounds became muffled. Gushing water ran past his ears. He opened his mouth to yell but swallowed salt water. He tried to cough it out but only swallowed more. Fear gripped him. He opened his eyes to a world of black water. He spun and twisted. He saw a leg kicking but then it was gone. A black blur brushed past him. His chest felt like bursting. He kicked and flailed. Sounds returned.

Sir William coughed cups of water and sucked in cold air. He moaned with each exhale and gasped with each inhale. The rollicking surf spat on his face. The wind pushed him, and the currents toyed with his limbs. He searched for his bearings and noticed his arms.

They were covered with brown flecks. He realized something was sticking to his face. He wondered what it was when his knees struck something hard below the surface, and the waves pushed him onto his side. He rolled over and felt coarse substance beneath him.

His arms were pulled taut and his entire length scraped across what felt like gravel. Some of it got inside his waistband, and he realized it was sand. He was forced over and a great compression seized his stomach. Water flowed past his lips.

"Sir William!" a voice said.

He saw the shape of a man's face close to his own. "Sir William!" the voice said again.

Sir William focused his eyes. It was a round face talking to him. It was the portly fisherman.

"Joseph," Sir William whispered.

"Aye!" Joseph smiled back, his face strangely speckled.

"Wh—what is on your face?" Sir William asked.

Joseph smiled. "Oats. Same as yours."

Sir William moaned as he struggled to sit up. Joseph assisted him. Around them swirled clusters of oats, ripped timbers, and smashed crates. Scattered up and down the shore were prone bodies. "The sloop?"

Joseph shook his head. "She's broken up, sir."

"Our crew?" Sir William asked, trying to stand but stumbling to his knees.

"Tom and Jimmy didn't make it, sir," Joseph said. "Michael is alive."

Michael stepped into view, standing behind Joseph. "And so are you, sir."

Sir William kneeled in the sand, sitting back on his heels. He wiped the oats that still clung to his face and looked across the bay. There were no ships left in the bay, though large pieces of timber still churned amidst the waves. Beyond the bay, he saw the light of the makeshift lighthouse, and he remembered.

"The *Two Sisters*?" he asked.

"I don't know," Joseph said.

"I forgot all about her," Michael said.

Sir William forced himself to his feet. "Come," he said. "They might need us."

Sir William, Michael, and Joseph arrived at the pier to find that Captain Reid and his crew had successfully reached the large schooner with the towing lines. The steady activities of all involved had eventually drawn the attention of several more from town. With a throng of helpers, including Burbridge, Graves, and Monty Jones, a mass of men were pulling in sea chantey rhythm to safely haul the *Two Sisters* to harbor.

Sir William and the two fishermen found spaces in the line.

"You had a good haul of fish on your left," Lieutenant Graves chanted. "Heave!"

As Sir William pulled, he recalled Jimmy O'Leary straining at the oars.

"You had a good haul of fish on your right," Lieutenant Burbridge yelled.

Sir William could still hear Tom's doubt about towing the *Merchant*.

"Heave!" Lieutenant Burbridge yelled.

It took hours and was late evening before it was over. The wind had settled to a stiff breeze and the hail had long since stopped. The *Two Sisters* was moored near the *Vigilant* and the exhausted men had scattered about the pier. Some fishermen disappeared into pubs while others slipped into hotels or returned to their homes. The York dining room was teeming with others who had been involved. Captain Reid returned to his hotel room. Sir William sat on the steps of the hotel along with Burbridge, Graves, Joseph, Michael, and Matthew.

"At last," Joseph said. "Our work is done."

Sir William, his body wracked with pain, lowered his eyes and said nothing.

"Hey, you," a familiar voice said.

Sir William looked up. It was Monty Jones and a woman with an infant child.

"Go away, Jones," Michael said.

"Shut up, Kellerman," Monty said. His taut, scarred face appeared fierce.

"Hey, you, Mister Royal Hillary or whatever you go by," Monty Jones said, stepping closer.

"You want me to throw this wretch in the harbor?" Lieutenant Burbridge asked, stepping up and straightening his clothes. "I think I've got enough spunk for at least that."

Sir William held up his hand and waved off his defender.

"Oh, yeah," Monty Jones said, his mouth twisting and his face reddening. "That would be like you, now wouldn't it? Just throw us away, you do. Well, I want you to meet someone, Mister Courage-Is-All-It-Takes."

Sir William understood the anger. The night was a disappointing mix of success and failure. He nodded his surrender and looked up at the couple. "Pleased to meet you, Mrs. Jones."

The woman stared at him. She was not pretty, and was dressed in a ragged, filthy dress. She was covered with two shawls, neither of which looked warm. She held a small infant son with a pale, pointed face bundled in a tattered blanket. The woman stared at him, her dirty face hollow and streaked with tears.

Sir William's neck grew stiff with pain. He lowered his gaze.

"No," Monty Jones said, pushing his face closer to Sir William, his breath putrid. "You got it wrong. It's not Mrs. Jones, Sir Hill-of-Beans. It's Mrs. Jimmy O'Leary and baby James. I was thinking you might want to explain to her how far that two pounds is going to go and how it's so much better than having Jimmy O'Leary coming home tonight."

Sir William shuddered. He snapped his gaze back to the destitute woman.

Her spittle struck his cheek and rolled down.

Chapter 10

It had been weeks since the rescue of the *Vigilant* and the other ships, and Sir William's health had suffered ever since. Today was his first day out of the house, and only because his brother-in-law had insisted they take a morning ride.

"Whoa." Sir William reined his horse back. The clear skies and bright sun were a pleasant surprise for the otherwise cold February morning, and the snow-covered countryside reflected brightly to silhouette Major Tobin only a few paces away. Sir William shielded his eyes. "I always meant to get up this way with Ambrose. We never did."

"I miss the old colonel," Major Tobin said, turning his horse around and walking back to position alongside Sir William, facing the opposite direction. "But not as some have been missing you." The major's eyes roved until settling on Sir William. "People close to you are worried," he said in an odd tone.

Sir William looked at him. His brother-in-law was dressed more casually than usual, though his tan pants and red shirt were finely pressed. His riding coat, gloves, and hat were of fine suede. His black boots glistened in the morning light. "The rescues drained me," Sir William said. His horse shifted. He noted the height of the rising sun and wished it were warmer.

"You've seemed absent these few months," Major Tobin said. "Can I help?"

"Emma put you up to this?" Sir William asked, turning his horse to face the same direction.

The neck of the major's horse twitched, and he stroked its mane. "My sister is worried."

"Why?" Sir William asked. "I am recovering, that is all." He looked everywhere but at the major. He knew he had been depressed, but he was feeling better today and did not desire to talk about it. His horse stepped uneasily.

"I think your horse is ready to run," Major Tobin said. "Let us race to the hill."

Sir William smiled. This was more the brother-in-law he was used to. "I accept the challenge."

Major Tobin smiled. "Best hope you are a fast rider!" The major snapped his reins and bolted ahead. Snow and dirt kicked high.

Sir William kicked with his heels and yelled. "Hee ya!" His horse sprang into motion, shifting quickly into a gallop. The air was cold.

The major raced straight up the path toward the base of the hill. The path was only wide enough for two horses abreast. His hunched-over frame with arms and elbows flailing made it difficult to pass without being forced into the snow.

Sir William considered breaking right to race across the field. It was a shorter distance, but the snow was deep. He maintained his position, closed in from behind, and squinted to protect his eyes from flying snow and mud.

Try as he did, he could not close the distance, and his brother-in-law charged up the hill to beat him. The major reined up his horse and laughed, his teeth as white as the blanketed countryside. "Ha!" Major Tobin shouted. "You lose!"

Sir William reached the top and pulled up. "You did have a bit of a head start!"

"Come now, Sir William," Major Tobin said. "I've never known you to make excuses."

"None are offered," he said, tipping his head in mock bow. "You are the winner of the race to the hill."

"Then I have proven who is the better man," Major Tobin said, holding his arms out wide.

"Says you," Sir William said. "There's still the matter of getting home." He snapped his reins to slap the rear of his horse and raced down the other side.

The cold wind chilled his face. The force of it rushing past his ears reminded him of being at sea with flapping sails and the pounding of his horse's hooves sounded like waves breaking upon rocks. The depression returned. He saw the face of the O'Leary woman. He could hear the sarcasm of Monty Jones. Sir William kicked the ribs of his horse and galloped faster.

Suddenly his horse stumbled, and Sir William soared through the air. He rolled in the deep snow alongside the path. He immediately worried about the horse but also instantly felt anguish over losing again to the major. He struggled to his feet, saw his horse standing unhurt, and then looked up, half-expecting to see his brother-in-law galloping by with a huge grin.

It didn't happen.

He looked ahead toward home and there was no sign of the major. He looked back toward the hill and spotted him making poor time through deep snow, apparently having tried to cut across the lower field in a shortcut to the fork. Sir William laughed. He was bruised, and his horse was flustered, but he took the reins and led his horse to walk home the winner.

"I swear there are two boys in the house today," Emma said, wiping the bloody scrape upon Sir William's forehead with a warm cloth.

"Your husband, dear sister," Major Tobin said, "will do anything to win a horserace—even fly!"

"And what of your measures?" Sir William asked. "Shortcuts aren't chosen for any other reason but to be first."

"A most unfortunate strategy, I admit," Major Tobin said, sipping a steaming cup of tea. He extended his legs to rest his feet on the footstool in front of the fire in the great room. He was wrapped in a quilt. "I've had better ideas."

"I'll get Hattie to fix you both some warm stew," Emma said, kissing Sir William on the cheek.

"Tell her to bring some brandy for my tea," Major Tobin said.

The men sat quietly for several long moments.

"I've been thinking about something lately," Sir William finally said.

The major peered over the top of his teacup, lowered it, and said, "I doubt that very much. More like you've been sulking."

"I have an idea that may warm your insides more than any brandy can."

"I doubt that even more," Major Tobin said with a grin. "But if it be so much a constant breath that must flow through your lips, I will indulge you to share your idea with me."

"You are too kind." Sir William smiled. The major was sounding like himself. "How I should be so fortunate to merit such keen interest is indeed a mystery. Nevertheless, I will seize the opportunity."

"My, my, you do love to tease one another, don't you?" Sarah asked. She looked stunning in her velvet-trimmed dress as she entered the room and glided across the floor to sit on the seat made for two, directly opposite the two men. "Emma reports quite the morning contest between you two, but I was unaware it was still continuing."

"Sweet Sarah, how nice to see you," Major Tobin said. "I would rise to greet you, but I am in a cocoon."

"Good morning, Sarah," Sir William said. He crossed to her, bent down, and kissed her on the forehead. "No contest here. We were about to discuss my intention to draft an appeal addressed to the king and to be circulated among the Admiralty."

"Well," Sarah said, nodding to the major. "I am impressed to learn of the company your conversation entertains."

Major Tobin yawned. "I have no idea what he's talking about. This is the first I've heard of it."

Sir William crossed to the center of the room. "The captain of the *Vigilant* offered to personally take any letter of mine to royalty."

"Charming," Emma said, bringing in a tray with two bowls of hot stew and a small decanter of brandy. "No doubt in gratitude for saving his rank."

"That is splendid," Sarah said.

"Ah, brandy," Major Tobin said, reaching for the decanter. "I doubt the captain will ever recall his promise to you. He was likely numbed by the cold and spray." He poured a shot of the amber spirit into his tea. "Nothing like a stiff brandy to warm the bones."

"And stew," Emma said. "This is all the more needed for grown men trying to run about as young boys." She placed one bowl of stew atop the table at her brother's side and turned to Sir William. "Where would you like yours?"

Sir William motioned to the table between his customary chair and where Sarah sat. Emma placed his bowl and took her seat beside Sarah.

"I think highly of the captain," Sir William said, not missing a beat. "I am inclined to take up his offer."

"Capital!" Major Tobin said. He tipped the decanter to pour a generous amount of brandy into his stew.

"Caesar!" Emma said.

"It's just to warm me up, sister."

"But not in your stew," she said.

Sir William watched the distractions then loudly exhaled.

"I'm sorry, dear," Emma said. "Please go on."

"I've a thing or two on my mind I'd like to tell the king," Sarah said.

"What do you think of an organization designed to help those shipwrecked at sea and on land?"

Sarah and Emma sat smiling. The major sipped his tea and shrugged his shoulders.

"Well?" Sir William prodded.

"How does one shipwreck on land?" Major Tobin asked.

"Yes, how?" Emma asked.

Sir William looked at Sarah, and she raised her eyebrows and nodded.

"If you lose your husband at sea"—Sir William paced as he spoke—"and have no income other than what he received for his daily labors, then there can be as much wreckage at home as there is at sea."

"I see." Major Tobin gulped another swig of brandy and tea. "This is about those sorry mates who drowned during the rescue." He set his cup down and partially loosened his blanket. "William, you can't blame yourself for that loss of life. No one would have been saved if not for your efforts. Besides, I heard that the captain of that sloop was reckless and was earlier responsible for forcing the *Vigilant* onto Conister in the first place. No, sir, you are not responsible."

"Indeed not, Sir William," Sarah said. "You were courageous."

The major raised his teacup. "To courage!"

Sir William frowned. "Regardless the fault, the wreckage remains." He placed his hands on his hips. "All is not well."

"Is this man never satisfied?" Major Tobin asked the women, leaning forward to seize their gazes. "Does he never rest?" He reached for his bowl of stew.

"The king of England rules the greatest maritime nation in the world," Sir William said. "That is why I am going to write an appeal."

"An appeal?" Emma asked. "What do you mean, dear? For what?"

"I am calling for the establishment of a national institution for the purpose of preserving lives that have been upset by shipwreck. It must not come down to capricious acts of charity but it must be a guarantee of rights—for everyone! Not just Englanders, either. I'm saying all nations, all peoples, and the world." Sir William stood, his hands extended, his heart pounding, his energy high. He smiled at his family. "What do you think of that?"

The major gripped his spoon of stew with his teeth but delayed pulling it out. He looked at Sir William but then lowered his eyes.

Emma sat, hands folded in her lap, displaying a bright and warm smile fixed and unmoving. She hardly blinked.

Sarah sat in a similar pose but her eyes moved without a corresponding move of her head, first one way toward the major and then the other way toward Emma. She returned her eyes to look at Sir William and blushed. "It's a fine idea," she said sheepishly.

"The world?" Emma asked. "We've only recently made peace with America."

The major pulled the spoon out of his mouth and slowly chewed. "It is a somewhat larger appeal than I had expected." He swallowed. "Perhaps we should just focus on, say, taxes. Aye, there's plenty to say about that."

Sir William dropped his arms and shook his head, exhaling long and slow. "I don't mean the whole world right now. I meant I expect it could spread around the world. Of course, there are steps between here and there. But do you understand the vision? Do you think it's a good idea?"

"Who'll pay for it, dear?" Emma asked, her voice as quiet as a soft rain, but a dampening one.

"England," Sir William said in somber tone.

Emma exhaled. "Whew! I'm glad for that. No more IOUs?"

The major stood and clumsily unwrapped himself from the quilt. He poured a shot of brandy into his teacup and quickly tipped it down his throat. "Ah! Compliments to Hattie," he said, crossing to Sarah and Emma and planting kisses on the cheeks of both. He turned and bowed to Sir William. "Very impressive, Sir William. Well beyond anything I know anything about, but bold in the typical Sir William Hillary fashion." He held one thumb up. "It is now convenient for me to resume my intended activities for the day, so I will excuse myself."

He turned and bowed to the ladies. "I trust, dear sister, you will consider my mission satisfactorily completed since your husband, no doubt, has returned to the former glory of being himself." He bowed once more to Sir William and then walked swiftly across the room to disappear down the hall.

Sir William looked back at the ladies. They stared at him with all the pleasantry their soft, affectionate countenances could produce.

"Never mind," Sir William said. "I will write it, and then you will understand." He crossed to his seat, picked up his bowl of stew, and departed for his study. The women said nothing.

He walked down the hall, glimpsed the major hurrying out the front door, and trudged to his study where he sat at his desk and ate his now-cooling stew.

Hours passed. Emma entered at one point to see if he wanted anything, but he silently motioned her away. Sir William wrote page after page, then crumpled page after page. He paced. He sat. He wrote again. He crumpled pages again.

He stared at his shoes, he stared out the window, and he stared into space. He wrote until his wrists hurt and his fingers ached. He got up, dressed warmly, and walked outside.

He walked along the garden in its winter repose. He recalled what it had looked like last summer and what Emma had said to him all those years ago. The bursting of color and thickly hanging fragrance seemed so foreign now. Emma was right. One would never know what this little plot of ground was capable of displaying judging by its bottled up buds and barren sticks. It was all there somewhere in the roots, but presently unseen.

He looked toward the bay and relived the rescues. He ached to communicate what the experiences had done to him and what it should mean to all.

He thought about visiting the vicar and then decided against it. He thought about visiting Matthew Hanby and then decided against it. He thought about venturing to see Michael Kellerman, and then Joseph but decided against every idea that came. He thought about Colonel Ambrose St. John and wished he were alive. He wondered if he'd visit him now if he were, and then decided he wouldn't, despite missing him.

There was nothing to do but write it down. If he couldn't write it, then he didn't yet have it clear. If he didn't yet have it clear, no one else would either. He returned to his study.

He skipped dinner. He resisted Emma and Sarah both trying to coax him out of his seclusion. Finally, he spoke so miserably and rudely to them that they left him alone. He was so uncomfortable that he wondered if it was worth it, but he couldn't leave it unfinished.

He again crumpled up all the papers he'd written. He felt incapable and out of energy. He stretched out on the floor and tried to sleep. He sat in his chair and tried to rest. He curled up in a ball and sat in the corner of his study and buried his head in his knees. Finally, he prayed.

"What do You want?" he asked. His mind was unable to grasp what he felt. "What do You want me to do?"

It was not until the middle of the evening that it all started to come together. Nothing in his efforts had changed. The method was the same. He wrote and crumpled and wrote and crumpled until one time he stopped crumpling what he wrote. Then he wrote some more. And then some more.

The dreadful storms of the last autumn prevailed with unusual violence. On some occasions, it has been my lot to witness the loss of many valuable lives, under circumstances where, had there been establishments previously formed for affording prompt relief, and encouragement given to those who might volunteer on such a cause, in all probability the greater part would have been rescued from destruction. At other times I have seen the noblest instances of self-devotion with the certainty that families would be left destitute if they perished in the trying. Nevertheless, they tried.

As Sir William labored with his pen and his heart, it dawned upon him that there was more working inside of him than the experience of the last shipwreck. It was something he'd seen in the face of Michael Kellerman when Michael had seen little Mike on the beach that one dreadful night. It was the story of Red Kelly leaving behind a family with no one to care for them. It was Jimmy O'Leary, his skinny frame rowing tirelessly to his own death, and the faces of his wife and baby now destitute. It was the words of the mean-spirited Monty Jones. There was truth in those words.

It was one thing to risk your life for another. That required sacrifice enough. But to risk the welfare of those dependent upon you seemed to be an entirely deeper level of sacrifice. His Quaker upbringing suddenly quickened his heart with the realization that Scripture hadn't said God loved us so much that He gave His life. It claimed He loved us so much that He gave the life of His *Son*.

To ask men to risk their own lives was one thing, but to ask them to risk the lives and welfare of their sons, their families, while they ventured to rescue others was getting close to the kind of love that God had demonstrated. Could a man love like that?

Sir William didn't like the question, and he didn't know the answer. If somehow assurances could be made, assurances rooted in compassion for loved ones, assurances that families would be taken care of should family providers perish in the doing of noble deeds, then men might be more inclined.

He wondered if that made the sacrifice less noble.

He didn't know.

Regardless, it would be worth it because more efforts to save others in dire need might happen. He prayed again. "Are these my thoughts or Yours?"

These are not arguments founded on the visionary contemplation of remote or improbable dangers. Their urgent necessity must be obvious to every mind. So long as man shall continue to navigate the ocean, and the tempests shall hold their course over its surface, in every age and on every coast, disasters by sea, shipwreck, and peril to human life, must inevitably take place; and with this terrible certainty before our eyes, the duty becomes imperative, that we should use every means to obviate and to mitigate the disastrous consequences.

Sir William wrote page after page in service to such ends. However, as he wrote, he became convinced that passion without a plan was simply zeal without knowledge—ultimately useless to effect the kind of change needed. He knew it wasn't enough. He became specific, turning his mind to practical steps involved, so others might read them and run.

To the consideration of such aforementioned things, I most respectfully beg leave to submit:

That a national institution should be formed, equally worthy of Great Britain, important to humanity, and beneficial to the naval and commercial interests of the United Empire; having for its objects,

First, The preservation of human life from shipwreck; which should always be considered as the first great and permanent object of the Institution.

Secondly, Assistance to vessels in distress, which often immediately connects itself with the safety of the crews.

Thirdly, The preservation of vessels and property, when not so immediately connected with the lives of the people, or after the crews and passengers shall already have been rescued.

Fourthly, The prevention of plunder and depredations in case of shipwreck.

Fifthly, The succor and support of those persons who may be rescued; the prompt obtaining of medical aid, food, clothing, and shelter, for those whose destitute situation may require such relief, with the means to forward them to their homes, friends, or countries. The people and vessels of every nation, whether in peace or war, to be equally objects of this Institution; and the efforts to be made, and the recompenses to be given for their rescue, to be in all cases the same as for British subjects and British vessels.

Sixthly, The bestowing of suitable rewards on those who rescue the lives of others from shipwreck, or who assist vessels in distress; and the establishment of a provision for the destitute widows or families of the brave men who unhappily lose their lives in such meritorious attempts.

Sir William wrote the steps in the order in which they would happen, though it was this last point that moved him the most. Fishermen like Jimmy O'Leary and Red Kelly and others could not be viewed with any less dignity than those who had been honored or publicly recognized in other areas of society. Income certainly determined the ease or labor of a man's life, but it couldn't be confused with an equation of his worth or goodness.

A wicked man might be poor, it is true. And a rich man might be good. But just as easily the reverse could be correct—a wicked man could be rich and a good man could be poor. Therefore, no standard of social status ought to influence a man's decision to risk his life for another.

Clear the decks of all unfair advantages and let each man's conviction on whether or not to risk his life for aid of another be on the same terms, regardless of station.

Sir William wrote with feverish intensity, writing page after page of justification of his cause and his call for a national institution. He called for permanent establishments in all greater and lesser seaports, provisioned with lifeboats, anchors, cables, hawsers, and future inventions designed to preserve life at sea. He called for the national distribution of life jackets.

Finally, at just after midnight, with the beginning of a new day, he wrote the final words:

That every stranger, whom the disasters of the sea may cast on her shores, should never look for refuge in vain.

Douglas, Isle of Man, 28th February, 1823

Sir William slapped down his steel pen and placed his hands behind his head, interlocking his fingers. He smiled and then yawned.

He pushed his chair back and raised his feet to rest atop his desk alongside a stack of pages. He stared at the pile for a long time and then stood and stretched. He felt satiated, his vision thus recorded, his burden eased. He slowly strode across the room, feeling aches for the first time in several hours.

He stopped and looked back at his writing implements. He returned to his seat and dipped the pen into the inkwell. He tapped the steel tip on the edge of the small jar while smoothing a piece of paper with his other hand. He bent his wrist and circled the pen a few rotations without allowing the ink to reach the surface. When the loops felt right, he applied the perfect pressure to form a grand *D* and wrote another letter welling up from inside.

Dear Augustus,

You must have grown so much by now . . .

Chapter 11

For much of the remains of that year, Sir William ventured to stand in front of the quayside comptroller's office, dressed in top hat, suit, and cane. Almost every week he stood, hoping a prized letter would arrive by the Whitehaven packet. It was now September, and there was no sign of what he had been hoping for.

Mungo Murray, the comptroller in charge of collecting and tabulating all the fees and surcharges related to the maritime industries, became a familiar sight to Sir William. The fat man with the dusty black suit sat hunched over his desk. The mail was often left in bundles upon a long table inside Murray's office. Many folks passed in and out of the large, square room, retrieving their letters and packages and settling with the comptroller any postage due.

Not being a talkative type and never mistaken for courteous, Murray this day surprised Sir William with a lukewarm greeting. "Hey, Hillary."

"Huh?" Sir William craned his neck to look back from the table, where he had just begun sorting through the piles of mail, searching for his own. "Are you addressing me?"

"Yup."

"Yes, well, good morning." Sir William resumed sorting through the stacks.

"You looking for these?" Murray asked.

Sir William turned and beheld a banded stack of letters held up in the man's pudgy hand. Murray looked up and frowned. "You've been panting for over six months down here. You're always here on arrival day. I thought I'd save you the trouble of sorting." He leaned forward and held out the short stack.

Sir William retrieved his mail.

"Actually," Murray said, "it dropped to the floor when the packet man dumped it on the table. I figured you'd be here today, so I set it aside."

"Thank you," Sir William said, turning to leave.

"Yup."

Sir William stepped outside and immediately shuffled through the letters, instantly spotting the return addresses. Nothing.

"Wait!" Murray said.

Sir William heard the fat man's chair scrape the floor. Mungo Murray filled the entire doorframe. He held an elegantly wrapped letter inches from his nose. "Here's another one," Murray said. "It's from someone beginning with an *A*."

"Augustus?" Sir William felt giddy.

"Nope."

Sir William felt like he'd tasted spoiled seabird. "Oh."

Mungo Murray extended his short arm to hold the letter in front of Sir William's face. "I wouldn't be too disappointed," Murray said. "It's a royal seal."

Sir William examined the return address. The giddiness returned. The letter was from the Lords of the Admiralty. He took the letter and turned away. He walked all the way down the quayside admiring the fine envelope, the elegantly scripted lettering, and the royal seal.

He entered the York Hotel and crossed to his favorite table in the back corner near the smaller fireplace. There was always good light from the side window and a pleasant view of the inmost part of the harbor where it narrowed and turned southward, becoming a river. He placed his hat and gloves and cane on the chair beside him.

"Morning, Sir William!" Matthew Hanby called out from near the entrance to the kitchen.

Sir William waved and sat down. He pushed the packet of mail aside except for the one with the seal. He savored looking at the royal reply in his hands. "Could you bring me an opener?" he called out to Matthew.

Matthew brought a knife. "Something special?"

"I believe this is the reply to my proposal," Sir William said. He displayed the return address and the seal.

"Royalty!" Matthew pulled his chin in tight and smiled. "Quite the nobleman you are!"

Sir William slid the knife to perfectly slice the envelope open without cracking the wax. "I want to preserve the seal," he said, savoring the moment like a cup of fine tea. "This may be historic, you just don't know."

"What sort of proposal?" Matthew asked, sitting down.

Sir William smiled. "I'll read it, and then you tell me." His heart was beating so rapidly he could feel it tapping his chest. He puffed the envelope with his breath and placed two fingers inside. He slid out the one page letter as if it were made of brittle glass. He unfolded it. The first sentence jumped out at him.

"Your appeal advocates a worthy consideration," he read aloud. He rushed through the transitional content and found another choice phrase. "The Admiralty wishes success for this undertaking," he read a little louder. He scanned further and saw another stirring phrase. "It should not be immediately dismissed," Sir William said with a hearty tone.

"What?" Matthew asked. "What shouldn't be dismissed? What did you propose?"

Sir William saw the word and suddenly felt sweaty about his neck. His stomach knotted. "However," he read aloud, his voice lowering.

"Uh-oh," Matthew said.

"There being no precise information . . ." He began to mumble, skipping entire groups of words. "No steps at present to be taken . . . Regrettably. Admiralty." Sir William set the paper down and stared at the table.

"I'm sorry, Sir William. Really." Matthew stood up. "I'll get you some tea. Would you like that?"

Sir William nodded and then shook his head. "No, no thanks, Matthew." He stood and shrugged. "I think I'll take a walk."

"Come back for some beef at lunch," Matthew said. "I'll make your favorite plate."

"I had a good idea," Sir William said. "It was to help preserve lives hurt by shipwreck. I really thought they'd see the merit of it." He looked at his friend.

Matthew stood smiling. His mouth moved to speak, but no words came forth.

"I'm sorry," Sir William said. "I didn't mean to be awkward."

"I'm sorry you're disappointed," Matthew said. "Come back for lunch."

Sir William replaced his top hat and tugged on his gloves. He hooked his cane on one arm and gathered his mail. He nodded and left.

Outside the weather was pleasant, but inside Sir William felt out of order. He doubted he would return for lunch. He walked along the pier.

"Good day, Sir William," Michael Kellerman said.

Sir William looked up to see his friend, wearing his wide brimmed fishing hat, sitting on a crate mending nets. A teenage boy worked another net beside him. "Hello, Michael."

"A cloud has covered you, sir," Michael said, still focusing on his work. "Can I help?" Michael looked up. His bushy eyebrows had a trace of gray. The boy worked on.

Sir William lifted one foot to rest on the crate beside Michael. "I managed to have a proposal distributed among some of the most notable among notables, including the Lord Commissioners of the Admiralty. I had hoped they would help us form a lifesaving organization."

"That would be useful, sir," Michael said, working intently.

Sir William scanned the entire quayside along the pier. Boats and ships traveled safely. Fishermen and merchants moved in multiple directions. Seagulls hovered and squawked. It all looked so peaceful when the south wind wasn't blowing. "It was very much inspired by the exploits we've known, Michael," Sir William said. "It was a plan to get us a lifeboat and assistance for widows."

"None of them sympathetic, sir?" Michael asked, peering up at Sir William from under his fisherman's hat.

Sir William waved the packet of letters in a semi-circle. "Oh, they're sympathetic all right."

"Congratulations then, sir."

"But that is all they are," Sir William said.

"Oh," Michael said, lowering his gaze back to his work. "Sounds like a common sea to me, sir."

The boy lifted the net he was working on and showed it to Michael. "Poppa?"

"That's good, son," Michael said.

Sir William looked at the boy and then at Michael. "Is this your son? Little Mike?"

The boy looked up and squinted.

Michael smiled. "He's not so little these days, sir. He's fifteen years old."

Sir William smiled and extended his hand. "I'm pleased to see you again, young man. Do you remember me?"

"I think so, sir," little Mike replied. He was thin but had a healthy build. His thick, wavy hair stirred in the gentle breeze.

"He remembers you, sir," Michael said with a warm smile. He ran a hand through his son's hair.

"I certainly remember you," Sir William said.

The boy grinned.

Suddenly, many memories came back, and Sir William felt bold. He exhaled and folded up the royal letter, crumbling the seal. Most of the red wax fell to the pier. He stuffed the letter into his pocket. "Maybe I will print more. Maybe I should send it to all the noblemen in England."

"Then there are others who may listen?" Michael asked. He stood up and held his net high, inspecting it closely. "Sir?"

"I'll widen the circulation to include every nobleman and merchant I can muster," Sir William said, his voice firm and steady. "Have a nice day, Michael. Be strong, little Mike."

Turning back the way he had come, Sir William suddenly felt hungry. He imagined returning to his favorite table at the York Hotel, enjoying some hot beef, and working up a list of potential patrons. He bounded up the steps of the hotel.

"Already?" Matthew said as soon as he saw him. "Nice to see you again."

"Ha!" Sir William said. "I'll have the—"

"—the beef, I know," Matthew said. "Onions? Cider?"

"Yes."

"You're a little early."

Sir William smiled. "Might I have a pen and paper while I wait?"

"Anything else?"

"They've rejected my appeal for an institution devoted to helping people in matters of shipwreck," Sir William said. "I need more ideas of whom I can send a second appeal to. I'll send hundreds."

"They must hear you in person," Matthew said. "You'd have a real chance, I think."

"What do you mean?" Sir William asked.

"Go there and tell them yourself," Matthew said. "Sometimes I've got to get to the kitchen and do things myself if I want them done right. As a matter of fact, I'd better get there now, or there'll be no early beef for you." He winked.

Sir William watched his friend scurry away and then gazed out the window. He looked up the harbor and saw the Whithaven Packet preparing to leave. He watched her slowly move away from the pier and churn the sea toward England. *Tell them myself?* "Matthew!" Sir William yelled.

Matthew burst forth from the kitchen. "What is it? What?" Matthew looked around the dining room and then at Sir William. "What's wrong?"

Sir William smiled. "You're brilliant!"

"I am?" His tiny eyes bobbed like buoys. "How so?"

"For telling me to go to England," Sir William said. He pointed out the window toward the distant sea.

"Did I tell you that?" Matthew asked.

"That's what I heard," Sir William said. "And that's what I'm going to do."

Chapter 12

Sir William traveled by steamship across the Irish Sea and overland coach across the English countryside to London. He had sent several hundred copies of his appeal ahead of time to every potential supporter he and Emma and Sarah could think of. Even Major Tobin had suggested a few names. It was Captain Reid who arranged for him to meet two men who were impressed enough with his appeal to want to meet the author of it.

Sir William met with these men in the drawing room of the Checker Club in the center of London. George Hibbert and Thomas Wilson were men of influence and saw merit in his idea. Hibbert oversaw the West India Merchants and had formerly been a member of parliament from Sussex. Thomas Wilson was a liberal parliamentarian from Southwark.

"This project is best served by a philanthropic model," Wilson said, puffing on his cigar.

Hibbert nodded, his droopy jowls framed by fuzzy white sideburns and shaking like gelatin. "I quite agree. You'll waste your time running after government underwriting."

"Forget parliament," Wilson said, walking across the room and blowing smoke high into the air. "It is the wealthy you must pursue."

Hibbert stood up, his gray suit tight and wrinkled, his large belly straining the buttons on his waistcoat. "Much more likely to succeed, I quite agree." His bottom lip jutted out.

"I propose we help you gather an initial group of founding members," Wilson said. He waved his hand in the air as if painting a picture. "I can see it being very appealing to the sorts I know."

"But," Sir William said, "don't you think it good to have some government involvement?"

"Definitely," Wilson said. "Not for underwriting but for credibility." He crossed to the billiards table in the center of the room and picked up a copy of Sir William's appeal. He shook it while dragging on his cigar. He blew a great cloud of smoke, and then clinched the papers in his fist. "This is a supreme concept. It is a worthwhile endeavor, and I see it being of tremendous value to insurance underwriters and shipmasters and everyone else whose interest is best served by safety at sea."

"And on shore," Sir William added. He stood and stuck his thumbs into the side pockets of his silver vest. "I am delighted by your interest."

"I can interest a few political supporters," Wilson said, crossing to him and placing a hand on his shoulder.

Hibbert walked over and firmly gripped Sir William's hand. "I know of several merchantmen I want to share this concept with." His forehead layered with wrinkle upon wrinkle. "This is a fine proposal for all of England."

"What say you, Sir William?" Wilson asked, squeezing his shoulder uncomfortably hard. "Any key contacts of your own to add to the mix?"

"I have one key contact of royal blood," Sir William said.

"Good, good!" Wilson said, releasing his grip. "Who might that be?"

Sir William breathed more easily. "The Duke of Sussex."

"Prince Augustus?" Hibbert asked, his jowls and wrinkles and bottom lip doing what they did.

"It has been many years, but I served him as equerry," Sir William said.

"King George III's sixth son. Excellent. And he will receive you?" Hibbert said, peering at Sir William.

"I believe I can revive the relationship."

"Then we know what we must do," Wilson said, taking another long drag and then pausing to stare at the carpet. He blew a swirl of smoke toward the floor and appeared mesmerized.

Sir William looked at George Hibbert, who stood with his arms folded and one fist under his triple chin. He nodded vigorously. Sir William shifted as both of his new friends seemed deep in thought.

At last, Wilson looked up. "I think we ought to call for a meeting," he said, very slowly at first. "At Bishopsgate."

"Ah, yes," Hibbert said, smiling widely for the first time. His teeth were tiny, and some were capped in gold. "The tavern. The perfect choice."

"I'm familiar with it," Sir William said, liking the sound of it. "The tavern at Bishopsgate is well-known for hosting events of all kinds."

"Particularly important ones," Wilson said, his cigar wedged into the corner of his mouth. "Important ones like this." He turned serious, studying Sir William with a sober stare.

Sir William shifted again. "Thank you."

"One other thing," Wilson said. "You will need to be prepared to share your passion in the midst of our assembly."

"I can do that," Sir William said, standing straighter.

"Having read your appeal and having heard what Captain Reid said about you," Wilson said, his stare remaining fixed, "I'm sure that you can."

Hibbert folded his arms behind his back and walked around the billiards table, his head tipping low. "You're thinking of someone else?"

"I can do it," Sir William said. "I already know what I'll say." He took a small step forward and held out his hands. "I'm the best one to address it."

Wilson returned to looking at the floor. He blew another swirling cloud of smoke and then looked up with a big smile. "I've got it—Wilberforce!"

Hibbert's mouth dropped wide open and then formed into a smile; then the entire weight of the man shook with a deep belly laugh. "Brilliant!" he said. "Absolutely brilliant!"

"William Wilberforce? You think he should present it instead of me?" Sir William stumbled over his words. "But . . . well, he is a powerful man, yes, but, well—"

Wilson smashed his cigar into a small tray on a round table near the wall. He rapidly waved his other hand. "No, no, no," he said, crossing over to Sir William and standing close. "I don't mean in place of you. I mean ahead of you."

"Yes, indeed!" Hibbert stepped alongside Wilson.

"Wilberforce is a man of tremendous influence," Wilson said. "I think it wise to send you to him and let you share this vision directly with him. If he likes you as much as I think he will and should he believe in the concept of what you are proposing, then his support will prove invaluable."

Hibbert nodded like a drooling canine. "You agree, Sir William? You agree?"

Sir William smiled and then found the whole scene utterly humorous. He laughed, then shrugged, then held open his arms, still laughing.

Hibbert's face twisted. He turned to Wilson. "Does he agree or doesn't he?"

Wilson pulled out another cigar from his inside pocket. Sir William nodded, still chuckling his amusement.

Wilson grinned and bit off the end of his smoke. "He agrees," Wilson said and shook Sir William's hand firmly. "I'll set it up, Sir William. We'll help you see this thing through."

Chapter 13

"Welcome," the servant said. "He will see you now." The servant led Sir William down a long hallway, past several rooms, and finally into a formal living room. The man Wilson had arranged for him to see was seated on the far side of the room. The man waved the servant away and motioned for Sir William to approach.

"I've read your appeal," he said. "I know why you've come."

Sir William tipped his head, unsure what to say. "Thank you for seeing me, sir."

William Wilberforce was a puny man for having such an enormous reputation. His eyes were impressively luminous, as if lit from behind, and his grin was ingratiating. "The opulent have a duty," he said. "If they can manage to see past the glare of their privilege, they might even recognize it as such—but don't count on it."

His body appeared contorted and sickly despite his proffered amusement. He reminded Sir William of Prince Augustus Frederick, who had also been of a sickly deportment but with a beneficent soul.

"Fight for it, yes," the little man said. "But never count on it." He lifted his head. His lengthy, upturned nose pointed high as he surveyed Sir William. There was nothing fearful or intimidating about Wilberforce. His posture was poor, and he sat nearly limp with relaxation. He seemed so harmless for a man who had done—and was still doing—such powerful things to fight slavery. "Because I understand why you're here, we'll have to be brief, I'm sorry to say."

The sixty-five-year-old parliamentarian lowered his head and lazily tipped it sideways. He placed both hands on the black velvet arms of his chair and grimaced as he pushed himself to stand. His head rose only to Sir William's chest. The little man with the big life looked up and motioned Sir William to retreat a few steps. Sir William respectfully complied, backing away so swiftly that he accidentally knocked over a stack of books. They had been piled so high they towered taller than the small table plastered with loose papers held in place by a large, open Bible.

"My apologies," Sir William said, stooping to gather the books.

"Leave them," Wilberforce said. "Come here." He led Sir William to a window overlooking the streets of London below. "What do you see?"

"London," Sir William said. "In all its glory." He paused. "And shame."

"Said well enough. It is a convolution of many things, but, despite what humanity thinks, a man can only give what he has been given. There are poor and there are wealthy and there are those in between. It has always been a stubborn delusion on the part of the men of wealth and power in our society that they are there by their own grand works or by their wits, or at least by the same of their forefathers. I do not believe such nonsense." His voice suddenly weakened, interrupted by a violent cough.

He removed a hankie and patted his mouth, then fumbled with a small tin he removed from his silk vest, momentarily getting tangled with his gold watch chain. Flipping the tin open, he pinched a small amount of white powder from inside and jammed it tight to his nose and inhaled. He stood still for a moment, his head tilted back. A quiver ran through his body, and he stuffed the tin back into his vest.

"I do not approve of such remedy," he said, a tiny tone of bitterness in his voice, the first of such Sir William noted. "Yet my ailments leave me with no recourse." Wilberforce resumed his gaze out the window.

Sir William knew about the colitis and the pained eyesight, and he willingly deferred to the great little man in respect of his achievements and in honor of his station.

"You will need patrons, of course," Wilberforce said. "Such are the requirements of the Divine. Helps us to work in tandem, I believe."

Sir William valued the important man's views, but it was answers and assistance he needed, not insights and inspirations. It was time for action. "Mr. Wilberforce," Sir William said, "I am fascinated by what you are saying, however—"

"Yes, yes, you grow impatient." Wilberforce turned back toward his chair. "Nevertheless, despite your emotional willpower, it will take what it takes." The tiny man painstakingly lowered himself into the chair in a series of staged movements.

"Yes, but I—"

"—need to listen, my friend," Wilberforce said. "What I am telling you is valuable." He sat back and exhaled, momentarily closing his eyes and then opening them. "It will prove helpful in future felicities." His tiny eyes slightly widened and the friendly grin reappeared.

Sir William suddenly surrendered with a hearty one-syllable laugh and bounded over to sit on the footstool near the esteemed abolitionist. How foolish he had been. If William Wilberforce were prepared to lecture him, then he would be wise to listen. "Forgive me," Sir William said. "Go on."

William Wilberforce closed his eyes again, drew in a long and gentle breath, and slowly blew it out. His eyes opened, and his countenance changed. Color rose and his cheeks tightened as he fixed his gaze into a penetrating stare into Sir William's eyes.

"Men do reap what they sow," Wilberforce said. "It is true. But they can only sow what is given to them." The man did not blink. "Men do not create seed. It is unfortunate that men of achievement do not often recognize the source of their wealth and the unique purposes they are called to discover and fulfill."

His bottom lip quivered and then relaxed. "They mistakenly believe that if other men simply worked as hard or as wisely as they, then those other men would also experience as much gain. This is untrue—although it is convenient to believe so."

He suddenly blinked and smiled. "As you know, I was born surrounded by extreme wealth and command nearly unlimited money. Yet that has not been enough. My labors have been extensive, and still the battle rages." He shifted, his face wrinkling as he moved.

"There is no doubt," Sir William said, slightly bowing his head, "about the enormity of the task you have undertaken to make the nation aware of the horrific nature of the slave trade. Few have persisted as you have."

"As John Wesley once told me," Wilberforce said in a voice suddenly melodic, apparently made so by the sweetness of his memory, "unless God has raised you up for this very thing, you will be worn out by the opposition of men and devils. But if God be for you, who can be against you?"

"I am prepared, Mr. Wilberforce," Sir William said, sitting up straight.

Wilberforce softened and grinned. "We are only prepared for what we expect."

Sir William shifted.

"No matter," Wilberforce said. "There is One who will see to your preparation for what you don't expect."

"Can you help me?" Sir William asked.

"I already have," Wilberforce said, straight faced.

"Will you subscribe to the organization? Will you speak at our meeting?"

"You are aware that I participate in nearly seventy philanthropic efforts?"

"I was not aware."

"You are aware that I give a full twenty-five percent of my income to the poor?"

"I was not."

William Wilberforce looked at Sir William for a very long time. Sir William did not dare breathe.

"I will contribute what I can," Wilberforce said.

Sir William breathed, but he was not finished with the small, powerful man. "Is it possible that any of the members of your famous Clapham Sect might assist?" Sir William asked, his heartbeat increasing. He knew he was pushing, but those men were well heeled and had done much to help Wilberforce in his fight against the slave trade.

Wilberforce smiled. "I am continually amazed that even despite all the wisdom I myself have come to discover surrounding the subject of subscribing to a noble cause and that as admirable and necessary as persistence is, it is most uncomfortable when aimed back at you." He chuckled with more energy than he had shown till now. "Ascribe that to our carnal natures, I imagine."

"I make no apologies," Sir William said, surprised at his own confidence, momentarily feeling like he wasn't doing the actual speaking, though he knew he was.

"You realize, of course," Wilberforce replied, "that I wrote my own appeal last year on behalf of the Negro slaves in the West Indies."

"Of course," Sir William answered quickly, wanting to move Wilberforce on to the point of his question about the sect.

"And that the Clapham Sect are equally committed toward those ends."

"Which, in the main, is focused on abolishing the slave trade, I understand," said Sir William. "But if I am not mistaken, the many legislators, bankers, diplomats, and businessmen comprising the sect are equally committed to godly life in public service, philanthropy, and goodwill."

Wilberforce's smile lengthened. "You are not mistaken. I, however, cannot speak for the individuals who have joined me in that quest. I will make mention of your appeal to them, but can presently only commit what I personally can do. I will attend the meeting at the tavern, as you have invited me to do, and will do what I can to support you. Tell Wilson I'll introduce you if that is what he wants." William Wilberforce withdrew his smile, lifted his hands, and grew quiet. He suddenly looked tired.

Sir William understood the gesture. The conversation was over. "You have honored me with your time and your professed commitment," Sir William said, rising and bowing. He shook the man's hand, being careful not to grip it too hard, but was surprised how firm the handshake was. He smiled. "See you at Bishopsgate."

William Wilberforce nodded and closed his eyes. He waved a final goodbye without opening them. A servant arrived and showed Sir William out.

As he strolled down the lanes of London, he couldn't help walking toward the famous tavern on Bishopsgate Street. The large block of a building was famous for its guests, its meeting rooms, its dinners, and its wine cellar. Perhaps it would one day be famous for what would take place in a few weeks.

Chapter 14

The meal had been the finest Sir William recalled eating in quite some time. Not since his days traveling with the prince had he enjoyed such delicious fare of sweet flavors and smoky scent. The fish was fresh and seasoned with a mild dusting he could not identify. He thought the wild game must have been farm raised and flowing with royal blood for there was no gameness to it. It filled the table with a pleasant scent of roasted wood but filled his mouth with both a crunchy and soft medley of spiced flavors, similar to mint but with something more.

The small, round breads were too hot for immediate touch but finally discovered as warmly delicious once they cooled enough to be placed upon the palate. One bite and a mist of dairy cream butter simply escaped the doughy piece to cascade the length of his tongue. It was blissful.

He was never much of a drinker of spirits because of its effect upon his stomach, though he ventured to tip his wine glass and sipped the sparkling white coolness that tasted like berries stripped of their tartness and left with a mild sweetness. Everywhere he looked, the wines flowed freely—dark reds and sparkling whites, soft blushes and even a nearly clear one with slight golden cast.

"Sir William," Prince Augustus said, seated beside him. "You and your friends have done a most splendid thing. Behold." He waved his arm to sweep the room.

Archways, sculptures, chandeliers, and magnificent wall hangings were punctuated by a range of colors contributed by flowers and fabrics and wallpapers and further accented by crystal, silver, and fine china.

There were several bishops, eminent politicians, well-known men of the court, and active naval officers, as well as several chairmen of key banks and business enterprises, all seated at various tables. Sir William smiled at his old friend. "Thank you. But in none could I be more delighted than you. Thank you for making time to be counted among us."

"I wouldn't miss it, old friend," the prince said. He was thin and moved slowly, but his color was good and his voice steady. He set his silver down and pushed his plate a few inches back. "Most magnificent," he said, raising his wine in toast. "To the firm establishment and indefinite longevity of your most movingly proposed institution."

The men raised their glasses in tribute to the cause and chattered away until it came time for Wilberforce to move to the dais to introduce Sir William. He rose from a nearby table, surrounded by many of his Clapham Sect supporters. The entire assembly of nearly two hundred hushed as the little man stepped upon a small box behind the lectern.

"We were lucky to get him," Wilson whispered to their table. "I understand he's traveling to Essex this very night."

Sir William's heart quickened. *Essex?*

William Wilberforce began speaking to the impressive gathering of churchmen, reformers, parliamentarians, and royalty. "To those of us of favored status it might seem no stimulus is present . . ."

Sir William leaned toward Wilson. "Do you have a pen or quill?"

"Still working on the speech, eh?" Wilson smiled and called a member of the wait staff over. The man returned with an inkwell, powder, steel pen, and sheets of paper. Wilson pointed to Sir William, and the man set them down before him.

Wilberforce continued, "But if we place ourselves in the situation of those who have to expose their lives to peril and hardship and who may, at a moment of danger, though never thinking of themselves, be somewhat slow in risking their lives for want of not leaving their families vulnerable, but who would hasten to brave the storms and waves if they could be certain their families would not be forsaken, then we may grasp our essential responsibility."

While Wilberforce spoke on, Sir William scratched a note. He blotted out a few words and wrote a few more. He quickly reviewed it and then signed his name. He blew on the ink and powdered it, folded the letter, and stuck it inside his left vest pocket. He looked up.

The assembly was rapt with attention. Not everyone in attendance was a friend to Wilberforce—some were quite well understood to be his political adversaries—but all respected his presence and his oratory.

"Such reply is the duty of the opulent to provide," William Wilberforce said, "and who better to emphasize such reply than the man whose proposal has drawn us here tonight. Gentlemen, I present you Sir William Hillary." He stepped down from the box and moved it aside. The room erupted with applause. Wilberforce rejoined his table, sitting next to the archbishop of Canterbury and the bishop of London. He nodded to Sir William.

Already? Sir William cleared his throat. His mouth felt terribly dry. Wilson nodded to him and glanced toward the dais.

Sir William stood. He walked stiffly toward the lectern. The crowd offered courteous applause, though far less deafening than Wilberforce had received.

His black tails, shiny gray vest, and puffy white shirt matched the wardrobe of most there, although there were a few powdered wigs atop men wearing colorful silks and white stockings.

He tilted his head down and pulled out his notes from his right vest pocket. He didn't read them. He focused on breathing deep. When his heart slowed, he looked up.

He surveyed the room with darting glances in several directions as the crowd hushed. It seemed a long time before the group became as quiet as he. He noticed Prince Augustus nodding for him to begin.

He looked at William Wilberforce. Some of the Clapham Sect members sat at the same table, flanking the bishops. They were looking directly at him, their faces gentle and still.

Suddenly his mouth opened and the words flowed. His notes dropped from his hand. He spoke of donations and subscriptions, resolutions and purposes. Then, to his delight, on his point of lifeboats being positioned around the coasts, men shouted approvals, at first randomly, but then growing in intensity and number.

When he spoke of the formation of district branches, men openly vocalized their approval, and when he spoke of awarding medallions in recognition of acts of self-sacrificing bravery and made mention of the provision of relief for widows or families left behind, he received a rousing standing ovation that echoed through the large room for several long seconds.

Sir William looked for Wilberforce but could not see him in the towering crowd, now on its feet. He looked for the prince and Wilson and Hibbert and saw them standing in vigorous support.

As the applause tapered and men resumed their seats, there remained one standing near the front. Sir William nodded to him, releasing him to sit, but he did not. The man raised his arm.

Sir William glanced at Wilson, who only shrugged his shoulders. He looked at Hibbert, whose countenance revealed nothing. The prince sat motionless, his chin resting on one hand, his eyes fixed on the lone figure. Sir William knew the prince well enough to know that his expression meant he didn't know what to make of it.

Sir William looked to where Wilberforce had been and found him. Just seeing him felt encouraging. Wilberforce raised his eyebrows and tilted his head toward the standing man, encouraging Sir William to yield the floor.

"Yes, kind sir," Sir William said to the man. "Do you wish to speak or ask a question?"

"Yes, I most certainly do," the man said. He was thin and balding, though the hair around his ears was black and neatly combed. His face was pointed, and his nose was long and slender. His mouth seemed quite large for such a thin face but his teeth were small and perfectly straight. They were clearly visible as he spoke. "I would like to challenge something you've submitted." He wore a fashion similar to Sir William's, though it appeared slightly baggy and it drooped near his shoulders. "That is," the man said with a smirk as he glanced around the room and then returned his gaze to Sir William, "if it is permitted to disagree."

Sir William was uncertain. He didn't know the man, and the atmosphere had been so perfect to lead into the next section where the archbishop of Canterbury, Dr. Manners Sutton, was scheduled to assume chairing the assembly in order to pass nearly twenty resolutions, all of which needed to be proposed and hopefully carried. He nodded slowly.

"To manufacture medallions and pecuniary awards," the stranger began in a much louder voice than previously, "for heroics, and to promise recompense for the widowed, may very well motivate some of lesser character to exaggerate their own actions, or worse, manufacture their own disappearance in order to secure, under such false pretense, their rights as you seek to define them." His screeching voice rang with a tone of mischievous pleasure.

Sir William interpreted the man's widening grin as satisfaction with himself. "Well—" Sir William began.

"There is another, though no less significant point," the man said, louder. "Since when do we contrive to pool resources with the intent of motivating men to help men? Is it not their duty?" The man's confidence grew. His hands became instruments as he spoke. He pointed and gestured and shook a fist. He included hearers on all sides. "Is it not a fair expectation of society upon men, regardless of their station, to anticipate their aid, solely on the grounds of holy humanity rather than the artificial prop of financial reward?"

Sir William was disappointed. He held up his hands at the precise moment the man finally paused. "I respect your questions," Sir William said. "I have asked myself, or at least my conscience has nudged me to consider, a similar question."

"Is conscience to be ignored?" the man asked, more than a trace of disapproval in his voice, his finger pointed directly at Sir William.

"Indeed not," Sir William said. "My own heart posed the question of whether it is less noble to rescue under promises and assurances rather than under risk alone. Perhaps it is!"

An ominous buzz swept over the crowd. The opposing stranger smiled large and nodded in all directions.

The perfect atmosphere had been corrupted. Sir William noted the men seated around the man. He recognized some of them and knew them to be good men, churchmen. However, the man speaking was unknown to him.

"Then again," Sir William said, "perhaps not. It would certainly render such heroics more likely. In view of such, more lives would be saved. Further, if any lives were lost in the effort, no ever-increasing weight of grief would be added, since the grief of loss would be grief enough. It would not be made worse by financial ruin and the poorhouse."

A few men clapped, and men seated at various tables around the room spoke supportive words.

"Do you think it virtuous to scorch the very divine plan of our Maker," the skinny man asked, "who Himself gave His only Son? Is that not the model of truth we are all to follow?"

Sir William was offended. His pulse was rapid, his forehead and neck hot. He wanted to strike a blow to the man's face to shut him up. If sincere compassion and well-thought planning wasn't sufficient, perhaps physical assault would do. He breathed deeply.

The growing buzz in the room seemed out of hand when suddenly another man from a table full of churchmen stood. Sir William didn't recognize him either. *Who invited these two buffoons?*

"I appreciate your enthusiasm and good intentions," the second man said to the first, only one table away.

Sir William wondered if a plot was afoot. He quickly looked to Wilberforce, who sat calmly inspecting his nails and offering no supportive eye contact. Sir William's throat constricted.

"But if one is to reference the most Holy Scriptures," the second man continued, "we would do well to be accurate."

The first man had been smiling but suddenly looked perplexed.

"Did not the Father issue forth a sovereign call for His Son's willing sacrifice with the foreknowledge and promise that despite the price paid, He would not let His Holy One see decay?" the second man asked.

A few men cheered with laughter and clapped.

"Christ did not die for us for the purpose of pecuniary rewards!" the skinny man protested, his face twisting into an unattractive snarl.

"Do the Scriptures not reveal that the burden of our Lord's sacrifice was made the more bearable by the joy set before Him?" the second man asked with a soothing calmness. The atmosphere was shifting fast. Sir William felt hopeful.

The second man continued. "Do they not clearly reveal that the Lord was further enabled to bear the shame and suffering of His cross because He was promised a joyful outcome as a result?"

The skinny man stuttered, and spittle flew from his mouth.

The second man spoke with peaceful confidence. "What was the joy set before Him but the promise that He was purchasing a future security for all of us? Do not the proposals presented here today resonate with an identical spirit?"

Some men stood up to clap. Others added loud cheers from around the room.

The second man raised his voice. "Shall those willing to risk their lives for others do so without the same assurance that attended our Lord? Is it not the divine model that, should they perish in the effort of rescuing others, they may do so knowing their families will not see decay by destitution?"

The crowd suddenly burst with the relief of laughs and smiles and sporadic applause until it grew into a rousing display. Shouts of "Hear! Hear!" resonated throughout the room. Most stood and clapped.

Sir William looked at the second man, who nodded to him and sat down. He had no idea who he was. There was nothing distinguishing about him.

Sir William next looked at Wilberforce who, though still attending to his nails, sat smiling. His table of associates were laughing and applauding.

Not far away, the skinny man was timidly regaining his seat, though his face was as red as the wine upon his table.

Sir William was startled by a tap on his shoulder and realized the archbishop of Canterbury was beside him. He bowed his head and shook Dr. Sutton's hand and then embraced him and kissed him on the cheek. The archbishop returned the greeting and lifted his hands to address the crowd and get down to business.

"We must now submit the motions for your voting," the archbishop said, barely able to be heard. "All right! All right! We need some order to proceed!" He turned and smiled and leaned to whisper in Sir William's ear. "I think it's going your way."

Sir William stood tall, but his entire body was quaking. He scanned the audience and saw countless men standing in jubilant applause. Even William Wilberforce was standing atop the seat of his chair. Sir William looked at his own table, and the prince shouted a cheer, his face glistening with sweat. Sir William thought of his own son, Augustus, and wished he were here.

When it was over, the twenty resolutions had been unanimously carried in support of the formation and operation of the National Institution for the Preservation of Life from Shipwreck. They gave it the name and purpose Sir William had asked for. He and his friends had done it.

Afterward, he looked for the unknown man who had spoken in support of the measures, but the man was nowhere to be found. Sir William did find William Wilberforce and asked him who his rescuer was.

"I don't know," Wilberforce said. "Someone who knows the Text."

"I'm glad for that."

"No doubt."

"I have a request, if I may," Sir William said, reaching into his left vest pocket.

"I must soon depart," Wilberforce said. "I've a journey this very night."

"I have a son," Sir William said. "He resides at Danbury. I think."

Wilberforce looked down and smiled, reaching for the note. "I will see that it gets delivered." He opened his mouth to say more but was interrupted by several persons desiring his attention and was quickly swallowed up by the crowd.

Sir William watched him be swept away.

It was time to go home.

Chapter 15

"It would be proper to invite local officials to a formal celebration affair," Sir William said. He opened and closed his evening vest. He had purchased the gray silk garment in London and liked the way he felt with one hand in a side pocket while his other hand trailed about in circular motions. "Do you think it would be indulgent to carry an unlit pipe?"

Emma and Sarah sat nearby within the great room at Prospect Hill, together sewing a large quilt. "It would be most sage-like," Sarah said. "The embodiment of wisdom."

"You understand the questions behind his question, don't you?" Emma asked. She looked up at Sir William, that loose curl dangling again. It always made her skin seem so deliciously white. "I advise not," she said. "It might prove too tempting to light, dear husband."

Sir William laughed. "But would it suggest an air of intellect?"

"Quite so," Sarah said with a giggle.

"You naughty child," Emma said. "Encouraging him so!"

"I would never smoke it, of course," he said.

"If you did," Emma said, smiling but not turning away from her sewing, "I would never kiss you again."

"Ah," Sir William said, raising both hands. "Then it's an idea that I surrender in forfeiture. Too high a price!"

"See," Emma said. "He's already wise."

"That is no secret," Sarah said.

"How can I not be?" Sir William asked, crossing to his favorite lookout from the window. "With the two of you constantly speaking such affirming words, I am likely to believe I can do all things."

"Hmm," Emma said, holding up her end of the quilt. "We may want to consider tossing out a few barbs here and there, if only to help your ego, my love."

"My ego?" Sir William asked, studying the outlines of the shapes in the bay. "I wasn't aware I had one."

"Ah," Sarah added. "Perhaps you do not yet know all things."

Sir William crossed to the table in front of the two women and looked down at the latest issue of the *Isle of Man Weekly Gazette*. He saw the headline again: "Sir William Hillary awarded Gold Medallion!"

"Ah!" he said. "You must be referring to this article of interest. I hadn't noticed." He grinned and waved one arm in a circle as though holding the imaginary pipe.

Emma and Sarah exchanged glances. "I daresay I'm shocked he hasn't memorized it yet."

"And they say women are vain!" Sarah teased.

He could feel an eyebrow rising. He smiled. "So much for an endless supply of affirming words."

The ladies laughed.

"What do you think, dear?" Emma asked. She stood and held her end of the quilt while motioning Sarah to do the same. It was large enough to cover his bed. It was colorful, thick, and perfectly stitched.

"You are geniuses!" Sir William exclaimed, drawing near and inspecting their handiwork. "We should frame it and hang it in our little gallery."

"We most certainly will not," Emma said, nudging into him. "We will finish it and spread it over our bed and grow warmer."

"Well done," Sir William said. "My sincere commendations to both of you. However, it may be an opportune time to purchase some new paintings, now that I'm thinking of it. What do you say?"

"Oh, dear," Emma said, sitting back down.

Sarah followed. "Another expense?"

"An investment," Sir William said. He moved to the fireplace and stoked the burning logs. The flames brightened and jumped. He placed another log on top. "You can't lose with informed selections. If we ever need to, we'll sell any one of our collection for more than we paid."

"He is always so certain," Sarah said with admiration.

"We are doing well, aren't we?" Sir William asked, holding the insides of his vest collar and dropping his elbows. He smiled at his family.

"Look at him," Emma said, also admiring him. "He's as proud as a clipper with royalty aboard."

"And how could I not be with such delicate damsels amidships? I have both queen and princess in view at all times. I must be king."

"I think you must be crazy," Emma said.

Sarah giggled like a schoolgirl.

He feigned a stern look in their direction.

The ladies sat down and lifted the quilt to block his looming broadside.

He fired fluff instead. "Let us dine on Athol Street tonight."

They lowered the quilt, their eyes wide and faces aglow.

Sir William nodded. "Ah yes, no complaint of expense now."

"You tricked us," Emma said.

"Shame on you, Sir William," Sarah said, nearly pouting. "You mustn't tease a lady. It is unfair!"

"I did no such thing," he said with grand smile. "Go and prepare yourselves. I will make the carriage ready."

The ladies moved quickly, folding the quilt and leaving the room, filled with animated chatter. Sir William felt warm.

He was seeing his visions come to pass. He loved his wife and the woman who was like a daughter. His dream of inspiring the nation toward caring for the shipwrecked was becoming increasingly established. He returned to the window. The promised donations for the first year of operations had turned out larger than he had imagined. District associations were being formed in various port cities of England as well as one in Douglas. He looked at ships at peaceful anchorage within the bay.

The Danbury estate had not failed, no creditors had come knocking, and his investments looked healthy. Even the mine was reporting a rich tap into copper.

He panned across to Douglas Head and the resplendent Fort Anne, all lit up. Someone had moved into the residence and put much work into her.

He gazed downward at the harbor. He was looking forward to talking to the fishermen again. He wasn't sure if they read the paper or not, but they must certainly know by now that a great fund was now available to purchase a lifeboat and cork jackets and to provide relief to widows in distress. Soon they would be training lifeboat men with regimented discipline. It was all as he had hoped. It was good.

"Dear?" Emma's voice broke his introspection.

He turned to see her standing at the entrance to the great room. "Yes?"

"The carriage? Remember?" Her eyebrows rose high and that same lone curl bounced down.

Sir William smiled. Dinner was next. "I was just thinking."

"Of course," she said, her smiling face serenely beautiful.

Athol Street was lined with fine places to dine when one wanted to run into friends. Sir William was not disappointed with their restaurant selection. The intimate room of the Misty Rudder was filled with round, draped tables encircling one large fire pit in the center. Lieutenants Burbridge and Graves dined with their wives only two tables away. Major Tobin was with Phillip Garret and another couple with a very young lady in attendance. Sir William didn't recognize them, but all had sent warm greetings and hearty congratulations to his table.

"Compliments of Major Caesar Tobin," the waiter said, displaying a two-year-old Madeira. He poured a half glass for Sir William.

Sir William sipped the wine and nodded. The major returned his smile from across the room. Sir William poured full glasses for Emma and Sarah.

Emma enjoyed the roasted duck and Sarah the curried rabbit. Sir William thought the baked cod tasty but wasn't as interested in eating as he had thought. He bypassed the wine the waiter had poured him and sipped his cider. It was cool and sweet.

Emma slid her fork from her lips. "Mmm, this is exquisite. Would you like to try some, dear?"

He shook his head.

"Sir William," Sarah said, wiping the corner of her mouth with her linen. "You have barely touched your fish. Is it not delicious?"

"It is wonderfully prepared," Sir William said, noticing Major Tobin rising from his table along with Phillip Garret and the unknown man. "I haven't appetite for too much."

Major Tobin appeared beside their table. "We'll not interfere with your cuisine for too long," he said, nodding to his sister and to Sarah. He fixed his gaze on Sir William. "You know Mr. Garret."

Sir William shook hands with him.

"But," Major Tobin continued, "you do not know Deemster John Christian. He's new to our community, having been recently appointed a judge. He temporarily resides at Fort Anne until his home in Ramsey is complete."

Sir William stood.

The new man was tall, balding, and with a stocky frame. He was well dressed, with a large pocket hankie nicely puffed and a very long and thin black mustache. His face was round and friendly.

"I am pleased to make your acquaintance," Sir William said. He waved his hand in the direction of his two ladies. "This is my wife, Emma." She rose and extended her hand, which the deemster politely kissed. "And our nearly adopted daughter, Sarah."

John Christian nodded and kissed her hand. "The pleasure is mine." He looked at Emma. "You are Caesar's sister, I understand."

"I am," Emma said, resuming her seat. Sarah did the same.

"You are both as lovely as Caesar bragged." He turned to Sir William before the ladies could do anything more than blush. "I am most interested to meet the man who founded this fascinating lifeboat institution. If I had on my hat, I'd take it off, sir."

"Thank you, Deemster," Sir William said, shaking the man's hand. It was a powerful grip. "I am most humbled to meet the one who now resides in the formidable Fort Anne. It is a residence unlike any other and much the satisfaction of my own taste. Congratulations to you also, Deemster."

"Well, for a season it is ours," Christian said. "But you and your lovely ladies are welcome to join us anytime." He turned and pointed to his table. "That is my wife, Helen, and my daughter, Susanna."

"An invitation we will be sure to reply to," Sir William said. He tipped his head.

"Well, well," Major Tobin said, placing his hands on the shoulders of Phillip and the deemster, "we'll not interrupt your meal any longer. I thought these two gentlemen would make fine candidates for the local branch of your new organization, Sir William."

"That is a worthy idea, Major." Sir William tipped his head again.

"Good," Major Tobin said. "Perhaps we can all enjoy the company of our mutual parties later, after the meal."

"That would be most fitting," Sir William said.

"We will enjoy that very much," Emma added.

The major turned his friends around, and the three of them walked back to their table. Sir William resumed his seat.

"Ah," he said with a smile and then picked up his knife and fork and sliced into his fish. He shoved a forkful into his mouth and chewed. "Mmm, delicious."

Over the summer Sir William withdrew monies through Sarah to underwrite several more published appeals. He was on a roll, and his reputation was growing. He wanted to strike while the iron was hot, while he was being recognized as a man of ideas who could get things done.

The new lifeboat, the *Nestor*, and cork jackets arrived by steamship. The major and John Christian agreed to train the lifeboat crew while Sir William wrote, published, and distributed another pamphlet he had nightly labored to author. He made over seven hundred copies. His proposals were expensive to publish in light of the scale of distribution he sought, laborious to write, and challenging to draw interest in, yet he persisted.

He envisioned a better lifeboat, one powered by steam. He valued the invention by Lukin and the subsequent contributions by Greathead and others, but improvements were possible.

He submitted a detailed plan for a forty-foot cork-floored vessel. It was propelled by steam-powered paddle wheels protected by large wooden fenders. It was heavily lined in various places with thick cork, in order to minimize the possibility of tragedy that airtight compartments left likely. Those could be corrupted by being smashed, whereas cork could not. He sought to improve the hinged scuppers and also designed a vertical center-house to protect steam engines by keeping the fires burning in the worst of storm and sea.

He finally proposed a tower of stone to be built upon Conister as a sanctuary in times of storm.

Despite his unrelenting efforts, every proposal was rejected.

There had been no worsening of weather, no tragedies to awaken the slumbering, and, he was sternly told by the men who oversaw his organization in England, "The single lifeboat already awarded to Douglas is considered sufficient for now. We do not have endless funds."

"I swear it must be true," Sir William said one day to a hovering flock of seagulls. He stood near the place where Colonel St. John used to sit and feed them. "The worst of storm and sea is rooted in the complacencies of men rather than atop the seas."

The birds screeched their replies.

Chapter 16

The two-paddle steamer the *City of Glasgow* was making excellent time en route from Scotland to Liverpool. Sixty-two passengers and crew were enjoying being ahead of schedule when a sudden change in weather darkened not only the sky but their festive mood. The three hundred–ton ship panted its way through the churning sea, the engines groaning.

"She's threatening to be fierce," the gray-headed but trim Captain Carlyle said. "This may be no ordinary gale."

Suddenly, a terrible screeching of metal seized his attention. Then came a huge clanging sound, and then a loud, singular pop. The port-side paddlewheel slowed. "Anderson! See to it and report straight away!"

"Aye, Captain!" Anderson shouted. The middle-aged, lanky Anderson, in striped shirt, buff jacket, and dark trousers, raced below. A few well-dressed passengers still braving the weather above deck made way. He reached the center ladder, grabbed the rails, and slid the length without ever touching a step.

A gentleman approached the captain. "What was that wretched noise?"

"We'll know soon enough," Captain Carlyle said. "It could be a blown engine."

"Blown engine!" The man's face tightened. "Thank goodness we have two."

"We'll not make Liverpool with one," the captain said, looking back toward the center stairs.

"We have to go back to Greenock?" the gentleman asked.

Captain Carlyle looked up at the telltales streaming from the pole atop the wheelhouse. "No, the wind blows from west-northwest. We can make Douglas. She has a bay well-able to provide protection from any wind from the north. We'll be safe enough to effect repairs, if needed."

Anderson leapt back up the center ladder two steps at a time. He rushed beside his captain's ear. "Port side engine busted," he whispered. "We'll need a few hours to fix, Captain."

"Very well," Captain Carlyle said. "Tell Hanley to make for Douglas. We'll shelter in the bay until we're running again."

"It'll be a limp to get there, sir," Anderson said.

"Is there another choice?"

Anderson shook is head and ran to the wheelhouse.

"Are we in any danger?" the gentleman asked the captain.

"No," the captain said. "Just delay."

Despite the parade of rejections, and despite having never heard from either of his children, Sir William enjoyed the fall. When dry, October was an attractive time of year on the Isle of Man. The hillsides were ablaze with color. It was also a good time to begin getting a feeling for what kind of winter season might lay ahead. Lots of rain and early discarding of leaves usually meant a hard winter, while blue skies and mild temperatures could mean a mild winter, although there were no guarantees.

The weather had been bright, blue, and mild, but severe winds had moved in from the northwest and since moved southward. Sir William worried about the large paddle steamer that had arrived to anchor in the bay.

He had sent word to town to learn of her predicament and discovered that she had anchored to effect the repair of a blown engine. After hours passed and she remained, he sent for further information and this time learned the captain of the steamer had sent a boat to shore asking for machine parts and other items to help with the repairs. It seemed they couldn't properly remedy the problem without some assistance.

The necessary parts were procured, but one of Michael Kellerman's friends claimed the job would likely require several more hours to complete. As evening came, Sir William worried the backing wind was changing the stakes considerably, and the cloud-streaked moonlight was threatening to disappear completely. If the wind moved too far south and east, the steamer would be endangered.

With the day grown old, Sir William bundled himself warmly and left for the shore despite Emma's objections over the late hour.

The wind blowing up Prospect Hill was a bad sign. If it continued this way a heavy sea would roll into the bay and threaten to push the steamer aground. Sir William hoped to advise their captain to take shelter in the harbor or, if able, to quickly put out to sea.

It was near eleven at night when Sir William reached the shore. He joined a small contingent of men already there. He saw Joseph and Michael. "I thought we'd have a bigger shore party than this."

"Not tonight," Michael said. "You'll find most in the pubs celebrating the reduction of the potato tax."

Sir William had forgotten, his mind having been so far removed from some of the local issues of late. "Any news on the repairs aboard the steamer?"

"Look!" Joseph exclaimed, pointing to the large ship. "She's turning to sea."

The steamer was moving away, past Conister Rock and into the passage of sea between it and the pier.

"Thank God!" Sir William said. "The winds are getting very strong. She's just in time, I think."

"I think not," Michael said. "Look."

The steamer struggled against the incoming rollers. She looked impressive at first but only for the first three or four waves. Suddenly, the port paddlewheel ceased turning and clouds of steam rose from her. The vessel stopped making forward movement and turned sideways to the rollers and listed.

"Gentlemen," Sir William said. "Tonight becomes the night we first launch the *Nestor*. Pray your training will serve us well."

"Aye," Joseph said.

The lifeboat was moored in the harbor, having recently been used in training. Sir William and five men reached the quayside to huddle in front of the comptroller's office. They put on their cork jackets while crates and tarps blew past.

"The *Nestor* is too small to ferry passengers with," Sir William shouted above the increasing roar of the wind.

"With this weather," Michael said, "the steamer could shoal and shatter. Whatever we do, we must be snappy."

"The steamer has adequate hawser aboard," Joseph said. "I saw it myself when aboard her with parts earlier today."

"Then that's the plan," Sir William said. "We retrieve the hawser and pull her to safety."

"She's three hundred ton," a husky man said, just arriving.

"Who are you?" Sir William asked.

Michael answered for the big man. "Sir, this is Isaac Vondy. He's new to the isle. He's an engineer who helped the steamer with her repairs."

Sir William nodded at the man. "Vondy, yes. I recall Major Tobin telling me you trained for coxswain and were quite good."

"He is, sir," Michael said.

"Will you join us?" Sir William asked.

"Towing a three hundred–ton vessel is more than the little *Nestor* can do in these conditions," Vondy said.

"The steamship still has one good paddle," Sir William said. "That will help."

"It'll have to," Michael agreed.

"Are there any other lifeboat men to help?" Sir William asked.

"None sober," Joseph replied.

"I'm in, sir," Vondy said. "The paddle will help."

"We're only seven, but it will have to do," Sir William said.

It wasn't an hour later that the *Nestor* reached the struggling ship. The wind had backed and now blew from the east with terrible force.

The *City of Glasgow* had drifted close to Douglas Head, but with her one good engine was able to avoid crashing into the rocky shore below Fort Anne. Her captain ordered the hawser thrown overboard to Sir William and his crew.

The tiny lifeboat rocked and splashed. The steamship sputtered and banged.

"The second engine may quit any time," Vondy said. "Row hearty, men."

The double-banked oars made rowing easier than in the pleasure boats owned by Hanby, but it was still exhausting work. With their backs and arms ripping with pain, the men managed to drag the hawser all the way back to the pier. A few men onshore made it fast. The *Nestor* tied up to the pier and began to disembark.

"We need all hands to pull her," Sir William shouted.

Joseph ran for the pub. "I'll get as many as I can. Michael! Help me!"

Michael followed.

Suddenly the line went taut. The steamer's bow turned toward the harbor entrance and seemed ready to make a straight line in but kept turning. A huge roller lifted her, both paddles completely clearing the water. Her bow pointed high, and the hawser snapped. The large ship crashed back to the sea and immediately turned toward the rocky outcroppings under Fort Anne.

"Michael! Joseph!" Sir William shouted. "Never mind! We need you here!"

Michael stopped so fast he fell to his hands and knees. Jumping back to his feet, he rushed to join Sir William in the boat. Joseph had already reached one of the pubs and disappeared inside.

The *City of Glasgow* struck rocks. Her bow caved.

The neurotic wind wrought havoc. It had inched northeast by east. "We must row straight into the rollers," Sir William said, "then pass the steamer and turn and ride the rollers to her stern." It was a variation of the plan they had used to rescue the *Vigilant*, only now in reverse.

"Then what?" Vondy had to shout to be heard.

"We take another hawser ashore and try to hold her from repeated slamming," Sir William yelled back.

"We ought to try a double hawser."

"Good idea! Let's hope she has two more aboard."

The men followed the plan and rode the fast rollers to shoot alongside the rocking steamer. The steamer bucked and the panicked passengers appeared at the stern rails. As soon as the *Nestor* was near they started to jump aboard the tiny lifeboat, trying to time their jumps with the rising and lifting of the waves.

"No! Wait!" Sir William pleaded. No one listened. No one could hear. Every passenger aboard the steamer jumped. Only the crew kept their heads.

"Oh, God help us," Sir William moaned. "There are too many!" He watched the flailing arms and floating heads visible above the churning foam and twisting waves. "This is bad." He reached out and began to haul bodies aboard. The lifeboat crew followed suit, and the boat was quickly filled beyond capacity.

Still, among the waves more desperate people cried out in anguish.

Sir William frantically pulled in more.

"Wait!" Vondy cried. "We'll capsize. We must run to the pier and return."

"They'll drown," Sir William shouted.

Vondy grabbed one of Sir William's arms. "If we take on any more, we'll all drown."

Sir William was angry. He glared at the man and then looked at the interior of their tiny craft. It was extremely low in the water and not an inch of space remained. He nodded. "You're right, man."

The men resumed their stations. They had turned the overcrowded craft toward the pier when a giant roller shoved the *City of Glasgow* into the tiny *Nestor*. Timber snapped.

The rudder disengaged. The helpless lifeboat, its sides crushed inward, spun sideways and instantly filled with sea. Sir William and his entire contingent washed overboard.

He was as helpless as the lifeboat now smashing to pieces against the jagged precipices jutting from the coast below Fort Anne. He was powerless to control his movements, caught in a rushing whirlpool of wet. It was cold and bitter. His eyes stung.

He saw a screaming woman and a child floating face down.

A powerful current yanked him under. It wrapped the length of his frame and twisted him deeper. His torso seared with pain, and his cork jacket bunched up around his neck.

A great force curled him backward like a hunter's bow. Suddenly, he rushed upward, broke through the surface, and flew amidst spray and foam.

He slammed against a sheer cliff face and slumped into a heap upon a rock ledge, instantly nauseous.

Dazed, he focused his eyes, then tugged his cork jacket into place. Before him, he saw a little boy floating face up with eyes closed. He yanked the child to the ledge. He lifted the lad and placed the boy's mouth near his ear and felt breath. He bent the boy over and repeatedly squeezed his stomach. Water gushed from the boy's mouth and he stirred.

A woman screamed.

Sir William looked up and saw dozens of people flung back and forth by the violent seas. Some were fighting, others were limp, and one woman was hysterical with fright. He saw splashing water approaching her and thought it a shark.

It was not. It was a man swimming hard to reach her. It was Isaac Vondy, bullying through the maze of hostile waters. Sir William cheered him on and then looked for others.

The little boy was coughing and hacking. He curled up and clung to Sir William's leg. Sir William stretched his arm to reach a floundering man a few feet away. Sir William's ribs burned with pain. As the man grabbed his hand, he realized he was seeing through one eye. The other was swollen shut.

Vondy laced his arm around the screaming woman's neck, underneath one of her arms, and towed her to another ledge only a few feet away. He shoved her as far back as he could, climbed upon the ledge, and dove in for another.

Sir William gritted his teeth, hauled the floundering man to safety, and did as Isaac Vondy had done. Holding the bottom of his cork jacket, he leapt into the sea.

He reached another man who was face down in the surf. Sir William dragged him to another ledge, one closer to where the violent force of current had pushed him. He propped the man upon the rocky outcrop and saw Michael already there aggressively working to revive another passenger.

The steamer engine screeched. Only then did Sir William give the steamer a thought. He turned back to the sea and looked for the vessel. It was so close that it towered high over his head. It was sideways to him and a giant paddle wheel cranked through the chopping seas.

The massive ship lurched sideways and pushed straight toward Sir William. He twisted to move but suddenly cramped and went under. He gasped and swallowed a mouthful of salty sea.

A hook seized his collar and yanked him up, his collar choking him. He pierced the waters on his back and was pulled to safety. He rolled onto his hands and knees to see Isaac Vondy, his meaty hands as able as any hooks.

They turned to see several others caught in the vortex of wind and weather and sea. Michael crouched nearby.

"Let us not rest," Sir William said, his body stiff with pain, his lungs sounding much like the weakening steamer engine chugging for air.

"Aye," Vondy said, preparing to leap again.

Their bodies wracked with pain, much of their clothing torn or washed away, the three lifeboat men stood in a row. Along the rocky ledges were several they had already rescued, all of them revived but each of them weak and vulnerable. Dozens of others, either floating or flailing, were being tossed about by the turbulent seas. "There are so many," Sir William said, his breath short and rapid. "How will we succeed?"

"Ahoy!" Joseph's strong voice pierced the stormy night.

The three men spun to see the portly fisherman standing up in a Matthew Hanby pleasure boat, with two other boats behind, full of jolly seamen.

"Get to shore!" Hanby shouted from another boat. "We'll get the rest."

Sir William stood, absorbing the sight. He offered a weak wave and then turned to help Isaac and Michael lead the rescued across the rocky ledges to the grounds of Fort Anne, where men stood with torches.

"Fear not, souls!" a familiar voice shouted. "We'll assist you!"

Sir William looked up to see Deemster John Christian and members of his household. They were in nightcaps and gowns and heavy cloaks. They carried blankets and helped the weary passengers ascend the steep ridge.

"Nothing is impossible with courage, hey, Sir William?" Michael asked, stepping beside him.

Sir William only nodded. His heart felt warm, but it hurt too much to speak.

Chapter 17

Less than one week later, the *City of Glasgow* remained seaworthy after several days of drenching in the surf at the base of Douglas Head in the midst of an unrelenting storm. Now, under blue skies and with assistance from a considerable number of locals, she limped into harbor for repair.

"Isaac, Joseph, Matthew, and Michael ought to be awarded medals and some financial reward," Sir William said with hoarse voice. He lay under a pile of blankets and was topped off with the newly completed quilt. His knew his eyes were red and his face pale.

"The *Nestor* needs to be replaced," Deemster Christian said. "She is a total loss."

"Yes," Sir William said and then sneezed hard. He reached up from under his covers and blew into the hankie already clutched in his hand. "I know."

The deemster sat at the foot of Sir William's bed, writing things down as they spoke. "Fortunately, there are no widows."

"Not a soul was lost," Sir William said. He reached into the bowl of hot water on the small round table beside his bed. He squeezed the rag inside and placed it on his brow. "I was certain men would perish that night. It is uncanny no one did."

"An act of God," the deemster said. "That ought to help us recover funds for a new boat since there are no widow supports to pay."

"I hope so," Sir William said. "Do you think they will take it well? I mean, losing the *Nestor* after one voyage?"

"We will make our requests known," the deemster said. "We will see."

"Hear! Hear!" Major Tobin blurted, barging into the room. He held the latest copy of the *Isle of Man Weekly Gazette*. "Once again the darling of the press we are! Sort of." He strode across the room and tossed the paper onto Sir William's bed. "My, you look hot. You must come out of there soon lest you sweat away to nothing."

"I'm overcome with this infernal flu," Sir William said.

"What'd the paper say?" the deemster asked, reaching for it. "May I?"

Sir William nodded and blew his nose.

"It's mostly favorable," Major Tobin said, sitting in a chair by the fire and putting his feet up. Rapidly melting snow dripped to the floor. "But I wouldn't make request of the lifesaving institution for a new boat just yet." He folded his hands behind his head and craned his neck to peer back at Sir William. "Timing, you know!"

"What on earth are you talking about?" Sir William asked, his throat sore and his nose wet. "What do you mean? Who times the storms and determines the conduct of the seas? We need to replace the boat as quickly as the organization can respond."

"Well then," Major Tobin said, turning back toward the fire, "at least be sensitive to the politics of the situation."

"Politics?" Sir William coughed. "That has nothing to do with it."

The deemster stood up and held the paper out to Sir William. "It may."

Sir William stared at the paper for a moment and then pushed back his layers of warmth to sit up and grab it. His nightshirt was clinging to him. "What's it say?" He quickly thumbed the pages.

"Some of the rescuers are believed to have been under the influence of alcohol," the deemster said.

"Nonsense." Sir William located the story and read.

"Inebriation is being claimed as the reason the lifeboat was lost," the deemster said, returning to his seat. The chair creaked as he lowered his bulky frame. "And it claims that is why the Hanby pleasure boats were delayed."

Sir William tossed the paper down. "Utter nonsense! Caesar! Throw this trash into the fireplace where it belongs." Sir William propped himself against the headboard with two pillows and tucked the blankets under his arms.

Major Tobin groaned as he slowly pushed himself out of the fireside chair and retrieved the papers. "Gladly, dear brother-in-law." He tore the paper lengthwise and dropped it into the fire. Taking the poker, he jabbed the offending periodical between the logs, where it was quickly consumed.

"Blame the politics of the potato tax and other varied interests," the deemster said. "That story is meant to satisfy many aims."

"It's preposterous," Sir William said. "There was nothing but the utmost devotion to saving life that night."

"There was considerable praise mentioned," the deemster said.

Hattie strolled in with two steaming bowls atop a large tray. "Stew has arrived."

"Ah, Hattie," Major Tobin said, offering a wave. "Might you have—"

"William?" Emma suddenly appeared in the room. "This just came today. Mungo Murray had it sent up, knowing you were laid up in bed." She crossed and handed the envelope to him.

"From the Institution?" Major Tobin asked.

Emma shook her head.

Sir William read the return address and smiled. He looked up.

"Might I be left alone?

"Is everything—?" Major Tobin started, but Emma hushed him.

"Of course you may," the deemster said, rising and moving toward the door.

"Follow me, Deemster," Hattie said. "I'll serve this to you in the dining room."

"I'll take yours if you don't mind, chap," Major Tobin said. "Unless you want it?"

"No, no," Sir William said. "Go ahead."

Emma leaned close and kissed his cheek. "You're clammy dear. I'll send Hattie later with more stew." She turned away and then stopped. "Enjoy your letter."

Sir William nodded. He waited until everyone had left and the door was closed. He viewed the return address again. It was from Essex.

It was from his son.

Chapter 18

Many months later, Sir William and Major Tobin strode across the lawns of the home on Prospect Hill, each dressed in formal attire, complete with top hats and canes.

"After all these months, annual subscriptions to the Institution have sunk like an anchor—by over £8,000," Major Tobin said. "I think the fervor is lessening. Add to that the fact that your appeals previously contained a request for funds to build a stone castle on St. Mary's Isle, and it's hardly beyond one's imagination as to why you hear, 'Too expensive!' as many times as you breathe."

"Not a castle," Sir William said. "A tower of sanctuary for the safety of the shipwrecked until help can arrive."

The major stopped at the gate. "If you could cease from proposing so much progress so soon, we might at least get another lifeboat."

"The whole economy of England is presently suffering," Sir William said. "I don't take it personally. You said it yourself once. Timing. Besides, this is a special day. Let's not talk about it." He opened the gate and motioned toward town. "Come along, brother. To my joy!"

Phillip Garret galloped his horse up the hill toward them. He tugged the reins and slowed to approach Sir William and the major. The two men met him in the road.

"Good day, gentlemen," Phillip Garret said. "I was just heading to your house, Sir William. Caesar, your servant told me you left the farm early to come up here. I need to speak with the two of you."

"Very well," Sir William said.

Caesar shook Phillip's hand. Sir William started walking.

"You are fancily dressed," Garret said. "What am I not aware of?" He nudged his horse to lumber beside the men as they descended the hill toward town.

"We're meeting—" Major Tobin began.

"A special guest," Sir William interrupted. "He is arriving via paddle steamer." He stopped for a moment and removed a hankie to pat his forehead. "It is hot."

"It is July," Major Tobin said.

"Your guest must be special," Garret said. "No doubt he will be impressed by the sight of the two of you."

"What is it you wished to see us about?" Sir William asked.

"Serious business, I'm afraid."

"'Tis the season for serious business, it seems," Major Tobin said, sounding more lighthearted than concerned.

"It has to do with the mining association at Laxey," Phillip Garret said.

"Did she strike another deposit?" the major asked, stopping and looking up at Garret.

Sir William stopped, intrigued.

"I'm afraid not," Garret said. He dismounted and walked beside the others as they resumed their descent. "We are swiftly running short on cash and still no substantial new lodes. There's talk of cutting our losses and shutting down the efforts."

Sir William stopped. "Nonsense!" he said with a snap that surprised even him.

He was not oblivious to the sideways glance Garret shot to his boyhood friend, the major. Garret's face tightened. Of course, an accomplished man such as he was not used to being spoken to in such commanding fashion.

Sir William modified his tone. "I apologize if I sounded a little, er, passionate. I am only certain that we should not give up on what we've all set out to do."

Phillip Garret seemed to ease. "None of us want to, Sir William. It's not so much a question of what we want to do, though. It's getting to the point that we have to do something. Our subscriptions are nearly exhausted, yet no significant deposits have been unearthed. We need to sell more shares at a time when no one feels at liberty to buy or we must cease operations. No one wants to borrow. What else can we do?"

"Laxey has been debt free until now," Major Tobin said.

"I will purchase a further share," Sir William said.

The major turned his head quickly.

Garret brightened. "That would be most helpful, sir."

"Not I, actually, but Miss Sarah," Sir William said, trying to sound less eager. "She-she recently acquired some interests from somewhere and has been asking me where to discharge some of it. I will recommend the mine. I believe it's important not to quit. We struck one lode, we may yet strike others."

"Can I count on you then?" Garret asked. "I mean, on Miss St. John? It will be in her name?"

"Yes," Sir William said without looking at him. He could still feel his brother-in-law watching him.

"You will be proxy?" Garret suggested.

"Yes, yes," Sir William said. He was feeling annoyed and was aware his tone didn't hide it.

"Very well. Then I'll not disturb the two of you further," Phillip Garret said, remounting his horse. "However, I shall pass this good news on to Stapleton and the others. Good day." He galloped away toward Athol Street.

Sir William walked briskly and mopped his brow.

"Emma will love this news," Major Tobin said with no hint of humor, hurrying to catch up and walk beside him.

"Let us not spoil the arrival," Sir William said.

The paddle-wheel steamer sat steady, tied securely to the pier. A long line of passengers disembarked. The tariff collections agent was already aboard, the collection chest tucked under one arm, and his derby pressed so tightly upon his head there could be no chance it would blow off.

"Do you see him?" Major Tobin asked.

"I'm not sure what he looks like," Sir William said. He was sweating in his suit.

"There's an interesting countenance on that one," Major Tobin said with a smirk, pointing to a young man in military dress.

The young man, who looked to be in his mid twenties, suddenly stood before them. He was dressed in an army uniform with a captain's rank on his shoulder. "Sir William Hillary?"

Sir William straightened. He hoped the shaking of his body wasn't visible. "I am," he said with as much authority as he could muster.

The lad began to smile and then repressed it. "Captain of the Sixth Dragoon Guards, Augustus Hillary, reporting. Former captain, that is."

Sir William laughed and opened his arms wide. "Augustus. Son." He hesitated to close his arms, but the young soldier nodded his permission. Sir William hugged him hard. "I am pleased."

"And I'm pleased to see you, sir," Augustus said.

Sir William released his grasp, but placed his hands upon his son's shoulders. He tilted his head toward the major. "Major Tobin. This is my son, Captain Augustus Hillary." Sir William dropped his hands to his sides. "He has completed his time of service and has now come to visit us."

"It is an honor, sir," Augustus said, extending his hand.

The major briskly shook it. "The honor is mine. Two Hillarys within arm's reach. I am most fortunate."

"How is Elizabeth? And your mother?" Sir William asked, retrieving the bag from his son's hand.

"Mother is not well."

"She is ill?" Sir William asked. The major relieved him of the bag.

"Gravely, sir," Augustus replied, with no apparent emotion.

Sir William felt a chill travel the length of his body. "I was unaware."

"I know," Augustus said.

"Elizabeth?" Sir William feared the answer.

"My sister has married well. She is happy."

Sir William exhaled. He placed an arm around his son as they headed up the pier. "We will make time to discuss this."

"Of course," Augustus said.

The three of them walked up Prospect Hill, though it would have been easy to find a carriage. "Tell me, Father," Augustus said. "I want to hear about your lifeboat adventures. I have read many fine things."

Sir William relished the slow walk and his chill was soon displaced by warm feelings. He noted his son's disposition and listened to his genuine interest. Despite the failure of his marriage to Frances, despite the financial hardship he had induced, despite the reality of Danbury Place falling into some disrepair, his son seemed glad to be near him.

Chapter 19

"I never expected this," Augustus said, grunting hard.

Sir William would have laughed if not for the grim circumstances. He was, of course, delighted that Augustus had exceeded his original intention of a short visit and had remained until now, just two weeks before Christmas.

Today the furious south wind arrived.

The *Nestor* had not been replaced. Sir William rowed beside his son in one of Hanby's recently modified boats. Isaac Vondy, Matthew, Joseph, Lieutenant Graves, and Lieutenant Robinson—another recent come-over—rowed with them.

It was an outrageous sea stirred into a tumultuous fit by a raging storm, and it was freezing cold. Sir William craned his necked to get a bearing. He fixed his eyes upon the struggling ship not far away.

The *Fortrondet* was a small ship in big trouble. She was sideways to the rollers and could swamp at any moment. She had snapped two anchor cables and was at the mercy of the gale.

"She's moving straight for Conister," Lieutenant Graves shouted.

"If she doesn't fill first," Vondy said.

"Release anchor," Sir William shouted.

Augustus and Joseph stopped rowing long enough to reach down and pick up the large anchor fastened to a secured cable and tipped it overboard. Sir William watched the line unravel.

"Pray she holds us steady," Sir William said. "Manage your oars."

The seven men worked in cooperation with each other and the cable to ride the rollers in as straight a line as possible given the circumstances. Suddenly, the *Fortrondet* lifted.

"She's free!" Joseph exclaimed. "She may not swamp!"

Sir William knew better and braced himself.

The small ship appeared safe for a moment but then dropped down and pushed hard and fast into the breakers around St. Mary's Isle.

"Father!" Augustus shouted.

Sir William suddenly wished he had left his son on shore. "Courage, son," he said, almost involuntarily.

Cracking timber pierced the howling night wind, and the *Fortrondet* suddenly ripped open to flood with water. It slammed against the ancient reef.

"She's breached," Vondy yelled.

"We steer to her lee," Sir William ordered, knowing they could find a lesser wind on the far side of the wreck. "It's our best hope."

"Aye!"

The men pulled hard, their anchor holding well, but it was a bucking ride to rush past the bow of the helpless vessel to finally bob on her lee side with less violence. They were soaked. Sir William wondered if his own lips were as blue as those of his crew.

"Help!" a man cried.

A gargantuan wave swept the deck of the *Fortrondet*. Sir William and others tossed lines and stretched forth their arms. They had hauled ten men on board when Sir William sensed another presence. He turned and saw a launch from a navy cutter pulling near.

"We're from the HMS *Swallow*," the coxswain yelled through cuffed hands.

Sir William had noticed the cutter around the harbor earlier in the day but hadn't realized they were still in the area. "We're full," he shouted back. "Can you assist?"

"Aye!" the coxswain said.

The naval launch cut into the breakers, its anchor cable keeping them safe from getting too close to the rocks. They tossed multiple lifelines into the sea and hauled in the other crewmen.

Sir William ordered his Hanby lifeboat to shore. Beside him, Augustus rowed with as much energy as if he had just started. He noticed the young man's beaming face.

When the National Institution for the Preservation of Life from Shipwreck heard news of the rescue, they quickly dispatched word that rewards and medals were in order. In the spring, they awarded Sir William a commemorative emblem and sent several medals of silver to the lifeboat crew, including one for Augustus. With the arrival of the medals came news of Frances's death.

On a warm day in April, Sir William took Augustus for a long walk and wound up at his favorite table in the York Hotel.

"She is gone," Augustus said, his face streaked by one lone tear. He lowered the letter. "I should have gone back."

"It is troubling to me as well," Sir William said. He looked out the window.

"Did you love her?" Augustus asked.

Sir William looked at his son. "Yes."

"Why did you leave?"

An old, deeply familiar pain rose from his stomach and gripped his throat. His eyes burned. It was difficult to swallow. "Things don't always go as planned," he said slowly, "or as hoped."

"I always wondered why she never expressed any hope you might return," Augustus said. He looked across the room. "You're famous. At least with most people."

"She didn't want me to return," Sir William said. "I disappointed her. I let her down." He took a deep breath. "I caused much pain."

Augustus looked at him, his eyes welling. Sir William didn't know what his son was feeling.

"If it isn't the courageous baronet and his son," Matthew Hanby said, striding up to the table, his apron as alive with colors as the spring weather outdoors. "I cannot stay long, but I wanted to greet you both."

Sir William forced a smile. Augustus stared out the window, his face turned away from the friendly proprietor. Sir William lowered his eyes and tried motioning with his head. Matthew didn't notice.

"I recommend the vegetable soup," Matthew said. "New recipe from Marseilles. I'm sure you'll enjoy it."

"Thank you," Sir William said. "We'll have a plate of sliced beef with two side dishes. Also a couple of boiled potatoes and some of that yellow squash if you still have it. Fried and slivered onions and a small decanter of red wine. And cheese."

"Wine?" Matthew asked. "Excellent. The house?"

"The house will be fine," Sir William said.

"No soup?" Matthew asked.

Sir William looked to his son, but Augustus remained staring out the window. "No soup."

Augustus turned around; his eyes were clear. "Yes, thank you," he said. "The soup sounds like a fine addition."

"Two?" Matthew asked.

Sir William nodded. He held up two fingers and Matthew left.

"Are you all right?" Sir William asked.

"Of course," Augustus said. He picked up the linen and tucked it into his collar.

"It's been nearly a year since you arrived last July," Sir William said, tapping his spoon on the table. "It has felt like a month. It's been good to have you."

"I should have visited her," Augustus said. "I knew she was not well. I just kept putting it off."

"Augustus," Sir William said, setting his spoon down. He hunched over and leaned closer to his son. "You have done nothing wrong. You have always honored your mother, and she knew that. She loved you very much."

"I loved her," Augustus said. His tears returned and flowed down both sides of his face. He wiped his face with the back of his sleeve and then dabbed his eyes with his linen. He looked out the window.

"As did I," Sir William said, his voice soft.

Augustus shot a hard gaze at his father. "They hated you, you know, despite all you've done."

"Her family?"

"Who else would hate you?" he asked, wiping his nose with his sleeve.

"Not the sleeve, Augustus. Use your handkerchief."

"I hated them for that. You know they're ferociously mad about you inheriting Danbury." His lips trembled. "You're a hero!" Augustus said, using the appropriate linen this time. "They never said good things about you. I couldn't wait to leave. That's why I didn't go back."

"Why did you take all these years to write?" Sir William asked, wishing his voice hadn't wavered.

Augustus sat still.

"I'm surprised they didn't poison your mind against me," Sir William said. Old resentments began moving across his mind. He pushed them away.

"Here you go, gentlemen," Matthew said, placing two steaming bowls of soup before them. He also placed a basket of hard rolls in the center of the table and a small ceramic jar filled with spread. "I'll be back with your beef in a little while. Enjoy."

Augustus waited until Matthew was out of earshot. "Mother always defended you," he said. "Mostly when they weren't around. She told me everything wasn't your fault."

"She was kind," Sir William said. He set a roll down beside his bowl of soup and picked up his spoon.

Augustus did the same. As he sipped the hot soup, his eyes widened to peer up at his father. "I like Emma and Miss Sarah."

Sir William smiled and tasted his soup. It was hot and flavorful. Matthew scored again. He broke his roll and dipped a piece into the steaming liquid.

Augustus laughed. "That was never permitted." He broke his roll and dipped it into his soup just like his father did.

The two ate quietly for several minutes. Matthew arrived with the beef and the decanter. "I'm sorry I was late with the wine, Sir William."

"No trouble," Sir William said. "The soup is delicious."

"Yes," Augustus said. "Great for dipping rolls."

Matthew returned to the kitchen.

"What will you do with Danbury?" Augustus asked, his mouth full with a soup-soaked roll.

"Make sure you taste the beef before you lose your appetite," Sir William cautioned. He used his fork and knife to lift a slab of beef onto his plate. He scooped a pile of crispy brown onions and layered them on top. He also dished a heap of squash and smacked his lips. "I love Hanby's beef. I bet you will, too." He lifted another piece and reached across the table to plop it on his son's plate.

"Don't forget the onions," Augustus said, snapping his fingers and pointing to his plate.

"Ha!" Sir William said. "You help yourself."

Sir William tasted his favorite Hanby dish and was not disappointed. It was hot and juicy with a rich, smoky flavor.

"So, what about it?" Augustus asked. "It's in ruins, you know. It's not livable without major renovations."

"I plan to sell it. Is that okay with you?" Sir William asked, pausing in mid-chew.

Augustus sliced a piece of his beef, stabbed it with his fork, and rolled it around in the gravy. He put it in his mouth. "Mmm, this is good. No, it's no problem with me. I don't want to go back there."

Sir William chewed his dinner and poured two glasses of wine. "It's a fine meal, don't you think?"

"Sir William!" a booming voice called from across the room.

Sir William turned around to see Deemster John Christian and his daughter, Susanna, entering the hotel. "Deemster!" Sir William stood up and wiped the corners of his mouth. "Come! Come and join us!"

The big man was dressed in finery, as was his pretty daughter. He was in a shiny black suit and ruffled shirt. She was in a white dress and large bonnet. They approached the table. The deemster extended his hand. Susanna smiled and blushed, her eyes lowering. "No," the deemster said, his voice still loud despite his being right beside their table. "We'll not interrupt you and your son."

Augustus stood and offered his handshake to the deemster. "No interruption at all," Augustus said. "Please join us."

Sir William noticed his son's eyes lingering on the pretty young lady, who blushed.

"Matthew!" Sir William boomed across the room in an uncharacteristic way. He was surprised at his own volume. He knew it wasn't due to the wine—he had taken only a sip. "More plates and beef and glasses for our guests." He sat down. His face hurt he was grinning so large.

"This is a pleasant surprise," the deemster said, pulling out a chair for himself.

"It certainly is," Sir William said, watching his son fumble with a chair for Susanna.

Chapter 20

"William, you cannot!" Major Tobin scolded him so boisterously that, if not for the spray streaking up from the pier, he would have been certain his brother-in-law had just spat at him.

"Father," Augustus pleaded, "let us do it." He leaned forward at an amazing angle to hold his footing against the gale. "You have nothing to prove."

"It has nothing to do with proving anything," Sir William said, his eyes refusing to move from the frightening sight, his rain gear flapping. He put on his cork vest. "It has to do with helping them." He pointed to the steamer impaled on Conister Rock. "There is no time."

"But the flu took so much out of you that you barely made it through our last few rescues, especially the last two," Major Tobin said. "And you've been complaining of your joints. Let the younger men go."

"I think not," Sir William said. He charged to the new lifeboat, the *Preservation*. The Institution was still struggling with weak subscriptions and not doing all he had hoped, so he had underwritten this new lifeboat himself. "Ready oars," he barked. "Courage, men."

He saw the usual faces. Lieutenant Robinson, Major Tobin, Isaac Vondy, Michael, Joseph, Matthew, Augustus, and the others were gathering the cork vests and taking their places. Lieutenants Graves and Burbridge would have been among them had they not been in England.

"This is no ordinary storm," Isaac Vondy whispered to him.

He nodded. "Ready to push off," he ordered, his eyes lingering on his son. Augustus was tall and lean but strong and wiry, and he knew how to swim. "Where's your life jacket?"

"We're one short," Augustus said.

Sir William quickly unfastened his.

"No, Father."

Sir William held it out. "Put it on."

"Father, please."

"Put it on or disembark."

Augustus took it and fastened it tight. "What about you?"

The storms of the last two seasons had been furious and frequent. Sir William had led no fewer than a dozen rescues, and his bones had soaked for so long in the salty brine that he felt brittle. "I'll be fine."

They rowed out of the harbor. The incoming tide resisted every stroke.

"Brace!" he shouted.

Everyone bent down. A massive wave crashed atop their backs, flooding the craft with freezing seas. Suddenly the boat lifted and the water gushed through the scuppers. The men sat straight up in unison. They lifted their oars, the boat dropped into a trough, and they pushed on.

Sir William spotted the wreck.

The *St. George* was a strong steamer and had cables of chain, but neither the muscle of her two powerful engines nor the forged links of her anchor chains had proved able to resist the crazed violence of the south wind. It had pushed the ship away from entering the harbor and then shifted to southeast by east, manhandling the vessel with a rush of incoming tide. It had forced her onto the rocks of Conister, where she had ripped open and was flooding fast.

Sir William peered through squinted eyes, the spray and salt threatening with every blink. He hoped he wasn't seeing what he thought he saw. "They'll drown."

His men were too fixed on rowing to understand what he was communicating.

Sir William watched a small craft being lowered off the side of the steamer. It was not a Lukin-type craft with airtight properties, and was therefore immediately upset. Several crewmen were pitched into the breakers around the wreck. Their small craft was instantly shattered against a sharp reef.

"With all your heart, men," Sir William shouted. "We've much to do."

The men heaved and hauled. They straightened stiff, leaning backward and pulling hard. Sir William knew the strokes. Their legs were ripping with pain, their backs knotting with spasms.

"We can go where they can't," Sir William said. "Starboard oars, hard to port!" He pushed the tiller to angle them more precisely. They bore in fast.

Sir William saw crewmen aboard the steamer hauling in mates with lifelines from over the rails. "All oars!"

"Plan?" Vondy groaned from his station.

"I think we rush by," Sir William shouted. "We gain those who can jump."

He saw anger flash across Vondy's face, though the engineer nodded.

"The plan is weak, I know," Sir William said. "But the storm is fierce."

"We can only rush once," Isaac said. "We'll not be able to beat back."

"We've a sail," Sir William said. "We can loop around and rush again."

"Too much time," Vondy said, rowing hard.

"We can't do with oars and sail what the steamer hasn't accomplished with steel chains and steam," Sir William said.

Vondy frowned. "Aye."

The *Preservation* rode high on a crest and soared in close.

"We get one chance," Sir William shouted. He used his entire body weight against the tiller arm and pushed the tiller to veer in as close as he dared. His crew braced for a steep drop into the trough between two large waves.

Again the lifeboat rose high on a crest and Sir William saw the steamship crew gathered at the side rail of the severely tipped *St. George*, readying to jump. With the sliver of a cloud-draped moon behind them they looked eerie. One of the men aboard the steamer stood atop the rail in a precariously balanced position, ready to jump.

The steamship rose. The hull was scraped and a shredded net hung like moss over the side. The man on the rail fell overboard and disappeared into the foam. The massive vessel slammed down, lodging between two rows of rocks.

Sir William pushed hard on the tiller, and the lifeboat rushed in on the back of a raucous wave. The speed was beyond any he had known in any kind of transport. The wave stood up as though it had been on its knees. That's when he saw what he'd never seen before nor had ever heard described.

The oars of the lifeboat lifted completely out of the water, and his crew elevated above their seats. It defied common sense. His men floated above the boat, their hands gripping the oars.

Without warning the stern jolted, and Sir William launched over their heads, the tiller slipping from his hands. He kicked something or someone and heard his men yell as he flew over them.

He was immersed in a thickness of sea, spread-eagled and rushing forth at great speed. Foamy currents swirled about his ears. He clamped his mouth and eyes shut. He spun like he was being sucked down a drain. He needed to breathe but dared not. *I cannot breathe. I cannot swim. No jacket.* Sound disappeared. Only water existed.

His face was violently compressed. His head buzzed with pain. Salt water gushed into his mouth. His lungs deflated, and he dropped.

His right hand instinctively clutched to form a fist of bitter rage but a burning tube rushed through his fingers and then ceased. He became part of something large, his entire body plastered upon some ark, his hand in a bloody grip of hemp.

"Take hold!" someone shouted. "For the sake of all that's holy, man, open your eyes and take hold!"

Sir William opened his eyes. He was flat against the side of the steamer, his body pressed against the shredded netting, his right hand in a death grip around a thick line of rope.

Above him was a seaman, reaching. "I can pull you," the young man said. It was not just any man. It was Augustus.

His son pulled him aboard the deck of the steamer. Sir William felt unbearable pain throughout his sides and chest. He lay on the slanted deck as others peered down. He struggled with short breaths.

"Ribs," Lieutenant Robinson said. "You've definitely injured your ribs. We must wrap you and keep you from breathing too deeply."

"Wait! You're all here?" Sir William said. "The *Preservation*? Is she gone?"

"No," Matthew said. "I don't know who governs your journeys, Sir William," his friend said with a laugh. "But we were all thrown clear over the rail to land right on the deck of the *St. George*.

"The *Preservation* flew over the ship," Augustus said, excitement filling his voice. "It is afloat in a calm channel between this old hull and Conister."

"It's a miracle," Matthew said.

"You must . . . lower to boat . . . attempt . . . riding . . . shore," Sir William said.

"We wrap you first," Lieutenant Robinson said.

After the bandaging, Augustus and Matthew helped Sir William walk with difficulty to the opposite side of the ship to survey the situation. There was indeed a calm channel of sea between the steamer and the reef. It was protected by large sections of rocks and the sinking *St. George*. His brother-in-law and Isaac Vondy were down there in the lifeboat. They looked up.

"That's twice I've seen you fly," Major Tobin said. "And now you've taught your crew to do the same. Not us."

Sir William wanted to laugh, but it hurt to breathe. He waved to the two men and then looked to the shore side of the reef. The water was rough there but calmer than what was slamming the *St. George* on the opposite side.

Sir William pointed to the lee side of Conister. "We must all get in the lifeboat and take cover there," he spoke slowly, haltingly, careful to take shallow breaths. "It should prove safe harbor enough."

"How do we get there?" Augustus asked.

Sir William smiled as best he could manage. "With . . . courage."

"I say we arrange a lifeline," Lieutenant Robinson said. "We transfer everyone to the lifeboat."

Within thirty minutes, the entire group of salt-soaked and shivering men was crammed into the lifeboat. "There are only six oars left," Major Tobin said. "The others have been smashed."

"I count thirty-six of us," Vondy said. "Are all saved?"

"We lost one over the rail," the *St. George* captain said.

A great groaning of wood and steel suddenly seized their attention. They looked up and saw the steamship rise and swing, its stern turning toward the sea.

"Hard a port!" Sir William yelled, his sides bursting with pain.

Some grabbed oars, but there was no time.

The *St. George* swung past, missing them by only inches but sending an enormous wave that swamped them. The lifeboat flipped, and all thirty-six men fell into the sea.

Inverted but afloat, the *Preservation* bobbed. One by one and two by two, men appeared around her.

"I count . . . thirty-six!" Lieutenant Robinson shouted.

"We are indebted to Providence," Joseph said, bobbing beside him.

"No doubt . . . we are," Sir William said. "But we are not yet home. Let us hold fast our dependence upon Him."

The lifeboat floated in a circle on the safer side of Conister, opposite the direction of the oncoming wind. The treacherous reef acted as a windbreak. The men held on.

"Did you miscount?" Sir William suddenly asked. "*Augustus?*" His rib cage was on fire with pain.

"I am here," Augustus said. "Right beside you."

Sir William turned his head and saw his son.

"I am safe, Father," Augustus said. "Are you in pain?"

"No, no," Sir William said with great relief, despite the burning.

"We are again saved!" Joseph said.

"Look!" Major Tobin said with astonishment. "We are in that patch of sea you intended."

Sir William clung to the hull and laughed, though it hurt. "Well," he said, his speech broken and halting, "it doesn't always happen the way you think, hey?"

As the wind weakened and the sea eased, the men flipped the lifeboat over and climbed aboard. They were low in the water but safe.

From his place in the center, Sir William watched with the others as the battered *St. George* disappeared below the sea. With the early light of dawn, the weary men saw harbor boats moving swiftly toward them to escort them back home.

On land at last, Sir William was transported to his physician's office on Athol Street, where Sarah and Emma soon arrived, along with many others. He gripped their hands and kissed Emma's face while Sarah wiped her tears.

He was amazed by how many people he saw. Lieutenant-Governor Cornelius Smelt, looking gravely ill, stood smiling nearby. "You are a miracle, my boy," his friend said. "A miracle. If not, then you are a real fish!"

Deemster John Christian was also there, with compassionate face, red eyes, and trembling cheek. Susanna was there, and, if Sir William's eyes weren't fooling him, she was holding his son's hand and resting her head upon his shoulder.

"Is he all right?" he heard Major Tobin ask. Then, shoving his way in to peer at him was his brother-in-law. "Jolly well, man! He flies on earth and sea! How did you do it?"

Sir William smiled and then looked deep into Emma's eyes. He could see his face in her pupils, at least it seemed like he could. He was sure he could.

"With courage," Sir William whispered, "nothing is—"

"I know," Emma said, placing her soft hand upon his lips.

Chapter 21

Sir William listened intently as Emma read the letter from Lord Exmouth, a charter member of the National Institution for the Preservation of Life from Shipwreck:

> *You proved your professed principles, which have been often expressed in warm language and earnest spirit, by your embracing of dangers that would otherwise have appalled the boldest of our youth. When your age is reflected upon and your promptness, energy, and perseverance witnessed, others can only feel lost in admiration. We may only wonder if you received that noble impulse from Divine inspiration in the cause of humanity and Christian endeavor. How truly gratifying it must be to have set your friends in the world so noble an example. It shall be admired by generations yet unborn.*

Emma set the letter down and picked up a wet towel from a basin next to his bed. "Nicely done, William." Her red hair was hidden under her morning bonnet. He looked for the tenacious curl leading the lone charge atop her porcelain forehead, but it was tucked away. She squeezed the towel and mopped his brow. It was cool.

Sir William had broken six ribs and suffered a cracked sternum. He was mending, but with no few bouts of discomfiting pain. The doctors bled him daily but offered little else. He refused to take opium.

Sarah covered his feet with warm towels.

"If you dry them with your hair," Sir William said, his voice weaker than he intended, "then I'll know I've passed through the pearly gates."

"Fortunately for us," Sarah said, "you are in error." Her eyes looked moist. "You are where you belong. Among us."

"Fortunately for everyone," Emma said. "Especially those who wreck on rocks." She returned the towel to the basin and ran a hand through his hair.

"Augustus?" Sir William asked. "Where is he?"

Emma looked into his eyes and smiled. Her lips were pink and moist. "Visiting."

"Again!" Sarah added. She gently rubbed his feet through the towels.

Sir William chuckled and then groaned.

"Don't laugh, dear," Emma said. She slid his covers down to his waist and lightly grazed his bandaged ribs with her hand. "If you can help it."

"Paper," Sir William said. "Ink."

"Oh, no," Emma said. "For what?"

He looked at her and mouthed the words.

"The tower? You mean the castle? Oh, no, it's much too soon for you to be writing appeals for donations."

"You exaggerate," Sir William replied. "If we already had it built on Conister, I'd be in much better shape."

Emma's eyes softened. Her forehead was as white as cream. "I am proud of you, William. But you can propose your stone refuge when you're feeling better."

"There has been a breakthrough at the mine," Sarah said. She replaced the towels with fresh, hot ones. "It has struck great amounts of lead, silver, and copper. It is yielding nearly fifty tons per month and is promising to pay dividends of £1,000 per quarter. It was all in the *Gazette*."

"Along with a whole lot of praise for you and your endeavors," Emma said. She stroked his cheek.

Sir William lifted his arm, groaning a little.

"Be careful, dear," Emma said. "Don't exert yourself."

He reached for her face.

"If you want writing implements that much," Emma said, taking hold of his hand, "I'll call Hattie to bring them."

He bent his wrist and twisted his hand to break free of her hold and reached for her cap. He stuck two fingers under the edge and tugged out a solitary curl to rest upon her forehead. He dropped his hand to the bed and smiled.

"May I enter?" Hattie called from the hallway.

"Of course," Emma said.

"We have guests," Hattie said. "Mister Phillip Garret is in the house wanting to see Sir William. There are two other gentlemen with him. I believe they are the new bankers."

Sir William motioned his wife to draw close. "Prop me up," he whispered.

"You cannot possibly take company," Emma said.

"Get me a loose, silk nightshirt and bed cap," he said. "I'll need to be sitting in a chair for them, my love."

"No," Emma said. "It is still too early."

"You three ladies can help me to my chair," he said. "I insist." He moved and groaned.

"William, please," Emma said.

"If you let me meet these men," Sir William said, trying hard not to grunt, "I will buy you pearls for that bonnet." He winked.

"As if that will change my mind," Emma said. Her soft white face flushed pink.

Sarah rose to move behind her. "She doesn't need any pearls to make her lovely."

"Hattie?" Sir William called out.

Hattie approached to stand beside the two women.

"I am in need of all three of you," he said. "Please help me get into that chair."

"You are impossible," Emma said. "Hattie, please get a nightshirt from the wardrobe."

With no little difficulty, the feat was accomplished, and Emma helped make Sir William presentable. She kissed him. "I will return shortly to interrupt this visit if you allow it to go on for too long."

"Yes, Emma," he said. "It must be important, or I'm sure they wouldn't have come."

"Let us hope." She left the room.

Hattie returned with the guests.

"Sir William!" Phillip Garret said in a surprisingly cheerful tone. "Can nothing keep you down? You look remarkable." He extended his hand.

Sir William took hold, but it was Phillip Garret who launched the vigorous shake. Sir William's rib cage pulsed with pain. He forced a smile and then looked at the other two men.

"Sir William, do you recall Mr. Forbes and Mr. Wulff?" Phillip Garret asked.

Forbes was in typical banking attire and looked sharp, if a little tired. Wulff was dressed with all the right colors and materials, though a little slovenly when it came to proper tucks and folds and buttoning. His face was large and square and his lips thick and creased. His hair was black, thin, and wiry. The two men stared at him with dimwitted smiles.

"Gentlemen," Sir William said. He lowered his hand and nodded.

"Tell him, Edward," Phillip Garret said.

"A joint-stock bank, sir," Forbes said.

"A joint-stock bank?" Sir William asked, trying not to grimace from his discomfort.

"Precisely," Phillip Garret said. "Your name is something of—shall we say—a *draw*, to potential investors. Forbes and Wulff here were mightily impressed."

"Yes," Forbes said, moving a half step forward. "Yes, I daresay it is so."

"Tell him about the bank concept," Phillip Garret said, appearing either excited or annoyed. Sir William wasn't sure.

"Oh, yes," Forbes said. "The economy is expected to turn better, as I'm sure you are aware. Much better. The times will soon be good on the isle, you know, and ripe for developments and such, but it's difficult—yes, difficult, you might say—for any of the existing local banks to underwrite any of the said developments." He paused and scratched his mustache.

"Aw!" Phillip Garret threw up his hands and then smiled. "You see what's happening here, don't you, Sir William?"

"I'm afraid I don't." Sir William allowed a scowl upon his face. It was due to the pain he was feeling, but he didn't care what they attributed it to, the conversation was already so confusing. "Gentlemen, what is it that you want to speak about? How does it concern me?"

"What's happened here," Phillip Garret said, looking out of place with his good looks and fine clothes, "is that everyone is becoming so enamored with your exploits no one's quite sure if you're human."

Sir William laughed. He hadn't realized they were intimidated. "Rubbish, men. Say what you've come to say," Sir William said kindly. "I'm open to hearing it."

Wulff stepped forward. "The local banks have too limited resources to finance anything of substance in the way of developments, sir.

We believe if you lend your name to a new consortium venture, we would all do well selling shares for upgrading a local banking facility. This way, we will be in prime position to meet the demands of the approaching opportunities expected within the isle."

"Do not shareholders in such a structure assume total liability?" Sir William asked.

"Yes," Wulff said.

Sir William liked the fact the man did not hesitate.

"We know how to manage assets," Wulff said. "The proposed structure, although carrying a different type of risk, offers an enormous likelihood of profits for many years to come."

"Yes, yes," Forbes chimed in. "We are offering to transfer our existing exceptional business for twenty-five hundred shares. An additional seventy-five hundred shares will be put up for sale to local investors. You, if you like—you don't need to, of course, but if you like—may buy any number of shares, though we haven't come expecting that."

"Why *have* you come?" Sir William asked. The pain in his ribs was becoming too much for him to remain seated. He shifted.

"That's the rub," Garret said. "There's no effort here for you to subscribe any large amount of shares. It's simply that if you bought just a handful, your participation would be like a beacon that would give confidence to others to get aboard. It is a good arrangement. With such a consortium in town, we could begin looking toward even more profitable developments."

"It would also put you into a, shall we say, favorable position with the bank, sir," Wulff added.

The three pairs of eyes looking to read his every gesture and expression were too much given the pain he was in. "I like it," Sir William said. "Of course, I make no decision now, but I will give it serious consideration."

Wulff and Forbes smiled and looked at Phillip Garret.

"You won't regret it, Sir William," Garret said. He extended his hand.

Sir William nodded but didn't offer his hand. "Good day, gentlemen."

"Yes, yes—good day, sir," Forbes said.

"It's a privilege, sir," Wulff said.

"Fine. Thank you, Sir William." Phillip bowed slightly and retreated from the room. Wulff and Forbes followed him out.

The men had not been gone seconds when Hattie came in announcing another visitor. "Someone else to see you, sir. Shall I send him away?"

"Yes," Sir William said. "Please call Emma and Sarah and help me into bed. I should have listened to my wife. I will die from this pain."

"Of course, you should have," Hattie said. "I'll get the ladies and send the deemster away."

"The deemster?" Sir William perked up. "John Christian?"

"Yes, don't worry," Hattie said. "I'll send him away politely. He's such a gentleman."

"No, wait!" Sir William spoke so loudly a sharp pain cut across his rib cage. "Get the ladies," he said more softly, "and get me into bed. Then, welcome the deemster into my chamber."

The trip back into the bed was much more difficult but was finally completed. Sir William's feet had swollen, so Sarah placed fresh hot towels on them.

Hattie returned with Deemster Christian. After a lengthy exchange of pleasantries, the ladies left Sir William with his friend.

"You look well," the deemster said, standing alongside the bed. "Considering all you've endured."

"That bad?" Sir William asked.

Christian smiled and drew up the chair at the end of the bed to situate himself closer to the head. It creaked as he sat.

"It is good to see you," he said.

"And you."

Sir William closed his eyes to rest, waiting for the deemster to lead the way. After several long moments, the silence was broken.

"You have possibly noticed for some time that your dear son has demonstrated a certain fondness for my princess, Susanna?"

Sir William opened his eyes. "I have noted certain tendencies." He smiled, looking at his elevated feet wrapped in towels. "I submit that you may have noticed a certain return of affection from that most properly behaved young lady of yours."

The deemster nodded. "I have." He leaned closer. "A certain question has been brought to me by said young gentleman." He licked his lips. "Might you be familiar with the subject of his query?"

"I daresay I could guess it."

Hattie arrived. "Do you need fresh towels?"

"You needn't bother," Sir William said.

"Do you wish to guess?" the deemster asked with a laugh. "Or would you like me to say?"

"Most definitely." Sir William forced himself up higher, despite the pain. "Do say!"

"Your son, Augustus, has asked me for my daughter's hand in marriage. He asked in a most admirable manner, I want to add."

Sir William silently studied his friend.

Christian's face tightened. "You know that, as deemster, difficult judgments are often mine to make." He opened his mouth to speak, but Hattie returned.

"I said I didn't need any," Sir William said, surprised with his impatience.

"I know," Hattie said. "Lady Emma overruled." She fumbled with removing the existing towels for what seemed an infinite amount of time.

"Hattie, do hurry," Sir William said, fearing he'd blow up if she didn't finish quickly.

"I'm doing it proper-like, sir," Hattie said without increasing her speed.

The deemster lowered his gaze and waited. Hattie finally finished and left the room. Sir William waited.

"As a deemster, I have several times been called upon to make a difficult decision," Christian repeated.

"Yes, yes, man," Sir William said. He took a deep breath and offered a smile though it felt weak.

The deemster slowly looked up, and his face transformed to a huge grin. "This was not one of them. I easily granted what he sought."

Sir William stuttered a laugh.

The deemster burst out with a hearty guffaw.

"You did that on purpose," Sir William said.

Christian enthusiastically nodded. "I did."

"You old pigeon!" Sir William said.

"Ha! You should have seen your face."

They laughed. Sir William held his side.

"It seems our children will wed sometime after you are well."

"I am blessed," Sir William said. "Nothing could make me happier."

"Well," the deemster said, "there may be some additional news that may further sweeten the day."

"I can't imagine what that might be."

"Our house near Ramsey is complete."

"The one you've been waiting for in Milntown?" Sir William asked, suddenly serious.

"Yes," Christian said. "Do you know what that means?"

"Fort Anne will be available."

The deemster stared at Sir William for a long time. "Well?"

"Will you at least remain there long enough to hold the reception there?" Sir William winked.

"Ha! You would remind me of my obligation! We will hold the reception there and then move elsewhere on the isle. Hopefully, you will end up with Fort Anne."

Sir William took a slow, deep breath. It didn't hurt so much.

Chapter 22

S ir William stood holding his glass of sparkling champagne. "We are favored!" he exclaimed.

He was dressed as sharply as his son, who had that morning stood at the altar of St. George's Church in a black suit with long tails and crimson vest. The bride, Susanna Christian, was draped in a flowing silk dress of silver, with a train nearly fifteen feet long.

"To long and prosperous living, rooted in purpose and framed by courage," Sir William said to all in attendance.

Emma stood beside him. She was dressed in peach silk with intricate patterns of lace. She lifted her glass. "May this day always be remembered as a day of happiness that never subsides in both the Hillary and Christian households."

Sarah and the bride's parents rose from the same table. "Cheers!" the deemster said.

"Hear! Hear!" Major Tobin led the replies from his nearby table. Joining him were Lieutenant-Governor Cornelius Smelt, Lieutenants Burbridge and Graves, and their wives.

The west side ballroom of Fort Anne proved a grandiose setting for the afternoon reception, which was attended by the most eminent from all around the eastern coast of the Isle of Man.

The day was cloaked with the slightest fog under a flat gray sky, but the rains had held off and the temperature was pleasant. Fort Anne rose from the misty grounds, filled with gaiety, colorful costume, and a string quartet.

Sir William, Emma, and the others resumed their seats, and the music began.

Sir William whispered into Emma's ear, "I have seldom felt so happy."

A ship's horn blew from the entrance to the harbor.

"A most appropriate punctuation," Sarah said, lifting her glass of champagne. "To Sir William and Lady Emma."

The table replied in kind, lifting their glasses to clink against Sarah's.

"How so?" Emma asked.

"I believe the honorable baronet's ship has come in!" Sarah said, laughing. Her blue eyes glistened.

Sir William surveyed the scene. "Yes, dear Sarah," he said, watching Augustus dance with Susanna. "It is clearly a time of harvest. I am grateful."

The ship's horn blew again and was replied to by the lighthouse at the end of the pier, as harbor and vessel spoke through the fog.

The day flew by, as did the following year. Augustus and his new bride relocated to Milntown near Ramsey, and Sir William acquired the Fort Anne.

His fame and wealth grew, and he received generous donations to build his stone tower on Conister Rock. After one more year, it rose up from Douglas Bay.

Emma squeezed Sir William's arm as they gazed from atop Douglas Head, strolling along the grounds of their magnificent new home.

"It has all come together so well." He took in the sweeping view of Douglas, the pier, and the glistening bay. He allowed his eyes to linger for no short time upon the new stone edifice in the middle of the bay.

"It is just as you said," Emma said. "A tower of refuge."

Sir William admired its majestic form rising up from the center of Conister Rock. The tower had been built in the fashion of a thirteenth-century castle. "You were right," he said. "It is part castle." He kissed Emma's forehead. "You have to admit that 1832 isn't such a bad year, wouldn't you?"

"It is stunning," she said.

"I have always known it was possible," he said. "I don't think it is given a man the precise route he must travel, but he is allowed a vision that compels his every step—like a force that draws him. For me, I never lost hope."

"You are the eternal optimist," Emma said. She tugged his arm toward the house. "We've much to make ready."

"Nonsense," Sir William said, resisting the tug. "Hattie and the staff will see we're well prepared. We still have several hours."

"Yes, dear," Emma said, "but do not deprive me of the joy of helping to make our lovely home ready for our guests. Besides, Augustus and Susanna will be arriving early, as will Caesar." She leaned to tug harder, her face aglow with joy.

"Very well, my queen," Sir William said, moving on. "It will be good to see Augustus, won't it?" He let go his hold and turned to face her, walking backward. She looked grand in her fanciful summer dress.

"It will be wonderful," she said, "as will be the entire affair." She shielded her eyes from the overhead sun and slowed her pace to make eye contact. "We haven't danced in a while, and the ballroom is perfect for it." She smiled and cocked her head sideways and then laughed. She resumed her walk. "It will be nice to see Augustus, too. We see him so seldom since they moved to Milntown."

"That is his home now. The colliery requires much effort," Sir William said.

"And no little funding," she said. "Colliery sounds so much cleaner than coal mine."

"Agreed, on both points," he said, turning around to walk beside her. "You know, Dumbell will be attending tonight."

She laughed at the name. "Willard?" she asked. "The lawyer?"

"Do you know any other dumbbells?" he asked with a wide grin.

"You might guess at that," she said.

Sir William chuckled. "He's been persistently chasing my time. He and his partner, J. C. Bluett, want to share something with me about Falcon Cliff. With all the growth we're seeing, they're suggesting a development of gentlemen's villas right there." He pointed to the sloping woods directly behind the center of Douglas.

"No doubt," she said, retaking his arm. "Remember dear, tonight is all fun and pleasure. You'll not run off to drone about matters of business, will you?"

Sir William clasped her hand and lifted it to his mouth. Her skin was soft and smelled fresh. "I've been known to explore a plan or two at parties." He winked.

Emma smiled at him, her red curls shining in the sun, her face as porcelain as always. They reached Fort Anne and stepped inside.

Part 3

A man makes plans, but God orders his steps.

Proverbs 16:9 (par)

Chapter 23

"Bring out your dead."

The man's voice echoed through the dark streets of Douglas as he pushed a small barrow. The wooden wheels groaned under the weight of infants' corpses.

Other men teamed up to push larger barrows carrying the bodies of older children. A plough horse pulled a flat board wagon heaped with adult bodies.

Sir William was dressed in dark clothes, his face mostly covered by a large scarf, only his eyes visible. He watched the barrows and wagon roll down the south side street, collecting the dead.

It was a risk to venture where the sewers were open on both sides of the street and where scores of men, women, and children had suddenly fallen ill and died. It was a risk, but not a mystery.

Cholera had swept the Continent for a year. It had been only a question of time before it crossed the sea and touched the isle. Despite the expectation, none were prepared for this. It arrived with a terrifying shriek that didn't come from the wind but from the broken hearts of mothers and widows.

Sir William watched in horror as he saw wailing mothers clinging to the dead bodies of their infants while their husbands pried them loose for deposit into the barrows. Elderly people lay sprawled atop the wagons. No age was spared.

"Anne," one man whimpered. The limp body of a young man in his early twenties hung from his arms. "We have no choice. It could spread."

The woman became hysterical, trying to keep her husband from carrying the dead lad to the barrow. *Anne?*

Suddenly, Sir William felt his stomach sicken. That man was Michel Kellerman. The body of the dead youth being heaped atop the other bodies must be little Mike.

Sir William bent over and yanked down his scarf just in time. He vomited onto the street. He wiped his mouth with his gloved hand.

"Bring out your dead."

Sir William whirled around to see another cart full of corpses only a few feet away—the faces pale and silent. He bent over again, staggered to the middle of the street, and then rushed away toward the distant fire burning at St. George's.

Although many women cried out in anguish, he was sure he could hear Anne Kellerman's cry above all others. Her once-quiet voice was now horribly loud and bitter. "Why?" she wailed. "*Why?*"

He sped past several barrows and left the south side to head up Athol Street and up the hill toward St. George's cemetery. It was just before sunrise and torches still lit the graveyard. A bonfire burned in the back.

There were more men with barrows. They lined up like people waiting to board a ship, only they were men dressed in rags with cargoes of corpses. Some of the bodies were large with limbs dangling over the sides. Most were the tiny forms of children—of babies.

"God in heaven," Sir William bemoaned through his scarf. "What has befallen us? Why must this be?"

He saw the vicar standing nearby with a lantern and pointing downward while shouting to others. A short, squat man pushed his barrow to the spot where the holy man indicated and tipped his barrow with much difficulty until three tiny bodies from within fell like rag dolls into a giant hole in the ground.

"Mass graves?" Sir William's voice cracked as he arrived beside the vicar.

"We've no choice, Sir William," the vicar said. "You there. Roll it over here. Be careful, man."

Sir William looked into the pit before him, detesting the stench. He felt faint.

"You shouldn't be here, William," the vicar said. "Go to your own. It is safer there."

Sir William staggered away.

"Look out, man!" a barrow pusher yelled, nearly running into him. The barrow jerked and a body rolled out. It was a small boy.

Sir William stooped to pick up the dead child.

"Are you crazy?" The man bumped Sir William aside and used a large forked branch to roll the child over and over until he fell into the pit. "You don't touch them," the man snarled.

Sir William stood in the midst of the creaking barrows, thudding bodies, and crackling torches. Barrows and bodies were rolled and pushed from every direction.

He saw two men carrying a full-grown body wrapped in a sheet. They were struggling with the dead weight. "Let me help you," Sir William said. He moved next to the center of the body where it arched downward to the ground and looped one arm around the middle and pulled up as best he could.

"Careful, Sir William," one of the two men said. "Be certain you're only touching sheet."

Sir William recognized the voice. He turned his head to see Joseph lifting the feet of the corpse behind him. "Joseph?"

"Aye, sir," Joseph said, his face looking black from soot or grime or something else.

They walked past the pit.

"Why not there?" Sir William asked, motioning to the pit with his head.

"His dying wish was to be burned, sir," Joseph said, motioning with his head toward the back of the cemetery. "He believed it safer for all."

Sir William took a better look at the large fire burning from inside a shallower pit in the rear of the graveyard. It looked like an ordinary bonfire, and he was shocked to see bodies being swung into the flames. All of the workers had scarves double- and triple-wrapped around their faces.

Joseph stumbled and dropped his end of the body. The sudden shift caused the other man to drop his end, and Sir William collapsed under the weight of the cadaver. The sheet partially opened, and a shiny black boot of fine leather protruded.

"Sorry, sir," Joseph said. "I tripped on a root. Forgive me." He quickly covered the boot and picked up his end. "You there," he said to the other man, "hurry along."

The other man lifted up his end, and Sir William was able to resume his position in the middle. He thought about the boot.

"This man is a gentleman?" Sir William craned his neck around.

Joseph looked aghast. "You don't know, sir?"

"Know what?"

"I thought that is why you assisted us," Joseph said.

"I assisted you because I saw the weight was too much for you," Sir William said, his head turning forward and back, wanting to continue the conversation with Joseph, but not wanting to trip. "Who is it?"

"Why, sir," Joseph said, sounding astonished. "It's Lieutenant-Governor Cornelius Smelt."

Sir William's boot heel stuck in the dirt, and he fell face down.

Chapter 24

The spacious hall called the west side ballroom graced the Fort Anne residence with a feel of nobility. It was twice the length of the center of the grand home, predominantly stucco, and large enough to hold more than one hundred persons—and half of them in hoop skirts.

Anyone arriving at Fort Anne would pass through the hall, which Sir William had since adorned with tall paintings of natural and biblical scenes on each wall. The living quarters were in the center of the massive residence.

A gravel walk trimmed with shrubbery and variegated flowerbeds completely encircled the estate. At the easternmost end was another lengthy hall-like structure, adding balance to the architecture but without a roof of any kind. The walls and window openings appeared to enclose another ballroom but instead encompassed a serene arrangement of winding footpaths, Romanesque statuary, tall grasses, stone benches, and sparkling pools.

The outbuildings featured stables, a greenhouse, servants' quarters, and a coach house. The grounds had roaming green lawns occasionally broken by fancifully shaped gardens with low walls, Spanish chestnut trees, and gravel paths—three gardens in all.

The great yard tapered as it neared the harbor to the north and the sea to the east, affording a sweeping view of Douglas, the sloping woods of Falcon Ridge behind, the new shipyard where construction was underway, the bustling quay, prestigious Prospect Hill, the bay with the Tower of Refuge atop Conister Rocks, and all the way around to the newly built lighthouse at the end of the pier and the Irish sea beyond.

A switchback trail led from the top of the Douglas Head landscape to the great stone seawall below. The stately perimeter of quarried stone was thick enough to permit casual strolls atop it, five abreast, and ran the length of the shore from the innermost point of the harbor, where a pleasant cove and beach was part of the Fort Anne property. Beyond that, it was all rocky coast and twitching seas.

Sir William stood atop the seawall. He was dressed in the saddest pair of trousers he owned. He wore no vest, no puffy shirt, no cuff links or fanciful topper. He wore a wide brimmed straw hat and a loose, un-tucked shirt. In one hand he held the wooden handle of a thick brush, and in the other, a bucket of lime.

Joseph and Isaac stood by, each with a bucket and brush of his own.

"We will start with the seawall," Sir William said. "It is logically the outermost line of defense."

"I don't know if we'll ever reach a point beyond it, sir," Joseph said. "It's quite the large wall."

"Are you certain it will work, Sir William?" Vondy asked.

"No, I am not certain. It is merely rumored to be a deterrent to the cholera epidemic."

"May I purchase some for my own home?" Vondy asked.

"You may take as much as your own house requires," Sir William said. "As may you, Joseph. Now, let us be diligent."

The men labored through the hot summer sun and dumped bucket after bucket of lime wash atop the wall. They used rags, brushes, and brooms to spread as much as fast as they could.

When evening came, Sir William paid the men in pounds and sent them to their homes with a donkey cart filled with lime and a few boxes of food. "Let us continue tomorrow," Sir William said. "We've barely covered one quarter of the wall, I know, but let us not rest until we are done. After that, the house."

Sir William watched the tired men lead the donkey cart down Douglas Head trail to the town below.

It was good that Fort Anne was remotely located, and it was risky to have those affected on premises. He didn't have the heart to tell Emma of little Mike. It had been hard enough telling her about Smelt. He determined he would visit Michael after this was all over to see how the poor family was doing.

He looked at his lime-stained breeches and the buckets nearby. He surveyed his home. The flickering amber of lantern light was just beginning to appear in a few lower-level windows. Emma and Sarah were in the sewing room, no doubt. He knew he would find Emma sewing and Sarah reading one of those Jane Austen romance books.

He looked across the quay to his former residence at Prospect Hill. The sun had already begun to lower behind it, the sky a maze of purples and pinks. It was gloriously beautiful.

He crossed to the garden shed that was tucked inside the tree line at the west end. He put the lime wash away and rinsed off the brushes with well water. Emma had pleaded with him to let the servants do the work, but he didn't want to risk exposing them to the others from town.

She also had difficulty understanding his insistence they sleep in separate rooms for now and why even a peck on the lips was forbidden. His women and servants would remain isolated until the plague passed. There would be no exceptions.

Augustus had written, wanting to return from his colliery in Cumberland to help, but Sir William would have none of it. These were tragic days, and extreme measures were in order.

As he walked the length of the west side ballroom, he enjoyed perusing his collection of paintings. There were many more in the gallery, but some of his finest, certainly his largest, hung here. Like the setting sun behind the western hills of the isle, these too were beautiful. And yet just down the hill people died horrific deaths and dead children were pried from their mothers' arms.

The days remained dark and dreadful until the cold, calm days of December. The cholera tapered and seemed gone, though some were still dying from the lingering effects.

"I've called for this meeting because of the extreme circumstances we are now witnessing," Sir William said. He thought about that day at the tavern in London with Wilberforce and Prince Augustus in attendance. He wished such men were here now. But this was the York Hotel and these were not those men.

"We've our own serious matters to attend to," the lawyer, Willard Dumbell, said. He was dressed in his royal blue suit and shiny powder blue vest, and he sported his chestnut cane and gave it an occasional twirl. "Although we appreciate the meal, an Athol Street location would have been more preferred."

"Oh, shut up, Willard!" Major Tobin said, sitting nearby. "I admit the wine is somewhat watered down, but it'll do, you old stick!"

"Really, Major," Dumbell said. "You do remind me of the sort of class in attendance."

The major spun in his seat next to Sir William. His eyes were wide and glassy.

"Gentlemen! Gentlemen!" Sir William said. "Please."

"My wine is never watered," Matthew said from across the room. He and some helpers were setting out large servings of food along a large table.

Others in attendance scoffed.

"Of course you don't," Sir William said, feeling a little embarrassed. "Gentlemen, I understand we are all under pressure and each of us knows someone who has succumbed. But we must take it upon ourselves to assume some positive leadership in order to confer hope to those who have such little means during these difficult times."

"No doubt you want us to launch a lifeboat." The speaker was a man familiar to Sir William, but he couldn't place the name. He was seated alongside Dumbell, his face taut and scarred.

"To whom do I have the pleasure?" Sir William asked.

"Monty Jones," the man said. "Former fisherman. Present shoemaker."

Monty Jones sat at the table with Willard Dumbell and J. C. Bluett, another lawyer.

"I recall now, yes," Sir William said. "I am happy to see you well."

"Ha!" Monty Jones blurted.

Sir William continued. "But you are mistaken in supposing I have asked you here on matters pertaining to the lifeboat. Unless, of course, you invoked that word as an example of offering aid to those in need. If that is what you meant, then you are most correct."

Jones smirked and cast a sideways glance toward Dumbell, who kept his eyes on Sir William. Behind them, Matthew and his helpers brought out large plates of hot beef and steaming onions and situated them on the long table.

"The 'lifeboat,' in this case," Sir William said, as emphatically as he knew how, "may be defined as an emergency board of health."

"That sounds interesting, Sir William," Phillip Garret said, entering the dining room. He took a deep breath. "Mmm, that beef smells wonderful."

"Thank you," Matthew said very loudly. He glanced at the major and returned to the kitchen, his helpers trailing behind.

"Ah, Mister Garret," Sir William said. "I am happy to see you. Your sharp thinking will greatly aid us today, I am certain."

Phillip Garret was as neat as a pin, dressed in dove gray and topped off with a silver derby. He wore white gloves and boots so shiny they glowed. He scanned the tables for a seat and took one beside Edward Forbes and John Wulff, who were seated in the back. Sir William hadn't noticed them until now. "Thank you, Sir William," Garret replied as he settled himself. "Do continue."

Sir William remained standing beside his favorite table by the window. "I was saying th—"

"Can you move a little to the side," Monty Jones said, not too politely. "The glare from the window is disturbing me."

Sir William took a sideways step. "An emergency board of health ought to be put into place to help with clothing and fuel and food," he said. "And we ought to begin voluntary subscriptions today from among us—the wealthiest of our town."

He waited for a comment, but the only noise came from the kitchen. Matthew reappeared with his team, carrying all manner of bowls and plates of hot foods, breads, and sauces. The clinking of glass managed to catch the major's attention as Matthew placed bottles of wine at one end of the long table.

"It is in our best interests," Sir William said. "Only the other day I was whitewashing my own facilities due to no availability of local men to hire for it." This wasn't his personal motivation, but he felt it sufficient provocation for many of the men present.

Sir William saw some men, including Phillip Garret, nodding, and so he continued. "Consider what other forms of labor you might be required to personally assume should our working class continue to be decimated by the plague."

"I get it," Monty Jones said in a disrespectful tone. "Shudder the thought of having to sweat, so throw some bones to the poor, eh?"

Willard Dumbell placed a hand on Monty Jones's arm. "I see the merit of your idea," Dumbell said. "Truly, it is a wise and compassionate gesture."

"What?" Jones asked.

Sir William was not about to allow Jones floor time as he once did that strange man at the tavern in London.

"May I ask who invited you here, sir?" he asked. "This was to be a meeting of gentlemen, and though I do not doubt your sincerity, I think a shoemaker would hardly be interested in subscribing to such endeavors as we are gathered here to discuss today."

"Oh, I see," Jones said. "Too good for me, eh?" The man stood up, his fists clenched.

The major stood up so fast that his chair fell over backward. His eyes locked onto the smaller man.

"Whoa! Whoa!" Willard Dumbell said, slowly rising and again taking hold of his friend's arm. "I confess it was I who invited Mr. Jones and for good reason." Dumbell motioned his friend to sit.

The major waited until Jones sat down and then picked up his chair and did the same.

"I suspected this meeting might be to affect some charity," Willard Dumbell said. "I thought that shoes might be a good staple to provide for some of our locals. New shoes might also offer a sense of safety. Some think the illness is spread through unclean footwear, you know."

"I am grateful for your forward thinking," Sir William said. "I did not realize that, uh, Mr. Jones was proposing a donation of leather goods."

"No donation!" Jones snapped. "I'm no rich man like you, Sir Baronet."

Willard Dumbell shot a disgusted look to his friend and the shoemaker became silently red-faced. "As I was about to explain," Dumbell went on, "Mr. Jones is not in such position to entirely contribute, though he has expressed a happy willingness to offer them at greatly reduced prices." Willard Dumbell bowed his head and sat down.

"Well," Sir William began.

"I think you all should eat now," Matthew said. "Otherwise, you'll not taste my food when it's hot and good."

Sir William saw the pleading look on Matthew's face and conceded. "Gentlemen, let us help ourselves to the table. We'll continue this, uh, discussion after we've delighted ourselves on Hanby's most expert fare. I do say, his steaks are magnificent!"

Sir William smiled as he noticed Matthew Hanby beaming while the others lumbered up to the table. Phillip Garret chatted with Forbes and Wulff and then quickly snaked through the crowd to approach Sir William. "William!"

"Yes?"

"Count Wulff, Forbes, and myself in," Garret said. "It's the right thing to do. Just like the lifeboat and the tower. Always one to see it first, you are!" He shook Sir William's hand.

Sir William opened his mouth, but Garret did not wait to hear his words. The man quickly returned to join the others at the food table.

"This beef is delicious!" Wulff exclaimed loudly enough to seize Sir William's attention. The banker ravenously cut into another juicy piece. "Mr. Hanby," Wulff said, "it bleeds well. Excellent!"

"I told you so," Matthew said. "Here, try some wine."

The meal lasted nearly an hour, but eventually Sir William made his case and the board was formed. Emergency assistance would be provided for the relief of the poor.

Afterward, Matthew asked for a moment to speak to him. "I thought you might want to know," Matthew said softly. "Kellerman has lost his mind. Joseph told me." His head hung low.

"What do you mean?" Sir William asked, patting his friend on the shoulder. "Where has he gone?"

"No one knows," Matthew said, sadness all over his face. "He's just gone missing. He lost everyone."

"Everyone?" Sir William asked. "He lost another child?"

Matthew looked up. "He lost his wife and his children. They're all dead. The cholera took them all."

Chapter 25

S ir William kicked open the door.

It was pitch black and ice cold inside. He stepped back into the street and searched for something to see with. A mutilated copy of the *Isle of Man Weekly Gazette* blew down the narrow, grimy street. He snatched it up and formed it into a cone. He lit it with a match from his pocket and returned inside the home.

The fluttering torch cast ominous shadows of varying lengths to jitter across the walls and floor. He noticed the wobbly chair with the spindle legs lying broken in the center of the room where the table with the triangular shelf used to be. There were no dried flowers anymore.

He snapped the legs of the chair and placed them atop the cold ash in the fireplace and started a small fire with the newspaper and furniture pieces. Squatting down in front of it, he turned around on the toes of his shoes.

"Michael?"

He didn't expect an answer. He stood up and took a better look, now that the fire was burning and his eyes were adjusted.

There wasn't a stitch of cloth in the entire room. There was a bunk bed frame against the opposite wall. He didn't remember seeing that before. Like the rest of the furniture, it had been smashed in some way. Nothing remained hanging on the hooks around the fireplace, though implements were scattered about. There was no life, not even a crawling spider or scurrying rat.

A bag of English guineas lay in disarray against a corner as if it had been thrown. Sir William replaced the gold coins into the bag and pocketed it.

Outside, the air provided little refreshment to the staleness from within Kellerman's home. The stench of the sewers only allowed so much blowing breeze to remain untainted.

Sir William considered the sewers and the barely private outhouses along the street. He understood there was one outhouse to every ten flats. He wondered if that sort of hygiene had had anything to do with the spread of the deadly disease.

Where can he be? Where would I go, if I were in his place? Sir William stood up straight and looked up the hill. *Yes, of course.*

He ran across the south side, crossed over to Athol Street, and turned up the hill to St. George's Church.

That name had meant much over the years. He had married Frances in a St. George's Church. He had seen his son marry in this one. He had been involved with a glorious rescue of a ship by the same name. And now, he might perchance find his missing friend here.

He reached the entrance to the old church. The iron gate was cold to his touch in the December air. It squealed as he pushed it open. The light dusting of snow that remained on the hill was not to be seen on the streets below. Nevertheless, the thin winter blanket lay undisturbed here, though it did little to cover the scars of the plague. The earthen mounds made it obvious where the mass graves were. The indentation in the ground near the rear of the cemetery marked well the fire pit where many had been cremated.

Sir William stopped and surveyed every corner of the graveyard. Most of the markers were small white stones, though there was a section where simple sticks in the shapes of crosses stood all in a row, some of them leaning. There were a few mausoleums along the far edge. He turned around.

It was not possible to see the bay from this angle. He crossed nearer to the tombs and found a space where a sliver of the bay could be seen, at least during this time of year when little foliage remained to block the line of sight. He stared at the distant waters and was suddenly overcome.

He remembered the day he had gone fishing with Michael Kellerman. The man had only wanted to bring home some fish for his family.

Sir William wept.

He leaned against the gray slab of a tomb and slid down to sit in the snow-dusted pine needles and sticks. He rested his arms atop his knees and hung his head. He stayed there a long time.

He heard a squirrel bounding and hopping. He raised his head and stared.

Heaven help me.

It was not a squirrel.

He could have stood and run over but standing required too much time. Instead, Sir William raced on all fours to the hidden place behind the adjacent mausoleum, where Michael Kellerman lay writhing in the undergrowth.

"Michael," Sir William said, rushing to his friend's side and turning him over on his back. "You are alive."

Michael's skin was ashen, his face streaked with vertical lines of grime from his eyes to his throat. His eyes were set in a frightful stare. His lips were chapped and caked with dried blood. His hair was matted to his head like tar and his clothes were badly torn, almost shredded. In his clutches were a bonnet in one hand and a child's toy in the other.

Sir William dug his hands underneath his friend and pulled him up to embrace him. He squeezed him and rocked him, tumbling to fall against the back of the tomb. He twisted around to sit without releasing his protective embrace.

"Michael, Michael, Michael," he sobbed. "Michael, my friend, Michael."

Michael blinked. "They're gone," he said in a voice Sir William did not recognize. "Forever."

"For now, Michael," Sir William said, rocking him. "For now, but not forever."

Michael's eyes returned to a blank stare, but his mouth never ceased moving, forming silent words of sorrow.

February was blustery cold. The stately Fort Anne was blanketed in snow, its massive chimneys blowing large plumes of smoke into the night air, and its windows lit with the amber glow of oil lamps.

Sir William sat reading the newspaper in his favorite chair in the sitting room beside his master bedroom on the third floor. He wore his silk robe with paisley print and chewed on the mouthpiece of his unlit pipe. Beside him the marble-faced fireplace roared as the two year–dried hickory blazed with colorful leaping flames.

Outside, the cloudy sky moved and folded like gray molten fabric being tugged against the bottom side of the heavens. Rapid flashes of lightning appeared briefly in various places, backlighting the clouds. Booms like cannon fire rumbled from all directions in a series of echoes that rattled the windows of his home and likely the nerves of sailors at sea.

Emma and Sarah had gone to visit Augustus and the Christian household at Milntown near Ramsey. Augustus was visiting for a short time before returning to the mine in Cumberland.

Sir William was alone except for his staff of servants and Michael, who, although not yet fully recovered, was progressing nicely as a groundskeeper and, so far as Sir William knew, enjoying his modest cottage on the south side of the Fort Anne property.

Sir William, now sixty-two, gazed at the surroundings of his sitting room. The artwork was impressive, some of the finest pictures he had hoped to acquire now hung throughout his home. His investments were modest but consistent, and his reputation was solid and, he hoped, worthy of his title of baronet.

A large Bible lay open atop the stand alongside his chair. He had positioned it there in much the same way he had noticed the one in Wilberforce's apartment in London. He had even taken care to open the Bible in the same rough location, a little more than one-third of the way into the big book. He picked it up. For the first time he noticed the book and chapter he had unwittingly opened to. It was the book of Job.

Rabbit's foot. He smiled at the thought.

That's what the Bible was to him. He liked to keep it around. He hadn't read it at length in a very long time. Wilberforce certainly read his. He had told him so. Good for him.

Rumor was that the final passage of the slave emancipation bill that Wilberforce had labored his entire political life for was to be passed sometime this year. Sir William hoped so, for he also knew the magnificent member of Parliament was quite frail. Sir William closed his eyes and prayed for William Wilberforce. "May he see the fruit of his works, Lord." He opened his eyes and looked down at the Scriptures. He read a line from Job: "It collapsed on them and they are dead."

The verse stood out in the midst of the text. All else went gray. He immediately thought of Michael but didn't know why. He turned the page. It felt like onionskin in his hands. Another passage caught his eye: ". . . afflicted Job with painful sores from the soles of his feet to the top of his head."

Of course, Sir William thought. *The sufferings of Job.* Absorbed, he read the entire account. Finally he set the Bible down and considered it. He closed his eyes and the thunder boomed outside.

It boomed again.

And again.

Sir William sat up. He heard a fourth boom. *That isn't thunder!* He stood up and walked to the window and looked across the harbor toward the bay. *Unbelievable!*

He knew her shape. The five hundred–ton *Parkfield* had left Douglas Harbor earlier. It was supposed to be near Liverpool by now and then journey across the Atlantic Ocean to an American city, New Orleans. But there she was, fore and aft lights burning and firing emergency rockets. She was dragging her anchor chains and moving swiftly toward Conister.

He remembered the tower. It would offer some hope for the passengers and crew should they wreck, but Sir William hoped it wouldn't come to that.

He reached into his robe pocket and examined his watch. It was just after midnight—only three hours after her launching her maiden voyage. If she wrecked it would be ruinous to so many. He knew there were over sixty passengers on board. There was little time.

"Hattie!" Sir William yelled. "Hattie!"

It would be of little use to shout. She was on the second floor fast asleep. He knew it would take much time to stir the servants to prepare his horse. He would do it himself.

He quickly got dressed, rushed down two flights of stairs, despite his hurting joints, and raced out of his house.

Michael was in the yard, already standing by with two horses.

"Michael!" Sir William was astonished. "How did you know? Are you up to it, man?"

"I saw the rockets," Michael said. "I know you. It wasn't difficult to figure."

"God bless you, man," Sir William said, mounting his horse. "You needn't come, Michael. It is still soon for you."

Michael mounted. "I insist, sir."

"Very well," Sir William said. "With courage then."

"With courage, sir."

They galloped hard and fast into town.

By the time they had raced down the trail from Douglas Head, across the bridge over the river, and alongside the quay at the harbor, others had flocked to wonder at the predicament of the *Parkfield*. Among them were Joseph and Matthew.

"What is she doing back here?" Matthew asked.

Two tall men stepped up beside the hotel owner.

"Graves!" Sir William exclaimed. "Burbridge! You've returned!"

"Well, we can't jolly well leave all the exploits to you, now can we?" Lieutenant Burbridge said, older and with redder eyes.

"Good to see you, Sir William," Lieutenant Graves said, thinner but appearing well.

"And you," Sir William said, dismounting.

"I'll tie him up, sir," Joseph said, taking the reins and beginning to walk away. Suddenly, he stopped and noted Michael. "Kellerman? May I tie up yours also?"

Michael slid down from his mount and handed the reins to his old friend.

"Matthew," Sir William said. "We'll need the *Preservation* and maybe that modified boat of yours—if we have enough men."

"Modified?" Lieutenant Burbridge inquired.

"We've enabled double banks of oars," Matthew explained.

"That'll help," Lieutenant Graves said, raising his voice over the gusting wind. "But she's a large vessel. We'll need more."

"I'm on that!" Major Tobin said, rushing to the group. "I've four mortars." He shook the hands of his old friends.

"Precisely," Sir William said. "We'll need to fire hawsers to them from two mortars along the shore of the bay and two more from the end of the pier. We'll ferry passengers while the hawsers keep her from breaking up at Conister."

"My word!" Lieutenant Burbridge said. "That tower looks magnificent. It may come in handy."

"I hope not," Sir William said. "But if so, then thank God it's there."

"Thank Hillary," Matthew said.

"She's snapped!" a man yelled from the end of the pier. "All cables gone!"

The men rushed to the edge of the pier. The *Parkfield* had snapped the last of her anchor cables and was now rushing, stern first, on a swift sea directly for Conister. Suddenly, her stern dipped low and her bow swung around. There was a horrific crash.

"I'm afraid she's struck," Sir William said. "Major, attempt the mortars, they may help. You others, follow me, we must hurry. No telling what follows."

"Tragic!" Lieutenant Burbridge said. "I'm with you."

"Count me in," Lieutenant Graves said.

"Wait, Sir William," Major Tobin said. "You stay and look after the mortars. You can't risk another rescue. I'll go."

"I can't hit a mountainside with those things," Sir William said.

Isaac Vondy rushed to the group. "I'm here. Who is going?"

"Seems we all are," Sir William said.

"I'll fire the mortars if need be," Lieutenant Graves said.

"Very well," Sir William said. "Let's be snappy."

The men donned their cork jackets, ran to their stations, and in less than four minutes the *Preservation* was launched. Sir William manned the tiller while Burbridge, Michael, Vondy, Joseph, Major Tobin, Matthew, and others manned the oars. There were fifteen all told, and they muscled their way out of the harbor, rounded the point of the pier, and rode the bucking waves.

"She's a mean spirit," Lieutenant Burbridge grunted while rowing and breathing hard.

"We fight this old hag each time," Vondy said through gritted teeth. "We'll beat her Irish temper again."

"Can anyone tell me what the *Parkfield* is doing back here?" Matthew asked, straining to keep up with the stronger men.

"The captain must have turned her around midway," Sir William guessed. "He obviously judged a return trip safer than a crossing."

"He judged wrong," Vondy said. "Look!"

The rudder grounded and the large ship lifted and sank, each cycle bringing her closer to the highest rocks jutting from Conister. A great shattering added to the violent sounds of the storm.

A boom echoed from shore. All heads in the lifeboat turned but none stopped rowing. A black streak shot between them and the stranded ship and splashed into the sea.

Another boom sounded. A few seconds later another black streak shot across their view and something struck the rear quarter of the struggling *Parkfield*. It was the weighted end of a hawser rocketed from shore.

"Sure hope Graves sees us," Major Tobin said. "Those might help the *Parkfield*, but they could capsize us."

A third boom echoed.

Seconds later another streak flashed by and a weighted hawser landed atop the big ship. The passengers and crew cheered as they feverishly worked to secure the line. A fourth boom sounded and again landed a hawser within the bounds of the wrecking vessel. It was made secure.

"That will help," Sir William said. "I hope."

Suddenly a large wave pitched them high into the air. They were above the *Parkfield*'s angled decks and the passengers and crew craned their necks to watch Sir William and his men hurled high.

"It seems I'll fly yet!" the major said, his voice wavering.

Sir William could not believe it. Just as he had seen once before, his crew lifted from their seats as if they were floating above the thwarts they sat upon. They clung to their oar handles, but this time they had one other advantage. Sir William had learned from the Lukin accounts and had seen to it that his men were now fastened with safety lines. His men were safely tethered and were arrested in mid-flight.

Sir William rose high enough that he was unable to hold to the tiller arm, but he stopped short of sailing over the heads of his men as his safety line drew tight, tugged hard on his waist, and pulled him downward into the safety of the *Preservation*.

The lifeboat dropped into a deep trough, waves of towering water on both sides, then lifted as the sea beneath swelled and shot them forward into a mass of churning water. He pushed the tiller hard and, to his astonishment, the tiny boat answered, veering right to run alongside the struggling *Parkfield* just outside the treacherous breakers around her.

Men and women jumped, some of them clutching children, and each of them landing safely in the boat.

"Astounding," Sir William said, securing the passengers.

They were zipping past the bow of the big ship when suddenly the *Parkfield* lifted and then dropped fast to wedge between two columns of jagged rock. The bow split open, and others aboard the *Parkfield* tumbled to the foot of the tower. Two splashed into the sea.

Sir William cast cork buoys fastened to lines and reached two people in the surf. They clutched the lines, and Sir William strained to haul them in. Michael and Major Tobin assisted, and the two were recovered.

"Resume oars!" Sir William shouted.

The lifeboat skirted the area long enough to pull all those in the surf on board and then whirled around Conister to find a patch of calmer sea on the lee side. Sir William craned his neck to see the tower filling with grateful souls.

The people were wet and shivering, but they were alive. Husbands held their wives, and mothers clutched their children atop the parapets. Ominous though the castle appeared, the tower of refuge had no frightful tale to tell.

Sir William looked at his crew. They were all smiles, gazing up at the high tower, rising so eerily into the early morning sky. He spotted Michael now at the opposite end of the small boat. The widower was surveying the scene of stranded shipwreck survivors peering down and waving from above.

At first, Sir William thought Michael to be sobbing, but then he realized his friend's face was simply shivering, drenched with cold seawater. He wasn't crying, but he wasn't smiling. Only staring.

Chapter 26

"Wilberforce is dead," Sir William said, setting the *Isle of Man Weekly Gazette* on the stone bench.

"What's that?" Emma asked, sitting on a cushioned seat in the center of the garden within the eastern walls of the estate. The August sun was hot. Her bright yellow dress and parasol dazzled his eyes.

"You look lovely," Sir William said, standing and crossing to the dribbling fountain near her.

"Thank you, dear," Emma said. "Who died?"

"Wilberforce."

"Oh, that is sad," she said. "He was a saint."

"Yes," Sir William said. His thoughts traveled back to the time in the little man's apartment and to the evening at the tavern on Bishopsgate.

"He did much to abolish that horrific slave trade," she said.

"It's amazing, really," Sir William said. "The emancipation bill was passed on July twenty-sixth, just three days prior to his death."

Emma picked up her fan and waved it back and forth. "That is amazing."

"Someone in parliament was quoted in the paper," Sir William said, walking amongst a row of periwinkles. "I think it was Buxton who said it. He said that on the very night they closed out the minutest of details in the House of Commons, Wilberforce departed."

Emma stopped fanning. "Really?"

"Think of it," Sir William said, using his pocketknife to cut a short-stemmed flower from the purple plants and fixing it in his lapel buttonhole. "His life and labor ending on the very same day."

"That is most remarkable," Emma said. She resumed her fanning while lifting her face toward the sun. She closed her eyes.

"Be careful not to burn," Sir William said. "You know how easy that is for you." He walked around the pool with the center sculpture of a woman in Roman robes holding an urn. He approached the vine-covered arbor.

"Yes, dear," Emma replied without opening her eyes.

"The man was indeed remarkable," Sir William said. He examined the wine-colored berries on the vines. They were hard and smaller than he had hoped, but they were ripening in the sun, and the leaves were a hearty green. "His fight against slavery was marked by several defeats. Do you remember?"

"Generally, yes," Emma said, rising and walking around the sculpture while twirling her parasol.

"Defeated in '91 and then again in '92." Sir William retreated from his inspection of the arbor and looked down into the rippling pool at the base of the sculpture. The colored rocks at the bottom seemed to pulse with transforming shape. "He was soundly outvoted several times—for years. I remember it well."

"I am impressed, dear." Emma rested her parasol on her shoulder and laced her other arm within his. "I knew he had enemies, but I never realized he endured that many defeats."

"It wasn't until 1807, I think, that he had his first real victory," Sir William said.

"Blessed good for him," Emma said. "He never gave up."

Sir William looked up at the carved urn held in the arms of the statue. It gleamed in the sunlight. He wished the water flowed through it. "The slave trade was enormously profitable. Greedy men got roused and resisted him."

"Heartless men," Emma said.

Sir William stopped alongside the red, white, and yellow roses near the archway leading to the front lawns. "Such men are like those thorns—poking the sides of humanity and bleeding every noble deed, I suppose." He stared at the roses. "It makes sense to me now."

"What does, dear?" They wandered past the roses into the front lawn and casually strolled away from the house.

"Wilberforce said something to me one time," Sir William said. "He said—nearly predicted really—that opposition was certain to come. He sort of cautioned me, I think."

"It hasn't been easy. No one reads your appeals and suddenly funds them. It has taken much time."

"Perhaps. There was that one man—remember I told you about him? He stood up to oppose me at the tavern."

"Yes, I remember. But there was another who opposed him. Shut him up, if I recall. An angel, perhaps!" She smiled.

Sir William smiled and looked at her. Her usually marble white skin was flushed pink from the sun, her eyes as green as the leaves on the vines. Her galaxy of tiny freckles appeared more prominently upon her neck and shoulders now than in winter. He turned her around. "We must get you out of the sun."

They walked toward the front entrance.

"Wilberforce was a great man. All England will miss him, especially the people set free."

Emma squeezed his arm. "He was faithful to his call, as you are to yours."

Sir William patted her hand.

"How is Michael Kellerman doing, dear?" Emma asked. "I haven't noticed him for a few days."

They reached the door. He held it open for her. "Good that you ask. I gave him a few days off. He wanted to go fishing. It's been some time since he lost his family and, well, you can imagine, the remainder of the summer will only mark further anniversaries he has no cause to rejoice over."

"Yes," she said. "I do pray for him. He is doing well, don't you think?"

Sir William remained holding the door open. "Mostly, yes. He is scheduled to be around today. I think I will go look in on him. It is good that you've mentioned him."

Emma stepped into the house. "I will find Sarah, and we will take the carriage into town. Is there anything we can do for you while we're there?"

"Yes. Stop by Home's Bank and deliver my letter. It's on my desk. Give it to either Mr. Forbes or Mr. Wulff. It is my agreement to their proposal."

"Ah," Emma said, kissing him on the cheek. "The stock bank thing?"

"The joint-stock bank thing, dear," Sir William said, kissing her forehead. It was warm and moist. "We've been deliberating on this for quite some time. It is time to make it happen."

"Do be careful with these men," she said. "Honestly."

"Yes, dear. And you wear a large bonnet when outdoors. You're reddening considerably."

"I will," she said. "Don't forget my advice. I don't like that man—Wulff."

"You don't like his name, dear." Sir William purposely raised his eyebrows and tilted his head to urge her on her way.

She blew him a kiss and sauntered away.

He watched her every step to the stairs and then closed the door.

He faced the harbor. It was alive with activity today. Many triangular shapes of canvas cut through the waters, and a paddle wheeler chugged alongside the pier. He didn't notice any small boat that looked like Michael's and so thought to visit his friend in his cottage.

He headed toward the west end of the house, past the carriage house and gardener's sheds, beyond the stables, and up the gravel walk to Michael's quaint residence at the rear of the property. The gravel crunched under his calf-high boots.

He rapped on the wooden door. There was a wreath of dried sticks hanging on it. The door quickly opened and the wreath fell. Michael stood at the door fully dressed, save for his stocking feet. He looked well.

"Michael, good friend," Sir William said. He picked up the wreath and extended his other hand.

Michael shook his hand with a moderate grip and then took hold of the wreath. "Sir William. Come in, sir."

Sir William entered the small but nicely furnished home. Michael replaced the wreath on the door and closed it.

With the curtains closed, it was stuffy and mostly dark but for one tabletop lantern beside the wall under the window.

"It's dark in here," Sir William said.

"I'm sorry," Michael said, quickly moving to open some curtains.

"And warm. How can you stand it?"

"I'm sorry," Michael repeated and pushed open a window along the front wall. "Is that better, sir?"

"Anyway you like it is fine, Michael," Sir William said, feeling a little dizzy watching his friend scurry about. "I was only saying. No need to trouble yourself for me. What say we take a stroll?"

"If you like, sir." Michael began reluctantly tugging on a pair of crinkly boots.

"Michael," Sir William said, softening his voice, "what would you prefer?"

Michael stopped tugging. "I prefer to remain, sir."

Sir William nodded and sat down at the wooden table with the lantern on top. He motioned to the opposite seat.

Michael shucked off his boot and sat. "Thank you for the fishing time, sir."

"How did you do?"

"Very well. I've delivered quite a catch to Hattie in the kitchen."

"Did you keep any for yourself?"

"No, sir."

"Michael, be certain to retrieve your entire catch and store it on your own ice."

"No, sir. It's too great a catch. It would spoil."

"Very well," Sir William said. He glanced out the window. "However, I do insist you retrieve enough of the catch to stock on your own ice."

"Yes, sir."

"Might we leave the front door open, Michael? It's a bit thick in here for me."

"I'm sorry, sir," Michael said, hurrying to the door, opening it, and scurrying back to his chair. He gazed at Sir William.

The men sat silent for a long moment.

Michael's eyes darted from place to place.

"You seem nervous," Sir William said.

Michael nodded.

The silence continued.

"Well?" Sir William asked.

Michael nodded again.

Sir William could hear muffled voices outside. A lady laughed. He looked out the window and saw Emma and Sarah talking with the stableman outside of the carriage house. He looked back at Michael, whose eyes were lowered.

"Michael," he said, "how are you doing?"

"Well, sir . . ." Michael looked up, then darted his eyes away to the window, the fireplace, and then down at the table to remain for several seconds. He lifted his eyes and finally looked at Sir William. "Really, sir, I'm fine."

Sir William could hear Emma and Sarah talking and then the squeaking of springs and the creaking of wheels. He heard the noises of hitching the horse, the snapping of reins, and the rolling of wheels upon gravel, punctuated by the stomping of hooves. He was sure it was Sarah's laugh that he heard last as the sounds faded into the distance. He kept his gaze upon Michael.

Michael's eyes were red. "I am a wretch, sir."

Sir William didn't move. He was warm and could feel a drop of sweat rolling down the center of his back. He could imagine what it was doing to the appearance of his summer coat but still he sat.

"The object of wrath, I think." Michael's jaw tightened.

Sir William peeled off his coat and vest. He tugged his shirt from out of the waist of his pants and opened his cuffs. "Michael, talk to me."

"I don't know what to say." He shrugged. "I am a wretch. Forsaken by God." His cheek rippled like rollers crossing the sea.

"Ah, I see," Sir William said. He reached forward with both hands and pushed open the window over the table. The breeze was not cool, but it was moving. "You are angry with God."

"More like He is angry with me, sir," Michael said, appearing defiant as his face lifted and his lips pursed.

"Despite the catch?" Sir William said. He placed his hand over the top of the lantern and blew. The flame went out.

"What?"

"The catch. You said you had quite a catch of fish."

"A far cry from a fair exchange!" Michael said. His voice was strong.

"Exchange?"

"A string of fish for a family of four is no kind of trade." Michael's eyes became glass.

"I see. You are speaking of Anne and little Mike and Peter and Sylvia."

"People don't speak of the dead, sir." Michael's eyes lowered. The anger evaporated almost as quickly as it had come.

"You are a mix of feelings today, my friend."

Michael looked sideways, showing only the top of his head to Sir William.

"Michael, tell me more. What are you feeling?"

Michael snapped his head back, his face flushed red, his neck mapping with thickening veins. "I'm angry! I'm full of hate."

"You hate God?"

"I hate me! I am a wretch. What has God got to do with me? He does not even know that I exist, and if He does, He doesn't care." Sweat poured from his glistening hair and ran down the sides of his face.

"Why? Because your wife and children are gone?" Sir William remained calm, although he felt far from cool. Sweat still rolled down his back, and he wished they could have this conversation outdoors.

Michael rose to his feet. "Yes! They were snatched from me." His lips peeled back, baring his teeth. "Why? For no reason except that I am cursed."

He yanked the table away from the window and lifted it high over his head, scraping it against the rafters. He struggled to get it free of the interference to throw it down.

Sir William stood and held his arm. "You broke the furniture of your last home," he said with a low but firm tone. "Anniversary or not, you will not repeat such activity here."

Michael's face trembled for a moment, and his nostrils flared.

He loosened his grip on the table and allowed Sir William to lower it to the floor. Michael crossed the room to sit in a different chair.

Sir William arranged the table and crossed to the front door. He stood in the open doorway and then turned to face his friend. "You will walk with me. Put on your boots."

"I don't want to, sir."

Sir William stood in front of the man and looked down at him. "I don't care whether you want to or not. Put on your boots. I want to tell you about a story I recently read."

The walk along the seawall was refreshing. The breeze from across the harbor blew stiffly, and the sight of activity on the quay felt enlivening to Sir William. He walked the entire length of his seawall with Michael. They turned around and walked back the other way.

"I appreciate your efforts to help me, sir," Michael said, his tone indifferent. "But if I understand this tale of Job you've just shared, then I can only believe that, like him, my family was stolen by God, my future cursed by God, and my body ripe for disease at any time from God, all because God can do what He likes whenever He likes."

"Then you don't understand the story," Sir William said. "Many people interpret that story in a similar way. They think God randomly makes us suffer and we'd best accept that because He's God."

"I don't see any other conclusion, sir." Michael looked toward the harbor. "It rings true to me."

Sir William stopped and watched a schooner tying up near them on the opposite side of the harbor. He could see that Joseph was one of the men helping to tie her up. Beyond him was a group of well-dressed tourists preparing to go out for a ride in one of Hanby's pleasure boats. Sir William looked for his carriage but didn't see it. He turned toward his friend. "Your conclusion is incorrect, Michael."

Michael looked up at Sir William. "Then tell me, sir. I mean no disrespect, but if there's a point to this then please tell me."

"We all suffer," Sir William said. "It is a part of life. Everything we set out to do is resisted in some way."

"Maybe," Michael said. "But you have a great home, beautiful women, a fine—what do you call it?—repudiation, and no little money."

"Reputation," Sir William said, laughing. "Although repudiation sometimes fits."

"I have nothing," Michael said. "What little I had was snatched from me. I have lost everything."

"Did you have a brother who owned sugar plantations in South America?"

"What?"

"Did you have relatives who were friends of royalty?"

"I don't know what you mean," Michael said.

"Did you inherit an estate upon the death of a former wife or ever have sufficient funds to invest in speculative mines?"

"Of course not!" Michael said, his voice becoming higher-pitched.

"Such has been true for me," Sir William said. "But these are not works to boast of. They are gifts to be grateful for."

"I don't understand what you mean to tell me, sir. I know well enough I am poor." He walked a few steps away and thrust his hands down.

"That is not my point," Sir William said, following Michael. "The presence of wealth is nothing to be proud of, and neither is deficiency of wealth something to be ashamed of."

"Sir?"

"A man must not judge himself by his circumstances. That is not the measure used by God, and it is one we must avoid."

"I've heard that before, sir. From a friend of yours, I think."

"And?"

"As a matter of fact, it was the same man who gave me that bag of coins you returned to me. He claimed he heard it from you."

"And?"

"I do not believe it."

Sir William's heart sank. "Michael, my friend." His tone became sympathetic. He hoped not too much so.

"Please, sir." Michael's voice shook. "I do not welcome this conversation. I have little interest in what you are saying. May I be dismissed, sir?"

"Michael," Sir William said. "Listen to me. The point of the story of Job is that no matter what kinds of sufferings any of us encounter, and we all experience some sort"—he grabbed his friend's shoulders and held him firmly—"there remains a supply within us, sufficient to enable our rebound. A demonstration of something greater and more powerful than despair is promised."

Michael stood blank-faced. "May I leave now, sir?" Michael's voice trembled, but he didn't move.

Sir William released him. He exhaled and lowered his head. "I am sorry, Michael. I meant well."

Michael's face trembled.

"Yes," Sir William said softly. "Yes, you may go."

Michael partially turned as if expecting to be halted. He waited in a half-turned position, staring at Sir William. He took a hesitant step.

Sir William lowered his gaze and turned his back in order to give the man a sense of release. He heard Michael's steps move down the walkway and then heard them becoming more rapid and at last, in a full-out run. He turned around. Michael ran along the wall, leapt to the hillside and raced, occasionally on all fours, up the side of the hill toward the lawns atop Douglas Head. He disappeared over the ridge.

Chapter 27

"We are surrounded by three lovely ladies," Sir William said. He raised his glass of sherry from off the large rosewood dining table.

The large dining chamber in the center of the Fort Anne home was furnished with a mix of mahogany and rosewood furniture. Marble planters were filled with leafy plants. Romanesque statues as tall as men stood in the adjoining hallways, while statuettes of similar style, though smaller in form, were poised on every shelf.

Oriental carpets covered large areas of the floor, and the finest silk draperies hung from every window and in two of the four archways. The chandelier hanging in the center of the room held upwards of one hundred candles.

The fireplace displayed fine porcelain figurines arranged neatly atop the mantle while the fire blazed, the chandelier shone, and the food steamed.

"I should have been so lucky to find just one woman only half as beautiful as any of these," Major Tobin said. "I would be a content man."

"Hear! Hear!" Augustus said. "I am indeed content!"

The six of them clinked their crystal glasses.

"To be single is no deep burden," Sarah said, "when a family such as this is near."

Emma, Sarah, and Susanna wore luxurious dresses with heavily laced bodices and frilly petticoats peeking out at the bottoms. They were looped up with flowers picked from Sir William's gardens. The men were in fine black suits.

Hattie arrived with the next course.

"Lamb cutlets!" Major Tobin said. "I do have a taste for those!" Hattie scooped three of them onto his plate.

"Save some room, Caesar," Emma cautioned. "There is more to follow."

"This is an exquisite feast," Susanna said. "I do wish father and mother could have come. They would be indebted to Miss Hattie for life."

"As indeed all should be," Hattie said, arriving to serve Susanna with one cutlet and sauce. "If I recall," Hattie said, ladling from the bottom of the serving dish, "you appreciate a little extra juice upon yours."

"Mmm," Susanna said, "you rightly recall. And it does smell so delicious, Hattie."

"Roast duck and green goose to follow," Hattie said, moving around to Augustus. She looked across the table. "There will be plenty of raspberry creams and cherry tartlets, so prepare to loosen your belt some."

"Hattie!" Emma said. "Don't be crude."

"Where's the brandy?" Major Tobin asked. "I cannot provide you a perfect score until I taste the brandy."

"You are a most vile and unappreciative guest, Major," Hattie said, wagging a finger in his direction.

"Ha!" Sir William said. "You've been rightly found out at last, Caesar."

"All hail Caesar!" Major Tobin said.

"Snow and hail on Caesar!" Hattie said, returning to the kitchen.

The group laughed.

"Augustus," Sir William said, "tell us more about the coal mine. How does it fare?"

Augustus gave a sideways glance to his wife and then looked down the length of the long table toward his father seated at one end. "It is costly on the front side, Father. As you know—"

"We know!" Major Tobin said. "Our own mine at Laxey was costly at first."

"Indeed it was," Sir William said.

"It's coming along though, Father," Augustus said. He stuffed a large piece of cutlet into his mouth.

"Well," Sir William said, looking at Emma at the opposite end of the table. She was busy slicing her cutlet. "We understand the process. Don't fret, son. She'll yield greater amounts as time goes on. I've heard Cumberland is a good mine."

"I share your enthusiasm, Sir William," Susanna said. "As do my parents. We are yet hopeful."

"Indeed, you should be hopeful," Sir William said. "In fact, you have more reason to be, not less."

"How so, Father?" Augustus asked, reaching for one of the several baskets of hot breads.

"I've recently purchased shares in a joint-stock bank."

"So you did it then?" the major asked, sipping his drink.

"I did." Sir William smiled and lifted his glass. "Another toast!"

"Hear! Hear!" Major Tobin said, lifting his.

Sarah wiped one corner of her mouth with her linen while lifting her glass with the other. "Bravo! Has the baronet more to report?"

"Joint stock?" Susanna asked. "What is that, sir?"

Sir William laughed. "Something we will all enjoy jointly."

Augustus and Susanna lifted their glasses, their faces filled with confusion, though Augustus smiled.

"Not I!" Major Tobin said with a quick laugh. "But I'll toast with you just the same."

"There's still time," Sir William said to his brother-in-law.

"Time for what?" Emma asked, a neutral look on her face as she lifted her glass.

"Time to become a fellow shareholder, of course," Sir William said. He stood. "Lady Sarah may enjoy her fifty shares, and my fine son and his lovely wife now own seventy-five shares, as do Lady Emma and myself!"

The major stood and the others followed.

"Hear! Hear!" the major said. "To many more shares of many more revenues." He tipped his glass nearly upside down to swiftly empty it down his throat. "Ah! May the funds never cease to flow!"

The others followed in more moderate fashion and resumed their seats.

"What manner of banking is it, Father?" Augustus asked as Hattie returned.

"Green goose!" she announced. She used both hands to hold a large silver-covered platter and set it down on the table in front of Sir William. She lifted the cover, and a cloud of steam rushed to his face.

"Mmm," Sir William said. "We feast as royalty tonight."

Hattie sliced two thick pieces and placed them on a second plate, right beside Sir William's dish of cutlets. She recovered the platter and moved to the other end to serve Emma.

"Thank you, Hattie. It smells lovely." Emma looked across the length of the table. "Tell us, dear. Explain the joint-stock bank. It's never been completely clear to me."

"Certainly," Sir William said. "It is a consortium of investors who have pooled resources with Home's Bank in order to be more suitably positioned to finance development on the isle and most especially here in Douglas."

"It is a fact," Major Tobin said. "We are booming these days."

"Quite," Sir William said. "As the community continues to experience such happy progress and stimulating growth, we stand to make additions to our fortune by lending money to a diverse portfolio of developing projects."

"Like what?" Augustus asked.

"Tell them about Falcon Ridge," Sarah said. "That one is particularly interesting."

"Yes," Sir William said, feeling chipper. "Most interesting. It seems there is an increasing demand for gentlemen's villas as more and more come-overs are seeking summer homes here. They're eyeing the wooded slopes of Falcon Ridge, just behind the center of town."

"Excellent proximity to Athol Street," Augustus said, nodding.

Hattie finished serving two large pieces of goose to the major, but he touched her hand and nodded for a third. "You're a hungry one!" Hattie said, complying. She carried the platter to the other side of the table.

"And the ridge affords lovely views," Sarah added.

"I see it," Susanna said with a large smile. "Gentlemen's villas? Your motives in this are quite clear, my sweet sister."

Sarah laughed and waved her hand. "Nonsense!" she exclaimed. "I am the happiest spinster on the isle. Can any gentleman provide for me as my own adopted mother and father have? I'll not be moving anytime soon."

"Although she may find herself strolling atop the walk at the seawall a little more than usual," Emma said, smiling.

Sarah and Susanna laughed.

"This goose is absolutely to crow for," Major Tobin blurted. "Hattie, you are a genius."

"Geese don't crow," Hattie said as she finished serving Augustus and Susanna. "But I'm happy for any man that crows over my cooking."

"I am as happy as a goose," Major Tobin said.

"As loony, maybe," Hattie said. "Don't worry, I'm fetching the brandy next."

"Ha! You are well trained, dear Hattie. Well trained."

"Then you are feeling positively about this bank deal, Father?" Augustus asked. "Mmm, this goose melts upon the tongue."

"Yes," Sir William said, placing a large chunk of meat into his mouth. "Mmm, it is delicious. The spices are most active."

"What do you think, Lady Emma?" Augustus asked.

"I think I am full," Emma said with a pleasant smile, gently pushing her plate away. "There is only so much this tiny frame can hold."

"Tiny?" Sir William asked. "Nay, dear woman. Perfect, I say."

"Ha!" Major Tobin bellowed. "Sixty-two and still frisky as any young cadet."

Emma smiled. "I am glad you approve, dear husband. Let us hope you still value my opinions as well."

"Touché!" Major Tobin said. He grabbed a roll and buttered it thickly.

Sir William grinned. "I always will."

"Is there another conversation here I do not understand?" Augustus asked with a smirk.

"Wulff!" Emma said.

"Brandy!" Hattie announced upon entering the room.

"Not wolf, duck," Major Tobin said. "It's my favorite dish that Hattie makes, and she's saved it for last. No doubt for my pleasure."

"As is everything that goes on in the world, Major," Hattie said, pouring his first. "All exists for the pleasure of Major Caesar Tobin." She lightly tapped him on the top of his head and moved to Sarah.

"Well-trained and well-schooled," Major Tobin said. He lifted his glass and drank a singular toast to Hattie.

"Emma refers to a man by the name of Wulff," Sir William said. "She does not trust him. He's one of the bankers."

"It's hard to trust a man who has difficulty looking you in the eye," Emma added.

"Wulff's been around," Major Tobin said. "Home's Bank has previously done well. There are no grievances against him so far as I know."

"I see," Augustus said. "But you don't trust him, Lady Emma?"

Emma exhaled. "I don't know. It's an intuition thing."

"Well then." Susanna lifted her glass as soon as Hattie filled it. "You know that I do not drink brandy, but I shall lift my glass in toast to godly favor upon this venture. May His will be done."

"Fair enough," Sir William said. He lifted his glass and took a sip. It burned.

"When will we get a taste of that duck, Hattie?" Major Tobin asked her.

"When it stops quacking, I'm certain," she replied.

"Quack! Quack!" Major Tobin said, lifting his glass. "I propose a toast. May we all age as perfectly as this fine wine." He gulped it down.

Part 4

In this world you will have trouble. But take heart!
I have overcome the world.

John 16:33

Chapter 28

Sir William and Emma walked the grounds of Fort Anne. He moved slowly and with less flexibility. His thinning hair was mostly gray with a few strands of black.

"I'm impressed with Falcon Ridge," Emma said. "Over the last several years, it has taken a better shape. The gentlemen's villas under construction ought to be filled in a few months, I've heard."

"Yes," Sir William said, a handful of envelopes in his grasp. With the other hand, he pressed much of his weight onto his cane. "Supposedly by summer." They exited the eastern garden and stopped at one of the new stone benches he had installed about the property. He groaned as he sat. "These blasted joints of mine feel as dry as dust."

"It's the rheumatism, dear," Emma said. "You should soak this afternoon."

"I desperately want to speak with your brother about aspects of the development."

"He's too ill to leave the farm. Perhaps we should visit him this week." She sat beside him. Her lime-colored dress flowed loosely. She removed her sun hat.

He thumbed through the envelopes, reading the return addresses. "I keep waiting for this stiffness to lessen with the warmer weather."

He held up an envelope and smiled. "Like last year."

"If it's too much, dear, I can have the sedan chair brought for you."

"No!" he said. The spring sun was too warm. He could feel beads of sweat on his forehead. "I detest that thing. It makes me look wretched." He fumbled with a small knife from his pocket.

"Let me help you."

"Bah!" He sliced the envelope open.

Emma put her arm around his neck and leaned on his shoulder. "The sedan chair makes you look like royalty," she said softly.

"Bah!" he said again. He read the letter, shook his head, and replaced it with the others. "You should keep your hat on. You know how quickly you burn."

"Yes, dear," she said, replacing it. "I'm serious about the chair."

"I don't want to discuss it. Let's go around to the front. I want to see the harbor." He groaned as he planted his cane and pulled himself up. "If it isn't my knees, it's my back."

Emma assisted him as he straightened.

He stepped forward. All his joints burned, but he plodded on. "Come along, Emma."

"You are stubborn," she said, lacing her arm in his.

They moved slowly to angle across the front yard and toward the northern edge of the grounds.

"What did Augustus have to say?" Emma asked.

"Hm?"

"The letter." She pointed to the packet in his hand.

"Oh." His lips felt cracked. "Challenges at Cumberland. He wants to visit, but his hands are full with the mine."

"Did he ask for more money?"

"Ah!" Sir William stopped and carefully pointed with his cane. "The harbor is active today." He lowered his cane and shifted his weight upon it.

Emma squeezed his arm and rested her head on his arm.

"I miss braving the storms," he said. "I miss working with the others."

"I know."

"I wonder how Michael Kellerman is doing," Sir William said. "We haven't heard from him in a while."

"I heard he purchased a small cottage by the river in the hills behind Woodville."

"Good for him," Sir William said. "I hope he has found his peace." He gazed past the harbor and to the Tower of Refuge in the center of the bay. "His own cottage, you say?"

"You paid him well, dear," Emma said. She stepped in front of him and looked west. "Look at Falcon Ridge. It's grand!"

He looked to his left and saw the development on the sloping hill behind Douglas. Every time he looked at it he felt ill. "I wish Caesar were well."

"Whenever I see a new dwelling built there," Emma said cheerfully, "I am grateful you went ahead with your plans to be involved with it. It is good for Douglas, don't you think?"

"Let's go in, dear," Sir William said, feeling lightheaded. "It is too warm."

Three days later, Sir William sat staring through the rain-streaked windowpanes of his library. It was his favorite sanctuary these days. The surrounding walls of books helped him feel connected. His nearby writing desk was important should he find the strength to write one more appeal. He shifted in his seat while Sarah looked on.

"I'll help you, sir." Sarah reached around him and adjusted the pillows in a better way and arranged the blanket perfectly.

He thought her lovely. Her blond hair and blue eyes had never changed their shade that he could tell. Her face was not as slender as he remembered from long ago but still appeared soft and feminine, despite the wrinkling. Her smile remained endless all these years. "Thank you, daughter."

"You've had a stream of visitors today," she said. "Are you sure you aren't ready to rest upstairs?"

"You know how business is." His voice was raspy. He cleared his throat. "Water would be nice."

She poured him a glass from the pitcher on the side table. "Always my pleasure, Poppa." She placed a very small pillow behind his neck and kissed him atop his head.

"Sir," Hattie said, appearing in the doorway, "Mr. Dumbell to see you."

"Send him in, Hattie." His voice sounded weaker than he preferred. He cleared his throat and struggled to adjust the pillows around his hips and lower back. "Help me with my posture, dear." He fumbled with a blanket to cover up the props.

Sarah handed him the glass of water and quickly made his pillows right. The water felt cool on his throat.

"Sir William!" Willard Dumbell shattered the tranquility. "Good day, sir."

Sarah exchanged courtesies with the lawyer and left the room behind Hattie.

Dumbell was dressed sharply in blue, with no sign of the rain. Hattie had no doubt intercepted his cloak, gloves, and hat. He held loosely to his cane.

"Do come in, Willard," Sir William said. His voice was strong.

Dumbell stepped before him and tipped his head. He sat down in the chair opposite, placing the cane across his lap. He sat so straight that Sir William felt inclined to straighten himself. The shifting dislodged the pillow behind his neck to protrude from one side.

"As you know," Dumbell said, "the lottery for the sale of the remaining Falcon Ridge lots is scheduled for June, and we ought to consider a proper promotional strategy to ensure our success."

"Promotions?" Sir William wanted to appear slightly dull. Better to elicit whatever ideas Dumbell had than to begin making suggestions too soon. He reached up to adjust his pillow. The angle of movement was painful but he fought his own private war to maintain a peaceful countenance.

"Yes, sir."

Sir William allowed his smile to relax but offered no speech. He adjusted the pillow around his neck and lowered his arm. Sweat rolled down his back. It begged a scratch.

"Yes, well, uh, there is cost related to such a strategy," Dumbell said. "I thought you might want to discuss what you are prepared to do."

The rain pattered against the window. Through the wet glass, the lawn was a blur of green and the distant bay a muddled gray.

"What *I* am prepared to do?" Sir William asked. His emphasis pleased him. "I was hoping you came here to tell me we've sold some reasonable number of lots. That would be news."

Willard Dumbell's neck lengthened, appearing straighter and more rigid than before. "But of course." His head cocked to one side.

Despite the water-streamed glass, Sir William saw tiny crests of white snake around the bay, bursting into spray, only to be reformed elsewhere and burst again.

"Sir?" Dumbell repositioned his head to be in line with Sir William's gaze. "You must realize the importance."

"Of what?" Sir William said, returning his eyes to peer into Dumbell's.

"Of promotions, man," Dumbell said, flustered well before Sir William had expected him to be. The man leaned forward, his legs spread and his cane planted onto the floor. "You must see how vital proper promotions are to our success. Do you not?"

"Of course," Sir William said. Behind Dumbell, through the window, the rains were lessening. Across the lawns, a giant tower of saltwater spray flew up but he couldn't make out if it was from the pier wall or the rocks of his own Douglas Head shore. He looked at Dumbell and smiled. "What about it?"

"There's a cost to doing it right." Dumbell punctuated his last word with a cane tap.

"Of course there is," Sir William said, nodding his head vigorously, despite the shots of pain it triggered in his spine. "But why speak to me of such? I have invested more than anyone at this juncture."

"Yes, you have," Dumbell said, relaxing enough to lean back in his chair. He replaced his cane atop his lap. "And you have the most to gain."

"Perhaps," Sir William said, purposely showing no emotion and staring right back at the lawyer. He knew Dumbell's negotiating tactics well and was determined to play every countermeasure to the fullest. Whatever frontage was displayed, Dumbell's own impatience and arrogance would force him to spill the entire matter of his purpose before too long. Dumbell's face was already glistening. "Is it too warm in here?" Sir William asked.

Dumbell's face contorted several times before the word came out. "What?"

"Sometimes the rain makes the air sticky. Shall I call for a hand fan?" Sir William asked.

Dumbell stood up and inhaled deeply.

Sir William tilted his head back to behold the man and was glad there was no corresponding tingling of pain in his vertebrae. "Perhaps you want to continue this discussion at a later date?" Sir William asked, feigning a misinterpretation of the man's stance.

Dumbell's posture slumped.

Sir William labored to hold back the corners of his mouth.

"Sir William!" Dumbell said louder. "You are the one who first suggested the lottery method of making the deeds available for general sale. You are the one with the most to gain and the most to lose."

"Yes," Sir William said as calmly as a flat sea.

"You are the one who took the measures of buying up the majority parcels at Falcon Ridge. You are the one paying the bulk of the land rents until the developments are sold. If we are to be successful in sales of sufficient amounts," he said, pacing about the room, "then we must prepare a strategy of promotion designed to accomplish such ends." He stopped with hands clutching his cane horizontally behind his back, silhouetted in front of the window.

The sun broke through a small patch in the cloudy sky and, helped by the wetness upon the window, made something like trails of rocket flares around the side of Dumbell's head. It appeared artistic to Sir William.

"Impressive," Sir William said.

"Thank you," Dumbell said. He resumed his seat opposite Sir William.

"If I were to continue to take on such a central role," Sir William said, "it would appear that I am singularly spearheading a personally designed scheme for profiteering."

"Aren't you?" Dumbell asked with a disturbing coolness.

"Falcon Ridge makes sense for Douglas."

"Of course. It just so happens to be enormously profitable—"

"I am not doing it for mere profit," Sir William said with slightly more volume than he intended. "Although to attempt it without a profitable outcome would be foolhardy."

"If it is to be profitable," Dumbell said, slowly spinning his cane upon his lap, "it must be properly promoted. If it is *not* promoted, then it will indeed become a foolhardy venture." He rested his head upon the upholstered chair, his eyes looking down his nose. "You must further underwrite some considerable promotions."

"Why do you not seek such support from the others?" Sir William sat up. The pillow behind his neck dropped behind his back. It did not matter. He shifted forward in his seat and threw off the blanket. He swung his legs to the side and pushed himself out his chair by pressing hard on the armrests. His joints pulsed with pain. He made short steps to the window. "Come here."

Dumbell sighed but followed.

Sir William pointed out the window. "Tell me what you see."

Dumbell frowned. He stared out the window for several seconds. "Weather," he said. "Too much weather."

"What else?" Sir William asked. "What else is out there?"

"I don't know, Sir William," Dumbell said, sounding distressed. "What? There are many things. Air. Water. Boats. Rocks. What?"

"Look harder!" Sir William said.

"I see opportunity." Dumbell suddenly spoke lightly. He smiled and breathed in deeply. "Yes, I see opportunity."

"For what?" Sir William asked. His knees shook with pain.

"To sink or to sail," Willard Dumbell said. "It is your choice." He looked smugly at Sir William. "What do you see?"

Sir William felt his shoulders lower. This was not going how he had hoped. It played out differently from when he and Wilberforce had stared out the window in London. "Something different than you."

His energy was tapped. He walked back to his chair, every step a concentration of control to make his frame appear comfortable and strong. At last he reached his chair and grabbed the armrests. His arms and shoulders bore all of his weight as he lowered himself into his seat. He looked up at Dumbell, standing in front of him.

"Let us hope you soon see it as I do," Dumbell said. "Or you will lose much money."

Sir William folded his hands in his lap. "I am weary of being the largest underwriter. There's no end to your justifications for requests. I will offer no more funds to the project. You'd best find support from others who have yet to do their part."

"That's your reply, sir?" Dumbell asked, his voice shaking.

Sir William closed his eyes. "I will consider it."

"Thank you," Dumbell said, his voice calmer. "I will show myself out."

Sir William opened his eyes. Dumbell was gone. Through the window, he saw the sun retreating and the rains return.

Chapter 29

The rains did not cease all summer long, a fact that kept many vacationers away.

"Sarah skipping breakfast, again?" Emma asked.

"I suppose," Sir William said, preoccupied.

Emma crossed to him and lightly massaged his neck. "You are so quiet today. What is troubling you?"

"I fear the Institution is quite low on funds," he said, crunching a piece of dark toast.

"Please don't think we can help them. You have done so much already."

"I don't know what Thomas Wilson is doing in London. As president of the Institution, I really expected him to be more productive in raising sufficient annual subscriptions."

"I agree. Though we should remember that finances are tight throughout the empire, dear."

"Yes." His tea was lukewarm. "But how can we preserve lives from shipwreck without ongoing subscriptions? It's not possible. It should be so much better established by now. After all these years, it all remains so tenuous."

"Like I said, my dear," Emma said between bites of crispy sausage, "make sure you don't go making any pledges. It will work out, you'll see."

"I wouldn't think of making pledges. We've spent enough money on Falcon Ridge and Cumberland."

"You don't mean more, do you?"

He nodded and looked at her sideways.

"More money?" Emma asked. Her hand fidgeted around the corner of her mouth. Sir William worried. She never did that. "How much more?" she asked.

"The summer weather kept buyers away, dear," he explained. "We've had to modify our plans."

"What do you mean, 'modify'?"

"A few more promotions," he said, not bothering to look up. He dipped his toast in the sausage gravy. "We've altered the type of lottery draw and a few other things. No worries."

"How much?"

"Don't fret, my love," he said, trying to keep the conversation calm. "Let's discuss the lifeboat issues. That's what's on my mind."

Emma was firm. "How much, William?"

"About four thousand pounds." He sipped his tea.

Emma gasped and started crying.

"Do not fear, Emma," Sir William said. He touched her elbow.

"Do not fear?" Emma pulled away and sat up straighter. She pushed her breakfast plate away and rose. Her cashmere gown flowed as she crossed to the fireplace on the near side of the morning room. "William, are we spending too much?"

"We are a little leveraged, dear. We are not in any kind of critical state. All will unfold nicely. You'll see." It hurt to stand, but he did and, with a bend in his posture, slowly walked near her but did not reach out. He held onto the mantle.

"William," Emma said, facing him. Her eyes were red. "You have undertaken extreme lines of credit from that Forbes and Wulff bank for the lands, the promotions, the rents, and for all I know, countless other things. Can we repay them?"

"You do not understand the process," Sir William said. "The bank could not issue such lines without guarantees from someone, so they came to me. It's a protocol. Nobody will actually have to pay them. The lot sales will cover the debts with large profits left over."

"The lot sales?" She shook her head, her hands rigid in the air. "What lot sales?"

Sir William didn't like it when she spoke in such a tone that her bottom teeth were bared. "I admit I did not anticipate the severe rains all summer long."

"You did not anticipate much, it seems."

Her rude reply was a sharp knife. It was like his anchor cable being cut. "Forgive me for not controlling the weather!" His voice was loud enough that he knew there would be no servants approaching the room anytime soon—so much for any hope of hot tea.

Emma shook her head. "What if the lots don't sell?"

His face was hot. Sweat rolled down his back. He clenched his teeth together and focused on breathing deep. After a few moments, he was able to speak with more control. "They will sell." He turned and slowly walked away.

"William!" Emma snapped at him.

He trudged away.

"William!" Emma shouted his name.

He left the room, wanting hot tea.

One week later, Fort Anne was covered in a silent blanket of snow. The doctor had left Sarah's bedchamber the evening before, suggesting she would recover in a day or two. He could not explain her extreme fatigue, the sudden weakness, or the rapid onset of chills. "She will be fine," he said. "Give her time."

Sarah lay with her bedcovers pulled to her neck, her face pale and trembling. Her eyes were squeezed shut, and her forehead was a maze of wrinkling. She mumbled, but neither Sir William nor Emma knew what she said.

"Try and rest, daughter," Sir William said. As much as the cold weather had aggravated his rheumatism, it hurt more to see Sarah unfit.

Emma kissed Sarah's forehead and tried to smooth out the wrinkling with her hand. "She is so warm."

"What is this sickness?" Sir William was frustrated. "Should we call the doctor back?"

"He said she would pass through it," Emma said. "Her fever needs to break. I will get some cold cloths."

"Hattie!" Sir William spoke loudly.

Hattie appeared outside the door. "Yes, sir?"

"Please bring some ice and cold cloths."

"Yes, sir." Hattie quickly rushed away.

"It is best for you to stay by her side." Sir William grunted as he pushed himself up to stand.

"Where are you going?" Emma asked, reaching for one of his hands. Her touch was warm.

"To our sitting room. I must ponder some things."

"Do not go down the stairs without assistance," Emma said, patting his hand.

"I won't. I won't." He kissed his fingertip and gently touched Sarah's cheek. "Be well, daughter." He kissed it again and touched his wife's nose. "Sweet Emma." He turned and began what seemed like a million steps to leave the room.

"No stairs, dear," Emma said from behind him.

"No stairs," he repeated without turning around.

The sitting room next to his bedchamber was toasty warm, thanks to Hattie. She never missed seeing the fireplaces lit in all the rooms he utilized the most. These days, the number of rooms he used was not great. He loved his library, was often found in this sitting room, still slept in his and Emma's bedchamber, and was good for at least two meals in the morning room. He rarely visited the dining room, and it had been nearly a year since the west side ballroom was filled, although a celebratory lifeboat dinner was due to happen there soon, unless he canceled it.

At last, he reached a comfortable chair. He slowly sank into the cushions. He fumbled with a few pillows, but it was too painful to try and place them just right. He missed Sarah. She always knew just where to put them.

When did I get old? Life had been so filled with adventurous experiences, and then suddenly he found himself flung into a different time and space. It was like that time when he had ventured out to rescue those aboard the *St. George*. So much precision and muscle and strategy to reach it and then—whoosh!—he was flying through some massive wall of sea. Before he could even imagine what was happening to him—slam! He was smashed against the hull with broken bones.

He smiled. He remembered he did recover from that rescue, and some of his greatest accomplishments followed—the Tower of Refuge, the numerous Institution awards and, most of all, the preservation of many lives. These were all good things, and yet it felt so vulnerable.

He grieved. It hurt too much to write further appeals.

Chapter 30

"The lottery was successful!" Sir William proclaimed. He stood at the foot of Sarah's bed.

Emma sat on a bedside chair, mending one of Sarah's things. "It's a miracle," Emma said. "Another fine outcome. We are fortunate."

Sarah sat up in bed, nursing a bowl of steamed oats. "These are so dry," she said, her voice raspy.

"Hush, dear," Emma said. "Just pretend you are eating the finest of seabird delicacies, to the chagrin of the baronet."

Sarah smiled weakly. She placed her hand upon her chest and coughed. "I'll try."

"It is what the doctor says will improve your strength," Sir William said. "Look how much better you have already become."

It had been one month, much longer than any had anticipated, but Sarah was finally improving.

"I do hope we may stop him bleeding me soon," Sarah said, squeezing her eyes shut while she chewed.

"We must do what he says is best," Emma said.

"Do you need me to sign any withdrawals, sir?" Sarah asked, setting her bowl aside and shifting to lie down. "There remains little in the account of my name."

"Don't trouble yourself about that now," he said.

"I want to be of help." Sarah coughed and held her head.

"Are you all right, daughter?" Sir William bent over and placed a hand on her knee.

Sarah took several breaths and then smiled. "Yes, Poppa." She closed her eyes.

"We should all begin receiving dividends soon," he said. "I hope we can resume making deposits instead."

Emma pricked her finger. "Ouch!"

"May I have some tea?" Sarah asked.

"Of course." Sir William started to rise.

"No, no!" Emma said. "You sit here, dear. I'll do it."

"I'm sorry," Sarah said. "It's just that my throat is so dry."

"Do not fret, Sarah," Emma said, setting down her sewing, sucking on her fingertip, and crossing to a table that bore a teapot and cups. "William, tea?"

"Yes, please."

Emma served everyone, including herself, and resumed a seat after moving another chair beside her husband. "I hope they distribute soon."

"It's important we do not appear too eager for profits," he said.

"William," Emma said with mild surprise, "we have no need to justify our reputation. You are well loved and have done much good for this isle, perhaps more than anyone. Besides, we *are* eager." She laughed.

"Most undoubtedly, sir," Sarah said, her voice faint but kind. She rested her teacup on the flat of her stomach and lowered her head to her feather pillow.

"One can never be too careful," he said. "Anyways, after a near failure with the lottery due to the foul weather last summer, we had to restructure the whole thing. It was nowhere near as profitable as first imagined, but it turned a slight profit, thankfully."

"Not that we've seen it yet," Emma said. "But we will, soon. Right, dear?"

"Quite right," Sir William said. "Mmm, the tea is perfect."

"As is everything you put your hand to, Poppa," Sarah said. She smiled and rested her eyes.

Sir William sipped his tea. It was hot and mildly bitter, just as he liked it. He also liked it when Sarah called him by such an affectionate name. "Well, it covered all the costs I had put our names on the line for."

"Thank God!" Emma said, sipping her tea. "Mmm, this is good."

"The profits were deposited into the joint-stock bank and are due to be passed to us," Sir William said, mildly shaking his head as he sipped some more tea.

"We have to rely on the good graces of Forbes and Dumbell for that," Emma said. "I hope they are as timely as they are shrewd."

Sir William swallowed. "And Phillip Garret. He is on their board. I wouldn't have made us all shareholders if not for Phillip's assurances. It seems his advice has proved sound."

"Mr. Garret will be at the Lifeboat Dinner, won't he?" Sarah asked, opening her eyes. "You can both flank him then and secure our dividends." She laughed weakly.

"Jolly funny, daughter," Sir William said. "Jolly funny."

"Be careful of your tea, dear," Emma said. "You might spill it."

"Will you take mine?" Sarah said, yawning. "I am tiring again." She closed her eyes.

"Of course, dear," Emma said, standing and reaching for the cup. She removed it to the tray and refilled her own. "I'm looking forward to the banquet. It's only one week away."

"Eight days, dear. Should we go through with it? It is a costly endeavor, and with Sarah still recovering, I'm wondering."

Sarah opened her eyes. She let forth an energized laugh.

Sir William observed the amusement on her face. He smiled. "What?"

"You proposing prudence while Lady Emma encourages a banquet," she said. "If that is not a reversal, there never has been one in the world."

The three of them laughed until Sarah's coughing begged them to stop. When it had subsided, and at Sarah's insistence, they saluted the upcoming banquet with one more sip of hot and bitter tea.

Chapter 31

"Hear! Hear!" Phillip Garret said from near the center of the long head table. He was dressed impressively in a black suit with long tails and white silk shirt. He held his glass high. "To Sir William, whose tireless efforts made possible such a grand organization as the National Institution for the Preservation of Life from Shipwreck!"

Sir William looked up. He would rather have seen Major Tobin standing there as he always had at special occasions past, but his brother-in-law was too ill to travel, so Garret would have to do. He was also sorry Augustus and others from the deemster's household were unable to attend, but the Cumberland Colliery predisposed them.

"Hear! Hear!" the crowd of men and women cheered.

The west side ballroom was lavishly adorned with fancily lettered banners, streams of wide and colorful ribbons, and several nicely arranged displays of newspaper accounts, medals, and nautical souvenirs. Hattie and the servants and some of the wait staff from the York Hotel milled about with trays and drinks.

"What's more," Garret said, "he puts on one fine feast!"

Sir William looked down the table. He saw many familiar faces. Joseph and Michael Kellerman sat at one end. Michael seemed well, occasionally smiling.

Lieutenant Robinson and Isaac Vondy sat at the other. Matthew Hanby, his wife, and both Burbridge and Graves and their wives sat near the middle on either side of him and Emma. Everyone was a little heavier and a little grayer but in good spirits. No one appeared to be as bottled up with rheumatism as he.

The *Preservation* lifeboat had been brought up on a carriage and situated in the center of the room in memoriam to those who had braved the seas but hadn't made it home. Despite a few scrapes, the lifeboat remained seaworthy.

The crowd was comprised mainly of lifeboat men and their families, although there were some subscribers and supporters.

Dumbell and Bluett sat at a table with Lieutenant-General Stapleton, and could it be? It was! He wondered why Monty Jones had shown up, but then Sir William remembered he had recently charged over two hundred–pounds worth of shoes from the man's store, which he had purchased for the south side children for Christmas. This must be Jones's way of showing appreciation.

Wulff and Forbes sat at a table with Mungo Murray, who had previously made token contributions to the lifeboat organization. He wished it had been more. The entire organization was suffering from a dearth of monies.

Lifeboats were falling into disrepair and damaged tools of the trade were not being replaced. Worst of all, widows weren't receiving what the Institution had promised to provide. For Sir William, that was unacceptable. It was the heart of what he had fought for—the most important purpose of all.

"Speech! Speech!" the crowd cried, begging for Sir William to address them. "Speech! Speech!"

He waved his arm and the crowd slowly grew quiet. He whispered to Graves, who in turn whispered to Burbridge, and the two old military men assisted his standing.

"Remain standing," he whispered to them. They no longer fit into their old uniforms but looked fair enough in their black suits. They each kept a light hold under his elbows.

"Thank you," Sir William said.

The crowd cheered. Some stomped their feet. A few whistled.

"You are kind." He leaned forward to peer around Burbridge's form to see Emma. He winked and she smiled. He looked back at the crowd. "Most kind."

They cheered again only this time standing and applauding. Sir William waited, though his knees and ankles pained him.

The crowd chanted. "Hillary! Hillary! Hillary!"

He again whispered to Lieutenant Graves, who raised his hands, motioning the crowd to quiet down. Several long seconds later it quieted.

"When I first dreamed of this organization being formed," Sir William said as strongly as he could, though he feared he wasn't loud enough, "I had this vision in mind."

He waved with his hand. "All of you. That was my vision." He heard a stirring behind him and turned to see someone handing a speaking trumpet to Phillip Garret, who passed it to Lieutenant Graves.

"Do you want to use this?" Lieutenant Graves asked.

Sir William took it and held it to his mouth. The back of his neck hurt. "You are the reason I dreamed of this organization," he said. "The reason the seas never intimidated me was because I saw a sea of faces." He lowered the trumpet and took a few breaths and then lifted it again. "Your faces and those of your loved ones."

Many applauded and more than one shouted, "Hear! Hear!"

"That is what we must always remember." His eyes welled, but he resisted allowing tears to fall. "That is what should ever be before us. Only then can we never lose courage in the doing of it." He lowered the trumpet. It was too difficult to hold up.

"Hear! Hear!" a man yelled from somewhere in the back. Another did the same, also in the back.

"It is the joy set before us," he said without aid of the trumpet and as loudly as he could. "It is the intended outcome of things that must inspire our actions and direct our focus."

He paused for cheers but all remained silent, except for those coughing. He suddenly was reminded of Sarah, and he wished she were here. Her coughing had worsened again, and she remained in her room.

"To those of you who have rowed by my side and those of you who continue to row today—you have kept the hope set before you and have never lost your courage." He used the trumpet again. "And with courage," he said, his voice suddenly filling with a great gust of strength. The crowd stirred. Applause grew from the back. "Nothing will be impossible!" He dropped the trumpet and waved.

The assembled guests rose to their feet in exuberant applause and rowdy cheers. The word *courage* echoed in cheers and chants throughout the great hall.

Lieutenants Graves and Burbridge helped Sir William regain his seat. Sir William whispered into Burbridge's ear.

The lieutenant nodded and then grabbed the trumpet. He faced the crowd. "Hattie! Hattie!" he shouted through the trumpet while the guests cheered.

Hattie, standing off to the side, came to the table. Sir William whispered to her, and she took the trumpet down to the end of the table where the vicar from St. George's church sat. He nodded, stood, and blessed the meal. He handed the trumpet back to Hattie, who fixed it to her mouth and bellowed forth, "Dinner is served!"

Suddenly, a large curtain was pulled back along the far side of the room, revealing several long tables covered with massive amounts of food. The crowd erupted and was soon forming multiple lines to the tables.

Sir William watched the energetic crowd and felt Emma squeezing his arm.

"No one throws a party like you, Sir William," Phillip Garret said, suddenly appearing behind Lieutenant Graves, who had since been seated, and tapping Sir William on the shoulder. "No one!" he repeated. "Lovely evening, Amelia. Well done."

Before Sir William could turn around and properly acknowledge him, he was gone, headed for the food and taking a place in line alongside Forbes and Wulff.

"He's got that right!" Lieutenant Burbridge said, nearly inverting his glass of wine. "Ah! A jolly good party this is." He flapped one arm like a silly bird. "And expensive, hey?" He winked and reached for the decanter.

"Sir?" a man interrupted.

Sir William turned and saw Michael.

"Michael!" Sir William was elated. He twisted in his seat so quickly that it hurt.

"Good to see you again, sir," Michael said. "I just wanted to say hello to you. I appreciate the banquet, sir."

"You are most welcome," Sir William said. "I am happy to see you. You must visit me sometime."

Michael smiled. "I will do that, sir. I will enjoy that." He nodded and stood there awkwardly for a moment.

"Here you are, sir," Hattie said.

Sir William turned around to see two plates of food set before him and Emma. "Thank you, Hattie." He turned around, but Michael was gone.

He sighed and then looked at his food. It was a hearty arrangement of meats and potatoes, even a slab of beef looking suspiciously like his favorite Hanby's special. It all looked perfect. He wished he were hungry.

Chapter 32

"Mr. Forbes has surrendered all his assets and has left the island with his family. You, sir, may be in a similar condition if you do not make these debts whole."

It was early evening on a cold February day, but Mr. Fletcher, having just entered from outside, did not shiver. He was dressed warmly, all in black, with a derby and heavy overcoat. He held a straight black cane with a carved lion head atop it. He carried a satchel and had tapped it several times while referring to some of the charges. He hadn't been hostile, but supremely serious.

Sir William was sunk deep into his chair in his library. "You are mistaken, I'm sure." The man's snow-tinged boots had left dribbles of water on the floor.

Sir William sighed. It had been a most distressing day, and now his floor was wet. First Emma had complained of being filled with such aches that she refused to leave their bed. He was already knotted up with the rheumatism, the heavy snows and blustery cold making it worse, and he had not been able to get warm all day long. He assured Hattie that he sometimes imagined it would be a relief to jump into the fireplace to get warm. Her only reply was to heap on more blankets.

"Tell me your name, again," Sir William said. "I didn't quite catch it. Who are you with?"

"Fletcher," the man said. "I am under the employ of Williams, Deacon, and Company in London."

"What does that have to do with me, Mr. Fletcher?" Sir William asked. "Oh, please do forgive Hattie for not taking your hat and coat. She's quite beside herself with duties today. Please remove them and sit down."

Hattie was as old as Emma but somehow stayed strong despite her age. She still cooked and cleaned and helped everyone with everything. Sir William didn't know how she could do it. She even tended to Sarah as if she were a doctor.

That had been harder to do since Sarah had begun taking the opium. It was her only hope, the doctor had said. But she still hadn't improved.

Sir William couldn't keep his mind from wandering. More thoughts of Sarah flowed into his mind. She was as ill now as she had been at her worst months ago and was now wasting away before their eyes. Her body had sores, and her skin was pasty. He couldn't bear seeing her in such a condition, but he made sure to be at her side whenever she was alert enough to understand he was present.

"Sir?" Fletcher said.

"Hmm? What did you say?"

"I'm fine, thank you," Fletcher said. "I prefer to stand." He was of average height, not too thin, and clean-shaven except for a thin mustache. His sideburns were neatly trimmed but long and square. "We are the clearing agents for Home's Bank and the joint-stock bank, both of which are entirely incongruous with good standing."

Sir William smiled. "What do you mean, incongruous?"

"In no condition to repay the multiple loans from William and Deacon, sir," Fletcher said. His mouth moved but barely anything else did. "Therefore, the joint stockholders are responsible. That is why I am here."

"Of course, what you say is alarming, but I can't see how it can be true. Many people come here asking me for money, but this scheme is a first."

"This is no scheme, sir," Fletcher said. "Perhaps you should not have been so generous when others came. For now, I suggest you find a rather capable advocate." Fletcher pulled from his satchel an envelope and held it out to Sir William.

"Please place it on the table here, if you would," Sir William said.

Fletcher placed the thick packet of documents down. "Is there an advocate you wish me to go to directly, sir?"

"I'll examine the documents," Sir William said, meekly raising a hand in surrender and then offering a friendly smile. "If I deem it worthwhile, I will alert Mr. Dumbell. He usually handles these sorts of things for me."

"I'm afraid not this time," Mr. Fletcher said.

"Pardon me?"

"I'm afraid a certain Mr. Willard Dumbell and his partner, Mr. J. C. Bluett, are also involved. To what extent I cannot say. Apparently, the fraudulent actions run very deep, involving a Falcon Ridge project and even corrupting a mine investment. The Kirk Lonan Mining Association, I believe."

"What?" As Sir William sat up, the pain raged up his spine and throughout his neck. "What are you saying?"

"Overvalued securities, unpaid advances," Fletcher said, blinking more rapidly. "You'll find it all addressed in the documents, sir."

"What have I to do with this?" Sir William asked, suddenly feeling too warm under his blankets.

"You were advanced monies for land purchases, promotions for a development called Falcon Ridge—"

"Falcon Ridge?" Sir William asked, struggling to tug off his blankets. "I paid off those debts with sales from the lottery."

"Do you have receipts for such, sir?"

Sir William succeeded in getting one blanket to fall on the floor and began extricating himself from the next. "Forbes arranged it for me. He'll tell you!"

"Forbes is gone, I'm afraid, sir."

"Well, it's true, there will be records, I'm sure of it."

"We've found no such records. There is also the case of your mortgage on Fort Anne."

"What of it?" Sir William asked, freezing in his upright pose, his hands full of rumpled blanket.

"It is collateral, sir. No doubt you understood that when assuming the loans."

Sir William threw the remaining folds of the blanket to the floor. "I am current on all my bills. I paid all the Falcon Ridge debts from the profits of the land sales. Besides, I have a steady flow of revenue from the Laxey mine that will address any shortfalls, of which I am sure there are none!"

Sir William found himself standing, but he was too angry to be impressed. Years ago he would have stood taller than this Mr. Fletcher, but his condition kept him bent over just enough to reach only the man's chin.

"You have holdings in the mine, sir?" Mr. Fletcher asked. "I don't recall seeing records of such, but if that is the case, your house may be safe."

"May be safe?" Sir William nearly spit as he protested. "May be safe! Are you a lunatic? There is no danger to my home! Do you know who I am?"

Sir William felt dizzy. It was all so confusing. How dare this man insult and accuse him in his own home. Sarah lay dying, Emma was upstairs in pain, he was reclining in his library in humble condition, and this man had the indecency to utter such atrocities.

"All is safe!" Sir William said with confidence. "My affairs are well in order."

"I am simply pointing out that our investigation revealed no shares in your name," Fletcher said.

"You are grossly in error. Check with Phillip Garret or Lieutenant-General Stapleton."

"Who, sir?"

"My most trusted friends, Mr. Phillip Garret and Lieutenant-General Stapleton."

"That is most disappointing, sir."

"What is that supposed to imply?"

"I imply nothing that I cannot simply state," Fletcher said with no loss of composure. "Both Garret and Stapleton had outstanding loans of their own and a deeply indebted position to each of the banks in question, which they quickly made whole through the sale of the entire ownership of mining stock. They made no representation of mining holdings in your name."

"Impossible!" Sir William said, his body trembling.

"I hope you are correct, sir," Fletcher said, turning to go. He stopped in the entrance to the library. "However, that does seem unlikely." He tipped his hat and was gone.

Sir William stared out the window, but it was too dark to see.

Chapter 33

The south wind howled.

It swept over the Irish Sea and bent the trees of Douglas. Vessels creaked and rocked uneasily in their harbor slips. Giant waves of chilling saltwater slapped the stones of the Tower of Refuge atop Conister Rock.

"I am betrayed," Sir William said to Emma. He wasn't certain she heard him.

Her lone red curl lay matted against her ghostly white forehead. Her eyes were closed and her breathing so quiet he stared at her midsection to make sure it was rising and falling. It was, but she shivered. He covered her with every blanket on their bed. He remembered when she and Sarah had made the quilt long ago.

It was a saturated spring, and the buds and flowers of this season were not what Sir William had planned for. They were less like fragrant flowers than poisonous berries with deadly thorns.

Down the hall, Sarah was close to death. It pained him to leave one for the other, not wanting either of them left alone. He tried to time their waking moments, but neither of them was often alert and the walking from room to room was becoming too much for his aching limbs. He considered all things to be hopeless and did not understand what manner to assume in such dire circumstance. There was no happy alternative.

"I am here," Emma whispered.

She had barely moved except for her dry lips. He dipped the corner of the linen from the breakfast tray she hadn't touched into the glass of water and dabbed her lips. She lightly sucked on the wet fabric. Her symptoms had been as Sarah's, only more rapid and aggressive.

Both lay deathly ill.

"I will not betray you." Her green eyes opened, and she smiled weakly. She barely turned her head to look at him.

Sir William imagined her lifting her head and looking at him through her wedding veil. He saw her sauntering toward the stairs in the center of Fort Anne and standing beside him to peer out the large window at Prospect Hill. He saw her twirling in her lovely gown as they danced at the governor's ball, remembered her body-shaking laughter from within the carriage and saw her sewing and smiling and staring into his eyes.

He felt her squeeze his arm, and he looked down.

Her curled hand lay motionless at her side. He looked back at her face, but her eyes were again closed. He looked at her midsection, under the layers of wool blankets. He couldn't tell whether or not she breathed. "Emma!"

Her eyelids fluttered almost imperceptibly.

He sighed. "My love, do not leave me. I cannot face these wolves alone."

Her mouth moved.

"Emma?" He leaned closer.

Breath flowed through her lips, but her words were indistinguishable.

"Emma, do not leave me." Tears rolled down his face. He straightened and wiped them with the back of his pajama sleeve.

She whispered again, this time articulating better but still unclear.

"What is it, my love?" he whispered back, leaning his ear to lightly graze her lips.

She breathed the word. "Courage." Her breath was warm.

Kneeling beside her, Sir William laid his head on the bed and curled one arm around her swirl of silvery red hair. His other arm gently rested across her midsection. He could feel his arm rising and falling as she breathed.

"I am afraid." His knees hurt, but he did not want to move.

Emma breathed, lifting his arm higher than moments ago.

Sir William lifted his head and smiled. "Emma?"

"Sir!" Hattie broke into the bedchamber. "Those men have returned. I couldn't stop them, sir! They have papers."

Sir William turned around. Hattie was red-faced and distraught. She was trembling. It bothered him greatly that some men would arrive in his home and have this effect upon her. She was always strong.

"Courage," he said softly and tried to stand. The bed was not sufficient to help him push his weight up, and he did not want to disturb his resting wife. "Help me, Hattie."

Hattie rushed over and struggled to help him rise from his kneeling position to stand. He teetered.

"Are you all right, sir?" Hattie asked, still holding his arms.

"Let go. I can manage, yes."

He was bent over, but he could walk slowly. He turned his head to look into Hattie's terrified eyes. "Stay with Emma." He hoped his calmness and smile assured her. She nodded and sat down on the bed beside Emma.

"They are removing things, sir," Hattie said, picking up Emma's hand.

Sir William turned his attention toward the door. "The dogs!"

"Oh, my!" Hattie shrieked. "Sir William."

"I'm taking care of it, Hattie." Nothing could stop him now. He would speak words to these men such as they had never heard. He would put a fire of such guilt into their hearts they would rush away in shame. Nobody entered a man's home and disrupted the peace, especially the peace of these women—ill women at that.

"Oh, Lord," Hattie sobbed. "Sir William! Sir William!"

"Be not afraid, Hattie. It takes only courage."

He shuffled through the door. Downstairs he could hear heavy scraping and many footfalls. "Who goes there?" Sir William yelled as loudly as he could, but he wasn't certain they could hear him. "Ahoy!"

The stairs were very far away, beyond the doorway to Sarah's room. It greatly angered him that he could not move more quickly. He was sure he was moving faster than he had in quite some days. He wished he weren't in his pajamas, but no time for such vanity now. The women's honor was at stake. His honor. The Hillary honor. All things honorable. *The dogs!*

He trudged down the center of the hallway and stopped in the window light that streamed across the floor from inside Sarah's room. He stopped and sideways stepped three or four times to turn his body to the left. At last, he could see her. "Courage, dear daughter. I will rout the dogs!" He stared at her.

Sarah lay motionless on her bed, draped to her chin in white satin covers. Light streamed in from the window beyond, cascading across her form, onto the floor, and into the hall. She looked as angelic as always. "Sarah!" he snapped, demanding her attention.

She didn't move.

Something shattered downstairs. Sir William turned his head. A man yelled something. His voice was familiar. Other men replied. Sir William returned his gaze to Sarah.

"Sarah!" he snapped again. He wanted to be certain she was not afraid.

She didn't move.

Sir William studied her. He watched her midsection. "Ah," he said. He could see it rising and falling, he was sure. "No matter. You rest. I'll be back soon." He smiled and spastically lifted one hand. "I've some life boating to do, don't you know?" He winked at her.

He took a step toward the stairs and then faced her one more time. "This is *our* tower of refuge, dear. Don't you worry. Courage, that's all it takes. Ask Emma, dear. She'll tell you." He blew her a trembling kiss.

Downstairs the sounds were great. Heavy items were being dragged. Glassware and silver implements clinked and rang.

"Blast!" Sir William muttered. The stairs were so far away and his knees and ankles felt so weak. "I'll make it." He swore it as an oath. "A little rest, that is all."

He ceased walking and bent his knees to lower to the floor. He placed his hands outward, palms down. His body burned. It was like he was at sea in winter and drenched through to his skin with stinging ice. He trembled as he leaned slightly forward, hoping to ease to all fours. A great wave of pain pushed him over. His palms slapped the hardwood floor. His elbows caved and his chest and chin slammed down.

He rolled to his side. Another shattering sound came from downstairs.

Sir William's head was spinning. He knew he was at sea. He was sure of it. He had mastered it before. He would do it again. "Oars!" he cried.

He rose up on all fours. He saw a tiny pool of red on the floor. He was relieved it was the floor and not the carpet. He reconsidered and thought the carpet might be easier to crawl atop. He inched his way on hands and knees toward the stairs.

"Who goes there?" he yelled. "Ahoy! I say!"

"Sir William?" the familiar voice rang out from two floors down.

"Aye! The master of this home," Sir William hollered back. He crawled with renewed determination. *I know that voice.* "You are to leave these premises at once!"

Someone was ascending the stairs, slowly at first. Other steps followed.

Sir William reached the edge of the top of the stairs and noticed the painting hanging on the wall of the second landing. It was one of his biblical collection. He peered down the steps, his hands now resting on his knees. "Declare yourself!" he ordered.

The ascending steps quickened. "Mr. Hillary?"

Mister? "Do not increase the offense," Sir William said. He tried to kneel, but the pain was too great. Better to rest with his palms on the floor. A man appeared on the lower landing and looked up at Sir William. He was dressed in black from head to toe.

"Sir William?" Mr. Fletcher asked. Two others arrived behind him. They were peace officers.

"That's more like it," Sir William said firmly. "I am a baronet. I will thank you to not forget it."

"Sir!" Fletcher reached into his vest pocket. "You're bleeding, sir." He produced a hankie and quickly paced up the stairs.

"Avast!" Sir William shouted, rising up on his knees. The pain was excruciating but respect was imperative. "Advance no farther, you . . . you . . . wolf or dog, take your pick!"

Fletcher stopped only two steps away and placed his hankie down on the step in front of Sir William. "Are you hurt, sir? Might I assist you?"

"Yes, you may assist me!" Sir William barked. "You may assist me by departing these premises immediately!"

"I cannot do that, sir," Mr. Fletcher said, producing a letter from his coat pocket. "It is all legal. We are seizing your assets to hold until proper liquidation can be determined." He set the letter down beside the hankie in front of Sir William.

Sir William fumbled with the letter for several seconds but could not remove the contents.

"Here, sir." Fletcher removed the letter for him.

Sir William snatched it and scanned it. "Who is this Mr. Jones?"

"One of many, I'm afraid," Fletcher said. "It seems you bought a few hundred pounds worth of shoes on credit, for which you never made good." Fletcher studied the painting on the landing and motioned to the peace officers. They reached to remove it.

"I'll make it good," Sir William said. "Leave that picture alone."

Fletcher looked again at the painting. "That's Joseph, isn't it? When he was in prison, it appears. Very fine. It will auction well."

"Leave it!" Sir William inhaled and lifted his chest as much as he could.

"I'm afraid I cannot. There are many more on that list than just Mr. Monty Jones, sir," Fletcher said, reaching forward and placing a hand on Sir William's arm. "Let me help you up."

Sir William yanked his arm away. The pain shot up his spine and into his neck and chest. "Help me? Don't be absurd!"

The officers lifted the painting off of the wall.

Fletcher withdrew his hand. "The others are listed below him, sir. His is the least of the debts you incurred. Your credit has been withdrawn, and your assets are presently being seized. It is not yet clear, but you may, in fact, retain the home. We will see."

The officers descended the stairs with the painting.

Sir William fought hard to stand. His legs quaked and his joints felt afire, but he was determined. "I will show you," he said through gritted teeth, "what courage can do." He lifted higher and higher until he stood at his full measure, over six feet, as tall as he had ever been. He was sure of it.

Fletcher's eyes grew wide.

"You've the fear of God in you now, eh?" Sir William said.

"Sir?" Fletcher extended both his arms. "Be careful, sir. You might—"

The wave rose from its knees and lifted the stern of his lifeboat so high that Sir William saw something magnificent—something he had never seen before.

His men elevated from their seats in the boat. They were flying like mighty warriors of the sea, rescuing the frightened and bringing them home. Sir William lifted high off the stern, his hands releasing from the tiller, and he soared like a seabird over the heads of his men into a massive swirl of sea. He spun, spread-eagled, as though being sucked into a giant drain. He need only squeeze his hand upon the netting and all would be safe. If any hardship were to follow, the Institution would make the widows secure.

Chapter 34

"There, there, sir," Michael said. "We'll be there soon."

"It'll be soon, sir," Joseph said. "You'll see."

The two fishermen looked so much older than Sir William remembered. He tried to recall their ages, but the jerky movement interrupted his thoughts. Sir William jostled side to side, forward and backward. "These infernal potholes!" he said again. "I wish they would use crushed gravel."

"They do, sir," Joseph said. "They have for some time. You know that."

Sir William remembered. Of course they do. Nevertheless, it was still bumpy.

His sedan chair was securely fixed in the back of the wagon, and his two friends had done much to make him comfortable, but comfort and carriages seemed exclusive of one another no matter what kinds of springs were employed.

"Dreadful," Sir William said.

The entrance to St. George's cemetery was overgrown, and the gate badly rusted. "How could the vicar allow this?" he asked his two coachmen. "He never let it slip this badly."

He noticed Joseph and Michael exchange glances in front of him and thought about what it meant. Ah. That's right. The vicar was gone. He had no idea who had replaced him. It seemed everyone was gone now.

"Here we are, sir," Michael said, stopping the wagon. He and Joseph climbed down and flanked him.

Sir William rested his eyes upon the tomb where Emma and Sarah lay. His chair suddenly rose high and was shaken more than was comfortable as his men worked to lift him in his sedan chair from off the back of the wagon. The lowering down was dizzying. "Be careful, gentlemen," Sir William said.

"Yes, sir," Joseph replied from behind him.

Michael was in front, his back facing Sir William and his hands gripping each of the two poles that supported the sedan chair. They bounded to the mausoleum and carefully set his chair down as near they could.

"Whenever you are ready, sir," Michael said. "Just say so." He and Joseph stepped aside and left him alone.

He stared at the tomb that bore Sarah's and Emma's names.

A thousand million thoughts flowed through his mind like an incoming tide and then left the same way. But he felt cleansed and renewed. Something about being near them helped soothe his soul. He looked up.

It was autumn, and the leaves had nearly all fallen. He could see a narrow portion of Douglas Bay through the bare branches. The bulky shape of the tower was mostly obscured, but he could make out the top part of one of the parapets. He was grateful his ladies had such a view. It was always comforting to view the sea.

A triangular white shape glided behind the maze of intervening branches of barren trees. Someone was enjoying a sail. There needn't be a fear of drowning. A lifeboat was near, and if it was not to be found, there was a tower to find safe haven in until help arrived. He was sure of that.

"Has the lifeboat been launched recently?" Sir William asked.

"Sir?" Michael stepped forward. "The lifeboat, sir?"

Sir William grinned, even though it hurt his neck to do so. "Yes, Michael. How many have been saved this season?"

Michael hesitated and looked at Joseph, who also stepped up.

"What is it?" Sir William asked. His smile disappeared.

"Many, sir!" Joseph said quickly. "Very many."

"We—we don't know the exact number, sir," Michael said.

Sir William felt relieved. "Tell me when you find out." It was a struggle, but he blew a trembling kiss toward his ladies in repose and then motioned to his men. "I am ready now."

Michael and Joseph lifted him.

"Have I ever told you two about the Essex legion?"

"I am not sure you've told us all, sir," Michael said with a kind smile. "Tell us again."

So he did—all the way home—to Michael's cottage by the stream.

The onset of winter came with a southern storm that seized all of Douglas with industry-stopping snows and property-damaging freezes. With few ships able to sail, the harbor was robbed of much commerce.

The bay had become a stormy burial ground for sailors swept into the sea. There was no lifeboat to save them because the *Preservation* had fallen into disrepair. For those who made it to the tower, there was little to offer them once they were ferried to shore after the storms. There were no provisions for them. Some suffered poverty so great they expressed wishes they had drowned.

Michael grieved.

In his little cottage by the stream behind the hills of Falcon Ridge, he had tended to his aging, ailing friend, Sir William Hillary, the baronet and founder of the near-defunct lifeboat institution. He had assumed care of Sir William since his dreadful fall down the stairs at Fort Anne on the very day his wife and adopted daughter died. It was nearly like the story of Job that Sir William had told him about so long ago. Michael had stood beside him through the tragic and embarrassing days in the courthouse and through the dreadful loss of all Sir William had owned.

Holed up in his tiny stone dwelling with heavy snow all around, Michael's own provisions were scarce enough for him, let alone his failing tenant. But he could not abandon him. He did wonder what had become of the man's friends and family. No one came forward to take care of him. No one offered to help. No one seemed to care.

Even the institution this great man had established was unable or unwilling to help. Michael didn't know which, but he figured something must have gone terribly wrong.

Everywhere the lifeboats had become derelict, and there were no more annual subscriptions to keep the organization alive. The local newspaper reported that nothing beyond a vestige remained of the organization both here and abroad. Presumably it still existed but had no funding and a rapidly decreasing membership.

"They lost the vision," Sir William said to him upon learning of the true state of things. "They didn't keep it before them."

"Yes, sir," Michael said.

"I must write another appeal," Sir William said.

"Yes, sir," Michael said as he always did, knowing his friend could not write nor even remember anything long enough to put more than two sentences together on the same topic.

"Is Caesar coming today?" Sir William asked.

"No, sir."

"When is the lifeboat dinner, Joseph?" Sir William asked, curled atop the cot along one side of the room.

"I'm Michael, sir," Michael said. "The dinner is in the winter."

"Is it winter, Joseph?" Sir William looked confused. "I mean Michael. Did I say 'Joseph'?"

Michael stood up and crossed to the area of his home where he prepared the meals. He studied his almost bare cupboards. "I must go fishing, sir." He turned and looked at his friend. "It is all I can think to do."

The baronet was curled and knotted, barely able to move. His eyes remained bright and at times his mind was quick. But he was a shell of what he had been, just like the organization he had once been so passionate about. It didn't seem real. Or fair.

Michael remembered his wife, Anne, and his three children, little Mike, Peter, Sylvia. Nothing was fair.

Where were the men who had deceived Sir William? Michael imagined them drinking and toasting in London, ladies at their sides—probably ladies that were not their own. It wasn't right. He wanted only one woman, but she was gone. There was no justice. He looked at his friend. His eyes had closed, and he lay there like a helpless child. He had been a good man. Michael shook his head.

"I must go fishing, sir," he said again. "We need something to eat, and the stores are very low. I would hunt, but the snows are deep. I will return as soon as I can. Will you be all right, sir?"

Sir William stirred and made a noise, but it sounded more like snoring than words.

"Wait," Michael said. He crossed to the trunk along the other wall and knocked the blankets and pillows off of it. He opened it and tossed out clothes and trinkets, a bonnet and some toys. He reached deep inside and retrieved the soft bag. He lifted it high, and it jingled. "The golden guineas," he said. "At last, something worthwhile to do with them. I shall buy you some food." He turned to Sir William. "I don't want to leave you, sir, but—"

There was a knock on the door. Michael opened the front door to his tiny home and grinned. "Joseph!"

The portly fisherman smiled. He was dressed in a heavy coat and furry hat. He held out his arms. Upon his wooly mittens was a box. "Beef!" Joseph said. "Hanby's! Courtesy of old Matthew himself."

"Ha-ha!" Michael slapped his friend's shoulder. "I may never spend these coins." He shook the bag.

"Where did those come from?" Joseph asked, entering and stomping his boots.

"It's a long story," Michael said. "You are in perfect time. You must dine with us."

"I have every intention to," Joseph said, removing his knit cap to reveal his matted gray hair.

The men embraced and prepared the meal at the small round table in the middle of the room. As soon as it was ready, they approached Sir William and gently nudged him.

"Hot beef and onions, sir," Michael said. "Mr. Hanby sends his warmest regards."

Sir William was motionless.

"Sir?"

The baronet opened his eyes. "Good man, Matthew."

Michael and Joseph smiled. "Yes, sir," Michael said. "He is."

"Joseph!" Sir William slightly turned his head. "Is that really you?"

"It is, sir," Joseph said, grinning large.

"Good men." Sir William closed his eyes, but he smiled. "Don't mind me. I am a garden in winter."

"Are you hungry, sir?" Joseph asked. "It's beef and onions from Hanby's. Your favorite!"

Sir William shook his head. "I'm not hungry."

Those were the last words he ever spoke.

Sir William died while Hanby's beef steamed on the table.

Chapter 35

Michael Kellerman did not want to forget 1847. He wanted to mark the year somehow. It was the year his life had changed in a way he had never seen coming—as though someone else had led him to a place he never knew existed but he was now deeply grateful to have seen.

It all became clear that snowy day over one year ago when Sir William had died in his cottage. His once-wealthy friend had been a remarkable man who died an impoverished death.

Today it was sunny and warm, and it all made sense.

He thought of Anne. His wife and children were gone, stolen from him senselessly.

Remarkable. He believed it now.

He took rocks from the bottom of the river that flowed past his home and stacked them into a tower—like the Tower of Refuge—at the end of the walk leading to his front door. It was important to keep the vision before him.

"What's it mean?" Joseph asked. "I don't understand."

"I didn't either," Michael said. "Follow me." He entered his humble home and opened the trunk. He removed the bag of golden guineas and placed them into his belt. "I know what to do with these now."

"A pint?" Joseph joked.

Michael led them out of the house. "I think not."

"What then?" Joseph asked, nearly bumping into the tower of rocks at the end of the short walk.

"Careful," Michael said. "That pile is there to remind me."

Joseph nodded. "Yes, but remind you of what?"

Michael smiled. "What I never knew. What I never believed."

"You are riddling me, Michael," Joseph said, sounding unhappy. "Where are we going?"

"To the harbor."

The walk to the harbor from the cottage was no easy task. The way was steep and winding until the path reached Falcon Ridge. The streets there were smooth, though the descent was sharp.

From there they would pass through the south side where Michael had once lived, then into town from behind the York Hotel, and then along the quay.

"What for?" Joseph asked. "What are we doing?"

"We're going to the boathouse," Michael said, his step sure.

"Why?"

Michael stopped and held up the coins. "We can do it! We can afford it."

"Afford what?" Joseph sounded distressed. "What are you talking about?"

"The lifeboat, mate," Michael explained with glee. "We will effect her repairs! She wasn't made to lie dormant in an old boathouse. Remember we had one long ago that was snatched by the south wind?"

"Yes, but—"

"Not this time," Michael said, his pace quickening. "Neither the sea nor neglect will steal her purpose now."

"Are you sure?" Joseph asked. "Are you sure that's where you want to put your money?"

"Quite sure. Absolutely positive."

"It didn't do a whole lot for Sir William, you know."

Michael stopped and stared at his friend.

"I mean, it didn't," Joseph said more gently. "Think about it. Wonderful he was, but in the end, desolate."

"What end?"

"What end?" Joseph scoffed. "Come now, Michael. I loved Sir William as much as you, but he was a sorry lot in the end. None of his friends were there for him. Look at what is left of the institution he labored so long and hard for. It's barely alive." Joseph shook his head. "No, you are better to invest those coins. Make them bigger somehow."

Michael smiled and patted his friend on the shoulder. "Is a man's life only measured during the days that he breathes? Is it not possible that he may have sown seed yet to burst forth beyond the length of his years?"

"You mean Sir William?" Joseph rubbed his chin. "I suppose."

"I not only mean Sir William," Michael said. "I mean Colonel St. John. I mean—"

"St. John?" Joseph's face twisted.

Michael held up the bag and shook it. "The colonel himself sowed this!"

"Really? Why?" Joseph felt the bag. "It's heavy."

"I don't think he knew why," Michael said. "But it goes for him, Sir William, me, you—anybody."

"Should I understand you now?" Joseph's face twitched.

Michael laughed so hard he bent over with his hands on his knees.

"Michael," Joseph's brow wrinkled. "I've never known you to laugh like this. Are you all right?"

Michael regained his self-control and placed a hand atop Joseph's shoulder. They resumed their descent. "Tell me, Joseph, do you think God loved Sir William?"

"Of course. The man risked his life for countless others. Of course God loved him."

"Yet"—Michael pointed in his friend's face—"he died in poverty."

"Yes, well." Joseph struggled for an explanation. "But that wasn't God's doing—"

"Precisely! Only I didn't see that when Sir William tried to help me understand things after Anne and the children died. I was angry and feeling quite sorry for myself." He stopped and grinned. "I'm not abandoned. Circumstances mean little." He rushed ahead, speaking over his shoulder. "They don't accurately reflect Sir William's life, and they don't speak the truth of mine."

Joseph ran to catch up. "What does all this have to do with repairing the lifeboat? And what will you do when those coins run out? Answer me that."

"I trust the Divine Author to know when the last chapter is complete." Michael nearly skipped down the steep hill.

"Last chapter of what? A man's life?" Joseph asked, his face flushed. He halted Michael by grabbing his arm. "When he dies, Michael. That's when it ends."

"I'm not speaking of the last chapter of a man's life, my friend."

"Then what?"

"His effect."

Joseph opened his mouth but said nothing.

Michael felt warm over his entire body. "Maybe there is no last chapter, Joseph."

Joseph scratched his white head.

"Circumstances are not what we should be interpreting," Michael suggested gently.

Joseph barely nodded.

"Focus on sowing the seed," Michael said. A cool breeze blew over the hill and caressed his face. The rising sun in the east shone in beams across the isle. He held up the bag and jingled it. "I don't know when it will bloom. I assign no terms. They likely wouldn't be honored anyway." Michael laughed and then became silent. He nodded at his good friend. "Come, there's work to be done."

Chapter 36

The south wind howled across the Irish Sea.

Snow swirled and crates blew down the narrow streets of Douglas. Windows were shuddered and lamps blown cold and dark.

St. George's cemetery was silent. The rays of the morning sun had yet to ascend the hills of the Isle of Man to creep into the graveyard and warm the bones within.

The Hillary mausoleum sat in the rear corner, deep in the shadows of bare-limbed trees. A dried leaf blew through the bars of the unhinged gate and tumbled over the gravesites and markers until it tucked itself against the corner of the framed entrance to the Hillary tomb. The wind increased, but nothing moved save the dead leaf. It finally fluttered away.

As the light of man rose from the east, the graveyard brightened with the early morning. Through a sliver of unblocked sight between the branches of naked trees, the wind-tossed waves of the bay were visible. They churned restlessly. Yet try as they might, they could not upset the brave boat piercing their green waters, blasting them into spray.

The heavily laden boat sat low, holding two courageous gray-headed lifeboat men, their resolute crew, and a handful of disheveled but grateful sailors. The bow of the noble boat faced the nearby harbor—where provision awaited those who had weathered the storm.

Bonus content includes:

Author's Note
Reader's Guide
A Conversation with Jon Nappa
Selected Bibliography

Author's Note

Despite the desperate condition of the organization at the time of his own impoverished death, the institution founded by Sir William Hillary has survived for more than 175 years. More than survive, it has flourished. Renamed the Royal National Lifeboat Institution (RNLI), Hillary's dream has resulted in the rescue of more than 135,000 lives since its inception. The numbers continue to grow to this day.

Sir William Hillary is honored as the founder of the RNLI, though that isn't all he got right. The asylum harbor he envisioned exists today, and his Tower of Refuge still stands atop Conister Rock in Douglas Bay. His appeals for steam-powered vessels were ahead of his time, and they were eventually adopted and resulted in countless lives being saved.

Today, the RNLI launches approximately twenty life-saving rescues daily, and it is still 100 percent funded by volunteer contributions.

Like a perennial planted in the garden on Prospect Hill, the effects of the vision and tireless efforts of Sir William Hillary live on. Some flowers are more fragrant than others—returning again and again, year after year, despite whatever circumstances surround their winter repose.

Reader's Guide

1. What was the significance of the garden scenes in the book?
2. What was the significance of the passage from Job that Sir William recited to Michael Kellerman?
3. What scene was depicted by the stairway landing painting removed by Fletcher's men near the end of the story? Why is this significant?
4. What are the similarities and contrasts between Sir William Hillary and William Wilberforce?
5. Describe a time when your circumstances were entirely misread by those around you. How did it make you feel?
6. What efforts have you made, or can you make, that can leave an impact beyond the days of your life?
7. If you try something noble with all of your heart and there follows no visible evidence that you've even made a dent, will you consider your efforts wasted? or pending?
8. Honestly, in view of what it takes to see something through to the end, will you keep trying no matter what the scale of difficulty? Or will you quit?
9. In the end, does the book *With Hearts Courageous* enlighten you? sober you? discourage you? or inspire you to greater resolve?
10. If you are not already, might you be willing to become a Storm Warrior-in-waiting?

A Conversation with Jon Nappa

Q: In your first novel, Into the Storm, you blended the timelines of Gilmore and Lukin for the purposes of the story. Did you do that in With Hearts Courageous?

A: No, this story mirrors the actual timeline of Sir William Hillary's life. In the broad strokes, it's reasonably accurate. The details are fictionalized, and the drama is heightened. In places I altered the record, though I believe I remained faithful to the truth of the experiences and events.

Q: Though both books feature exciting action on the seas and trace portions of lifeboat history, they are also very different. Into the Storm is more plot driven and With Hearts Courageous is a focused character study. Both were moving, this one deeply so. How does an author make that sort of structural choice?

A: By not setting out to write based on formula. The story will lead the way. The first book was rooted in the records of actual rescues performed at sea and lent itself well to an action-studded plot. The second does have a hearty dose of nautical action, but there was so much additional drama in the complicated life of Sir William. It turned out as a character study by its own insistence.

Q: Were the real-life characters similar to those you've included?

A: I used real names in many places but the characterizations are fictitious. In the case of major characters like Sir William, Emma, and a few others, I tried to respect the spirit of who they were but always without abandoning the creative license afforded in fiction.

Q: Did Sir William really go broke at the end of his life, and was the Institution he founded really on the verge of insolvency?

A: Absolutely. The irony of his life was that despite such noble intentions and courageous acts, his personal circumstances became tragic. Obviously, this fueled the theme of the story.

Q: Can you state the theme for us?

A: The theme of With Hearts Courageous is that circumstances do not tell the whole story. Many people find themselves in circumstances that seem to contradict the nobility or effectiveness of their efforts. This often raises questions and suspicions. People sometimes accuse others of secret sin or insincere motives, or they at least suspect that something is "off the mark" because the person's circumstances are unfavorable. The story in this book rejects that thinking. The lasting effects of Hillary's efforts are beautiful and priceless, though entirely contrary to the circumstances at the time of his passing.

Q: Were his financial arrangements as complicated as suggested?

A: Honestly, they were more complicated than what this book presents. They were extremely difficult to understand. At the root of it, I believe, was a desire to preserve and protect his wealth, though it backfired in the end. Like many visionaries, Hillary always had aspirations beyond his resources.

Q: The relationship between Sarah, Emma, and Sir William seems storybook. Was it really?

A: All indications are that it was. And both the women died around the same time. Sir William really did suffer great emotional, financial, and physical loss in short order.

Q: What drew you to this story?

A: Many things. For one, the theme I already shared about a person's effect lasting beyond the length of his or her days despite what circumstances may suggest. Secondly, it demonstrates how quickly mankind can lose vision if not for those who prop it up along the way. Many of the lifeboats that were built according to the original Lukin principles did fall into disrepair. The fire went out. The momentum was lost. It's one thing to launch, but it's another to sustain. Each presents a different set of challenges.

Q: Kind of like one solution makes the way for others?

A: Yes! Lukin helped rescue people who would never have survived without him. Hillary later recognized there were additional challenges, such as the widows and orphans who were left behind when a sailor was lost at sea.

Q: What's your biggest hope that readers will walk away with?

A: A simple awareness and appreciation of who Hillary was and what he did is the least I hope for. My greater hope is that the readers become encouraged to sustain the resolve they experienced in the first book, of wanting to launch their own unique lifeboats. I hope they won't let the passion fall into disrepair. I hope they will go to stormwarriors.org and sign up for free to become a Storm Warrior-in-waiting. Also, I hope With Hearts Courageous helps them remain unaffected by what accusers and naysayers may proclaim regarding their personal circumstances. They must press on, never quit, and stay confident that good seed sown will not return void, despite whatever length their days on earth and no matter the circumstances at that time.

Q: How is Storm Warriors International going?

A: It is progressing as planned. Our 501 (C) (3) status has been granted, allowing for tax-deductible contributions, and we are moving forward with much vigor. The website is available for people to sign up, and we will begin reaching out with moving stories from around the world that tell of real people in need of real help. It is something we can all help accomplish. We really can make a difference. We really can and we really will.

Selected Bibliography

Books

Cameron, Ian. *Riders of the Storm*. Weidenfeld & Nicolson: London, 2002.

Kelly, Robert. *For Those in Peril*. Douglas, Isle of Man: Shearwater Press, 1979.

Kelly, Robert, and Gordon N. Kniverton. *Sir William Hillary and the Isle of Man Lifeboat Stations*. Douglas, Isle of Man: The Manx Experience, n.d.

Internet Links

Storm Warriors International Inc, *http://www.stormwarriors.or*g

Royal National Lifeboat Institution, *http://www.rnli.org.uk/*

Manx National Heritage. *http://www.gov.im/mnh/*

Sir William Hillary, *http://www.isle-of-man.com/manxnotebook/people/residnts/whillary.htm.*

LaVergne, TN USA
02 December 2009
165797LV00001B/7/P

9 780615 323916